W9-DGZ-294

CRIME
FOR TWO

BY MEMBERS OF THE MYSTERY WRITERS
OF AMERICA

Edited by Frances and Richard Lockridge

J. B. LIPPINCOTT COMPANY · *Philadelphia* · *New York*

Copyright 1955 by Mystery Writers of America, Inc.
© 1955 by Mystery Writers of America, Inc.
Printed in the United States of America
Library of Congress Catalog Card Number 55-10460
FIRST EDITION

HOUSTON PUBLIC LIBRARY

R0109 090133

Acknowledgment is hereby made for permission to reprint the following: SIXTY GRAND MISSING by Robert Arthur (first published under the title NEAT IF NOT GORY), copyright 1941 by Short Stories, Inc., reprinted by permission of the author. THE ARMY OF LITTLE EARS by Charles B. Child (first published under the title THERE IS A MAN IN HIDING), copyright 1951 by Charles B. Child, reprinted by permission of the author. THE SWAMI OF NORTHBANK by Lawrence G. Blochman, copyright 1950 by Lawrence G. Blochman, reprinted by permission of the author. MYSTERY FOR CHRISTMAS by Anthony Boucher, copyright 1943 by Anthony Boucher, reprinted by permission of the author. THE SHADOW AND THE SHADOWED by Will Oursler, copyright 1951 by Mercury Publications, Inc., reprinted by permission of the author and Ellery Queen's Mystery Magazine. WHERE ANGELS FEAR TO TREAD by Stuart Palmer, copyright 1951 by Mercury Publications, Inc., reprinted by permission of the author and Ellery Queen's Mystery Magazine. COFFEE AND— by David Alexander, copyright 1952 by David Alexander, reprinted by permission of the author. INSIDE STUFF by Jerome Barry, copyright 1953 by Jerome Barry, reprinted by permission of the author. DEAD MAN'S CODE by Brett Halliday, copyright 1954 by United Newspapers Magazine Corporation, reprinted by permission of This Week Magazine. DIAMONDS IN PARADISE by Ellery Queen, copyright 1954 by Mercury Publications, Inc., reprinted by permission of the author and Ellery Queen's Mystery Magazine. A NAME FOR BABY by Thomas Walsh, copyright 1943 by Thomas Walsh, reprinted by permission of the author. DEATH BEFORE BREAKFAST by Q. Patrick, copyright 1951 by United Newspapers Magazine Corporation, reprinted by permission of the author. THE AMATEUR by Michael Gilbert (first published in the United States under the title THE UNSTOPPABLE MAN), copyright 1954 by Mercury Publications, Inc., reprinted by permission of the author and Ellery Queen's Mystery Magazine. DEAD TO THE WORLD by John D. MacDonald, copyright 1947 by Popular Publications, Inc., reprinted by permission of the author and Popular Publications, Inc. THE SECRET OF FORT BAYARD by Georges Simenon, copyright 1932 and 1943 by A. Fayard et Cie and Mercury Publications, Inc., reprinted by permission of the author and Ellery Queen's Mystery Magazine. THE DOG DIED FIRST by Bruno Fischer, copyright 1949 by Best Publications, Inc., reprinted by permission of the author and Mystery Book Magazine. ONE MORNING THEY'LL HANG HIM by Margery Allingham, copyright 1950 by Mercury Publications, Inc., reprinted by permission of the author and Ellery Queen's Mystery Magazine. HOMICIDE EXPERT by Lawrence Treat, copyright 1955 by Lawrence Treat, reprinted by permission of the author.

CONTENTS

Foreword	7
Sixty Grand Missing *by Robert Arthur*	9
The Army of Little Ears *by Charles B. Child*	21
The Swami of Northbank *by Lawrence G. Blochman*	39
Mystery for Christmas *by Anthony Boucher*	57
The Shadow and the Shadowed *by Will Oursler*	72
Where Angels Fear to Tread *by Stuart Palmer*	83
Coffee and— *by David Alexander*	107
Inside Stuff *by Jerome Barry*	122
Dead Man's Code *by Brett Halliday*	125
Diamonds in Paradise *by Ellery Queen*	137
A Name for Baby *by Thomas Walsh*	143
Death Before Breakfast *by Q. Patrick*	158
The Amateur *by Michael Gilbert*	164
Dead to the World *by John D. MacDonald*	175
The Secret of Fort Bayard *by Georges Simenon*	198
The Dog Died First *by Bruno Fischer*	205
One Morning They'll Hang Him *by Margery Allingham*	228
Homicide Expert *by Lawrence Treat*	246

FOREWORD

The editors would like to contend that the stories which follow were selected in accordance with well-established criteria—that abiding principles obtained or, at the least, some recognizable point system. Nothing of the sort was, of course, true. Selection was made entirely on the impulse of the moment, this being the manner in which all critical judgments are arrived at, whatever critics would prefer to have believed. A critic likes something, or he does not like it. (Or he has no response to it, one way or the other.) His extended remarks are rationalization, written in self-defense.

Since these stories have been printed before, we functioned as critics, rather than as editors. Someone, that is, had already pointed out to authors that the heroine's eyes, blue on page three, should not have turned brown by page ten. Someone had asked, with an editor's resignation, whether this sentence meant something and, if so, what? We were required merely to read a good many stories—which was no chore, since we like to read stories—and say "yes" to some and, often reluctantly, "no" to others.

On the stories chosen, we agreed in saying "yes." We were happier as we read them—more absorbed in what the authors had invented, more excited by what they said was happening, more anxious to turn next pages, more satisfied with final outcomes. Since all the submitted stories were good—members of the Mystery Writers of America, Inc., write only good stories—other editors might have made other selections. Many manuscripts which we decided to return we stroked wistfully as we sent them off.

The requirement stipulated in advance was that two persons be involved in the action, and, preferably, in the solution of the crime. We have followed this stipulation as far as we thought wise, seeking for Holmeses and their Watsons, for amateurs in co-operation with professionals, for couples (married or otherwise) who detected while they loved. We have not, as the reader will discover, always come up with anything so simple. Dogs have collaborated with humans.

7

(Cats have not, to the regret of these particular editors.) Small boys have helped their elders. In some instances, it would seem that the collaboration has been more in the commission of crime than in its punishment. And if the reader feels that the editors have sometimes cheated a little, a plea of *nolo contendere* is entered.

Formulas are incidental, to be adhered to only when convenient. The present point is that stories be told. Here they are, as they are in all mystery fiction, short or long. Here the emphasis is on what happened next, on ingenuity—on what, in this and associated crafts, are called "gimmicks." There are some fine gimmicks here, to our minds. There is also much good characterization and, here and there, phrases have been nicely turned. These are good things too, making the story grip the tighter. But it is always the story that counts.

FRANCES LOCKRIDGE
RICHARD LOCKRIDGE

Lewisboro, New York
February, 1955

SIXTY GRAND MISSING   Robert Arthur

*There are usually two answers to the question of how a writer
comes to write any particular story. The first answer is that he
is a writer and needs some money. To a writer the first answer
is quite sufficient. Every writer knows that the origins of many a
story lie in the murky swamps of the subconscious where millions
of hard-pressed brain cells, under the stimulus of urgent demand,
frantically combine thousands of nebulous idea-associations until
the conscious snatches on one and seizes it up, whereupon the
subconscious is able to relapse once more into its preoccupation
with Freud and Jung. This, however, does not satisfy the curious
public or the novice writer, who reiterate demandingly, "But
how did you get that idea?" There is no use in a writer's saying
he doesn't know. Anyway, sometimes he does. In this case I do.
This is a story about a crooked detective. Crooked detectives
were in the news when I wrote it, you see. I decided to explore
the idea of a detective whose partner and associates disapprove
of his actions. So I did. Incidentally, there is a twist here on the
theme of crooked cop that I don't believe has been used by Hollywood yet. It would make a terrific movie. Just give me the chance
and I'll work out a complete treatment for you in no time. Story
Departments, please take notice. (P.S.-Television, too!)*

ROBERT ARTHUR

Johnny Dresser sauntered into the precinct house dressed to kill at
twenty paces. His custom-tailored tan linen suit had a faint red stripe
in it, and the stripe reflected itself in his sand-beige tie—five bucks
at Brooks Brothers. The angle of his twenty-dollar panama was
jaunty, and his tan and white sport shoes clicked down on the scuffed
boards with a self-satisfied sound.

The squadroom door was open, and half a dozen cops besides the
sergeant at the desk got the full benefit of his glory. The little detective nodded at them.

"How's it, boys?" he asked. "Hot enough for you?"

The half-dozen cops looked at him, then looked away. Dresser, adjusting the tan linen handkerchief in his breast pocket to show another quarter of an inch, did not seem to notice.

"What's booked?" he asked the desk man.

The grizzled sergeant handed over a slip of paper.

"Two break-ins," he said, without inflection. "Here's the names and addresses. Kid gang stuff."

Dresser tucked the paper in his pocket.

"We'll get a line on 'em through the hock shops," he predicted. "Where's Sloppy Peters? He ought to be in by now."

The sergeant jerked his head. Dresser looked up as his tall, rangy partner ambled in from the street, wiping sweat from his face. Sloppy Peters' hair always needed cutting and his suits pressing. When he was engrossed on a job, he usually got his hands dirty in the search for evidence, rubbed his chin absent-mindedly, getting half the dirt on his face, and then wiped the rest of it off on his clothes. And no matter how often he apologetically promised Johnny Dresser to reform and be neat in the future, he always forgot.

"Hiyah, Slop!" the little detective greeted him. "How do you like the new outfit? Just delivered this morning, so I can take it along with me tomorrow. Nice for a rush job, huh?"

Complacently he flicked some lint from his sleeve. Instead of answering, the tall detective turned toward the desk.

"Anything on the fire, Mike?" he asked.

The sergeant shook his head.

"Dresser has 'em."

"Okay." Peters straightened. "I'll be around later then. There's a little matter of some misplaced dough I'm looking into right now."

He turned toward the door but Dresser's voice, lashing out, checked him.

"Hey, Slop!" The little man's jaw was thrust out. "What's the hurry? I asked you how you liked my new outfit."

Sloppy Peters paused, glanced back, let his gaze travel over Dresser's gaudy raiment.

"It looks like dough," he said tonelessly, then went on out to the street.

For a moment Johnny Dresser hesitated, as if on the point of charging after the other.

His lips were thin lines, his face tight with rage. Then he shrugged.

From his pocket he took a gold cigarette case, extracted an English Oval from it. With exaggerated slowness he lit the cigarette, blew a puff of smoke ceilingward, then, as if oblivious to the covert gaze of the silent cops in the squadroom, he sauntered out himself.

It was well after dark before Dresser appeared at the station house again, and in the intervening hours he had changed his clothes. The new outfit was even more resplendent than the last. Beginning with custom-made cordovans, it worked up through expensive, lightweight tweeds, custom tailored, to a fifteen-dollar silk shirt, ditto, a seven-fifty mogadore tie held in place by a platinum clip, and a forty-dollar snap-brim hat.

The sergeant at the desk—a different one, now—goggled at him for an instant. Then his face became blank.

"Sloppy Peters been in?" Dresser asked, his tone casual, but with a little rasp of anger beneath the casualness.

The other shook his head.

"Hasn't been in," he said. "Hasn't phoned in, either." His eyes met Dresser's. "Maybe he's working on that missing sixty grand from the armored truck holdup—the dough you couldn't find when you brought Nick Belmont in the other day."

"Maybe." The detective's lids half closed, but his voice was unchanged. "Maybe he is."

For an instant longer his eyes, dark and cold, stared into the sergeant's. Then, oblivious of the stares of the cops just inside the open squadroom door, all of whom had heard of the scene between him and his formerly inseparable sidekick, Sloppy Peters, that morning—as the whole neighborhood had heard of it by now—he sauntered out again.

On the precinct steps he paused to light a cigar—a two-bitter, the aroma testified—then he moved slowly through the darkness up the avenue toward Fourteenth.

At Fourteenth he paused to buy a paper, tucked it under his arm, then continued on a couple of blocks at a leisurely pace. Presently, tossing away his half-burned smoke, he turned into a cigar store on a corner.

"Hello, Dresser," the fat, shirt-sleeved man behind the counter greeted him. "If it was Christmas, I'd hire you to stand out front and be a Christmas tree. Where'd you get the pretties?"

"I won a little bet on a nag," Dresser told him. "Gimme a Triona."

"Tchk." The fat man made a little clucking noice, and withdrew a cigar box from the shelf. "Let you put your mitts on dough, and right away you start buying clothes."

The detective's eyes were cold.

"Never mind me," he said. "And put those weeds away. I want the two-bitters."

The fat man put the box away and withdrew another.

"I hear," he remarked, his shrewd, round face bland, "that the sixty grand Nick Belmont and his two triggermen heisted from that armored truck last Tuesday hasn't turned up yet. Too bad you couldn't find the dough when you busted in and took Nick the other night. You'd prob'ly have got a promotion out of it, even if you can't get a lead on the other two."

The fat man leaned his elbows on the showcase as Dresser took two cigars from the box, stripped the foil from one, and lit it at the counter lighter.

"Yeah," he said conversationally, "it was smart work, recognizing Nick from the description the truck driver gave before he died, and remembering Nick's brother-in-law owned a rooming house down the street by the junk yard. And the way they tell it, it was a nice job you did surprising Nick in his room and plinking him through the shoulder while he was throwing bullets at you."

"All in the job," Dresser said, tonelessly.

"Sure. Too bad, though, you couldn't find the dough in Nick's room. Sort of a mystery where it went to. Everybody knows that when Nick pulls a job, he always holds on to it until it's cut up. You took him before there was time to cut up the money, so he should of still had it. Wonder if anybody could have hijacked it?"

Dresser tossed down a dollar and looked at him.

"That's a very interesting thought," he remarked. "You think it up all by yourself?"

The fat man rang up the bill in the register and returned the little detective's stare blandly.

"If anybody did," he said, "and those two killers who pulled the job with Nick knew about it, there *might* be fireworks. So if somebody has that dough who shouldn't, this would be a nice time to take a vacation."

Dresser let blue smoke trickle from his nostrils while he stared into the fat man's eyes.

"It would be a good time for anybody to take a vacation, in this heat," he said at last, with cold deliberateness. "I'm heading for Maine for two weeks tomorrow myself."

"So I heard—" the fat man yawned sleepily. "Have a good time."

The detective let his gaze rest on the round, sweat-shiny face for another long moment. Then he turned toward the door. Almost through, he paused.

"If Sloppy's in anytime soon, tell him I'm looking for him," he directed.

"Oh, sure." The fat man half lifted a hand, let it drop. "I'll tell him. Sure."

Johnny Dresser looked at him again, his eyes half-lidded, then tapped cigar ash onto the floor and continued on out. The fat man smiled sleepily to himself.

The detective walked another block north, turned west, sauntered as far as Ninth, turned south for a few blocks, presently came back to Sixth and began working down again.

He stopped in half a dozen bars, giving each of them a chilly-eyed once-over, asking in each if Sloppy Peters had been in, getting always the same negative answer.

In an hour he worked his way south to the edge of the precinct district, then turned back, stopping in again at the same bars he'd cased on the way down.

In the second, the bartender signaled him.

"I heard a guy say he'd seen Sloppy Peters going into Luigi's, on

Eighth," he reported. "That was about five minutes ago, and the guy had just come in."

"Thanks." Johnny Dresser yawned, and adjusted his tie, using the mirror behind the bar to see himself in. He settled his hat more to his liking on his head, turned toward the door, and left as though he couldn't make up his mind whether it was worth going over to look for the big guy or not.

But once outside, his pace quickened, and he headed through the silent darkness, broken none too often by the distant lights on the long crosstown blocks, toward Eighth. Ahead of him, at the end of a block where the night crouched blackly in deep-sunk doorways, a red and green neon was blinking *Luigi's* into the darkness every five seconds. He was within fifty yards of it when the quick shuffle of footsteps came from a dark doorway he'd just passed, and a gun muzzle caught him in the back so swiftly he did not even have a chance to turn. He stood still, and his cigar-end glowed bright at his sudden indrawn breath.

"Okay, clotheshorse!" a voice like a shovel on a concrete pavement growled in his ear. "Forget how pretty you are and stand quiet, or you'll get a chance to see how you look in the new wide-open belly."

Dresser stood rigid as hands went through his pockets from behind, removing his gun, cuffs, and a wallet.

"Fifty bucks!" a hoarse voice like a laryngitis sufferer's reported. "It ain't here!"

"Stupe!" the shovel-on-concrete tones said. "You think he'd have the sixty grand in his pocket? He's got it hid some place safe, where he can get it but where it won't be found if anybody gets suspicious."

"So!" Dresser's tone was wooden. "That guy who said he'd seen Sloppy Peters in Luigi's. A plant!"

"Shuddup!" Laryngitis-voice said behind him. "If you'd of split with him, maybe you wouldn't be here now. That's what bein' greedy gets you."

"Clam up, Stupe! All right, Pretty. Start walking!"

"Where?" Dresser asked, without moving.

"To where you got the stuff planted."

"What stuff?"

"Lemme slap his ears!" Laryngitis begged hoarsely.

"I'll slap your nose. I'll handle this little chisel-hound. Listen! You got ten seconds to start walking. Nick had the dough. We hadn't cut it up. He had it in his room. You went there and took him. And the dough disappeared.

"It didn't get turned in. I know. It ain't in the room any more. It ain't in the house. The dough disappeared after you went in that room. You left Peters outside, and you had five minutes there alone to find it, after you put Nick out. Now you got it hid some place, what you didn't spend on duds, and you're gonna take us where it is."

"You're crazy," Dresser sighed. "If I had that sixty grand, would I still be hanging around this town?"

"Don't give us that!" Laryngitis rasped. "Where'd you get them duds? Outa your pay? Ha! Everybody knows you go hog wild buying duds when you get your hands on dough. And ain't you getting out of town tomorrer?"

"I bought the clothes out of anticipation," Dresser told them sarcastically. "Safety Transport has put up a thousand bucks each for you two intellectual giants, for shooting the guard. I was just spending it while I waited for you to come around and give up."

"Lemme slap his ears!" Laryngitis begged again.

"I'll slap your pants with a gun. Come on, Pretty, start walking. We know you got the dough. Peters knows it too. We heard about how he feels toward you now. Either we get it back or we get the satisfaction."

"Who am I to argue?" Dresser murmured, and shrugged. "But I'm going to turn around."

He turned slowly. The two behind him moved as he did, keeping out of his line of sight. He could see one was big, one slender, and that was all.

He began walking eastward. They crowded behind him, and the gun stayed jammed in his spine.

"Give out!" the shovel-on-concrete voice grated, when they had crossed Seventh and were still going east. "This is the way to Nick's room! And the dough ain't there!"

"There's a fire escape at the end of the hall next to Nick's room," Dresser said, in a disgusted voice. "Anybody could run down it and get back in three minutes. The fence along the alley underneath has a dozen boards out."

Shovel-on-concrete said something explosive.

"The junk yard!" he finished off. "All that scrap iron lying around!"

"All them tubs!" Laryngitis put in eagerly. "All them sinks! All them berlers! A hundred of 'em. He could of shoved it in a berler!"

Behind Dresser the two were breathing hard. The gun nudged his back forcefully, making him accelerate his pace. They came out on Sixth, and across the street was the junk yard which backed up against the house where Nick Belmont had been taken.

A rickety board fence staggered around the junk-yard lot, and rusty barbed wire crawled around the top of the fence. The avenue and the street were both deserted, dimly shadowed. In the darkness of the junk yard a cat merauwled at the scabrous backs of the rooming houses that looked down on the graveyard of bathtubs and boilers and toilet bowls.

Johnny Dresser crossed the avenue, went down the street, turned into an alley, and came to a pause halfway through it.

"Well," he said, "here we are. How do we do it?"

"Stupe, get inside," the shovel-on-concrete voice snapped. "Then, Dresser, you go through. Take one step after you're inside, and stand quiet. Keep a gun on him, Stupe. I'll follow."

The bigger of the two figures behind him detached itself, ambled to the fence, wedged into a space where a board was missing, and with a grunt shoved through.

"Next!"

Gun-pressure steered Dresser to the gap. He put his left foot through the opening, eased his body through, drew in his right foot, and moved one step away. Behind him, Stupe jammed a gun against him so hard he staggered.

Shovel-on-concrete slid through and joined them. They stood surrounded by piles of rusting iron. Pipes thrust out jagged arms at them. Discarded boilers hugged the ground like misshapen monsters, their shadows, cast by the half moon, wells of darkness. Bathtubs, some right side up and half full of rainwater, others inverted, lay around gleaming with a pallid whiteness. Discarded toilet bowls stood about maudlinly.

"C'mon," Laryngitis said, jiggling Dresser's kidney with the gun muzzle. "Where's it at?"

"Hell," Dresser grumbled, looking around. "They all look alike now. But I put it inside a boiler. One with a door still on. I'll know it when I see it. It's more over this way toward the middle."

He moved slowly away from the fence, toward a cluster of discarded sanitary apparatus of three generations. There were rusty boilers, bathtubs, sinks, toilet bowls, intermingled helter-skelter.

"Come on, quit stalling!" Shovel-on-concrete rasped. "Find it and let's get out of here!"

"With fifty old boilers lying around," Dresser told him sourly, "I can't go straight to it. I'll find it in a minute. I tell you, I'll know it when I see it. There's a firebox door on it, hanging by just one hinge."

He worked toward the center of the collection, and they stayed only inches behind him.

Ahead of him, a black tomcat leaped abruptly from a shadowy crevice and spat at them.

"Gee!" Laryngitis exclaimed. "A black cat!"

"Bad luck for Pretty Boy, if he don't produce before I count ten!" Shovel-on-concrete snapped. "I'm beginning to get the idea he's stalling."

"Hey!" Dresser remonstrated. "I said I'd recognize it, didn't I! Here it is."

He stopped before a massive apartment-house boiler, prone on its side, grated door over its firebox hanging loose by one rusty hinge.

"You want me to get it out, or will you?" he asked.

"You bring it out," Shovel-voice told him. "And if it ain't there, or you make any funny move, I'm just gonna pull the string and give it to you."

They stood back a pace. Dresser stooped, lifted the rusty iron door, wedged it back out of the way. Then he thrust an arm into the gaping black maw of the boiler and brought out an oblong package wrapped in newspaper.

"I wrapped it up," he said. "Like this, so if anybody looked in they'd think it was just old newspaper."

"Take it from him, Stupe," Shovel-voice grated. "And *you*, take this!"

He brought his gun down, barrel gleaming viciously, toward Dresser's forehead.

Dresser heaved himself backwards, the sight of the revolver clipping a red line down his cheek.

"Hey!" he shouted. "Give. *Give!*"

He caromed off the boiler and tumbled sideways. Shovel-voice lifted the gun to slash again. And then, not more than a dozen feet away, directly beneath the black cat that crouched on the inverted bathtub watching them, the night exploded in a javelin of flame.

The bullet screamed past Dresser as he fell, closer to his face than to the hand holding the gun. He hit a pile of junk and wriggled away on his side like a snake. Beyond him, Stupe was wailing.

"Gee, Phil! The cat! It shot at us!"

The night blew open again, but the cat wasn't there on the bathtub any longer. After the gun had gone off under its nose, it seemed to vanish in mid-air.

Red flame lapped out again. Shovel-voice dropped to a knee, got the gun up, and fired at the flash. A bullet screamed off metal, and the hole in the bathtub, where the overflow pipe had gone in, ejected gun-flare again.

"He's undera bathtub!" Stupe screeched, and slammed a couple of shots screaming off the rounded bottom of the tub. "We can't get at 'im!"

Dresser squirmed backwards. Shovel-voice had ducked back, and ignoring the tub, was shooting at him now. Dresser rolled. The bullets pinged up earth where he had been. Scrabbling at the package in his hand, he rolled on, over old iron, between tubs and boilers.

There was no more firing from the tub, because both Stupe and

Shovel-voice had ducked backwards out of the limited range from the pipe hole. Instead the tub itself was heaving mightily. It half rose, bucked and toppled, like a prehistoric monster getting to its feet.

Then it fell over backwards, ringing loudly against some old pipes, and a big man with a gun in his hand appeared from under it seeking something to shoot at.

The bullets coming Dresser's way stopped. Dresser got to one knee, yanked the gun free from the newspapers and string clinging to it, and fired. Stupe or Shovel-voice, he couldn't tell which, ducked at the shot, whirled to answer it, and the movement gave the lurching big man his target. The gun in his hand bucked. A dark figure gurgled, fell into a bathtub half full of water, and stayed there.

Dresser rose cautiously, and the gun that had just exploded swung toward him. He ducked down again.

"Hey!" he screeched. "It's me, dope!"

"Oops!" a bull voice roared. "Sorry, Johnny. There he goes!"

Halfway across the junk yard, taking advantage of the shadows, a dark figure was ducking from cover to cover, working toward the fence. Dresser yelled, but the double explosion of the big man's gun cut the yell off in his throat. By the time there was enough quiet for it to be heard, it was too late. The fleeing figure screeched, jumped convulsively, and collapsed across an outthrust arm of pipe.

Dresser put his own gun away, pulled himself free with a yank from the sheet-metal stampings, and strode over to the big man, who was peering down at the figure in the bathtub.

"Put away the cannon, Sloppy," the little detective said resignedly. "The way they fell, you stamped and addressed 'em both straight to the morgue. I wanted 'em alive, too. I wanted to talk to them.

"Phil Whip, the little one, and Wheezy Blaine, the big one. They know plenty that I figured on getting out of them about other jobs. It's too late now, though. When're you going to learn to shoot a prisoner nice and neat through the shoulder or the leg, instead of messing him up every time with a bullet in his face?"

"Gee," the big man said contritely, mopping his face with his hand and thereby spreading the dirt he'd acquired on it during his stay under the tub a little more evenly across his whole countenance. "I'm sorry, Johnny. I guess I was too anxious. But gosh, lying cramped in there all evening, I sure did get tired of waiting. I thought you wasn't ever coming."

Dresser looked morosely down at himself. The old iron and metal stampings might just as well have been barbed wire for all the difference the checked tweed would ever know. He fingered one of the yawning gaps in the imported woolen stuff, looked at the slashes in his cordovans, and groaned aloud when he found even his shirt was torn and his tie ripped. As for his new hat, it had a bullet hole in it.

"We don't get them alive and I don't even get my decoy scenery out of it," he growled. "And I spent about half my share of the reward money in advance, duding up!"

Sloppy Peters beamed down at him, happily unaware of the dirt that clung to his clothes, his hands, his face.

"Yeah, but look at all the credit you'll get," he argued. "You figured out the whole thing—having the lieutenant not say anything about you turning in the dough; letting everybody get the idea you hijacked that sixty grand and were gonna keep it. You made sure all the cops would know about it, and would spread it over the whole district, so that it was bound to come to the ears of those two killers and make 'em come out of hiding to get back the sixty grand they thought you had snaffled.

"Why, hell, Johnny, you didn't make one mistake all the way down the line. When the commissioner hears what a sweet scheme you cooked up to get those two killers, he'll maybe promote you."

"Nuts!" Dresser snapped, mournfully fingering the rents in his tweeds. "I made one big mistake and he'll jump all over me for it."

His big partner tried vainly to wipe loose some of the dirt on his hands and his face.

"What was that, Johnny?" he asked.

"He'll want to know why, once I finally had you in a bathtub, I didn't put in the soap and water, too," Dresser grunted.

THE ARMY OF LITTLE EARS Charles B. Child

*This story was an exercise based on the problem of how an in-
dividual could, in plain sight, walk up a road and turn a corner
and vanish. It is a very old problem, like the one about murder-
in-the-locked room; the author added to it the question of what
to do with a corpse in the heat of midsummer Baghdad, where
odors vary from rose gardens to sour drains.*

*The Army of Little Ears, obviously a Middle-Eastern auxil-
lary of the Baker Street Irregulars (and Praise to Allah!) was a
natural. The Grand Bazaar of Baghdad is infested by small boys
who act as light porters for customers; their fee is reasonable,
tourism has not yet produced the counterpart of the Egyptian
dragoman, and may that never happen.*

*The author remembers favorably these dead-end kids of Bagh-
dad and their extraordinary knowledge of local affairs. In this
story he has given them a leader, the son of Inspector Chafik.*

CHARLES B. CHILD

Chafik J. Chafik, of the Baghdad police, took his place at the breakfast table in his house on the Street of the Scatterer of Blessings. The
swarthy, neat little man, dressed for the heat of the day in immaculate
whites, accepted the homage of his family with the indulgence of a
Babylonian king. He glanced at his watch, announced, "I am four
minutes late," and dipped his spoon into the bowl of *liben* and honey-
colored dates.

Leila, his wife, a serene and graceful woman, asked, "My man, you
did not sleep well?"

She glanced at her son, a wide-eyed elf of a boy, and saw that his
effervescence was precariously corked. Her look constrained him.

Chafik said, "The Compassionate One willed me a bad night.
There were comings and goings and voices, and the most objection-
able voice was the voice of a cat." He looked at his son reprovingly.

Faisal began, "My father—"

Leila interrupted: "Faisal's cat had kittens."

21

"Five," the boy said proudly. "May I keep them? May I, my father?"

It was difficult for Chafik to deny his son anything, but he was incensed by his sleepless night. He signed. "Ah, what base ingratitude!" he said. "I took this animal into my house as a homeless waif and—"

He stopped, for he suddenly remembered that Faisal had been a waif, too. It was less than two years since the boy, then an eight-year-old orphan, had been one of the pack of homeless urchins who frequented the Baghdad bazaars. Chafik had taken him from that life to fill the gap in a childless, but otherwise happy, marriage, and had never regretted the impulse which had given him a fine son.

So, shocked by his unfortunate remark, the little man looked beseechingly at his wife.

Leila's head was lowered; she said nothing.

Chafik took refuge in attack. "Does not my sleepless night suffice?" he demanded. "Am I now denied the brightness of conversation? And must I have kittens underfoot, too?"

The telephone rang, and the Inspector padded on stocking feet to answer it. The caller was Sergeant Abdullah of the homicide squad.

Abdullah said in a voice of doom, "Sir, I trust you have enjoyed breakfast?"

"My stomach," Chafik answered, "is delicate this morning, and judging by your ill-omened croak it is well I left it unfilled. What horror have you to show me?"

"I regret, sir, a corpse." The sergeant went on to give details.

When Abdullah had finished, Chafik got his shoes from under the hall table, for Arab-fashion he did not wear them in the house. He picked up the shoes and returned to his family.

"The evil continues," he said. "Now I have a corpse. They found one on the premises of Mr. Topalian, the jeweler and antique dealer of the bazaars. And Mr. Topalian has vanished. Enough, therefore, of ungrateful cats and pestilential kittens. Respect my wishes and cast them out."

Faisal's wail followed Chafik to the street. The Inspector sought comfort in the wisdom of the Koran, and prayerfully hoped his thoughtless remark, which had distressed his wife, had escaped the notice of their adopted son. Knowing the sharpness of those faunlike ears, he was not sure.

"If the Devil had not given us speech, there would be less misunderstanding in the world," the little man said, as he drove away.

The establishment of David Topalian was in one of the far reaches of the great bazaar. Inspector Chafik, who had left his car outside the Imperial Bank, where the labyrinth of covered ways began, arrived on foot, and was received by the tall police officer who had telephoned.

Abdullah said, "Sir, the corpse is that of a man named Esiah Constantine. He—"

Chafik gestured for silence, extracted a record card from his tidy brain, and quoted: "Constantine, Esiah. Aged fifty-seven. Resident of Basra. Educated. Assisted in the archeological excavations at Ur in the Nineteen-twenties." He paused and then added, "Believed to be in possession of valuable antiques—allegedly he stole them from the excavations. I will now face his corpse."

They went down a short passage into a vaulted room, cool and shadowy, and brightened by silk prayer rugs on the walls. There were many treasures in the place, which was an exotic setting for the colorful Armenian dealer who normally presided over it in a velvet gown and embroidered skullcap. But Topalian did not preside today, and the corpse of Esiah Constantine was not exotic.

The body was sprawled in a low chair with its head bowed on an ebony coffee table. Two cups, which had been used, were overturned, and drunken flies crawled over the pool of sugary coffee. The back of the dead man's skull was crushed; on the floor was a bronze club shaped like a lion's paw.

Inspector Chafik looked at the club and said, "Ancient Assyrian—a warrior's weapon. Mr. Topalian has a large collection of such relics."

He examined the body, touched the mashed head, noticed splinters of protruding bone, and announced, "The killer stood on the right, possibly after pouring coffee to honor—and disarm—the guest. Three blows were struck. Wasteful energy; one was enough."

Sergeant Abdullah said, "Sir, the man has been dead some nine hours. It fits the time of Topalian's departure. He—"

Chafik wiped his hands on the coat-tails of the corpse. "Let us begin at the end, as detective stories are written," he said. "Who found Constantine?"

"The missing man's cousin, sir. George Topalian. I will produce him."

The sergeant brought in a handsome young man whose heavy-lidded eyes suggested that he kept late hours. He was nervous, and the ash of many cigarettes was spilled on his expensive, but crumpled, clothes.

"A candle that burns at both ends should at least gut itself neatly," Chafik said. "However, that is not my affair. Your name is George Topalian. You are twenty-three, unmarried, but not inexperienced. You work for your cousin, who is thirty years your senior. You discovered the unfortunate gentleman who lies here. Inform me of the circumstances."

The young man would not look at the body as he answered, "My cousin expects me to open the shop at 7:30, but I was perhaps half an hour late this morning. The door was still locked—"

Chafik interrupted: "Your cousin has a residence in the Jenub district; he also has a sleeping room above these premises. You feared he had stayed the night and would reprimand you for lateness?"

George Topalian's handsome face became sullen. He nodded.

"So you knocked?"

"There are witnesses. Neighbors—"

"They will talk later. With diffidence toward an elder, you knocked, and there was no answer. Then?"

"I unlocked the door and went in. I saw Constantine."

"You knew him?"

"I knew of him—that he was coming from Basra to sell something."

"What?"

"A chalice. The funeral cup of a Sumerian noble."

Chafik thought: So my records are correct—Constantine did steal treasures on that expedition years ago. Now he tries to sell them. And to what better dealer could he go than David Topalian?

Aloud, the Inspector said, "The killer apparently took the chalice away. I need a description."

The young man shrugged and answered disdainfully, "I can't help you. I care little about antiques; I like modern things. But any collector can describe the chalice; they all knew Constantine had it."

Chafik was disturbed because his records had missed this important fact, but he said, "So when you found the body, you ran for help?"

"First I went to see if my cousin was upstairs."

"Thereby establishing that nobody was hiding on the premises. Excellently done!" Chafik took out a packet of Ghazi cigarettes and offered one to the witness. "Now, your cousin's disappearance. When did you last see him?"

Topalian lighted the cigarette from the Inspector's match and answered, "Last night, about eight o'clock. We were closing. He told me to get porters for a customer's purchase."

"Several porters means a bulky object," Chafik said. "Was it the object that formerly stood outside in the entrance passage? I noticed a portion of lighter-colored floor. Observation is the fetish of my trade," he added apologetically.

"You observed correctly. It was a Meccan bridal chest. I found porters, escorted them to the purchaser's home, saw delivery made, left—"

"Wait," Chafik said. "I cannot stand on the curve of time and see all dimensions at once. Had the customer departed before you went for the porters?"

"Yes."

"And your cousin was here when you returned?"

"He had gone upstairs to rest and to wait for Constantine. I did not disturb him. Furthermore, I was in a hurry."

Chafik detected evasion in the young man's reply, so he asked with deceptive mildness, "You had an engagement, perhaps?"

Topalian stared down at his cigarette; his heavy lids concealed the expression in his eyes. "I was to meet a friend," he said.

"For the sake of tidy records, give me his name."

"We—he—we were to meet at the Shahrazade Cabaret. No, it was the Roxy. But he didn't turn up. I—" He stopped abruptly.

The Inspector would not let his confusion pass. "The sequence of events may refresh your memory," he said. "To whom did you take the chest?"

"To Dr. Ghaffari."

"Ghaffari, Mohammed," Chafik quoted. "Aged sixty-two. Ph.D. from London University. He buys antiques rather than food." The little man smiled, then asked, "At what time did you make the delivery?"

"I—I don't remember."

"Be at ease, the Doctor will remember. You see, I try to help you," Chafik said kindly.

"Ghaffari wasn't at home. He had an appointment, too. Before he left my cousin's shop he gave me a key."

"You were in the Doctor's house alone after you dismissed the porters?"

"For a few minutes. Why the Devil do you ask so many questions?" the young man asked angrily.

"How timely to mention the Devil! He was busy here, directing Constantine's murder, the disappearance of the chalice, the disappearance of your cousin—"

George Topalian interrupted vehemently, "Now you implicate my cousin!"

"I have made no accusation, yet. How much was he to pay for the chalice?"

"I don't know. He complained that the price was high, but he hoped to get it lowered. Besides, he had a buyer, an American—they are all foolish about antiques. So why should he kill?"

"An eloquent defense," Chafik said. "Let us, however, be factual and consider only the facts of his disappearance. Who saw Mr. Topalian last?"

The inquiry was addressed to the Inspector's assistant, who brought in a very old man clad in tattered battle dress.

Sergeant Abdullah said, "The next witness, sir. Shah Murad, the bazaar *charkachi*. Formerly of the Levise."

Chafik noticed with pity how the watchman strained to come to attention. "Did he see Constantine arrive?" he asked Abdullah.

"His evidence is that he saw the deceased admitted to these premises. Half an hour later, he states, Topalian left in a great hurry. Murad claims he saw him turn the corner into the Street of the Coppersmiths. Since then, so far as I can ascertain, no eyes have beheld the Armenian."

"What was Topalian wearing?"

"The robe he favors, sir. Also a hat with a brim, such as Christians wear."

Chafik said dryly, "An odd costume for a man who planned to disappear."

The Inspector went outside. The bazaar was roofed by straw mats which were rotted by the weather; sunlight and shadow made an intricate pattern over the unpaved way. The Street of the Coppersmiths was entered through a narrow arch a few yards from Topalian's shop.

The street was a place of thunderous noise and of sudden, leaping flames that brushed the workers at their forges with glowing color. Numerous passages, barely wide enough for a man on foot, led into mysterious reaches. Chafik shrugged, knowing the hopelessness of searching such a maze.

"Human tigers prowl this jungle at night," Chafik said. "If it were known that Topalian carried an object of value—" He finished the thought with a finger across his throat.

"A body," the sergeant said thoughtfully, "is difficult to hide."

"Its presence," the Inspector agreed, "would become evident in this heat in two days. In three days," he amended, flinching from the odors of the open drains. "You will instruct the police to alert their noses."

"That will be done, sir. But what of Constantine?"

"Yes. Constantine. The discovery of a dead Topalian would not answer the questions raised by the corpse he left behind."

The little man stopped, stared at the corner of the Street of the Coppersmiths, and ran. He was blocked by the crowd that had been attracted by rumors of murder.

"I swear I saw him!" Chafik exclaimed to Abdullah.

"Mr. Topalian, sir?"

"No. Faisal—my son. He should be at school."

"Boys look very much alike, sir, and there are many in the bazaar. They rush this way and that with great energy. It is the way of boys. I have daughters," the sergeant added smugly.

"Daughters undulate," Chafik said. And then, unhappily, he remembered the episode of the cat and kittens and his unfortunate remark at the breakfast table. He hurried back to the antique shop to call his wife.

"Leila," he began.

"Oh, my man!" There was relief in her voice. "You got my message?" his wife went on.

"What message? I am closeted with an uncommunicative corpse."

"I called your office to inform you that Faisal's school—"

"Yes? Yes? What, my wife?"

"They have reported he did not attend this morning."

Chafik was shocked and silent. He wanted to rush home, but duty restrained him and it was necessary to reassure Leila.

"A childish prank, my wife. I shall discipline Faisal," he added sternly. "Inform him, when he comes home, that his father will not speak to him for twenty-four hours." And with fond words for Leila, the Inspector hung up.

Then he beat his fists together and exclaimed, "All because of the cat. That monster and her kittens!"

"Sir?" Abdullah asked.

"Nothing, nothing." The Inspector sought escape in action. "I am going to Dr. Ghaffari, who perhaps can describe the object Constantine brought to Topalian. I assume he, like all collectors, knows about it," Chafik added. "As for yourself, check on the cousin. That young man's alibi was unsatisfactory. And, Abdullah—"

"Sir?"

"If you should see my son, reprimand him severely and send him home. He does not belong here, not in the bazaars, not now."

The man the Inspector wished to see lived at the back of the bazaars, in a house that thrust its ancient foundations into the river's slime.

It was once a Turkish palace but now housed many families; Ghaffari had rooms on the first floor.

As Chafik picked his way through the refuse of the streets, he had a feeling that he was being followed, and he looked around. He saw nobody suspicious, and was distracted by a boy who resembled Faisal.

The urchin wore a ragged gown and a wisp of turban. He skipped blithely on naked feet, balancing a basket on his head; light portering was the precarious livelihood of these waifs, hired for a few fils.

They grow up to become entries in my criminal records, Chafik thought sadly. This might have been Faisal.

The youngster passed, then twirled, like a ballet dancer, across the Inspector's path. He had a sharp, bright face, too-wise eyes, and an engaging smile. "Sahib?" he asked.

"I am not shopping," Chafik said. "And I have nothing to carry." He reached into his pocket for a coin.

The urchin ran backward before him. "Policeman Sahib, I am not to take money. I have a message."

Chafik stopped.

"I am to say that yesterday the Armenian merchant, Topalian, and his cousin, quarreled. About women. The young one has many women. The elder threatened to banish the younger from Baghdad, unless—"

"Who sent you?" Chafik demanded. "How do you know I am a policeman?"

The boy did a pirouette, kicked up his heels, laughed, and disappeared.

"Was it Abdullah?" Chafik wondered, as he walked on. "No, he would never send such a message by a seedling! So who?"

At Dr. Ghaffari's house, he rattled the heavy knocker.

The Doctor was a tall, stooped man who peered at the Inspector with tired, sunken eyes. His clothes were threadbare, but he had gracious manners and bowed as he recognized his visitor.

"I am honored, Inspector! Come in, come in! If I had known of your visit I would have prepared coffee."

"I am on duty, Doctor." Chafik was well aware Ghaffari had no coffee in the house. To save money for antiques, the Doctor bought the dross that merchants scraped from their sacks.

Ghaffari lived in three large rooms which opened off the entrance hall. Light came grayly through barred windows and touched the treasures that crowded every corner. The man had once been wealthy, but now his dinars were interred in this magnificent collection.

Chafik said, "I have come for help. You know about Topalian?"

"Yes, I heard. It's incredible. I saw him yesterday and he was in fine spirits and happy about an important deal. I cannot believe—"

The Inspector was in a hurry and stopped Ghaffari. "I am informed the deal concerned an antique which Constantine brought from Basra. It has vanished. Did you know of it? Can you describe it?"

"Can a man describe Paradise?" Ghaffari's eyes shone, and color touched his sallow cheeks. He went to a cabinet and reverently lifted a crystal cup which filled his two hands like a bowl of light.

"This," he said, "is Sumerian craftsmanship, but compared with the chalice you ask about, it is clay. The chalice is of this size and shape and made from a block of lapis lazuli worked so fine it shames an eggshell. Yet it is strong; gold is fused with the lapis. And the color! The sun-flecked blue of the canopy of God's Throne!"

"It would appear you have seen the cup," Chafik said.

"Constantine showed it to me in Basra years ago."

"So it is true then that he hid it from his superiors when they excavated the death pits at Ur?"

Ghaffari shrugged. "Who can blame him? But permit me to continue. The chalice is a funeral cup. When a Sumerian noble was buried, they put a cup filled with rare wine in his hands. And round about him were guards and attendants—"

"Slaughtered," said Chafik, "to attend their master's afterworld comforts. It is well I was not a policeman in those days. What value do you put on the chalice?"

"Value? You mean money? Inspector, one does not estimate such a treasure in dinars! I was shocked when Topalian said Constantine was going to sell. I had thought better of him."

Chafik was puzzled. The chalice was so rare that a warning circulated among the police of all countries would frighten away all prospective buyers. "And so," the Inspector said, "Constantine's murderer must be aware that if he tries to sell, he will be paid by the hangman."

The Doctor insisted on showing his collection and Chafik went politely from room to room. He was overwhelmed by the beauty he saw, and he felt pity for the man, living in poverty amid such wealth.

When they returned to the hall, the Inspector examined a large chest and asked Ghaffari if he had bought it from Topalian. The Doctor nodded, raised the heavy lid, and launched into a discourse.

"I believe this dates to the Queen of Sheba," he said. "The painted designs are Meccan, but there are traces of others underneath. However, the years have taken their toll, and perhaps I did not get a good bargain."

He pointed to cracks in the side of the chest and then let the lid fall. It closed like a slammed door and wafted odors of myrrh and frankincense into the room.

"I am told," Chafik said, "that young Topalian delivered this in your absence. You considered it safe to trust him with the key to your house?"

Ghaffari said, "I know the young man well and have always found him exemplary, except for—"

"Women?" Chafik suggested. They both smiled.

As he prepared to go, the Inspector asked, "Doctor, when you returned, did you find the chest open?"

"Open? Let me think." Ghaffari turned and looked at it. "Yes—yes, I am sure I found it open."

The little man salaamed and left. On the doorstep he threw down the stub of his cigarette, and, looking back a moment later, saw Ghaffari pick it up.

So he also denies himself the comfort of tobacco, thought Chafik. Surely the Compassionate One has afflicted him.

Anxious to telephone his wife for news of Faisal, he walked rapidly, and it was some time before he realized that a bazaar boy was running after him. He stopped, turned quickly, and the boy just as quickly backed away.

"Sahib! A message!"

"Another?" Chafik asked.

"Sahib, Hassan Ali, the beggar of the Street of the Leatherworkers, yesterday boasted he would rob the Armenian, Topalian."

The Inspector reached for the boy, and clutched air. The boy was as elusive as smoke. Bewildered, Chafik continued on his way.

"There is organization behind this," he told himself. "Only the All-Merciful knows if the intention is to hinder or help."

As if he had been sent in answer, a third boy appeared from nowhere with the same breathless "Sahib?"

"Deliver your message," Chafik said with resignation.

"I am to tell you to forget about Hassan Ali. After he boasted, he fell down drunk from drinking much arrack, and slept all night."

"I thank you," Chafik said. "The original rumor would have reached me on a police report and would have caused tribulation for both Hassan Ali and myself until the truth was known. Therefore I am grateful to whoever directs you, fleet-footed Father of Long Ears."

And courteously saluting the grinning urchin, he turned and left.

There was no news of Faisal. Inspector Chafik stood at the window of his office overlooking Al Rashid Street, and saw in the ugly, brown city the reflection of his mood. Somewhere among those half million people of all races and creeds was his son.

He reproached himself bitterly. Now he was sure Faisal had misunderstood the remark about the stray cat, had remembered that he had once been a homeless waif and, believing himself unwanted, had run away.

But I cannot divert men to find him, Chafik thought despairingly. I am a policeman. There is murder.

Sergeant Abdullah came in. He was as emotional as the stone image he resembled, and was excellent therapy for the distracted father.

In his usual ominous voice, Abdullah said, "Sir, I have checked the alibi of the younger Topalian. He lied. He was not at any cabaret. Nor did he go home last night. And sir, by careful inquiry I have learned that yesterday he—"

"Quarreled with his cousin about a woman," Chafik said.

"A fierce and wordy argument. But, sir, how did you know?"

"I have ears, many little ears. You re-examined Topalian?"

"He is stubbornly silent and refuses to detail his movements after he delivered the chest. I have detained him."

"Did you establish how long he stayed alone in Dr. Ghaffari's house?"

"There are no witnesses, sir. The porters departed immediately."

Chafik looked down at the signet ring on his left hand. "What else, Abdullah?" he asked, absently.

"One of those miserable urchins who frequent the bazaar—"

"I adopted one," Chafik said softly.

Abdullah went on, blushing, "The waif commanded me to tell you that four days ago Dr. Ghaffari purchased a chain and iron collar, suitable for a large dog. I could not detain my informant."

"It would be easier to catch a gazelle. These young messengers are bombarding me with wild rumors. Ghaffari has no dog. Yet, I wonder—I wonder."

The Inspector looked at his watch. "So late? I am going home. Continue to press the search for the elder Topalian. If his body does not appear within a few days, it will mean the man has left this city. Although why an honored citizen should turn murderer and thief is beyond me."

When Inspector Chafik reached home, he found his wife in tears; Faisal had not returned and it was already night.

The stillness in the house was heartbreaking. Chafik remembered the busy feet, the treble voice, the uproar of a lively boy, and he repented moments of anger when meditations had been disturbed. He held Leila and tried to comfort her with passages from the Koran, but grief overcame him and he joined her in tears.

"How fortunate that we are not English and do not find it necessary to inhibit emotion," he declared.

Presently he gave Leila a sedative, arranged for a neighbor to sit with her, and went out into the dark streets. He wandered, searching, and questioning the police patrols; duty would not permit him to assign men solely to the quest for his son.

At dawn Chafik went to his office and fell asleep in a chair. And it was there that Abdullah, arriving early, found him. The sergeant, too, was red-eyed and weary.

"Sir," he said with pity, "I regret I have no news of Faisal."

"You, too, have been searching?"

"I took the liberty, sir."

"Keep to your duty. We must both remember our duty," Chafik said, and added less harshly, "but thank you, Abdullah. Is there news of Topalian?"

"None. Today, perhaps, the noses of the police will discover—" the sergeant stopped suddenly, remembering the missing Faisal. Hurriedly he said, "I have to report a singular incident. There was another of the bazaar waifs outside as I came in."

"Yes? Yes?"

"He told me to tell you that Dr. Ghaffari has made large purchases of food. I held the child briefly, but his teeth were sharp." Abdullah tenderly nursed a wrist.

Chafik reached for a cigarette. "So the little ears are still busy. Could it be?"

No, it was too fantastic. "Yet, it is strange," he went on, "that a man who has never squandered more than fifty fils a day on his stomach these many years should suddenly indulge his appetite."

With little heart, but still pursuing this elusive notion, he began a busy day. Other things than the Topalian case required attention, and the Inspector occupied himself with these until the call to prayer reminded him that the day was ending.

Chafik thought: Another night. Darkness, and all it shrouds. My son—

Violently, he swept the papers from his desk and shouted, "To the Pit with duty! To the Pit with Constantine and Topalian! I will divert every man. I—"

Sergeant Abdullah appeared at the door. "Sir," he said, "a boy wishes to speak with you."

The boy was frightened. His bare toes curled and uncurled on the cheap carpet.

"What now?" Chafik asked.

"Sahib," the boy said breathlessly, "I am to say there is a man in hiding. The proof is his stomach's demands. He who sends me has found a way into the hiding place and has entered it to seek final proof."

The Inspector, with a tiger's leap, reached the boy, seized the slack of his gown, and shouted, "Who sent you?"

"I will not talk! I am Faisal's man!"

There was a ripping sound as the threadbare garment tore. Brown buttocks vanished through the door and disappeared down the gloomy corridor, as the boy outran the police.

"Imbecile!" Inspector Chafik exclaimed. "Imbecile!"

"I could not stop him," Abdullah said defensively.

"I am the imbecile! How could I doubt that Faisal was behind all this? He is of the bazaars. He mobilized his old friends and directed their inquisitive ears to help me. And I was too stupid to understand his messages."

The moment of relevation passed. "Faisal! Where has he gone? Into what danger? I must find my son, Abdullah!"

Chafik calmed himself and forced himself to sit at his desk and light a cigarette. "A man in hiding—misered fils spent suddenly on food. Oh, Merciful One! A chain and an iron collar but no dog! Abdullah, get the young Topalian from the detention room."

When the sergeant returned with George Topalian, Chafik stood on tiptoe in an effort to match the young man's stature.

"You are foolish and stubborn," he said, pointing his chin accusingly. "You gave me a lying alibi for the night your cousin disappeared, because you were with a woman, probably a married one since you protect her with your silence. You quarreled with your cousin about her because he had stern morals. So, enough. Tell me, when Dr. Ghaffari left the shop after purchasing the chest, did he slam the door?"

Topalian stammered, "Yes—yes, I think I heard it slam."

"Neither you nor your cousin actually saw Ghaffari reach the street?" the Inspector pursued.

"No, the passage leading to the door is at an angle."

"And when you returned with the porters, the chest was locked?"

"It had been padlocked."

Inspector Chafik's face was a mask. He reached into a drawer, grabbed his gun, and ran.

The crowds that filled the bazaars parted from the madman with a gun. He shouted, "Compassionate One, grant me time!" He was haltless, his pomaded hair was in disarray, and he had torn open his collar.

When Chafik reached the old house by the river, he hammered on the door and his voice cracked as he demanded admission. There was no answer, and he butted the door with his shoulder.

At that moment it opened and he fell into the dark hall.

He lost the gun on the tiled floor and scrabbled with bleeding fingers to find it. A figure materialized from the shadows and Chafik saw an arm raised to deliver a blow. He rolled clear and was shocked by pain as his shoulder hit the gun.

He seized it and rose to one knee.

In the smoky light from an oil lamp in an adjoining room he saw the dull gleam of metal—an ancient battle-ax poised for another blow. He steadied his wrist and fired twice.

The shots echoed in the vaulted hall. Inspector Chafik rose and looked down at the still form of Dr. Ghaffari, and said in prayer, "God forgive me." He turned quickly away.

He searched the rooms until he found a door hidden by a wall hanging. It was locked. He blew out the lock with his gun and did not feel the splinters that lacerated his face. He went down winding steps into the cellar of Ghaffari's house.

Ghaffari's prisoners were in an alcove strewn with straw. The man had an iron collar around his neck and was fastened to the wall by a chain. The boy was bound with rope, and both were gagged with tape.

Chafik released Faisal, saying over and over, "My son, my son." He took the boy in his arms and wept.

Faisal's lips were torn by the tape and he whimpered, "Father, it hurts. But, my father, there is the man."

Inspector Chafik used the barrel of his gun to force a link in the chain. He said, "Later we will remove the collar. It does not exactly adorn you, Mr. Topalian."

The antique dealer was unharmed, but shock had left its mark. He shook his head and said, "Ghaffari is a madman. Why did he keep me chained and feed me so lavishly? How did I get here?"

Chafik said, "After you sold Ghaffari the chest and he asked to have it delivered, he gave his house key to your cousin. Then he went out and slammed the door. But it was not the door he slammed. It was the lid of the chest. He was inside it."

"Then Ghaffari attacked me after George had gone for the porters!" Topalian exclaimed. "I remember a nightmare of suffocation."

"You had been bound, gagged, and probably chloroformed. And you journeyed, sir, in the chest, escorted in all innocence by your cousin, who was in too much of a hurry to heed the porters' grumbles about excessive weight. Your suffocation was real; you survived because there were cracks in the chest and because Ghaffari did not want you to die. Only one murder was planned for that night—Constantine's."

"Murdered?"

"For the chalice. Ghaffari admitted him to the shop, posed as your friend, and then killed him. Afterward, he put on your robe and hat and walked out boldly. He had correctly calculated the fading eyesight of the bazaars' ancient watchman. After vanishing into the maze of streets, he removed the robe and went home without exciting suspicion. He had the chalice, and he had his alibi."

Topalian shook his head. "But why didn't he kill me?"

"Because, sir, he couldn't dispose of your body. In this heat and in a house where there are other families—" Chafik raised his thumb and forefinger to his nose. "He had to keep you alive until the search for you as the murderer had died down. And if my son and his friends had not noticed the change in Ghaffari's shopping habits—"

The Inspector heard a noise upstairs. He checked his gun and ran. The Doctor's body was gone from the hall and a trail of blood led to one of the rooms.

Chafik followed it. The dying man was in a chair by the moonlit window. He had taken the chalice from its hiding place and sat holding it with both hands. The beauty of the lapis and gold transfigured his waxen face. In his last moments, Dr. Ghaffari forgot pain.

He slowly raised his head, recognized the Inspector, and whispered, "I did not take it for money. I could not let it go—into alien hands—far from our land."

The deep-set eyes became brilliant. "This," Ghaffari said in a suddenly strong voice, "is how the Sumerian was buried, holding his funeral cup. Where is my escort to the next world? The slaughtered ones—the—"

He bowed his head over the chalice; even in death he embraced it. . . .

When Inspector Chafik was able to leave with his son, Faisal looked up anxiously and asked, "My father, did I do well?"

"My son," replied the little man, "it was not well to distress your tender mother, and me, and I do not think it was wisdom to enter a murderer's house. But, my son, yes, you did most well, you and your army of little ears!"

"Then, if I did well, am I to be rewarded?"

"Ask, my son, ask!" Chafik said, embracing the boy.

Too late he saw the calculating look in those large eyes. Too late he remembered that Faisal had been whetted on the stone of the bazaars.

"My father," Faisal said innocently, "it is sad to be homeless, as I know. And have you not shown me that one must have compassion for a waif—such as the cat and her five kittens? I did what I did because of them. So, may I keep them?"

THE SWAMI OF NORTHBANK   Lawrence G. Blochman

*The origin of the detective team of Dr. Daniel Webster Coffee
and Police Lieutenant Max Ritter is a simple one. Collier's was
looking for a series character to replace the late William Mac-
Harg's O'Malley stories. I came up with a prospectus introducing
Dr. Coffee, who seemed to fill the bill. But in laying out the first
stories of the series, it became evident that while a hospital pathologist was the ideal prototype of a scientific detective, for the
purpose of plausibility he would need a cop to feed him crimes
to be solved. Somehow people just don't come around to a pathologist with puzzling cases the way they do to a private eye. So
the Coffee-Ritter association was formed to set a good example
to communities which do not have modern co-operation between
the working detective and the medical examiner or police laboratory. Thus, in addition to their original intent of being entertain-
ment, the Coffee stories have become an oblique attack on the
antiquated coroner system which still prevails in at least two
thirds of our states.*

*The team of two has since become a team of at least four, which,
after all, is what happens in non-fictional crime detection in this
age of specialization. In the second of the series, Dr. Motilal
Mookerji of Calcutta entered the Pasteur Hospital lab as resident
pathologist. And neither men could do without that able laboratory technician, Doris Hudson, who appears in most of the Dr.
Coffee stories.*

LAWRENCE G. BLOCHMAN

The precise little man with the bald head and the rimless octagonal
eyeglasses told a strange story. His name, he said, was Duncan Floyd
and he represented the Great Lakes and Southern Underwriters, who
had insured Sandra Farriston's diamond earrings for $50,000. He
was worried about Sandra's earrings and a Hindu crystal-gazer who
called himself Zygon, the Swami of Northbank.

"The only swami in Northbank I know of," said Max Ritter, Lieutenant of police detectives, "is Dr. Motilal Mookerji, and he don't

tell fortunes. He's resident in pathology at Pasteur Hospital. Came here from Calcutta on a scholarship. What have you got on this Zygon?"

Floyd had nothing definite on Zygon except that his methods of operation resembled those of a group of swindlers who had recently been preying on cities around Northbank. The swindler would be handsome and exotically dark. Endowed with second sight, crystal vision, and other occult powers, he preyed on well-fixed middle-aged women. Sometimes he used a jewel thief as accomplice.

"Madam," he would say, "you have come to consult me about a diamond ring. The ring was not stolen. You left it in such-and-such washroom. The maid picked it up before you returned, but terrified at being accused of theft, she has not dared dispose of it. It is hidden in—"

At this point the crystal ball would go dark and only a thumping big fee would make it light up again to reveal the hiding place. The ring, of course, would be there. One miraculous feat of divination like this was usually enough in a small city to assure the swami of a large and opulent clientele—until things got too hot and he moved on to cooler and greener fields.

"Has this bird Zygon been pulling stuff like that in Northbank?" Lieutenant Ritter asked.

"Not that I've been able to learn," the insurance man said.

"Then what do you expect the police department to do?"

"Sandra Farriston is giving a reception tonight," Floyd said. "Some big-shot concert manager is here from New York, and Northbank is turning out to gawk and kowtow. His name is Sewell. Sandra will wear her earrings, of course, and Zygon has been invited to put on some kind of séance. I'd feel a whole lot better if some of your boys were there, too."

"I'll look into the matter," Max Ritter said.

Ritter's first look took him to the sixth floor of the Northbank Trust Company building where Zygon, wholesaler of dreams and broker in the occult, conducted his business. The office door, which bore the simple device *Zygon—Consultation by Appointment,* was situated between a dentist's office and an advertising agency, thus giving a feeling of security to clients with guilty secrets or scoffing husbands. Entering, Ritter found himself in an eerie, dimly lighted atmosphere reeking of incense. Black velvet drapes parted, and a slim, bronzed, dark-eyed man with a tightly wound white turban asked in a soft voice:

"You desire to consult Zygon?"

"I'm looking for the dentist," Ritter replied.

"Next door," said Zygon.

Ritter backed out mumbling apologies and memorizing Zygon's features and build. He would be able to recite to himself a perfect *portrait parlant* when he examined rogues' gallery photos later. Meanwhile he would call on Sandra Farriston.

Sandra lived on Indian Hill, which was a fashionable part of Northbank at the turn of the century. Its old frame houses, with their hip roofs, their shingled turrets and cupolas, their gables and dormer windows dripping with gingerbread, were still impressive in spring and summer when the Boston ivy was in leaf and concealed their need for paint. Sandra's house had its own special impressiveness. It was not merely the home of a music teacher who eked out a bare subsistence drilling scales and trills into Northbank brats; it was the shrine of Sandra's glamorous past, the sphinx-temple of her enigmatic present.

Sandra's past was symbolized by the photographs and framed playbills which lined the walls of her staircase, showing a young and beautiful opera singer in the roles of La Traviata, Tosca, and Madame Butterfly, and testifying to her performance in the 1920s at the San Carlo of Naples, the Costanzi of Rome, the Municipal Opera of Nice, and the Opéra Comique of Paris. Also obviously part of her past were the diamond earrings, currently the worry of Duncan Floyd.

The two huge, flawless, pear-shaped stones, which she wore pendent from fragile platinum chains, appeared publicly just five times yearly: for the opening concert of the Northbank Symphony, for the annual two-night stand of the Metropolitan Opera Company, and for Sandra's two receptions, which were attended not only by the best people of Northbank, but by prominent musical figures from

Chicago, Cleveland, Cincinnati, and even New York.

Sandra's past was also symbolized—in malicious minds—by Josephine Farriston. According to Sandra, Josephine was the child of a dead brother. Sandra was grooming the girl for the opera stage. Josephine was away at some conservatory most of the year but she would be back for the reception. . . .

Max Ritter parked his car in the driveway at the side of the house, walked to the front, and twisted the old-fashioned bellpull.

The bell was not answered immediately. Deep inside the house Ritter thought he heard two angry voices. He could not distinguish words, but he was sure one voice was female and on the verge of tears. The other was a rumbling baritone.

Again Ritter rang. The voices stopped suddenly. After a brief silence Sandra opened the door. She was a stately, well-groomed woman clinging stubbornly to the hopeful side of fifty. Her young, unwrinkled face belied her white hair, and she was slender as few divas manage to be.

When Ritter started explaining why he thought he should attend her reception, Sandra cut him short with, "I am sorry, but I cannot insult my guests by having police present. Anyone invited to my house is presumed to be honest. I don't need you."

"Maybe I'd better come anyhow," the detective said.

"You are not welcome and you will not be admitted."

"Hold on, madam. You're going to wear those diamond earrings, and the insurance people—"

"You will not be admitted," Sandra repeated, "without a search warrant. And no court will issue a search warrant without evidence of a crime having been committed. There has been no crime committed. Good day." And she closed the door.

Ritter grinned and walked around the side of the house. He stopped grinning when he saw the girl sitting in his car.

The girl was young, in her early twenties at most; she had a pretty face and lively eyes. She wore a narrow blue ribbon around her blond hair.

"Hello," she said, "I'm Josephine Farriston. You're from the police, aren't you?"

"Am I?" Ritter countered. "Maybe that N.P.D. on my car door stands for 'No Passengers Desired.' I'd sure like to sit here and admire the fit of your pretty blue sweater, but I got work to do. Step down, sister."

"I've got to talk to you," Josephine said. "Did Sandra call you to keep Biff from coming to the party tonight?"

Ritter was suddenly interested. "Who's Biff?" he asked.

The girl's eyebrows lifted incredulously. She said, "Don't you know Biff Walters and his Catalina Catamounts? He played six months at the Blue Heaven Roof in New York. That's where I met him. When he finishes his twenty weeks at the Standing Room in Chicago, he's going to Hollywood to make a picture."

"Sandra doesn't like Biff?" Ritter said.

"And how! And vice versa."

"Why not?"

"Because I'm in love with him."

"And vice versa?"

"Very much vice versa. Biff wants to marry me. Sandra wants me to be an opera singer."

"What's the matter with a little of each?" Ritter asked.

"Sandra says opera is a full-time job. And she's afraid if I marry Biff I'll turn out to be a blues singer with his band. Which I'd love, only Sandra has spent so much money trying to make me the greatest Mimi since Bori that I just can't let her down."

"Unless Biff can beat all those silly ideas out of Sandra's head?"

"Biff will be at the party tonight, if that's what you mean—unless you keep him out. Biff knows that Sandra has spent about all the money she has to get me started, and he's afraid she'll do something foolish to get more until I click."

"That's not what I mean. Wouldn't that be Biff in the house right now, fighting with Sandra?"

"Now? Biff? Oh, no!" Josephine's whole body registered surprise.

"Well, somebody's fighting with her. Go in and see for yourself," Ritter said, stepping on the starter. "I got work to do, sister." He eased her gently from the car.

Ritter drove directly to the offices of the *Northbank Tribune* and asked the society editor to show him the guest list for Sandra's reception. He was delighted to find the names of Dr. and Mrs. Daniel Webster Coffee among those invited. Dr. Coffee was pathologist at Northbank's Pasteur Hospital and an old friend of Ritter's. Ritter sometimes consulted Dan Coffee when routine police methods were not equal to crimes of more than ordinary subtlety.

"Hello, Max," Dr. Coffee said when Ritter phoned. "Yes, Julia and I are invited, but Julia's in bed with the sniffles and I'm certainly not going there alone."

"You could take Mookerji," Ritter said.

"Nothing doing, Max. You know how I hate putting on a tux."

"Doc, you gotta go. You gotta do some scientific observing for me, and I'd like that swami of yours to get a look at another swami who maybe ain't only not kosher, but not even Hindu."

"Sounds intriguing, Max. Tell me more."

"Meet me at Raoul's for a short beer after dinner, Doc, and I'll brief you," Ritter said.

When Dr. Coffee arrived at Sandra Farriston's, stiffly uncomfortable in boiled shirt and dinner jacket, he was immediately aware of an odd uneasiness, not only in himself but in the other guests. Under the gay surfaces of this reception lurked something unpleasant, something almost evil. Whatever it was, Dan Coffee was unable to put his finger on it; he was inclined to laugh at himself for a melodramatic fool.

There was nothing ominous about the string quartet that played softly on the stair landing, nothing portentous about the caterer's flunkies who passed elaborate *canapés* and poured champagne from napkin-wrapped bottles. Even the corner of the room, converted by draped Oriental rugs into a den of mystery for Zygon, seemed far from sinister. The Swami of Northbank himself, resplendent in white silk tunic and purple satin turban, was only a swaggering mountebank as he stabbed cards out of a tarot deck with a jeweled dagger to tell the fortunes of goggle-eyed matrons.

It was only when the majestic Sandra took Dr. Coffee in hand that he realized the hostess herself was the focus of the strange uneasiness.

Sandra moved in a trance, her features expressionless, her body tense with some suppressed emotion. Dr. Coffee murmured apologies for Mrs. Coffee and introduced his spheroidal brown Hindu companion whose pink cotton turban looked miserable indeed in comparison with the magnificence of Zygon.

"Dr. Mookerji, my resident pathologist," Dan Coffee said.

"Am exuberantly delighted and honored beyond limits of ignorant vocabulary," the Hindu said, peering beyond his hostess for a gap in the field through which he might maneuver his global bulk in the direction of his supposed countryman.

Dan Coffee went through the ordeal of being presented to several dozen overdressed, overpolite, and overweening bores. Remembering his briefing by Max Ritter, he paid particular attention to Duncan Floyd, the bald-headed little insurance man; to Sewell, the white-haired concert manager from New York; and to a lanky, self-assured, broad-shouldered youth with a crew haircut to whom he was not introduced but whom he assumed to be Biff Walters, since the young man spent most of his time gazing earnestly into the blue eyes of Josephine Farriston. Whenever Dan Coffee felt ready to go under from boredom or uneasiness, he looked at the couple and felt human again.

After being social for half an hour, which was ten minutes beyond his normal limit, Dan Coffee was rescued by Dr. Mookerji. The Hindu drew him to false seclusion behind the grand piano and declared solemnly:

"Am convinced that so-called Zygon is fraudulent phony. When addressed with phrase in Hindustani inquiring as to point of origin, he riposted in English that he was unfamiliar with Hindustani language. Upon shifting to Bengali, received similar response. Punjabi likewise. Alleged Zygon claims Dravidian origin, purporting to speak only South Indian dialect with which am not personally conversant. Am of opinion that pseudo-swami is too pale-faced for Southerner. Dravidians usually tend to blackish tints."

"We'll report that to Lieutenant Ritter," Dr. Coffee said.

At this point Sandra Farriston mounted to the third step of the staircase and clapped her hands for attention. She moved her head slowly from side to side, so that her huge teardrop earrings swung in short, brilliant arcs. Her manner was gracious from habit, but her voice was taut as she said:

"If you'll all be quiet for a few moments, and crowd closer to this side of the room, Swami Zygon will give us an unusual demonstration of his occult powers."

Feet shuffled and the guests surged forward restlessly. Dr. Coffee saw Floyd, the insurance man, edging through the crowd to get closer to Sandra and the earrings. He saw Biff Walters put down his champagne goblet, clench his fists and stare at Sandra with something like hate in his eyes. Then Sandra touched the light switch and the room went dark—except for a blue glow from Zygon's crystal ball which shone directly upward to bathe his face with ghostly luminosity. His turbaned head seemed to be detached from his body, floating uncannily in the darkness. Zygon muttered a few cabalistic phrases.

Seated at the concert grand almost at Dan Coffee's elbow, Josephine Farriston struck a few chords and began to sing. She sang with a small, rather girlish soprano, the pathologist thought, but her voice had a pleasing, intimate warmth.

Dr. Coffee was watching the spectral face of Zygon glowing at the other side of the room when the head suddenly disappeared. The light below the crystal ball had winked out.

Josephine sang the closing phrases of her song in complete darkness. The piano still hummed with the final chords when the voice of the unseen Zygon again began muttering some mumbo jumbo.

The muttering grew louder and shriller—until it was cut abruptly by a knife-sharp scream. The shriek rose to a crescendo of terror and died quickly in a strangled sob. Then silence.

Dr. Coffee shouldered his way through the darkness, pushing aside the unseen guests who stood between him and the light switch. A confused murmur seemed to float on the black silence. Dr. Coffee pushed and elbowed until his outstretched hand touched the wall, found the switch. Light flooded back into the room.

Zygon was still—or again—behind his crystal ball. He was standing. Twenty feet in front of him Sandra Farriston lay stretched on the rug, her eyes closed. As Dr. Coffee strode toward Sandra, Biff Walters bent over her to shake her shoulder.

"Come on, Sandra," Walters said. "No more theatrics. This isn't the last act of *Rigoletto*."

Walters placed his hands under Sandra's shoulders, withdrew them immediately, and stared at his crimson fingers.

Dr. Coffee was still stooped over Sandra when Duncan Floyd pushed through the awe-struck guests.

"Good Lord!" Floyd exclaimed. "Her earrings are gone."

"She's dead," Dr. Coffee announced.

There was a shocked silence. Behind the grand piano Josephine Farriston gasped, then sobbed.

Dr. Motilal Mookerji waddled to the front door, threw it open, and spoke to a glowing cigarette-end on the porch.

"Leftenant Ritter, please enter without preliminary legal writs and warrants. Felonious crime has now been perpetrated."

During the next three hours the late Sandra Farriston's mansion was the scene of a grim and determined invasion. The police job seemed simple enough. Sandra had been murdered. Sandra's valuable earrings had been stolen. Nobody had left the house since the murder —Ritter himself would vouch for that. Whoever had the diamonds must be the murderer. Unfortunately, the diamonds could not be found.

A dozen detectives and policewomen had searched the sullen, frightened, or indignant guests. Another half-dozen detectives, aided by a worried, white-faced Duncan Floyd, hell-bent on preventing a loss for Great Lakes and Southern Underwriters, had gone through the house with rude and untidy thoroughness.

By the time the team of photographers and fingerprint men had packed up and left at midnight, only the following facts had been established:

Sandra Farriston had been stabbed to death with the jeweled Afghan dagger which belonged to Zygon. Because of its gem-encrusted hilt, no latent fingerprints could be developed.

The earrings had been torn from Sandra's ears, bruising the pierced lobes. The indication was that they had been snatched before Sandra was killed.

The fragile platinum chains from which the diamonds had hung were found under the piano with the twisted mountings—and without the stones.

Zygon had been searched to the most intimate recesses of his person and the diamonds were not found.

Nor were the diamonds found anywhere or on anyone.

Shortly after midnight, Max Ritter announced to Dr. Coffee, "I'm going to take Zygon downtown, Doc."

"Max, do you think Zygon is fool enough to commit murder with a weapon so easily traceable to him?"

"Zygon's no fool," Ritter replied, "which is exactly why he might do the obvious, counting on a logical guy like you or me to figure that he wouldn't do any such thing."

"He is Machiavellian impostor," Dr. Mookerji volunteered.

"I'd also like a little private jam session with the boogiewoogie boy," Ritter said. "The air will do you good, Walters."

"Biff doesn't know anything," Josephine said. "He was standing right beside me all the time I was singing. He kissed the back of my neck just before Sandra screamed."

"He was standing over Sandra when the lights went on," Ritter insisted.

"Where Biff goes, I go," Josephine said.

"That's fine, sister. I'd like to listen to your voice some more, too. I picked up a few new tunes this afternoon I want to try on you. You can both ride with me. Brody, you and Jenkins take the swami."

"Correction, please. Alleged swami," said Dr. Mookerji.

The caravan formed at Sandra's front door. As the pale, perspiring, and protesting Zygon was helped into one police car between two detectives, Duncan Floyd approached Ritter.

"Mind if I come along, Lieutenant?" Floyd asked. "You can understand my concern. I'll follow in my own car."

"Okay, follow. Doc, we seem to be a little crowded. Think that hot rod of yours is good for another two-three miles?"

"Dr. Mookerji and I will be hot on your tracks," Dan Coffee said. They were not very hot, because of the cold reluctance of Dr. Coffee's obsolescent carburetor to awake to action. In fact, by the time the pathologist and his Hindu resident had caught up with the caravan in Harding Park, the shooting had already started.

Dr. Mookerji had just remarked, "Were you observing, Doctor Sahib, that so-called swami was exhibiting gastric symptoms? Personally noted livid and anxious face, plus clammy skin."

"He probably ate too many of Sandra's rubber hors d'oeuvres," Dr. Coffee was saying, just as they came to the roadblock.

Three police cars were drawn up in echelon across the curving park road, with Duncan Floyd's car parked a little to the rear. Spotlights from the police cars slashed the night with hard, hot blades, raking the lawns, whipping trees and bushes. Flashes of gunfire flickered in the shrubbery.

When the first explosions beat upon the darkness, Dr. Mookerji seized Dan Coffee's arm. "Am perceiving signs of armed conflict, Doctor Sahib," the Hindu said. "Suggesting option for better part of valor."

"Let's park here outside the combat zone," Dan Coffee said.

The nervous staccato of police guns subsided with a few desultory shots and the whine of a ricochet bullet.

Biff Walters and Josephine were huddled in the back seat of Ritter's car. Ritter was standing beside the car, revolver drawn.

"Spurious compatriot is no doubt causing felonious shenanigans, eh, Leftenant?" said Dr. Mookerji.

"Yeah," Ritter said. "Zygon jumped when we slowed for the curve, and he landed running. He won't go far, though. He's wearing bracelets."

A shadow moving toward Ritter materialized as Duncan Floyd.

"I warned you he was a slippery character," the insurance man said. "I was afraid—"

A shout from the darkness interrupted him. "Over this way, Max. Looks like we winged him."

Six flashlight beams fingered the night, contracting as they converged on a tall plainclothesman standing beside a syringa bush. Dr.

Coffee followed the lights. Zygon was lying under the bush, his turban partly unwound and caught in the lower branches. His face was gray and shiny with sweat. A bright red stain was spreading across the front of his white tunic. The wounded man groaned as Dr. Coffee examined him.

"Get him to the hospital," Dan Coffee said. "Quick."

Pasteur Hospital was just over the hill. The intern on emergency duty started giving plasma to Zygon while the stretcher cart was being rolled to the elevator. In the operating room the resident surgeon took one look at the unconscious man and ordered X-rays.

Dr. Coffee, Dr. Mookerji, and Max Ritter followed the stretcher-cart to the X-ray department. They waited while the radiologist made a panorama of Zygon's midsection. As soon as the films were out of the developer and into the fixing bath, a technician gave the high sign and the little group crowded into the darkroom.

The resident surgeon glanced at the wet films, decided the bullet would have to come out, and went to scrub up while Zygon was rolled back to the operating room.

Dr. Coffee remained in the darkroom, studying the films. After a minute he gave a peculiar laugh.

"Apparently our friend Zygon has an appetite like an ostrich," he said. "Look at this."

Ritter peered over the pathologist's shoulder and the Hindu peeked under his arm. Dr. Coffee indicated a point on the film, just below the latticed shadows of the ribs. Two other shadows were clearly visible, shadows that must have been caused by two opaque objects several inches long and pear-shaped.

"No wonder we couldn't find the sparklers on him!" Ritter exclaimed. "He chewed the stones off the mountings and swallowed 'em."

"Some non-Hindu Indians quite notorious for ingesting strange foodstuffs," Dr. Mookerji said. "Gastric symptoms now explained."

"Anyhow, the case is solved," Ritter said. "Zygon killed Sandra and stole— Those are the earrings, aren't they, Doc?"

"They're certainly not smoke rings," the pathologist said. He was silent a moment as he re-examined the X-ray film. "Still, I'm not sure our solution is quite so simple. Where's Mr. Floyd, Max?"

"He's in the waiting room with Josephine and her boy friend. Brody's keeping an eye on 'em."

"Bring them to my lab, Max. I've a few questions."

Dr. Coffee carefully carried the wet film to his laboratory. When the insurance man came in, Dr. Coffee asked:

"Mr. Floyd, did you ever have Mrs. Farriston's earrings in your own possession?"

"Oh, yes," Floyd replied. "I had them appraised when I wrote the original policy about two years ago. And a few weeks ago, when the policy came up for renewal, we made a routine reappraisal."

Dr. Coffee produced the film. "Would you say, Mr. Floyd, that the objects shown in this X-ray photograph of Zygon's stomach resemble Mrs. Farriston's diamonds?"

"Good Lord!" Floyd excitedly extracted a micrometer caliper from his pocket and measured the shadows. "Those are the stones, all right. What a relief!"

"Where did Mrs. Farriston get the earrings originally?"

Floyd didn't know, but Biff Walters did.

"Josephine's father gave them to Sandra," Walters said.

"You mean Sandra's brother?" Ritter asked.

"I mean Sandra's ex-husband, Henry Sewell. He was there tonight."

"Is that true, sister? Was Sandra your mother?"

Josephine nodded, her eyes sad.

"Sandra thought it was a big secret," Walters continued. "She didn't even admit it to Josephine. But it's common knowledge around Carnegie Hall in New York that Sewell paid for Sandra's European successes in the late twenties. Sandra was never more than a third-rate singer, and she sang in French and Italian theaters because Sewell bought out the house on the nights she sang. You could also buy favorable criticism in the European newspapers in those days. When Sewell lost his money in the nineteen hundred twenty-nine crash, he left Sandra. She divorced him in Paris before Josephine was born, without even telling him she was about to bear him a child. Sandra was proud."

"Has Sandra been giving Sewell the shakedown?" Ritter asked.

"Never!" Josephine said.

"Look," Ritter insisted. "Sandra's been borrowing like mad for years. She's mortgaged everything she owns to keep this gal headed for a career. Her credit's been running thin lately, and she even had trouble financing her shindig tonight. But I found out this afternoon that Sandra deposited five grand in her bank account yesterday—in cash. I'll find out from Sewell if the five G's didn't come from him."

Walters said, "You're all wet, Ritter. Sandra didn't give Josephine the name of Sewell. She never told him Jo was his daughter. She wanted to keep the girl all for herself. We had a big fight about it this afternoon. I was trying to convince Sandra it would be better for Jo to be a hit blues singer than a bad prima donna, and—"

His speech was cut short by the arrival of the resident surgeon. The surgeon's gauze mask dangled from one ear and there was blood on his short-sleeved white jacket. He carried a gauze-covered metal cup.

"I couldn't save your man," the surgeon said. "He died on the table. But I got the bullet. I suppose you'll want it."

"What about the diamonds?" Floyd demanded. "The man swallowed two very valuable diamonds."

"Dr. Coffee will have to recover them for you when he does the autopsy," the surgeon said. He placed the cup on the lab workbench and departed.

"At least I can sleep tonight," the insurance man said. "Do you gentlemen need me any more now?"

Ritter shook his head. "Go on home," he said.

After Floyd left, Ritter lifted the gauze from the surgeon's cup. The bullet was slightly twisted, but it was not the usual shapeless mass of lead that is dug out of gunshot victims. It still resembled a bullet.

"Hell!" Ritter exclaimed. "This looks like a .32."

"Please, what is hellish about .32 bullet?" Dr. Mookerji asked.

"Every cop in Northbank carries a .38 police positive," the detective said. "If my boys didn't shoot Zygon, who did?"

"Dr. Mookerji and I had the opportunity," Dan Coffee said. "So did Mr. Walters and Miss Farriston."

"Floyd, too," admitted Ritter. "But I went over Floyd with a fine comb, and Miss Farriston and Walters here were searched, too. None of them could have been hiding a gun. After all, there are some things a guy can't swallow."

Dr. Coffee arose quickly as though a sudden idea had struck him from below. He grabbed his hat.

"Max, I've been stupid. Let's try to catch up with Mr. Floyd."

They had to wait several minutes for the elevator, and by the time they reached the ground floor, Floyd's car was gone from in front of the hospital.

"I know where he lives," Ritter said.

"Try his office first," said Dr. Coffee.

Floyd's car was standing in front of the office building. Ritter tried the door. The car was unlocked.

"He's careless," Ritter said.

"Or in a hurry," said Dr. Coffee. "Try the glove compartment."

There was nothing in the glove compartment but a tattered road map, a flashlight, and a square of chamois.

They rang the night bell. The sleepy night elevator operator took his time about answering. Yes, Mr. Floyd had come in a short while ago. Yes, he would take them up.

Duncan Floyd did not seem surprised to see them.

"Hello," he said. "I stopped by the office to draft my report to the home office. They'll be glad to know there won't be a claim to pay on the Farriston diamonds. What can I do for you gentlemen?"

"You can open that safe behind you," Dr. Coffee said.

"I'd be glad to," Floyd said, "except I've just had the combination changed, and I have trouble remembering it. We'll have to wait until my secretary comes down in the morning."

"Open it now," Ritter said. "Or I'll send for the Safe Squad."

"Well! What's the hurry? What the devil's in the safe?"

"Mrs. Farriston's diamonds," Dr. Coffee said.

Floyd laughed. "Doctor, you assured me the diamonds were in Zygon's stomach. You yourself showed me the film. I saw the X-ray photo of the stones with my own eyes."

"You saw what Zygon *thought* were the Farriston diamonds," Dr. Coffee said. "But the gems in the X-ray photo are imitations."

"Well! Appraisal by photo." Again Floyd laughed. "Aren't you exaggerating the miracle of the X-ray, Doctor?"

"On the contrary. If Zygon had swallowed the true gems, they could not have been seen in the photo. Genuine diamonds are perfectly transparent to X-rays. False diamonds, however, are made of strass, a brilliant glass with a very high lead content. Don't you know, Mr. Floyd, that lead is opaque to X-rays?"

"Remember the combination now, Floyd?" Ritter said.

"I'll—I'll try. I'd like to prove you're wrong."

Floyd crouched in front of the safe, twirled the dials. The heavy door swung open. Floyd spun about as he straightened up. In his left hand was a small chamois bag. His right held a revolver.

"Hands up, gentlemen!" he ordered.

The detective and the pathologist complied. The bald-headed little man dropped the chamois bag into his pocket and yanked the telephone cord from its baseboard connections. He backed toward the door, taking keys from his pocket with his left hand.

"I find you are right after all, gentlemen," Floyd said. "So I will require a few hours' head start." He opened the door behind him. "There's a ten-story drop outside that window, and you'll find this lock very difficult to pick."

As Floyd started backing through the half-open door, his expression suddenly changed. His head jerked back.

A high-pitched voice in the hall said, "Kindly elevate hands above head, subsequent to relaxing grasp on revolver gun!"

Floyd dropped the revolver. Ritter pounced on it. Floyd re-entered the room, pushed from behind by Dr. Motilal Mookerji, who was poking something into the small of his back.

"Suggest use of manacles, Leftenant," Dr. Mookerji said, "in view of apparent homicidal intent of smallish hairless gentleman."

Ritter snapped steel about Floyd's wrists. The Hindu withdrew the bunch of keys he had been poking into Floyd's back and handed them to Dr. Coffee.

"Please pardon intrusion, Doctor Sahib," the Hindu said, "but remarked you were forgetting keys on laboratory workbench. Therefore, knowing Mrs. Coffee's dislike of rude awakenings in small hours of nighttime, I—"

"Swami, I could kiss you," Max Ritter said. He was examining Floyd's revolver. "It's a .32 all right. He musta transferred it from his car to the safe before we got here. How about it, Floyd?"

Floyd refused to talk without advice of his attorney. So Dr. Coffee reconstructed the case from his own deductions.

"Sandra Farriston evidently made some deal with Floyd to dispose of her diamonds, replace them with exact reproductions, and then collect insurance on the loss of the replicas," the pathologist said. "The five-thousand-dollar cash deposit no doubt represented a down payment on what was to have been a long-range scheme.

"But Sandra wanted more money in a hurry. Her peculiar pride made her prefer dishonesty to seeking help from a former husband. So she obviously made arrangements with Zygon to steal the imitation earrings, so she could collect the insurance. This unforeseen haste threw Floyd into a panic. He was in it for himself, not for Sandra, and he was taking a bigger risk than she was.

"I can see no other reason for the desperate measures he adopted. Before paying a fifty-thousand-dollar claim, the insurance company would put trained investigators on the case—while the original diamonds were still in Floyd's possession. I was sure they must have been still in his possession, to drive him to commit two murders. To try to prevent being caught in a fifty-thousand-dollar fraud, Floyd came to you in the afternoon, hoping to stop the projected robbery.

"When Sandra refused police protection—for good reason, as we have seen—Floyd grew even more desperate. And when Zygon actually stole the earrings in the dark, Floyd stabbed Sandra with Zygon's dagger. Sandra's death would eliminate a possible witness against him. It would precipitate police intervention so that Zygon would be caught with the earrings on his person: thus there would be no claim to pay and no insurance investigation. And finally Floyd would be left in full possession of the original gems—and a very neat clear profit for his trouble.

"However, Zygon's method of hiding the gems upset Floyd's new plan. The earrings were still missing, and an insurance investigation was still an unpleasant possibility. So when Zygon made a break in the park and your boys started shooting at him, Floyd took the gun which he obviously kept in his car—you hadn't searched his car, remember—joined in the hunt and bagged his game. He might have got away with it, too, if it hadn't been for Dr. Wilhelm Roentgen."

"Roentgen?" Max Ritter interrupted. "I thought the resident surgeon's name was Smith."

"Dr. Roentgen discovered X-rays," Dan Coffee said.

"Am foreseeing only one unhappy possibility arising from otherwise happy aforesaid solution," Dr. Mookerji said. "To wit, as follows. If title to high-priced diamonds is reverting to golden-haired Josephine with silver-plated voice, will not same lady feel compulsion to pursue dismal operatical career?"

"That," said Dr. Coffee, "is a matter I think we can well leave in the hands of Mr. Biff Walters."

MYSTERY FOR CHRISTMAS   Anthony Boucher

*It's fitting that a story dealing with teamwork between two
detectives should itself have been produced by teamwork—that
type of teamwork, so valuable to writers and so little known to
readers, which can develop between an author and a truly creative editor. In 1942, when I'd begun selling my first detective
short stories to* Ellery Queen's Mystery Magazine, *Queen asked
me if I had any unsold shorts cluttering up my files; maybe something could be salvaged from them. Of course I did (is there any
writer who doesn't?). I sent him a batch of unpublished and (I'll
admit now) unpublishable stories; and the one in which Queen
saw possibilities was this, at that time called* The Mickey Mouse
Mystery. *Now Queen is, God bless and keep him, the kind of
editor who can not only tell you what's wrong but show you
how to make it right; he indicated a completely new angle from
which to approach the story—and that entailed, again fittingly,
the introduction of the character of Mr. Quilter and the produc-
tive the-whole-is-more-than-the-sum-of-its-parts teamwork between him and young Tom Smith.*

*Just to balance things a little, this story also brought about
the one occasion on which I've been able to catch Queen with
his editorial slip showing. He wanted to run it in the issue of
EQMM appearing just before Christmas in 1942, and said we
should therefore retitle it* Murder for Christmas. *I wrote back
that this was fine (aside from the fact that the title had, like almost anything a mystery writer can think of, been already used
by Agatha Christie); there was only one small point against it
—the story contains no murder.*

So, Mystery for Christmas, *starring Quilter & Smith, plotted
by Queen & Boucher.*

ANTHONY BOUCHER

That was why the Benson jewel robbery was solved—because Aram
Melekian was too much for Mr. Quilter's temper.

His almost invisible eyebrows soared, and the scalp of his close-cropped head twitched angrily. "Damme!" said Mr. Quilter, and in that mild and archaic oath there was more compressed fury than in paragraphs of uncensored profanity. "So you, sir, are the untrammeled creative artist, and I am a drudging, hampering hack!"

Aram Melekian tilted his hat a trifle more jauntily. "That's the size of it, brother. And if you hamper this untrammeled opus any more, Metropolis Pictures is going to be sueing its youngest genius for breach of contract."

Mr. Quilter rose to his full lean height. "I've seen them come and go," he announced; "and there hasn't been a one of them, sir, who failed to learn something from me. What is so creative about pouring out the full vigor of your young life? The creative task is mine, molding that vigor, shaping it to some end."

"Go play with your blue pencil," Melekian suggested. "I've got a dream coming on."

"Because I have never produced anything myself, you young men jeer at me. You never see that your successful screen plays are more my effort than your inspiration." Mr. Quilter's thin frame was aquiver.

"Then what do you need us for?"

"What— Damme, sir, what indeed? Ha!" said Mr. Quilter loudly. "I'll show you. I'll pick the first man off the street that has life and a story in him. What more do you contribute? And through me he'll turn out a job that will sell. If I do this, sir, then will you consent to the revisions I've asked of you?"

"Go lay an egg," said Aram Melekian. "And I've no doubt you will."

Mr. Quilter stalked out of the studio with high dreams. He saw the horny-handed son of toil out of whom he had coaxed a masterpiece signing a contract with F.X. He saw a discomfited Armenian genius in the background busily devouring his own words. He saw himself freed of his own sense of frustration, proving at last that his was the significant part of writing.

He felt a bumping shock and the squealing of brakes. The next thing he saw was the asphalt paving.

Mr. Quilter rose to his feet undecided whether to curse the driver for knocking him down or bless him for stopping so miraculously short of danger. The young man in the brown suit was so disarmingly concerned that the latter choice was inevitable.

"I'm awfully sorry," the young man blurted. "Are you hurt? It's this bad wing of mine, I guess." His left arm was in a sling.

"Nothing at all, sir. My fault. I was preoccupied . . ."

They stood awkwardly for a moment, each striving for a phrase that was not mere politeness. Then they both spoke at once.

"You came out of that studio," the young man said. "Do you" (his tone was awed) "do you *work* there?"

And Mr. Quilter had spotted a sheaf of eight and a half by eleven paper protruding from the young man's pocket. "Are you a writer, sir? Is that a manuscript?"

The young man shuffled and came near blushing. "Naw. I'm not a writer. I'm a policeman. But I'm going to be a writer. This is a story I was trying to tell about what happened to me— But are you a writer? In *there?*"

Mr. Quilter's eyes were aglow under their invisible brows. "I, sir," he announced proudly, "am what makes writers tick. Are you interested?"

He was also, he might have added, what makes *detectives* tick. But he did not know that yet.

The Christmas trees were lighting up in front yards and in windows as Officer Tom Smith turned his rickety Model A onto the side street where Mr. Quilter lived. Hollywood is full of these quiet streets, where ordinary people live and move and have their being, and are happy or unhappy as chance wills, but both in a normal and unspectacular way. This is really Hollywood—the Hollywood that patronizes the twenty-cent fourth-run houses and crowds the stores on the Boulevard on Dollar Day.

To Mr. Quilter, saturated at the studio with the other Hollywood, this was always a relief. Kids were playing ball in the evening sun, radios were tuning in to Amos and Andy, and from the small houses came either the smell of cooking or the clatter of dishwashing.

And the Christmas trees, he knew, had been decorated not for the benefit of the photographers from the fan magazines, but because the children liked them and they looked warm and friendly from the street.

"Gosh, Mr. Quilter," Tom Smith was saying, "this is sure a swell break for me. You know, I'm a good copper. But to be honest I don't know as I'm very bright. And that's why I want to write, because maybe that way I can train myself to be and then I won't be a plain patrolman all my life. And besides, this writing, it kind of itches-like inside you."

"*Cacoëthes scribendi,*" observed Mr. Quilter, not unkindly. "You see, sir, you have hit, in your fumbling way, on one of the classic expressions for your condition."

"Now that's what I mean. You know what I mean even when I don't say it. Between us, Mr. Quilter . . ."

Mr. Quilter, his long thin legs outdistancing even the policeman's, led the way into his bungalow and on down the hall to a room which at first glance contained nothing but thousands of books. Mr. Quilter waved at them. "Here, sir, is assembled every helpful fact that mortal need know. But I cannot breathe life into these dry bones. Books are not written from books. But I can provide bones, and correctly articulated, for the life which you, sir— But here is a chair. And a reading lamp. Now, sir, let me hear your story."

Tom Smith shifted uncomfortably on the chair. "The trouble is," he confessed, "it hasn't got an ending."

Mr. Quilter beamed. "When I have heard it, I shall demonstrate to you, sir, the one ending it inevitably must have."

"I sure hope you will, because it's got to have and I promised her it would have and— You know Beverly Benson?"

"Why, yes. I entered the industry at the beginning of talkies. She was still somewhat in evidence. But why . . . ?"

"I was only a kid when she made *Sable Sin* and *Orchids at Breakfast* and all the rest, and I thought she was something pretty marvelous. There was a girl in our high school was supposed to look like her, and I used to think, 'Gee, if I could ever see the real Beverly Benson!' And last night I did."

"Hm. And this story, sir, is the result?"

"Yeah. And this too." He smiled wryly and indicated his wounded arm. "But I better read you the story." He cleared his throat loudly. *"The Red and Green Mystery,"* he declaimed. "By Arden Van Arden."

"A pseudonym, sir?"

"Well, I sort of thought . . . Tom Smith—that doesn't sound like a writer."

"Arden Van Arden, sir, doesn't sound like anything. But go on."

And Officer Tom Smith began his narrative:

THE RED AND GREEN MYSTERY
by ARDEN VAN ARDEN

It was a screwy party for the police to bust in on. Not that it was a raid or anything like that. God knows I've run into some bughouse parties that way, but I'm assigned to the jewelry squad now under Lieutenant Michaels, and when this call came in he took three other guys and me and we shot out to the big house in Laurel Canyon.

I wasn't paying much attention to where we were going and I wouldn't have known the place anyway, but I knew her, all right. She was standing in the doorway waiting for us. For just a minute it stumped me who she was, but then I knew. It was the eyes mostly. She'd changed a lot since <u>Sable Sin</u>, but you still couldn't miss the Beverly Benson eyes. The rest of her had got older (not older exactly either--you might maybe say richer) but the eyes were still the same. She had red hair. They didn't have technicolor when she was in pictures and I hadn't ever known what color her hair was. It struck me funny seeing her like that--the way I'd been nuts about her when I was a kid and not even knowing what color her hair was.

She had on a funny dress--a little-girl kind of thing with a short skirt with flounces, I guess you call them. It looked familiar, but I couldn't make it. Not until I saw the mask that was lying in the hall, and then I knew. She was dressed like Minnie Mouse. It turned out later they all were--not like Minnie Mouse, but like all the characters in the cartoons. It was that kind of a party --a Disney Christmas party. There were studio drawings all over the walls, and there were little figures of extinct animals and winged ponies holding the lights on the Christmas tree.

She came right to the point. I could see Michaels liked that; some of these women throw a big act and it's an hour before you know what's been stolen. "It's my emeralds and rubies," she said. "They're gone. There are some other pieces missing too, but I don't so much

care about them. The emeralds and the rubies are the important thing. You've got to find them."
    "Necklaces?" Michaels asked.
    "A necklace."
    "Of emeralds and rubies?" Michaels knows his jewelry.
His old man is in the business and tried to bring him up
in it, but he joined the force. He knows a thing or two
just the same, and his left eyebrow does tricks when he
hears or sees something that isn't kosher. It was doing
tricks now.
    "I know that may sound strange, Lieutenant, but this is
no time for discussing the esthetics of jewelry. It
struck me once that it would be exciting to have red and
green in one necklace, and I had it made. They're perfectly cut and matched, and it could never be
duplicated."
    Michaels didn't look happy. "You could drape it on a
Christmas tree," he said. But Beverly Benson's Christmas tree was a cold white with the little animals holding
blue lights.
    Those Benson eyes were generally lovely and melting.
Now they flashed. "Lieutenant, I summoned you to find
my jewelry, not to criticize my taste. If I wanted a cultural opinion, I should hardly consult the police."
    "You could do worse," Michaels said. "Now tell us
all about it."
    She took us into the library. The other men Michaels
sent off to guard the exits, even if there wasn't much
chance of the thief still sticking around. The Lieutenant
told me once, when we were off duty, "Tom," he said,
"you're the most useful man in my detail." Some of the
others can think, and some of them can act; but there's
not a damned one of them can just stand there and look
so much like the Law." He's a little guy himself and
kind of on the smooth and dapper side; so he keeps me
with him to back him up, just standing there.
    There wasn't much to what she told us. Just that she
was giving this Disney Christmas party, like I said, and
it was going along fine. Then late in the evening, when
almost everybody had gone home, they got to talking about
jewelry. She didn't know who started the talk that way,
but there they were. And she told them about the
emeralds and rubies.
    "Then Fig--Philip Newton, you know--the photographer
who does all those marvelous sand dunes and magnolia
blossoms and things--" (her voice went all sort of tender
when she mentioned him, and I could see Michaels taking
it all in) "Fig said he didn't believe it. He felt the
same way you do, Lieutenant, and I'm sure I can't see why.
'It's unworthy of you, darling,' he said. So I laughed
and tried to tell him they were really beautiful--for
they are, you know--and when he went on scoffing I said,

'All right, then, I'll show you.' So I went into the
little dressing room where I keep my jewel box, and they
weren't there. And that's all I know."

Then Michaels settled down to questions. When had she
last seen the necklace? Was the lock forced? Had there
been any prowlers around? What else was missing? And
suchlike.

Beverly Benson answered impatiently, like she expected
us to just go out there like that and grab the thief and
say, "Here you are, lady." She had shown the necklace to
another guest early in the party--he'd gone home long
ago, but she gave us the name and address to check. No,
the lock hadn't been forced. They hadn't seen anything
suspicious, either. There were some small things missing, too--a couple of diamond rings, a star sapphire
pendant, a pair of pearl earrings--but those didn't worry
her so much. It was the emerald and ruby necklace that
she wanted.

That left eyebrow went to work while Michaels thought
about what she'd said. "If the lock wasn't forced, that
lets out a chance prowler. It was somebody who knew you,
who'd had a chance to lift your key or take an impression
of it. Where'd you keep it?"

"The key? In my handbag usually. Tonight it was in a
box on my dressing table."

Michaels sort of groaned. "And women wonder why jewels
get stolen! Smith, get Ferguson and have him go over the
box for prints. In the meantime, Miss Benson, give me a
list of all your guests tonight. We'll take up the ser-
vants later. I'm warning you now it's a ten-to-one chance
you'll ever see your Christmas tree ornament again unless
a fence sings; but we'll do what we can. Then I'll deliver my famous little lecture on safes, and we'll pray
for the future."

When I'd seen Ferguson, I waited for Michaels in the
room where the guests were. There were only five left,
and I didn't know who they were yet. They'd all taken
off their masks; but they still had on their cartoon costumes. It felt screwy to sit there among them and think:
This is serious, this is a felony, and look at those
bright funny costumes.

Donald Duck was sitting by himself, with one hand rest-
ing on his long-billed mask while the other made steady
grabs for the cigarette box beside him. His face looked
familiar; I thought maybe I'd seen him in bits.

Three of them sat in a group: Mickey Mouse, Snow White,
and Dopey. Snow White looked about fourteen at first,
and it took you a while to realize she was a woman and a
swell one at that. She was a little brunette, slender
and cool-looking--a simple real kind of person that didn't
seem to belong in a Hollywood crowd. Mickey Mouse was a
hefty blond guy about as tall as I am and built like a

tackle that could hold any line; but his face didn't go
with his body. It was shrewd-like, and what they call
sensitive. Dopey looked just that--a nice guy and not
too bright.

Then over in another corner was a Little Pig. I don't
know do they have names, but this was the one that wears
a sailor suit and plays the fiddle. He had bushy hair
sticking out from under the sailor cap and long skilful-
looking hands stretched in front of him. The fiddle was
beside him, but he didn't touch it. He was passed out--
dead to the world, close as I could judge.

He and Donald were silent, but the group of three talked
a little.

"I guess it didn't work," Dopey said.

"You couldn't help that, Harvey." Snow White's voice
was just like I expected--not like Snow White's in the
picture, but deep and smooth, like a stream that's running in the shade with moss on its banks. "Even an agent
can't cast people."

"You're a swell guy, Madison," Mickey Mouse said. "You
tried, and thanks. But if it's no go, hell, it's just no
go. It's up to her."

"Miss Benson is surely more valuable to your career."
The running stream was ice cold.

Now maybe I haven't got anything else that'd make me a
good detective, but I do have curiosity, and here's where
I saw a way to satisfy it. I spoke to all of them and I
said, "I'd better take down some information while we're
waiting for the Lieutenant." I started on Donald Duck.
"Name?"

"Daniel Wappingham." The voice was English. I could
tell that much. I don't have such a good ear for stuff
like that, but I thought maybe it wasn't the best English.

"Occupation?"

"Actor."

And I took down the address and the rest of it. Then
I turned to the drunk and shook him. He woke up part way
but he didn't hear what I was saying. He just threw
his head back and said loudly, "Waltzes! Ha!" and went
under again. His voice was guttural--some kind of
German, I guessed. I let it go at that and went over to
the three.

Dopey's name was Harvey Madison; occupation, actors'
representative--tenpercenter to you. Mickey Mouse was
Philip Newton; occupation, photographer. (That was the
guy Beverly Benson mentioned, the one she sounded that-
away about.) And Snow White was Jane Newton.

"Any relation?" I asked.

"Yes and no," she said, so soft I could hardly hear
her.

"Mrs. Newton," Mickey Mouse stated, "was once my wife."
And the silence was so strong you could taste it.

I got it then. The two of them sitting there,remember-
ing all the little things of their life together, being
close to each other and yet somehow held apart. And on
Christmas, too, when you remember things. There was
still something between them even if they didn't admit it
themselves. But Beverly Benson seemed to have a piece of
the man, and where did Dopey fit in?

It sort of worried me. They looked like swell people--
people that belonged together. But it was my job to
worry about the necklace and not about people's troubles.
I was glad Michaels came in just then.

He was being polite at the moment, explaining to
Beverly Benson how Ferguson hadn't got anywheres with the
prints and how the jewels were probably miles away by
now. "But we'll do what we can," he said. "We'll talk
to these people and find out what's possible. I doubt,
however, if you'll ever see that necklace again. It was
insured, of course, Miss Benson?"

"Of course. So were the other things, and with them I
don't mind. But this necklace I couldn't conceivably
duplicate, Lieutenant."

Just then Michael's eye lit on Donald Duck, and the
eyebrow did tricks worth putting in a cartoon. "We'll
take you one by one," he said. "You with the tail-
feathers, we'll start with you. Come along, Smith."

Donald Duck grabbed a fresh cigarette, thought a minute,
then reached out again for a handful. He whistled off
key and followed us into the library.

"I gave all the material to your stooge here, Lieutenant," he began. "Name, Wappingham. Occupation, actor.
Address--"

Michaels was getting so polite it had me bothered.
"You won't mind, sir," he purred, "if I suggest a few corrections in your statement?"

Donald looked worried, "Don't you think I know my own
name?"

"Possibly. But would you mind if I altered the statement to read: Name, Alfred Higgins. Occupation, jewel
thief--conceivably reformed?"

The Duck wasn't so bad hit as you might have thought.
He let out a pretty fair laugh and said, "So the fat's in
the fire at last. But I'm glad you concede the possibility of my having reformed."

"The possibility, yes." Michaels underlined the word.
"You admit you're Higgins?"

"Why not? You can't blame me for not telling you right
off; it wouldn't look good when somebody had just been up
to my old tricks. But now that you know--And by the
way, Lieutenant, just how do you know?"

"Some bright boy at Scotland Yard spotted you in an
American picture. Sent your description and record out
to us just in case you ever took up your career again."

"Considerate of him, wasn't it?"

But Michaels wasn't in a mood for bright chatter any
longer. We got down to work. We stripped that duck costume off the actor and left him shivering while we went
over it inch by inch. He didn't like it much.

At last Michaels let him get dressed again. "You came
in your car?"

"Yes."

"You're going home in a taxi. We could hold you on
suspicion, but I'd sooner play it this way."

"Now I understand," Donald said, "what they mean by the
high-handed American police procedure." And he went back
into the other room with us.

All the same that was a smart move of Michaels'. It
meant that Wappingham-Higgins-Duck would either have to
give up all hope of the jewels (he certainly didn't have
them on him) or lead us straight to them, because of
course I knew a tail would follow that taxi and camp on
his doorstep all next week if need be.

Donald Duck said goodnight to his hostess and nodded to
the other guests. Then he picked up his mask.

"Just a minute," Michaels said. "Let's have a look at
that."

"At this?" he asked innocent-like and backed toward the
French window. Then he was standing there with an automatic in his hand. It was little but damned nasty-looking. I never thought what a good holster that long bill
would make.

"Stay where you are, gentlemen," he said calmly. "I'm
leaving undisturbed, _if_ you don't mind."

The room was frozen still. Beverly Benson and Snow
White let out little gasps of terror. The drunk was
still dead to the world. The other two men looked at us
and did nothing. It was Donald's round.

Or would've been if I hadn't played football in high
school. It was a crazy chance, but I took it. I was the
closest to him, only his eyes were on Michaels. It was
a good flying tackle and it brought him to the ground
in a heap consisting mostly of me. The mask smashed as
we rolled over on it and I saw bright glitters pouring
out.

Ferguson and O'Hara were there by now. One of them
picked up his gun and the other snapped on the handcuffs.
I got to my feet and turned to Michaels and Beverly Benson. They began to say things both at once about what a
swell thing I'd done and then I keeled over.

When I came to I was on a couch in a little dark room.
I learned later it was the dressing room where the necklace had been stolen. Somebody was bathing my arm and
sobbing.

I sort of half sat up and said, "Where am I?" I always
thought it was just in stories people said that, but it

was the first thing popped into my mind.

"You're all right," a cool voice told me. "It's only a flesh wound."

"And I didn't feel a thing.... You mean he winged me?"

"I guess that's what you call it. When I told the Lieutenant I was a nurse he said I could fix you up and they wouldn't need the ambulance. You're all right now." Her voice was shaky in the dark, but I knew it was Snow White.

"Well, anyways, that broke the case pretty quick."

"But it didn't." And she explained: Donald had been up to his old tricks, all right; but what he had hidden in his bill was the diamonds and the sapphire and the pearl earrings, only no emerald and ruby necklace. Beverly Benson was wild, and Michaels and our men were combing the house from top to bottom to see where he'd stashed it.

"There," she said. She finished the story and the bandaging at the same time. "Can you stand up all right now?"

I was still kind of punchy. Nothing else could excuse me for what I said next. But she was so sweet and tender and good I wanted to say something nice, so like a dumb jerk I up and said, "You'd make some man a grand wife."

That was what got her. She just went to pieces--dissolved, you might say. I'm not used to tears on the shoulder of my uniform, but what could I do? I didn't try to say anything--just patted her back and let her talk. And I learned all about it.

How she'd married Philip Newton back in '29 when he was a promising young architect and she was an heiress just out of finishing school. How the fortune she was heiress to went fooey like all the others and her father took the quick way out. How the architect business went all to hell with no building going on and just when things were worst she had a baby. And then how Philip started drinking, and finally--Well, anyways, there it was.

They'd both pulled themselves together now. She was making enough as a nurse to keep the kid (she was too proud to take alimony), and Philip was doing fine in this arty photographic line he'd taken up. A Newton photograph was The Thing to Have in the smart Hollywood set. But they couldn't come together again, not while he was such a success. If she went to him, he'd think she was begging; if he came to her, she'd think he was being noble. And Beverly Benson had set her cap for him.

Then this agent Harvey Madison (that's Dopey), who had known them both when, decided to try and fix things. He brought Snow White to this party; neither of them knew the other would be there. And it was a party and it was Christmas, and some of their happiest memories were

Christmases together. I guess that's pretty much true of
everybody. So she felt everything all over again, only--
     "You don't know what it's done for me to tell you this.
Please don't feel hurt; but in that uniform and everything you don't seem quite like a person. I can talk
and feel free. And this has been hurting me all night
and I had to say it."
     I wanted to take the two of them and knock their heads
together; only first off I had to find that emerald and
ruby necklace. It isn't my job to heal broken hearts.
I was feeling O.K. now, so we went back to the others.
     Only they weren't there. There wasn't anybody in the
room but only the drunk. I guessed where Mickey and
Dopey were: stripped and being searched.
     "Who's that?" I asked Snow White.
     She looked at the Little Pig. "Poor fellow. He's been
going through torture tonight too. That's Bela Strauss."
     "Bella's a woman's name."
     "He's part Hungarian." (I guess that might explain any-
thing.) "He comes from Vienna. They brought him out here
to write music for pictures because his name is Strauss.
But he's a very serious composer--you know, like..." and
she said some tongue twisters that didn't mean anything
to me. "They think because his name is Strauss he can
write all sorts of pretty dance tunes, and they won't let
him write anything else. It's made him all twisted and
unhappy, and he drinks too much."
     "I can see that." I walked over and shook him. The
sailor cap fell off. He stirred and looked up at me. I
think it was the uniform that got him. He sat up sharp
and said something in I guess German. Then he thought
around a while and found some words in English.
     "Why are you here? Why the po-lice?" It came out in
little one-syllable lumps, like he had to hunt hard for
each sound.
     I told him. I tried to make it simple, but that wasn't
easy. Snow White knew a little German, so she helped.
     "Ach!" he sighed. "And I through it all slept!"
     "That's one word for it," I said.
     "But this thief of jewels--him I have seen."
     It was a sweet job to get it out of him, but it boiled
down to this: Where he passed out was on that same couch
where they took me--right in the dressing-room. He came
to once when he heard somebody in there, and he saw the
person take something out of a box. Something red and
green.
     "Who was it?"
     "The face, you understand, I do not see it. But the
costume, yes. I see that clear. It was Mikki Maus." It
sounded funny to hear something as American as Mickey
Mouse in an accent like that.
     It took Snow White a couple of seconds to realize who

wore the Mickey Mouse outfit. Then she said, "Philip,"
and fainted.

Officer Tom Smith laid down his manuscript. "That's all, Mr.
Quilter."

"All, sir?"

"When Michaels came in, I told him. He figured Newton must've
got away with the necklace and then the English crook made his
try later and got the other stuff. They didn't find the necklace anywheres; but he must've pulled a fast one and stashed it away some
place. With direct evidence like that, what can you do? They're
holding him."

"And you chose, sir, not to end your story on that note of finality?"

"I couldn't, Mr. Quilter. I . . . I like that girl who was Snow
White. I want to see the two of them together again and I'd sooner
he was innocent. And besides, when we were leaving, Beverly Benson
caught me alone. She said, 'I can't talk to your Lieutenant. He is *not*
sympathetic. But you . . .'" Tom Smith almost blushed. "So she
went on about how certain she was that Newton was innocent and
begged me to help her prove it. So I promised."

"Hm," said Mr. Quilter. "Your problem, sir, is simple. You have
good human values there in your story. Now we must round them
out properly. And the solution is simple. We have two women in
love with the hero, one highly sympathetic and the other less so; for
the spectacle of a *passée* actress pursuing a new celebrity is not a
pleasant one. This one sympathetic woman, to please the audience,
must redeem herself with a gesture of self-immolation to secure the
hero's happiness with the heroine. Therefore, sir, let her confess to
the robbery."

"Confess to the . . . But Mr. Quilter, that makes a different story
out of it. I'm trying to write as close as I can to what happened. And
I promised—"

"Damme, sir, it's obvious. She did steal the necklace herself. She
hasn't worked for years. She must need money. You mentioned
insurance. The necklace was probably pawned long ago, and now
she is trying to collect."

"But that won't work. It really was stolen. Somebody saw it earlier in the evening, and the search didn't locate it. And believe me, that squad knows how to search."

"Fiddle-faddle, sir." Mr. Quilter's close-cropped scalp was beginning to twitch. "What was seen must have been a paste imitation. She could dissolve that readily in acid and dispose of it down the plumbing. And Wappingham's presence makes her plot doubly sure; she knew him for what he was, and invited him as a scapegoat."

Tom Smith squirmed. "I'd almost think you were right, Mr. Quilter. Only Bela Strauss did see Newton take the necklace."

Mr. Quilter laughed. "If that is all that perturbs you . . ." He rose to his feet. "Come with me, sir. One of my neighbors is a Viennese writer now acting as a reader in German for Metropolis. He is also new in this country; his cultural background is identical with Strauss's. Come. But first we must step down to the corner drugstore and purchase what I believe is termed a comic book."

Mr. Quilter, his eyes agleam, hardly apologized for their intrusion into the home of the Viennese writer. He simply pointed at a picture in the comic book and demanded, "Tell me, sir. What character is that?"

The bemused Viennese smiled. "Why, that is Mikki Maus."

Mr. Quilter's finger rested on a pert little drawing of Minnie.

Philip Newton sat in the cold jail cell, but he was oblivious of the cold. He was holding his wife's hands through the bars and she was saying, "I could come to you now, dear, where I couldn't before. Then you might have thought it was just because you were successful, but now I can tell you how much I love you and need you—need you even when you're in disgrace. . . ."

They were kissing through the bars when Michaels came with the good news. "She's admitted it, all right. It was just the way Smith reconstructed it. She'd destroyed the paste replica and was trying to use us to pull off an insurance frame. She cracked when we had Strauss point out a picture of what he called 'Mikki Maus.' So you're free again, Newton. How's that for a Christmas present?"

"I've got a better one, officer. We're getting married again."

"You wouldn't need a new wedding ring, would you?" Michaels

asked with filial devotion. "Michaels, Fifth between Spring and Broadway—fine stock."

Mr. Quilter laid down the final draft of Tom Smith's story, complete now with ending, and fixed the officer with a reproachful gaze. "You omitted, sir, the explanation of why such a misunderstanding should arise."

Tom Smith shifted uncomfortably. "I'm afraid, Mr. Quilter, I couldn't remember all that straight."

"It is simple. The noun *Maus* in German is of feminine gender. Therefore a *Mikki Maus* is a female. The male, naturally, is a *Mikki Mäuserich*. I recall a delightful Viennese song of some seasons ago, which we once employed as background music, wherein the singer declares that he and his beloved will be forever paired, *'wie die Mikki Mikki Mikki Mikki Mikki Maus und der Mikki Mäuserich.'*"

"Gosh," said Tom Smith. "You know a lot of things."

Mr. Quilter allowed himself to beam. "Between us, sir, there should be little that we do not know."

"We sure make a swell team as a detective."

The beam faded. "As a detective? Damme, sir, do you think I cared about your robbery? I simply explained the inevitable denouement to this story."

"But she didn't confess and make a gesture. Michaels had to prove it on her."

"All the better, sir. That makes her mysterious and deep. A Bette Davis role. I think we will first try for a magazine sale on this. Studios are more impressed by matter already in print. Then I shall show it to F.X., and we shall watch the squirmings of that genius Aram Melekian."

Tom Smith looked out the window, frowning. They made a team, all right; but which way? He still itched to write, but the promotion Michaels had promised him sounded good, too. Were he and this strange lean old man a team for writing or for detection?

The friendly red and green lights of the neighborhood Christmas trees seemed an equally good omen either way.

THE SHADOW AND THE SHADOWED Will Oursler

One night some years ago my wife and I were out on the town in New York City. In a midtown bar I noticed a very slim, small red-haired man with ice-cold blue eyes watching a young lady in a booth. The young lady and her escort arose and departed apparently unaware that they were being observed. An instant later the man who had been watching them, gulped his drink and hurried out after them.

That was all. Out of that brief incident in a crowded Saturday-night oasis was born my character Mike O'Shaunessey, the Irish shadow who finds his exotic adventures amid the brick and mortar, the gasoline fumes and the alcoholic haze of Manhattan.

WILL OURSLER

Before me tonight on my office desk lies the folder. On the Manila cover, neatly typed in the upper left-hand corner, is its grim little legend: *Vashti Evir, alias Eve. Deceased.*

So be it. There are those who call the case my greatest washout. Mike O'Shaunessey's most fantastic flop, they like to say. And they may be right. I wouldn't be sure.

My part in the Vashti Evir extravaganza began on a sticky August night in New York. My first scrawled note in the folder, in fact, is dated August 21: *Mr. Timar Hambul will pay a large chunk of cash —to keep a lady alive for three days.*

Timar Hambul had made his appointment by phone for seven-thirty. I was waiting alone—here in our offices on West 46th Street —when he showed up. He came in at a slow swagger which gave me a chance to note the gray spats, the gleaming ebony cane, the little waxed mustache.

Friend Hambul was a man of weighty affairs. He wasted no time coming to his point. He favored me with a curt Arabic bow, introduced himself in his pure Oxonian accent, and stated with patronizing familiarity, "I'm in trouble, old man. I need your help. Following people, I'm told, is your business specialty."

I didn't answer. Shadowing to me is half-profession, half-art, and around it I've built my life and career. I have followed men and women on a hundred missions—from one side of the earth to the other. I stayed with one man nearly two years, and he did not even suspect.

The pompous little Arabian leaned on his cane. "You must keep her alive," he whispered. "My Vashti. You must keep her from harm. Only until Saturday, until our wedding. It is worth many dollars, O'Shaunessey. Ten thousand American dollars."

I leaned back in my desk chair, lighted my pipe. For no good reason I could think of I wanted to tell him to go to hell. Under the circumstances, I restrained the impulse. Instead, I asked, "Your Vashti—from whom is she in danger?"

His delicately curved lips twisted. "From herself! From a devil in her mind which would destroy her. It is pitiable, yes. But it will change—vanish—after we are married."

Pinpoints of light came into his dark eyes. "When she is with me, or with her parents, I do not fear. But she has threatened foolish things. And when she goes out alone, unwatched—" He shrugged. "It is then *you* must watch her, must protect her from her foolishness."

There were echoes in his story of the perfumed bondage of the East. But he was using legal American tender. He counted out $2,000 in crisp twenties. The rest would come, he informed me smoothly, at the conclusion of the wedding ceremony.

I switched on a desk lamp, reached out, and picked up the bills.

I insisted on details, naturally. With these, plus bits of gossip I'd read in the social columns, I was able to jot down Fill-In 1 for the files:

"Subject: Vashti Evir. Age nineteen. Hair black. Eyes ditto. Skin light olive. (But high coloring of cheeks and lips, in gospel according to Hambul.) Weight about 125. Height five feet three.

"Betrothed Timar Hambul. Age about 35 (he says). Marriage arranged by families in time-honored tradition. Wedding set for ten A.M. Saturday morning, August 25.

"Families Saudi-Arabian aristocracy. Floating international set.

Here on protracted vacation. Both sides loaded for bear with Arabian oil, so money no object. Anxious to unite powerful clans.

"Vashti wants out. Timar and the others won't let her off the hook. He tells me, 'She carries a little gun of pearl and insists she will blow off her pretty head, rather than marry me. But she will learn to love me, of course. After Saturday.'

"Why doesn't the lady take a run-out powder? Hambul says there isn't a chance. They would follow her to the last corner of the world. She knows they would find her, wherever she might go. It would be a matter of their high honor.

"Seems like she's beginning to play with the idea that they couldn't follow so easily into Mohammed's third heaven for unmarried maidens."

I was waiting, early the next day, just beyond the Park Lane's main entrance, as she came out. In the crowded street I managed to move in for a "close-up" of this poised Arabian lovely, as she stood a moment in the shadow of the portico.

She carried herself like some lovely ancient queen—with chromium trimmings. Cool serenity rode in the dark eyes and on the rounded red lips. But she was young and vibrant and alive. Hardly the sort to be planning self-destruction.

I took in the costume. Alligator shoes with Cuban heels. And alligator purse to match. Gray-green tailored suit that must have been made just for her. A tiny green sports hat with a feather. Brown suède gloves. On one wrist, I noticed, she wore a gold-link bracelet.

She made quite a picture waiting there, while the doorman signaled for a cab.

I followed in another taxi, of course. I'd notified Louie to be on hand. Louie and his cab have worked with me for many years—on a variety of problems in pursuit.

"Follow the dame," I told him, "but not too close. I may be hopping in and out. I've got a notion we're just on a shopping tour."

My notes of that morning in the folder:

"Subject stopped at a number of stores along 57th Street, between Fifth and Seventh Aves. Milgrim's. Bendel's. Bergdorf. Annine's

Gowns. Several other small shops. Subject made no purchases. Tried on twelve hats, four dresses, two coats, eleven pairs of shoes. Showed no sign of suicidal intentions.

"At 11:23 A.M. subject dismissed waiting taxi. Paid driver five dollars, took no change. At corner of 57th and Seventh, subject took plebian bus, headed down Seventh Ave. Followed in Louie's cab. Subject left bus at 34th St. and entered Macy's department store. Continued to shadow on foot.

"Subject highly uncertain. Looked over compacts in cosmetics dept. Also lipsticks. Examined odds and ends at ribbon and sewing counter. Tried on green bedroom slippers—special price $2.93—at sale counter on main floor. Did not purchase.

"Subject visited basement. Counter-shopped, but still purchased nothing. Then started upstairs via escalator. Stopped at each floor, beginning with second, to examine items of merchandise. Articles examined from basement to eighth floor include: slips, nightgowns, coats, hardware, wicker furniture, sporting goods, lawn mowers, garden hoses, kitchen linoleum.

"Arriving eighth floor, subject went directly to rug department. Pretended to look over rugs but now seemed highly nervous. Constantly glancing around. After about three jittery minutes a tall good-looking young man in a high straw hat swung around the corner.

"I was about fifteen feet distant, engrossed in bathmats, as they greeted each other. Could not hear what they said. But saw them clasp hands and talk in low, earnest tones, standing very close together."

She was not free, of course. She was out of the shackled world of the East. But she could not be her own agent, not even here in the mundane magnificence of Macy's rug department.

I watched them as they talked together, standing by a pile of rugs. They looked like any young couple in love. Once he leaned close and I saw his lips brush hers. She drew away quickly and glanced around. I lost myself behind the bathmats.

It lasted only a few brief moments, this secret rendezvous. I saw him press her hand and then she turned and started toward the escalator marked *Down.*

Half a minute later, I followed.

I was starting to wonder about Mr. Hambul's story. It didn't add up. Would a girl like this be plotting to take her own life? Or could the whole thing be an alibi for himself that Hambul was carefully building up in advance?

I did not mention the rendezvous when I phoned Hambul that night with my first report. My job was to keep the lady alive through Saturday morning. What she did otherwise, I reasoned, was her own business. And I had no desire to find myself in the middle of any Arabian triangle.

I did give him a running account of the shopping tour. I explained that I had operatives on duty outside the hotel, in the lobby, and in the suite across from hers, where our man would keep an eye on the corridor.

But I also reminded him that we couldn't be responsible for anything she might try within the sacred confines of her hotel suite.

Hambul insisted that was the least of his worries. "Her parents are always there, old man," he confided. And added with obvious relish, "Besides, her maidservant is actually in my employ. Never lets the turtledove out of sight. It is only when Vashti leaves those—those sacred confines. Only then—"

Always the perfectly logical answer. But I decided the moment had come to try him on what seemed an odd inconsistency. "Why not just take that little pearl-handled piece of death from her?" I asked in a casual tone. "The way you've got her hemmed in, it ought to be a cinch."

His reply was strictly of the East. The trapped animal only grows more desperate when it knows it is trapped. And she could obtain another weapon easily enough. "Better to pretend we take her threats lightly, to let her think she has escape at her fingertips."

We kept a round-the-clock vigil for the next two days. There was never a moment, except when she was within those sacred precincts

of the hotel suite, when a Mike O'Shaunessey operative was not close
at hand, ready to spring into action at the first suicidal gesture.

Only—there was no such gesture. With each hour that passed, I
grew more dubious of Mr. Hambul and his extravagant fears. Yet
far from diminishing, his terror seemed to mount to greater pitch each
time I called.

"She calls me twelve kinds of a fool," he mourned. "She would die
a hundred times before she would be mine. I have even tried to take
away the little gun, but she prevents me. She sleeps now with the
purse beneath her pillow." A long, almost wistful sigh. Then,
"O'Shaunessey, you must not let her out of your sight! Not for a
moment! Is that perfectly clear?"

I said we'd do our best.

She had several more of those secret meetings with her young
man. They were always brief encounters in out-of-the-way places. On
one of these occasions, my operative clumsily moved in too close.
He was collared by the boy friend.

From the operative's report of the incident:

"This unfortunate thing occurred, as I say, in the Piscatorial Division—that is, the fish department—at the Museum of Natural History.
The tall fellow grabbed me and wanted to know what I thought I
was doing. I told him I was just looking at the fish, that it was a
hobby of mine. He made a sound like a snort, then he said:

"'I don't know who you're working for but whoever it is, tell
the jerk something for me, will you? Tell him I'm no Arabian prince.
But I'm going to marry Eve—that's what I call her, Eve—and we're
going to live in a two-bit quonset some place and play canasta and
eat hamburgers and have babies, just like anybody else.'

"He went on that way. From his jabbering I gathered he'd met
the subject first in Paris during the war, when he was a GI. Her
family must have busted it up. But he must have nearly blown his
top when he read about her coming to America and getting engaged
to the other guy.

"While they were talking—before the guy crabbed the play—the
only thing I heard distinctly was the name Joe Kelly. Don't know
if it referred to him or somebody else."

Friday night she was still alive, I was reasonably sure. My night watches were at their posts—the man at the open door across the corridor and the one in the lobby downstairs. And I myself was watching the windows from the shadows across the street.

In just about twelve hours it would be over. Hambul would have wed his turtledove and I would have my fee. Hambul had preened himself, when I talked with him earlier. "Only a little while longer," he had murmured ecstatically. "I am so grateful. I would like to pay you in glittering gold coins. But it will have to be in dirty dollar bills."

Dirty dollar bills were okay with O'Shaunessey.

The lights in her room went out about ten. Half an hour later the lights in the rest of the suite went out too. The bride-to-be and her entourage had retired to their fitful rest.

I stood near the corner, just out of range of the street light. As the hours lengthened, the hush of this August night deepened. In the folder I find a note I scrawled as I waited, *It's too quiet. Is our pal Joe going to take this lying down? What the devil gives, anyway?*

About midnight, I heard the whistle.

It came from the open window on the third floor—in the suite across from hers. This was the prearranged signal from my operative. It meant the little lady was on her way out.

A moment later I saw her hurry through the entrance and into a cab.

With a curious, perverse pleasure, I realized I had no way of stopping her. I couldn't call in the police—she was committing no crime. And I had no intention of trying force.

My one bet was to leap into Louie's cab and take off in pursuit.

Here, from my notes in the folder:

"In Louie's cab trailed Vashti, alias Eve, on winding, irrational course. Subject apparently aware she was being followed. Seemed to be making a game of weaving in and out of side streets, Louie following with unprintable epithets. At 101st Street and Park, subject got out of cab. Paid fare.

"Louie switched off lights, parked half a block away. Subject stood waiting on street corner. In about two minutes a dark battered coupe pulled up by the girl. Man driving. Looked as if there might be third party in car. Subject got into coupe and they drove off.

"Continued tailing. Coupe drove at high speed, heading mainly west. Finally hit Hudson River Parkway. Continued north on Parkway to point just beyond the George Washington Bridge. Coupe pulled over onto grass and stopped. Subject and man got out.

"Couple headed toward shadows along bank of river. Louie pulled up on grass and I followed pair on foot. Saw them stop by tree close to embankment railing. About ten feet below were the swirling currents of the Hudson."

I remember tonight the sudden panic of that moment. Vashti and her boy friend were too close to that rail. It was too easy, too handy an exit, if they had elected that dire way out.

Of course it was insane. I was letting Timar Hambul and his welter of alarms distort my thinking. This was only another rendezvous—a few last stolen moments together. Nothing more.

They were barely twenty feet from me. But the forms were vague in the darkness. It seemed to me that they had some sort of package with them, but I couldn't be sure. One instant they were in my line of vision; the next, the foliage hid them.

For a long moment they were locked in embrace, silent, motionless, their lips clinging. At last they drew apart and talked in low hurried tones that I could not make out, whispers that were like little gusts of night.

Then abruptly Vashti Evir whirled. She seemed to be peering into the shadows, directly at the spot where I crouched, hidden and motionless.

"You there," she called out. "You in the darkness! I know you're there. Well, listen to me. You can't stop me, do you hear? I don't care how many of you there are. You can't stop me now, none of you!"

A pause. Then, "Do you hear me, up there? Do you understand what I'm saying? I won't be hemmed in. *I won't be hemmed in, ever again!*"

Her shouting attracted the attention of the man at the filling station, fifty yards away. He was standing outside, looking around, probing the darkness with his flashlight.

The flashlight found her. I couldn't see the man with her, only the girl. She was alone, by that rail. And it was then, at that moment —in that grotesque, impossible spotlight—that it happened. Vashti Evir, alias Eve, twisted like a dancer in a pirouette and flung her beautiful body over that rail and down into the river.

My reaction was automatic. I'm a strong swimmer. I couldn't let her die like that. I was throwing off my coat while running forward. At the rail I could make out her form swirling in the water.

There were sounds around me—the engine of the coupe starting up, Louie the cab driver running toward me, and the filling-station man yelling, "She jumped! I saw the girl jump!"

I kicked off my shoes and plunged over the rail.

She was there in the water ahead of me, not forty feet distant, a gray ghostly form in the shadowy half-light on the river. But there was no sound, no cry from those lips, no splash of struggle.

I lunged toward her with desperate strokes. But even as I swam I knew I was too late. I seemed to have known that from the start, as though it were a prearranged pattern I could not alter.

Ahead of me, she seemed to quiver an instant—then to sink. The swirling currents pulled her down into the darkness below.

There was only empty silence when I reached the spot. But a few feet off in the shadows I made out a small object. It was bobbing up and down on the tiny waves like an impudent signal of triumph— Vashti Evir's little green hat with the cocked feather.

It was when I reached out and grabbed the hat that I made the discovery. There was something clinging to the lining, some foreign substance which was sticky against my fingers. Uncertain what it was, I tried to dismiss the vagrant possibility that crossed my thoughts.

For a few moments I treaded water. There was no other sound. She had won her victory, just as she had promised.

The filling-station man's flashlight was searching the water, trying to pick me up. I turned and started back to shore. In one hand I clutched the little green hat.

The notes in the folder read:

"Vashti Evir, alias Eve. Drowned in plunge in Hudson River, near George Washington Bridge, Aug. 24. Body not recovered. Believed swept out to sea.

"Man with her just before suicide dive apparently fled in terror. Has not been located. No clues whatever to his identity.

"My story of suicide plunge verified by Louis Maddox, cab driver, and Paul O'Rourke, filling-station attendant. Both, like myself, saw her dive over the rail.

"Hambul claims Vashti put sleeping pills in the milk of maidservant on night of suicide. Holds me responsible, however. Has made variety of unpleasant threats. But is sailing for Paris in morning."

Vashti's parents and entourage returned to their white stucco domains in the Near East. Hambul, I learned, married a handsome French widow, in a sumptuous wedding in Paris.

The case of Vashti Evir was virtually forgotten, except by some of my competitors who like to recall it as Mike O'Shaunessey's most abject defeat—when he watched $8,000 in fees wash down the Hudson River.

But, of course, they haven't all the facts. Not quite all. Because in recent months we've begun to hear rumors. Rather curious rumors which drift into the office from a variety of sources. Reports concerning a Mr. and Mrs. Joe Smith and family living in one of those peaceful, Sunday-come-to-meeting communities somewhere out in the Middle West.

No precise details. They say he's an engineer and they live in a small cottage and have a couple of kids and a garden and a porch with wicker furniture.

Only thing unusual about them is Mrs. Smith. Seems she's a kind of mystery woman in town—a raven-haired, olive-skinned lovely who carries herself like an Oriental queen and could be a belle of local society except that she spends all her time with the husband and kids.

I never bothered checking the rumors. I had it figured out anyway —from the moment I realized what that foreign substance was that stuck to my fingers when I grabbed the little green hat.

The police assumed that substance was just a bit of flotsam from the river. After all, they had the evidence of Vashti's numerous suicide threats, and eye-witnesses who saw her make the fatal dive. They treated it as a routine suicide all the way. And I didn't attempt to change their minds.

Fact is, I really had no proof. It was only a suspicion on my part that her suicide threats to the terrible Hambul were all phony, that she had framed the whole show to give her the perfect way out. Or that what really dived into the water—just an instant before she and her Joe fled to the battered coupe and sped off into the night—was a weighted straw dummy which would sink swiftly, disintegrate, and slip out to sea.

As I say, nothing but suspicion. I could never see any reason to mention such a wild possibility to anyone, not even to the police. And I could see nothing whatever to be gained.

But sometimes, looking at the little green hat with the cocked feather, and the dried bits of straw inside, I find it hard to hold back a smile—an $8,000 O'Shaunessey smile . . .

WHERE ANGELS FEAR TO TREAD   Stuart Palmer

Where Angels Fear to Tread *was the sixtieth-some short story recounting the adventures and riddles of Miss Hildegarde Withers and the Inspector. There have also been nearly twenty novels in the series. The beginnings are lost in the mists of antiquity; it must be noted that, during the years, Hildegarde has taken on color from the ladies who have depicted her on the movie screens and television screens of the nation; she has a good deal of Edna Mae Oliver and Agnes Moorehead and Zasu Pitts and Helen Broderick and Marjorie Main all mixed together.*

This individual story was conceived and written when the author was living in lovely La Jolla, California—a few miles from the border. It was at a time when the airwaves were filled with broadcasts from little fly-by-night Mexican radio stations, advertising patent medicines, diagnosis of all ailments by mail, advice to the lovelorn and marriage counsel. It occurred to me that a man who ventured—on the basis of a letter—to diagnose and prescribe for illness, matrimonial or otherwise, was sticking his neck out. In other works, he was murder-prone. Dr. Charles Augustus Doan is a blending of several of these vocative charlatans. May his tribe decrease.

STUART PALMER

The honeymoon cottage, Miss Hildegarde Withers sensed immediately, was as deserted and melancholy as a last-year's bird's nest. "Dear me!" sighed the maiden schoolteacher uncertainly. A realtor's *For Sale* sign was not at all the warm welcome she had a right to expect from her favorite niece. What she had meant to be a surprise visit had reverse-English on it, and her departing taxi had left her and her suitcase stranded in the desolate reaches of a half-built suburb in the drizzling rain.

By peering through the blinds she could see hanging above the cheerless fireplace the framed Picasso print of the *Woman in White* which had been her wedding present to the young couple only last June. The letter box was stuffed with mail, but it was not the front of a house that told its story. Marching around to the rear, past the

empty gaping garage, she lifted the cover of the garbage can to discover coffee grounds, cigarette butts, empty pint bottles, and the
remains of a small table-model radio which appeared to have been
sat on by an elephant.

Miss Withers was about to tackle the lock of the back door with
a hairpin when she heard a loud "Hey!" and turned guiltily to see
a slatternly young woman in slacks climbing over the picket fence
from next door. "Say, didn't they tell you at the real-estate office to
ask at Rauthmeyer's for the key?"

"Why—it quite slipped my mind if they did," the schoolteacher
temporized. The door clicked open, and she was ushered into a little
kitchen stocked with modern gadgets, but in extreme disorder. The
house itself smelled dank and sour. "But isn't someone still living
here? Are you quite sure the house is for sale?"

Mrs. Rauthmeyer nodded. "Furnished, too. The folks who lived
here broke up a week ago. She's left, but he's still camping here off
and on." Miss Withers obediently followed her guide on a conducted
tour. There was dust lying thick on the bureau in the little back
bedroom which Joanie had written would always be kept ready for
Aunt Hilde, and the other chamber was a tangle of rumpled bedding
and soiled masculine laundry. The closet was jammed with feminine
garments. "Guess she just walked out in what she had on her back,"
the young woman suggested. "Probably she'll send for them when
she gets settled."

"You have no idea where she can be reached?" Miss Withers asked,
as casually as she could.

"Nope. We really didn't get to know the Sansoms very well, though
they did come over to play bridge one Sunday. He works nights, you
know. But even that bridge game broke up in a row when he took
her out of a business double and they went down six."

"But surely a nice young couple wouldn't break up over a game
of cards?"

"Easy to see you've never been married," Mrs. Rauthmeyer said
wisely. "When a wife and husband fight, it's never really about what
they seem to be fighting about. If you must know, I think that the
main trouble was that radio program Joan was always listening to.

Her husband hated it like poison—those war vets have jumpy nerves anyway, you know. Anyway, one night he up and smashed the radio to smithereens."

Miss Withers nodded. "Sinatra?"

"Huh? Oh, no, it was Dr. Somebody's Clinic on Family Relations, over one of those Mexican stations. Comes on at seven right when I'm getting supper, so I never listen." The door key jangled. "Well, if you've seen everything. . . ?"

Standing in the midst of the bedraggled living room which had once been decorated and furnished with such loving care and such high hopes, Miss Withers took a last look around. She shook her head at the stained carpet, at the shelves where *David Copperfield* and *Swann's Way* had been elbowed aside by a dozen thick volumes on the psychology of marriage, and last of all her eyes turned to the wedding picture silver-framed on the table. There were Joanie and Neil coming out of the chapel, looking incredibly young and ecstatic.

"Yes," the schoolteacher said softly, "I've seen quite enough." But typically, as they were leaving, she had to rush back inside and retrieve her umbrella. "I guess I'd lose my head if it wasn't fastened on," she observed tritely, as she returned. But young Mrs. Rauthmeyer's smile was mechanical, and as Miss Withers went on down the street she felt eyes on the back of her neck. "Thinks I'm a nosey-Parker," she told herself. But she had to go all around the block and come back from the other side across the vacant lot, before she could retrieve her suitcase and scramble in with it through the window she had managed to leave unlocked during her search for the umbrella.

Twilight was falling, but she dared not turn on any lights. With the aid of a pocket-flash the schoolteacher set out to search the honeymoon cottage as it should be searched.

Half an hour later she knew the worst. Her suspicions had been amply confirmed. But this was far different from her impersonal kibitzing on police homicide investigations in the past. This involved her own Joanie, whom she still thought of as a little girl. Why, somewhere in a trunk Miss Withers still had a sheaf of old letters, the first one printed in smeary red crayola, and thanking Aunt Hilde for the "lovely dolly that wears dipers."

She was so busy woolgathering that she did not even hear anyone outside until the doors burst open and they were upon her.

Three thousand miles to the eastward a grizzled little leprechaun of a man, wearing only a towel and a big black cigar, picked up the telephone. "Inspector Oscar Piper? San Diego, California, is calling." A moment later he heard an all-too-familiar female voice saying, "Oscar? Is that you? Do you know what's happened?"

"What's happened is that I just had to get out of a hot tub and I'm dripping all over the floor! Hildegarde, if you want to play guessing-games—"

"Wait, please don't hang up. I'm only allowed one phone call. Oscar, I got out here this afternoon to find that Joanie Sansom, my married niece, has disappeared without her clothes—"

"The girl ought to be easy to locate, if she's walking around in her skin."

"Stop trying to be funny! I mean without most of her wardrobe, and without even leaving a forwarding address. Oscar, there are signs that somebody tried to clean up bloodstains from the living-room rug with *hot* water, and only a man would do that—women know enough to use cold. And there's no pistol in the house!"

"So what? Maybe there isn't a 75mm howitzer, either."

"But there is an *empty* holster for an army automatic tucked away in a trunk under her husband's old uniforms, and a spare clip of .45-caliber cartridges. I just feel it in my bones that something's happened to Joanie. Nobody in the family really approved of her marrying that man because she'd only known him a few weeks and she admits she picked him up in the park . . ."

"Well," said the Inspector dryly, "I seem to remember that you picked me up in the Aquarium some years ago. Relax, Hildegarde. The girl's probably in Reno."

"Without her best dresses? If she was getting a divorce she'd certainly want to look her best at a time like this. Besides, the neighbors overheard them having a terrible fight one night about a week ago, and Joanie hasn't been seen since."

"It's out of my territory. Why don't you call in the local police?"

"*Call* them?" Miss Withers snorted. "Oscar, I guess I forgot to tell you that I'm in the San Diego police station, charged with illegal entry and grand larceny and I-don't-know-what-else." Her voice sharpened. "Are you laughing at me?"

"Just choked on my cigar," Piper hastily assured her.

"Oh. Well, anyway, while I was searching the house the snoopy woman next door noticed my flashlight through the window and called the police. I had my own suitcase with me, of course, and they took that as proof that I'd just finished looting the place. So here I am—they say my bail will be two thousand dollars."

The Inspector choked again. "Okay, Hildegarde. Put whoever's in charge on the line and I'll see if I can talk you out. But let this be a lesson to you . . ."

The toll-call ran through eleven dollars and ninety cents with tax while a suspicious Latin-American detective-lieutenant listened, and even when he had hung up there was little warmth in the brown shoe-button eyes. "Guess we'll have to turn you loose," he said reluctantly. "That New York inspector says you're just a meddlesome old battle-ax of an amateur detective, but that you've no criminal record."

She tossed her head, rather like a startled horse. "Well, I must say!"

"And besides," Detective-lieutenant Villalobos went on, "while you were phoning we opened the suitcase. The stuff inside must be yours all right—there's nothing that a young bride like Mrs. Sansom would wear even to a dogfight."

"Never mind that. Now that you've satisfied yourself as to my *bona fides,* what are you going to do about my niece?"

"We're reporting her to Missing Persons."

"Not good enough. Don't you see, you must arrest her husband at once! She wrote me that he is junior chemist for an oil company here in town."

Villalobos gestured with both hands. "We can't arrest anybody on your suspicions."

"Not even if I'm willing to sign a complaint?" Her fountain pen appeared.

"Okay," said the detective, when the deed was done. "It's you that's climbing out on a limb, not me." Picking up her suitcase, he escorted

her firmly outside and hailed a taxi. "Now, ma'am, you just run
along and let us do our job."

"But you'll really send out a broadcast on Neil Sansom, and stake
out a couple of your men in the cottage to grab him if he comes
home?"

"Sure, sure. Good-bye, Miss Withers."

"But Sansom works—" she started to say, and then bit her lip.
The taxi was moving away, and after all the man might be right.
In a way she was out on a limb. Moreover a tiny red light was flash-
ing off and on in the back of her mind, a warning that she had forgotten something she should have remembered. But what?

"Take me to the—the Signal Hill Oil Company plant," she told
the driver, on a wild impulse. As they crawled through the downtown
traffic, he switched on the radio and filled the taxi with hillbilly music.
The schoolteacher suddenly remembered something, and looked at
her watch, which showed a little past seven. "Can you get Mexico?"

"Sure can, lady. The Tijuana stations, anyway." After some fishing
around through bits of a sister-act singing *La Paloma* in Spanish and
a re-running of the day's races at Hollywood Park in Brooklynese,
Miss Withers at last heard a throbbing, feminine voice saying,
". . . work, work, work from morning to night cleaning and cooking
and washing and then when he comes home, he just eats and goes
to sleep, or else goes out bowling—he says. I'm just fed up, I am.
Sometimes I get to crying and can't stop." There was a short pause,
and then a man's voice: "That's her side of it, Doctor. But what
about me? I work hard at the office all day and when I get home
she hasn't even got her hair brushed, and around the house she's
always nagging because we haven't got a new station wagon like
our neighbors . . ."

"But it's in English?" Miss Withers wondered. "I thought—"

The driver turned to grin lopsidedly. "Sure—they only broadcast
from across the border to keep out of the jurisdiction of the Federal
Communications Commission. Some of 'em sell snake-oil. But this
Dr. Doan is pretty good—my old lady swears by him."

". . . and it is obvious here," a deep, oddly heart-warming baritone
was saying, "that the marriage of our good friends Mr. and Mrs.
Blank is gravely endangered by a growing anxiety-neurosis and sense

of emotional frustration on the part of both husband and wife. It is not easy to sublimate the emotions of courtship into the workaday relationship of everyday married life. . . ." The hypnotic voice went on and on, and as she jounced around in the back seat Miss Withers' prominent nose began to wrinkle.

"Only thus," the mellow tones continued, "can you both make the necessary adjustments and find domestic security and peace. Here is a copy of my new book, *Pitfalls of Love and Marriage,* with my compliments." There was a brief musical phrase, and then: "And to you of our radio audience—are you one of those who are puzzled and confused by the problems and conflicts of modern living? Do you need counsel? Then sit down and write me a letter—just Dr. Doan, Radio station XBYO, Box 131, San Diego. My help is free, as a public service. However, if you want an immediate answer on the air or in writing, just enclose a five-dollar bill to insure a number-one priority. And now for the mailbag as time will permit . . ."

There was a great deal more of the same, blasting forth the intimate secrets of a dozen or so unhappy human beings, with every problem glibly analyzed and solved in a few smooth sentences stuck full of the catchwords of psychiatry like a cookie full of raisins. When they arrived at her destination and the schoolteacher got out, it was with a deep sense of relief, for not even the cracking plant of an oil refinery smelled as bad as that radio program.

She approached a low white building surrounded by vast looming spheres and cylinders of shining metal, interlaced with a spider-webbing of pipes, and here and there erupting belches of flame into the sky. Miss Withers wasn't at all sure of what she was going to say to Neil Sansom when she found him. You couldn't just up and ask a young man if he'd murdered your niece—or could you?

As it developed, she needn't have worried. For Sansom wasn't at work today, nor had he shown up yesterday either. She received this news from a pudgy young man in soiled linen who said that his name was Hank and that he worked out of the same test tubes with Neil Sansom. "When I heard that there was a lady out here looking for him, I thought maybe it was his wife," he confessed. "The poor guy's been almost off his rocker for the past few days. We were afraid he might do something desperate."

"So was I," the schoolteacher admitted. "Or that he already has. But you *must* have some idea of where I could locate him?"

"Well," suggested Hank helpfully, "there are only 194 bars in the San Diego area. You could start with those." More dispirited than ever, Miss Withers thanked him and returned to her waiting taxi.

"Back to town, lady?"

There seemed nothing else to do. "The trouble with me," she told herself, "is that I'm acting like a mother hen instead of a bloodhound. If I only had half my wits about me I'd—but of course! *The wedding picture!*"

"Beg pardon, lady?"

She realized that she had spoken the last words aloud. "Turn around," said Miss Withers firmly. "I've decided to go down to Tijuana."

"But that's a long haul, and I been driving this hack all day!"

"I'm already too far out on a limb," she told him, "to turn back now. Take me across the border." She leaned back in the seat, nodding almost happily. This is what she should have thought of in the first place.

The man muttered something to himself, but made an abrupt U-turn. A moment later he switched the radio on again, bringing back the mellifluous tones of Dr. Doan: "And in conclusion I say to the young woman who signs herself Miss Puzzled that since her fiancé has shown fixed infantile behavior patterns and evidently is in the grip of a mother-fixation with schizoid tendencies, she should forget him and—"

"And *frammis* the *stanportis,*" Miss Withers put in tartly. "Driver, do you mind turning off that double talk?" They rode on in silence, in the wrong direction.

A few miles northward along the coast from San Diego sleeps the village of La Jolla, famous for Torrey pines, abalone shells, and for having the most mispronounced name in recent history. In one of the most secluded of its neo-Moorish beach homes, shielded from the street and the curious gaze of the tourist by a line of pepper trees, Dr. Charles Augustus Doan sat in his comfortably furnished study and listened to the sweet sound of his own voice.

Dr. Doan stroked his neat little Van Dyke complacently, making a mental note as the XBYO station-identification came on in staccato Spanish that the program just ending was his 2,940th. Then he loosened the cord that held the heavy wine-colored dressing gown around his ponderous body, and turned again to his hobby. Other men of standing might collect first editions or Flemish paintings, but the doctor fancied five-dollar bills. With the dexterity of long practice he removed these from the heap of letters which represented yesterday's mail. Through wide French doors he could look out as he worked upon the rain-washed, moonlit garden filled with cacti and rare succulents, to the garage at one side which held his two late-model sedans, and a little farther to the low vine-covered retaining wall and the shimmering Pacific beyond. Somewhere nearby a mockingbird was singing.

Not bad. Not bad at all for a man who only twelve years ago had been trying to eke out a hand-to-mouth existence as Professor Charles, mentalist and lecturer on sex (Miracle of the Unborn, 12 count 'em 12 genuine human embryos in bottles, carnival bookings available for next season, address care *Billboard*).

Though he had a competent staff, this was one operation which Dr. Doan always liked to perform in person. Into his pocket went the money, and into a wire tray beside him went the letters, to be dramatized on the air, answered briefly at the end of the program, or directly by mail. Letters without any enclosure went into the wastebasket unread, but luckily these were few and far between.

After a while there came a discreet tap at the door, and without removing the big corona from his mobile mouth, Doan said, "Come in, Patty."

The secretary was a pale, wispy woman on the rocky side of thirty-five, addicted to shapeless knitted dresses and open-toed shoes. As was her almost unvarying custom, Patty Givens gave a dry little nervous cough before she spoke. "Excuse me, Doctor—"

"All set? Everybody here?" Doan started to rise. "Might as well get it over."

"Er—no, Doctor. Dora and the writers are in the living room, but

Julio hasn't had time to get back from the studio. It's something else. A young man insists on seeing you. He's sort of wild-looking— perhaps I ought to call the police?"

"Police? Of course not," Doan cut in hastily. "Would I be doing my duty if I turned away a poor soul who is in need of counsel? Just explain to him that I don't keep office hours for consultation, but that I'll try to see him later—"

"You'll blamed well see me right now!" came a high, excited voice from the hall, and a young man entered the room as if blown by a high wind. His clothes were hung on his thin body scarecrow style, and there was dried blood above his eye.

The Doctor looked at him in cold, offended dignity. "My dear sir, you can't come bursting in—" he began, and then noticed that the uninvited guest was brandishing a large and nasty-looking automatic pistol. "Please sit down and put that thing away," he said quickly and firmly. Then his voice softened. "Something tells me that you are in serious trouble. You don't have to make threats to receive any help that it is in my power to give. Tell me about it, lad. Just what is your problem?"

"You are!" blurted Neil Sansom.

From the doorway Patty cleared her throat. "Doctor, hadn't I better call—?"

"Of course not," Doan told her sharply. "But you might get our visitor a stimulant."

"Save your liquor, I don't want it. I came here about my wife!"

"Ah, yes." The Doctor sighed. Even at his age, which was pushing sixty, there were a good many phone numbers in his little black book. Some no doubt had husbands. This was likely to be awkward, unless the fellow identified himself. "Perhaps, Miss Givens, you had better step outside and leave us in privacy," he suggested.

Once the study door was closed, even with her ear pressed close against a panel, Patty could only hear the rumble of their voices. She sighed, and then went back to the kitchen and—first making sure that the Mexican cook had left for the day—helped herself to a glass of cooking sherry, chasing it with a peppermint. "For my nerves," she told herself. Not that she lacked confidence in Dr. Doan's ability to handle any conceivable situation. . . .

When the buzzer sounded, summoning her, she raced back into the study and stopped short. There was the Doctor standing alone beside his desk, smiling as he ground out a cigar butt in the tray. "That awful young man—" she cried. "I didn't see—"

Dr. Doan nodded toward the garden door. "I gave him what help I could, but he is still in a nervously disturbed state and I thought it just as well that nobody meet him in the hall."

"Doctor, you're wonderful!" Patty gazed on him with dog-like devotion. Then she saw that Doan was holding the pistol.

"Yes," he continued, "I suggested that our young friend take a good stiff walk along the shore and cool off. And I convinced him that in his condition it would be wiser to leave the weapon with me." Doan dropped it into his desk drawer. "By the way, aren't we ready yet?"

"Oh, yes, Doctor! They're all in the living room waiting. I don't think they suspect a *thing*." Patty stepped quickly aside to hold the door, and Dr. Doan started down the hall. To a fresh corona he held a gold cigarette lighter bearing a caduceus made of tiny emeralds, and on the obverse *To Dr. Charles with gratitude from Lana,* which had been his birthday present to himself a year ago.

In the vast, underlighted living room, filled with arches and niches and wrought iron, were gathered the four people to whom Dr. Doan liked to refer as his fellow workers. Dora Dinwiddie, Lady of the Hundred Voices, was a veteran of vaudeville who never let anyone forget that in the early days of radio she had been featured on Ed Wynn's show. Dora played all the feminine parts for this program, from teen-age daughter to doddering crone, though in person she was a handsome forty, hung with bracelets and bangles.

Nearby, sprawled on the big divan were the Carnehan brothers, graduates of the Hollywood quickie studios, a pair of paunchy, graying adolescents in sweat shirts and slacks. Ray and Sam, known respectively as the Drinking One and the Chasing One, wrote and arranged the program, read some masculine parts, and ghosted Dr. Doan's books.

At the moment they were sharing their *Racing Form* with Julio Barnes, a thin, waspish man with the manner and the flying hair of a concert maestro. He handled music and sound effects, cut the recordings, and each evening drove down across the international boundary and supervised the actual broadcasting of the program from the little studio at XBYO.

It was a tribute to Dr. Doan that they all rose—even Dora—when he entered the room. Patty Givens assumed the role of hostess, and bustled around refilling their glasses and gleefully recounting how the Doctor had overpowered and disarmed the wild-eyed intruder by sheer mental force. But Doan cut her short.

"My friends and fellow workers in the cause of human welfare," he began in his honeyed baritone, "tonight I have a very important announcement to make, as you perhaps have guessed. Contracts were signed today between myself and a relative of a very big *politico* across the border, which will make us equal partners in *El Negro y Blanco,* the Black and White network, Mexico's first television chain. Originating in Tijuana but sent by wire to be rebroadcast from Mexicali, Nuevo Laredo, and Matamoros will be the new video program—'Judge Doan's Court of Human Problems'!"

There was a little stir among the listeners, the beginning of surprised congratulations, but Dr. Doan raised his hand. "As you know, we have waxed enough platters to carry the old show until the first of the year, when it will go off the air. You have all worked with me hard and faithfully, and therefore I have a sort of bonus, an advance Christmas present, for each." Doan produced a sheaf of envelopes from his pocket, much as he might have taken a rabbit from a silk hat, and handed them to the hovering Patty to distribute.

Dora Dinwiddie opened hers first. "A check for two months' pay!" she cried delightedly, and then read on, in a voice that suddenly went harsh: " 'In final settlement of all claims and obligations.' " Her bracelets fluttered and jingled. "But—"

"Oh, yes," said Dr. Doan. "You see, television is quite different from ordinary radio. For instance you, Dora, have a hundred voices. But you have only one face. The new show will require a completely new cast of characters for each broadcast, except for myself of course. Also a completely different sort of preparation and script, and a technical staff trained in the video field. It is with deep and heartfelt regret that I say good-bye to you, and I wish you success as you go on to other fields of service." The Doctor's smile warmly embraced them all, and then he bowed and swept out of the room.

The four of them stood there, flat-footed. It was Julio Barnes who first found his voice. "That—that *cabron!*" he whispered, and spat on the rug.

Ray Carnehan for once in his life put down a highball half finished. "Why, I owe my bookie more than the amount of this check! We'll get a lawyer and sue—"

Sam interrupted. "You know what we'll get in the Mex courts. Besides, our contracts are with the program that's being killed. Line forms here for unemployment insurance." He was thinking of the golden, laughing girls of the Hollywood Sunset Strip and how far twenty dollars a week would go with them.

"We've made Doan a million dollars and now he kisses us off with two months' pay that he'd owe us anyway!" Dora Dinwiddie cried, for once in her own true voice with the Iowa twang to it. "Slaving away for ten years on less than Guild scale for that flea-bitten chiropractor. . . ."

"*Judge* Doan now," Julio Barnes put in. "It's a wonder he didn't go the whole way, and ordain himself Father Doan!" He snorted. "The Confessional on the Air!"

Patty Givens cleared her throat from the doorway. "You shouldn't say such things about a brilliant man who's devoted his life—" But the four of them stamped out of the house, making rude remarks about what Dr. Doan could do with his life, and the front door slammed behind them. Patty peered out of the front window, in an odd state of fluttery happiness, as they held a further indignation meeting on the sidewalk under the pepper trees, and then she let go a sigh of relief as they separated and drifted away. In her opinion they were crude, vulgar people and unworthy to have shared in the Doctor's great work. She was happy to see the last of them.

She almost said as much to Dr. Doan as a little later he lay stretched out on the big red-leather couch in the study and—cribbing occasionally from his library on popular psychology—dictated answers to the day's mail. It was in moments like this that Patty Givens was cosiest, just the two of them alone in the big rambling house. She felt even more intensely than usual the glow of the sherry inside her, the tingling sweetness of the peppermint in her mouth, and the warmth of the tiny electric heater on her ankles.

It would have been altogether perfect if the Doctor would only let her close the doors into the garden and draw the shades. Sometimes the looming shapes of the giant cacti made her nervous. In the moonlight one Joshua tree in particular resembled a lurking man, with an arm upraised in warning. . . .

Patty was still busy with the Doctor in the study when the doorbell rang. A pause, then it rang again, and finally someone hammered as with a nightstick. "Just a *minute!*" the secretary muttered, and then hurried down the hall and flung open the front door. "You're here, thank heavens—" she started to say, and then her jaw dropped. For instead of the blue uniforms she was expecting, there was only a tall bony woman with a long face which vaguely resembled Man o' War, topped by a hat straight out of *Godey's Lady's Book*.

The apparition held an umbrella poised, ready to knock again. "I wish to see the Doctor at once," announced Miss Hildegrade Withers.

Patty coughed. "Oh—but well, you see the Doctor doesn't practice. I'm his secretary—you could write him a letter if you wish his counsel. . . ."

"I don't," said the schoolteacher. "But I've been tracking Dr. Doan all over Tijuana and back, and I'm not leaving until I see him. I—" Suddenly she stopped, her eyes curious and almost sympathetic. "What are you afraid of? I won't bite."

"Oh—why, I expected it to be the police at the door," Patty admitted.

"Why? What's wrong?"

"Nothing, really. But you see, I thought I saw somebody in the garden. I've imagined it lots of times before when I've had to stay and take dictation late at night, but tonight there really *was* something there. And the Doctor finally said I could call the police if it would make me feel easier. I just know it was that same awful young man who was here earlier, waving a gun. . . ."

"Oh, dear!" sighed Miss Withers. "A young man with a gun . . . but I suppose that a man like the Doctor has many enemies . . . ?"

Her remark was abruptly punctuated by the sound of a shot, incredibly loud and clear, from somewhere back in the house. "Oh, God!" shrieked Patty Givens. She whirled and ran.

Though left at the starting gate, Miss Withers made up ground on the straightaway and they were neck and neck at the study door. Flinging it open, she was met by the acrid stench of cordite. There had evidently been a fierce though brief struggle, for the desk drawer was gaping, papers and letters were scattered like autumn leaves, and the electric heater had been kicked over.

The big, bearded man in dressing gown and slippers lay crumpled on the floor between desk and couch, eyes staring at nothing. In a second Miss Withers satisfied herself that Dr. Doan was forever finished with human problems, including his own. Yet there was no wound, no bullet hole that she could see.

Patty Givens, who had snatched up a vase and rushed out into the garden like a tigress defending her cub, now came slowly back. "I heard the murderer—running away," she said, half choking.

Miss Withers came to the door and listened, but there was by this time nothing to hear except the swishing of the surf on the beach, and the distant singing of the mockingbird. Out of the corner of her eye she could see that the secretary was doing a nervous little dance step, an absurd hop which increased until her whole body was shaking. "Oh-oh-oh," moaned Patty, "I'm going to—"

"You are not either," said the schoolteacher, and slapped her. Then the woman subsided into great shuddering sobs, clinging to her like a scared child. It was at that opportune moment that the police finally arrived. Just her luck, Miss Withers thought, that when for once in her life she had been on the scene of a murder ahead of the authorities, she had to be entangled with a hysterical woman.

The officers took one look at the body and then one of them raced for the phone, the other shepherding the two women into the living room where he stood guard over them. Nor did he seem disposed to pay heed when Miss Withers tried to give him a few well-intentioned hints about the handling of the case. "Lady," he told her, "I only work the prowl-car beat."

Outside, autos arrived hastily, and there was the banging of doors, heavy steps in the hall, and the tantalizing sound of masculine voices that she could almost hear. The schoolteacher grew very tired of sitting on the sidelines, of listening to Patty Givens coughing and sniffing, and of the scent of peppermints. "This has gone far enough," she finally burst forth. "I demand to see the person in charge. After all, I've been working on this case longer than anyone else, even if I did guess wrong about the victim. . . ."

"Shut up—please," said the patrolman. "Your turn'll come."

When it came, Miss Withers was rather sorry she had insisted, for it was none other than her old acquaintance Lieutenant Villalobos who finally came into the room, wearing an old trench coat and a worried scowl. The shoe-button eyes flashed in recognition. "Oh, *no!*" he said, wincing. "Not twice in one day."

"Lieutenant, I didn't expect to see you in charge way out here. . . ."

"La Jolla happens to be part of the city of San Diego," he told her. "I was never sorrier." Wearily he took out a black notebook. "Now ma'am, how do you explain . . ."

"I came here, after bribing the people at Tijuana to give me Dr. Doan's home address, because I happen to know that my niece Joanie Sansom *always* listens to Doan's radio program. I thought that maybe she isn't dead after all, because if he'd killed her, Neil wouldn't keep their wedding picture around to look at. I hoped to persuade Dr. Doan to include in his next broadcast an appeal to her to come home or let us know where she is. . . ."

"And it was just a coincidence that you happened to be on the spot when he got killed. Is that your story?"

"But I wasn't! I was standing in the doorway, trying to get his secretary to let me see him, when the shot was fired. And for that matter I don't know if the man was murdered or not. I didn't see any wound anywhere."

Villalobos smiled grimly. "You should have lifted his toupee, then."

It was Patty Givens who gasped. "His *what?* But the Doctor didn't—"

"Oh, sure. They make 'em nowadays so nobody can tell. Anyway,

Doan was shot in the center of his bald spot at close range, the bullet angling down into his body. We figure the hair-piece must have got knocked off in the struggle, but the murderer took time out to replace it, neatly covering the wound. The gun itself—"

"An army .45 automatic . . ." whispered Miss Withers.

"I was about to say that the gun is missing, though we found an ejected .45 shell under the bookcase." The dark eyes narrowed. "You seem to know a lot about this."

"Put it down as a lucky guess," the schoolteacher said, somewhat feebly.

But she was saved for the moment by Patty Givens, who could keep silence no longer. She blurted out the breathless story of what had happened that evening, of the awful young man forcing his way in with the gun and how Doan had taken it away from him, of the session here in the living room when the Doctor fired his staff, and of how later she had seen someone or something moving in the garden.

Villalobos listened patiently, making notes only of the names and addresses of the four members of the staff who had been paid off. He tore out the sheet and handed it to a uniformed man. "Pick them up," he said.

"But, Lieutenant," objected Miss Withers, "don't you think it unlikely that people would commit murder just over losing a job?"

He gritted his teeth. "I've seen murder committed over eighty-five cents. Killers aren't reasonable."

But it was really Patty who answered the question. "You don't know them," she insisted. "They'd all been with the Doctor so long they thought they owned their jobs. Dora Dinwiddie has a young husband and she knows he'll walk out on her if she stops making big money. Julio Barnes was in prison once for trying to strangle a man in an argument over the proper way to adjust a microphone. And the Carnehans—they both live up to every dime they make, and Ray can't do without liquor any more than Sam can do without little blond extra girls."

"Surely there are lots of other jobs," the schoolteacher objected.

Patty shook her head stubbornly. "Nobody goes back to one of the big networks again after ten years with a shoestring station down here. This is the end of the line."

"Okay!" growled the Lieutenant. "I'm asking the questions. What you're saying is that one of the four people who got their final pay checks tonight thought it over and then sneaked back through the garden to get even with Doan. Is that it?" He tugged thoughtfully at his lower lip. "Now who besides yourself knew that the gun was lying there handy?"

"Why—" the secretary flushed. "Maybe I *did* mention about how magnificently the Doctor quieted and disarmed that young man, when we were all in here."

"So the Dinwiddie woman, both Carnehans, and Barnes knew the gun was somewhere in the study?"

Patty nodded, and started to speak, but Miss Withers interrupted. "There was somebody else who knew—the person from whom the gun was taken."

Villalobos' bow was exaggerated. "Could be. Also could be that that person's name is Neil Sansom. Anxious to swear out another warrant?"

"Certainly not! Because whoever did murder Dr. Doan, I'm positive that it wasn't my unfortunate nephew-in-law. If he had been going to commit homicide he'd have done it on the spur of the moment when he first arrived. I'm also positive—"

"If there's anything you're *not* positive about, let me know!" the Lieutenant told her. He turned Patty Givens over to a subordinate with orders to have her sign a written statement. "That'll be all for tonight," he told Miss Withers, taking her by the elbow and steering her down the hall.

"But, Lieutenant, I want to make a written statement too! And shouldn't we have another look around Dr. Doan's study? I was thinking of the papers on the floor, and the ash trays, and his checkbook. . . ."

"I said that would be all!" Villalobos repeated, in a queer, strained voice. But as they reached the front door, it was flung open and in came two bulky detectives, with Neil Sansom handcuffed between them. He looked sulky, scared, and guilty as Cain—but still in the pale, handsome face Miss Withers could see the boy of the wedding picture.

"Found him walking along the beach," was the report. "Says it was a nice night and he was just taking the air. But guess what we found in his pocket, Loot? A nice big .45 automatic that he happened to find a few minutes ago right below this house, left high and dry by the tide."

Neil only muttered, "Why shouldn't I have picked it up? It's mine."

"You poor boy," cried Miss Withers quickly, "don't say one thing more until I get you a lawyer. I'm Joanie's aunt from New York, and I'm afraid I've helped get you in a lot of trouble. Just tell me one thing—where is she?"

Neil Sansom seemed to be too tired to be surprised, even at this. "I haven't seen Joan since she knocked me cold with an ash tray and walked out of the house. I don't know where she is and I don't care any more."

Then his captors jerked him along, and Miss Withers found herself being escorted out the front door in what was almost the equivalent of the bum's rush. "That fellow in New York warned me over the phone that you'd get in my hair," Lieutenant Villalobos muttered through clenched teeth. "Good-bye, *please.*"

However, the schoolteacher had to give him credit for one thing. The man was courteous enough to have a police car take her back to San Diego. It was not until they passed the ferry terminal and pulled up outside the familiar big brick building with the barred windows that she realized the Lieutenant's hospitality included putting her up for the night.

After a sleepless night in a detention cell and a breakfast of mush and jail coffee Miss Hildegarde Withers did not think that anything could make her more miserable than she was already. But she had not counted on being hauled out to the house in La Jolla again shortly before noon, and coming face to face with her missing niece in the front hall.

The girl clung to her tearfully. "I was in Las Vegas," Joanie cried. "But I hired a plane as soon as I heard it on the radio."

"But, child, why didn't you let anybody know?"

"I was afraid if I wrote anybody or sent for my stuff, Neil would find out where I was and come after me. I wanted to give him a real good scare, but I really wasn't going through with a divorce. Only you see, when we quarreled he tried to spank me!"

"The beast!"

"No, he isn't! It was all my fault, every bit of it. And now they're going to hang him for murdering that awful Doctor—"

"No, they're not, child." Miss Withers tried to keep her voice confident.

"But yes they are!" Lieutenant Villalobos came briskly toward them, a look of smug satisfaction on his newly shaven countenance. "Just a few things to straighten out on the timetable, which is why I've got everybody rounded up here. Will you follow me into the living room, please? You too, Mrs. Sansom—you're the motive." Then he dropped back to take Miss Withers' arm. "Sorry we had to hold you last night, but you know how it is. By the way, I'll have to admit that was a good steer you gave me about Doan's checkbook."

"Was it?" She blinked. "And the ash trays?"

"Nothing in them but cigar butts."

"Oh," said the schoolteacher, her mind racing like a flywheel. But there was no time. The Lieutenant ushered them into the living room, already rather crowded with uniformed men and material witnesses. Dora Dinwiddie sat on the edge of a hard chair, playing with her bracelets. The Carnehan brothers, both stiff and sober now, shared the piano stool, and Julio Barnes and Patty Givens slumped in easy chairs. On the divan, manacled to a stony-faced policeman, was the guest of honor. Neil looked up at Joanie as they came in, let out a breath, and then turned back to stare at his shoe-tips again.

"I'll make this short and sweet," began the Lieutenant. "It's important that we have the times established. At eight-thirty last evening Miss Patty Givens came into the Doctor's study and told him that there was a young man insisting on seeing him. She has identified the prisoner as being that man, and he doesn't deny it. At that time Miss Dinwiddie and both Carnehans were waiting in this room, and Mr. Barnes was on his way here, right?"

They all nodded. "Okay. At eight fifty-five Dr. Doan rang for Patty Givens and showed her a gun he'd taken away from Sansom. . . ."

The brisk, confident voice went on and on. Miss Withers racked her brains, but no inspiration came. She felt that she was drifting in a boat without oars or rudder, caught in a swiftening current and with the roar of a cataract ahead.

"Okay. At approximately nine o'clock Dr. Doan came into this room and made a little speech, after which he distributed pay checks to four of his employees. Around nine-fifteen they left—" He referred to his notebook again.

"And I for one went straight home," said Dora Dinwiddie. "My husband will back me up!"

Sam Carnehan spoke up. "If it's alibis you want, I spent the rest of the evening with Mimi, the day cashier at the Casa. She's not supposed to date guests, so I imagine she'll deny it."

His brother Ray confessed to having spent the previous night in a round of bar-hopping, starting at the Beach and Tennis Club and ending up on Skid Row in downtown San Diego. Julio Barnes said he'd gone home, played his violin for a while, and then taken his spaniel out for a long walk. All alibis, of a sort, but nothing Miss Withers could get her teeth into. It had to be one of them.

Villalobos continued summing-up. "So after you four had left, Patty Givens and the deceased started cleaning up the dictation in the study. At this time Sansom was taking a walk along the beach and trying to cool off. Finally he wandered back from the beach and came up into the garden and Patty Givens saw him out there, and called the police. That was at ten fifty-eight. At a minute or so after eleven Miss Withers arrived and rang the doorbell, so Patty had to leave Doan alone in the study to answer the front door—"

"I wouldn't have," Patty cried. "Only I thought it was the police answering my call!"

The Lieutenant nodded. "I'm not suggesting that her arrival at that moment was a put-up job, but it did give Sansom the chance he was waiting for. Seeing that the Doctor was alone, he slipped in from the garden and grabbed the gun out of the desk, or maybe he even asked

Doan to return it to him. Anyway, once it was in his hand—"

"But what about the checkbook?" Miss Withers cut in desperately.

"Oh, yes." Villalobos nodded. "There were four stubs in it dated today, filled out properly for the four final pay checks. And there was a fifth check torn out, stub and all—*that* was the check he wrote to Neil Sansom, trying to buy his life!"

Across the room Neil started to rise, but felt the jerk of the handcuffs and sank back again. "Probably," continued Lieutenant Villalobos, "the shot was fired while Doan was bent over to write the check, thus accounting for the location of the wound. Sansom destroyed the check when he got outside, but then he lost his nerve. He remembered that Patty Givens could identify him—so he wandered up and down the beach, probably trying to get up courage enough to use the gun on himself."

Joanie leaned down and whispered in Miss Withers' ear. "He's innocent, I know he is! Neil wouldn't do anything like that in a million years. He couldn't!"

But the schoolteacher only sat there, still held in her nightmare. The Detective-lieutenant's reconstruction was the only possible one. There was nothing, nothing at all she could offer in its place. It was that, or else she had to take her pick of the four—Dora, the Carnehans or Barnes—and they all had the sort of alibis innocent people usually have.

Through Miss Withers' mind flashed the events of last evening, like film being hastily rewound on the reel. Neil's arrest, the Lieutenant's questions, the wait with Patty in the living room, the scene in the room with the body, the sound of the shot—

"I'm afraid, Lieutenant," she said a few moments later, "that my niece is going to faint. Perhaps I might get her a glass of water?" Without waiting for an answer she whisked out of the room, plunging past the uniformed man in the doorway so swiftly and erratically that she almost threw him off balance. In less than five minutes, however, she was back with the glass of water. But now there was a look in her eye which—had this been one of Oscar Piper's cases—would have made that wise little Irishman order full speed astern.

Lieutenant Villalobos, however, still had the bit in his teeth. "Now listen," he was saying to Neil, "you can save yourself and everybody a lot of grief by making a full confession. You killed Dr. Doan because you knew he had advised your wife to leave you, and no doubt a jury will take that into consideration. But it's an open-and-shut case—"

"Please don't shut it just yet," interrupted Miss Withers airily. "By the way, Lieutenant, I just noticed in the bathroom that you're having the plumbing opened up. An excellent idea. I was sure that the missing check and stub had been burned or disposed of right here in this house."

Someone in the room sighed, very softly. "What the—?" began Villalobos.

"And remember, I tried last night to tell you that I thought it odd the killer replaced Doan's toupee neatly over the wound. That would seem to imply a squeamish person, who had to stay in the room with the body for a while and couldn't stand the sight of blood. Did I mention to you too about how Patty Givens here went rushing out into the garden after the murderer, she said? Up to then she'd been timid as a mouse. And how did she know that Doan was murdered then? She barely looked at him and there was no visible wound."

"Oh-oh-oh!" screamed Patty furiously. "You horrible woman, to say such things! Why, I worshipped the ground he walked on!"

"No doubt you did," Miss Withers conceded. "Until he told you that you were fired too. What could be more natural than after getting rid of the rest of his staff he'd get rid of his secretary? They say there's nothing more aggravating than an office-wife, especially one that coughs and sniffs and eats peppermints constantly. . . .

"And that jiggling little dance step that Patty was doing in the study last night," the schoolteacher continued. "I thought at the time that she was only shaking with hysteria, but *it was really the open-toed shoes!*"

"That's enough of this nonsense," Villalobos cut in. "You're trying to pin this thing on the Doctor's secretary, but you're way off base. Haven't you forgotten that in your own statement you said you were talking to Patty Givens when Doan was shot?"

"Yes, Lieutenant—*but Doan was already dead when I rang the doorbell!* Patty Givens had killed him and thrown the pistol into the ocean—but not far enough—before she phoned the police. She thought I was the law, so she made a quick last-minute adjustment in the study and hurried to answer the door, thinking that she was about to give herself a perfect alibi. Because nobody can tell within five or ten minutes the exact time a body expires."

Miss Withers stopped for breath. Something had gone terribly wrong, for it should have happened—

Then a bullet ricocheted screaming down the hallway, and the sound of a shot boomed through the house.

For an instant everyone in the living room was paralyzed, and then the cool Bostonian accents continued. "What you just heard was a pistol cartridge that I snatched from the belt of that officer in the doorway and stuck into the filament of the electric heater," she announced. "When the heater got red hot, the thing went off. Of course I should have faced the heater toward the open door, so the bullet would go harmlessly out to sea, as it did for Patty last night." Miss Withers peered toward the secretary. "But it had to appear that there was only one shot fired, didn't it? You wanted to get rid of the *second* empty shell, but of course you didn't think it would be that hot. You worked it into the open toe of your shoe, and that's why you were dancing. . . ." Patty Givens suddenly stood up.

"There's no need to say any more," she told them dully. "Since you're tearing up the plumbing you'll find the scraps of the check anyway." Once started, she kept on talking endlessly, on and on. But long before she finally ran down, Miss Withers and the Sansoms were far away. It was a fine bright day, with little clouds like tufts of cotton wool.

"But you're coming home with us for your visit, after all?" Joanie was begging, Neil's arm around her and her head on his shoulder.

Miss Withers thought not. "You young idiots deserve a chance to get together and pick up the broken pieces without anyone else butting in," she told them. "Perhaps I'll come later on. Right now, I think I'll make a long-distance call to a certain hard-headed little inspector in New York and give him a piece of my mind. 'Meddlesome old battle-ax' indeed!"

COFFEE AND— David Alexander

*The detective "team" in this story, Tommy Twotoes and Terry
Bob Rooke, known as "Soldier," were introduced in my first
two mystery novels,* Most Men Don't Kill *and* Murder in Black
and White, *both published by Random House in 1951. The main
character, Tommy Twotoes, was (aside from his 300-pound avoir-..
dupois) based upon my great good friend, the late "Sunny Jim"
Coffroth. Coffroth was without question the greatest sports pro-
moter of all time, and I'm not forgetting Rickard or any of the
others. He was also one of the zaniest and most completely lov-
able human beings I have ever known. Twotoes was criticized
in some quarters as being on the fantastic side. The answer to
that is that I had to tone the real Coffroth down when I depicted
him as the fictional Twotoes, for I knew no editor of fiction would
accept the true-life article as being remotely possible. As for
Rooke, Tommy was crippled from alcoholic neuritis and needed
a pair of legs. I invented the Soldier to supply my hefty hero
with a means of locomotion. Rooke, I think, derived mainly out
of the nowhere into the here. He was depicted in my early novels
as being a veteran of the iron coffins (tanks) in War Number
Two and as liking his likker. In those two small respects, at least,
he resembled his creator.*

*The reception of Tommy Twotoes by the public was heart-
warming, not only in America but in England, France, and
half a dozen other European countries. His reception by certain
critics and by the reprint editors was not so gratifying. They
wanted a more "realistic" hero although I had had to tone down
the antics of a flesh-and-blood human being in creating him.
So I regretfully dropped him and created new heroes for the
books. Tommy stays alive in an occasional short story. I love
the old guy and would like to put him back in a novel some
day. But I can't, not until America recovers the most precious
possession it ever lost. I mean its sense of humor.*

DAVID ALEXANDER

Tommy Twotoes, the three-hundred-pound millionaire penguin-fancier, entered the office of Terry Bob Rooke, Private Investigator, on the loglike arm of old Killer Carney, the punch-drunk, rum-dum former heavyweight who was now a Bowery bum. Maybe I should explain right off that I'm Rooke, better known to my friends as "Soldier," and that my agency was subsidized by the slightly fantastic Mr. Twotoes when he began to fancy himself as a criminologist in the twilight of his hectic life, and figured he needed a front for his latest hobby.

To describe Mr. Twotoes as eccentric is to lapse into euphemism. Mr. Twotoes had been everything from a skid-row vagrant to a multimillionaire during the seventy-odd years of his intensely alcoholic existence. Among other things, he had promoted the fights of some of the greatest boxers of his time, which is one of the reasons he was acquainted with such characters as Killer Carney. The private detective agency for which I held the license was just one of his numerous conceits. He had a herd, or maybe I should say a covey, of penguins housed in an especially refrigerated miniature Antarctic on his estate in Tarrytown. Mr. Twotoes maintained you could learn a great deal about human beings from the study of penguins, since he claimed these flightless birds from the polar regions were the most completely amoral and unchristian of all living creatures.

The Killer, who supported the enormous, crippled Mr. Twotoes on his sturdy arm, was something of a character in his own right. As a result of old batterings and raw booze, he'd been on the Bowery for years. When he wasn't panhandling coffee money, he was engaged in baby-sitting for tenement mothers who couldn't afford the union wage scale of the Baby-sitters Local. Sometimes the Killer was paid a few nickels for his time, and sometimes he was rewarded with homemade wine or a dish of spaghetti; but more often he pursued his odd profession through sheer love of the work.

As he entered the office, Tommy was smoking his queerly wrought pipe, the bowl of which was fashioned in the shape of a nude woman. He took the pipe from his mouth, exuded billowing smoke, and boomed in his foghorn voice:

"Soldier! Have you made arrangements for Lieutenant Romano to receive us?"

Lieutenant Romano was an old buddy of Tommy's who was now attached to the Homicide Squad. That morning Tommy had called me to say that Killer Carney had burst into his home in Tarrytown, panic-stricken, and that the broken-down old pug had important information in connection with the town's latest murder, in which a middle-aged college professor named Stephen Dean was being held for the poison slaying of his beautiful young wife.

I said: "The Lieutenant is awaiting us, and you could have saved yourself a trip up in the elevator. If you've got the Rolls outside, we can drive right downtown. But how did a character like the Killer get mixed up with a college professor and a murder in Mulberry Mews?"

"You will hear in good time," said Tommy, "when the Killer tells his unusual story to Lieutenant Romano. In the meantime, we will pause for refreshment."

Tommy produced a blue crock of French brandy from a cavernous pocket of his coat; I produced glasses, and we all had a drink. After that I helped Killer Carney to the elevator and out into the street with the old man, who was so crippled from alcoholic neuritis that putting one foot in front of the other posed a problem for him. Ebony Black, the gigantic Negro who had lost an eye when he was a heavyweight in Tommy's stable, now acted as bodyguard and chauffeur for Mr. Twotoes. Ebony, clad in plum-colored livery, sat at the wheel of the Rolls Royce, which was parked directly in front of a fireplug. The antediluvian vehicle was so familiar on New York's streets, and its owner was so well known to the police, that Ebony Black was contemptuous of such small matters as traffic regulations.

Mr. Twotoes was always nervous when he was riding, and would permit his chauffeur to proceed at a speed of no more than thirty miles an hour, even on deserted country roads. During our ride down to Manhattan-West headquarters of Homicide on Twentieth Street, my penguin-fancying patron nearly suffered a nervous collapse as the car swerved suddenly.

"Sorry, boss," apologized Ebony, "but a ol' dog almost run under the wheels—ain't nothing makes me feel so poorly as hurting a dumb animal."

Mr. Twotoes, whose doughy moon of a face was even paler than usual, did not answer, but revived himself with a long pull at the blue crock. This time he did not pass it to me or the Killer, however.

"Professor Dean, he was a animal-lover, too," said the Killer. "His house was full of animals, it was."

"Killer," I said, "do you mean to tell me you visited the renovated stable in that sublimated alley in Greenwich Village where Professor Dean has his residence? You're moving in swanky circles these days."

"It ain't no stable," declared the Killer. "It's just a little brick house with kind of a concrete garden out in back. And it ain't in no alley, either. It's in what you call a mews, maybe because they got a lot of cats in it. A mews," explained the Killer, "is a kind of little court which has a lot of trees growing out of boxes in it."

We reached the Manhattan-West station and found Romano, the cop with the classic profile, sitting at a battered desk with a green-shaded light on it, and looking sour, like a man who always expects the worst and is seldom disappointed. He nodded at us.

"Yeah," he said, when Tommy started to introduce the Dean murder witness. "I know the Killer. He was one of the characters around and about your place when I was investigating the Danise Darlan Killing last year."

"He has important information for you, Lieutenant," said Tommy, as we lowered his bulk into the stoutest-looking chair in the office.

"Please don't be doing me favors," said Romano. "I got a clean-cut case of poisoning that is all wrapped up in tissue paper and pretty ribbons and ready to deliver to the D.A. for his birthday. This fellow Dean's young wife dies right after she and he have drunk a cup of coffee. Seems her cup was loaded with a little cyanide. Coffee and—, you might say. Seems the Professor's wife, who's about twenty years younger than he is, has been playing around with a pretty-boy artist named Porter, so we got motive. Seems the only alibi the Professor has is a witness who he claims drank coffee with 'em. We found another cup with fingerprints we couldn't identify, but that could easily have been a plant. The Professor claims this witness is a vag he's picked up and asked in for coffee at his nice little house—a very likely story indeed.

"The Professor claims this vag can testify his wife made the coffee, poured it out into three cups in the house, and brought the cups out to them in the garden. The Professor also says this vag can testify he told his wife he suspected her of trying to poison him so that she could inherit his insurance and marry Pretty Boy Porter, and that he challenged her to drink the coffee she'd prepared for him in an extra-big cup he always used. He says they had a heated argument over this, and that finally his wife grabs the big cup and drinks it down before he can stop her, and drops dead. He says the missing vag can testify to the truth of all this. Only trouble is, the vag lams the minute his wife comes down with a hard case of the death throes."

The Lieutenant scratched his classic Roman nose. "So I've got a perfect case until you come along and do me favors by producing the only witness who can knock the whole case to hell and gone."

He stared at the Killer with his brooding, liquid Italian eyes, and the Killer looked uncomfortable.

"How you ever happen to tell the Professor your name is Vanderlip?" he asked the Killer.

The Killer said: "Cecil Vanderlip was a pug which went nine rounds with me oncet when I was good. The name just come into my mind like that. Vanderlip seemed like a name which would please the Professor. The Professor had class."

The Killer looked guilty. He was sweating. "I don't never give nobody my right name if I can help it," he explained.

Tommy said to Romano: "Before the Killer tells his story, you are due an explanation as to why he did not come forward at once, as to why he left the scene of the crime, in which he was in no way involved, somewhat precipitately. The Killer is a derelict. To him, and to all his kind, the police are natural enemies. It has been half a century or more since I feared the police, but I can understand the Killer's attitude. I trod skid row of the San Francisco that existed before the fire, and I avoided the company of cops, just as the Killer and his cohorts do today. The Killer had no intention of withholding evidence, but he did not wish to involve himself with the police, since his standing in the community is somewhat ambiguous. He fled to me for advice. Being a law-abiding citizen, I have brought him to you."

I had to chuckle at Mr. Twotoes' description of himself as a law-abiding citizen. A good part of his fortune stemmed from Prohibition days, when he was reputed to have been the mastermind behind one of the largest and most profitable of the rumrunning syndicates. But Mr. Twotoes held that Prohibition was an onerous and unnatural law, and he deemed himself a public benefactor in assisting his fellow citizens to flout the Eighteenth Amendment.

Romano sighed patiently, like a man who has conditioned himself to the acceptance of the slings and arrows of outrageous fortune. He called a stenographer and said to Killer Carney: "Tell your story, please."

The Killer said:

"Well, it's thisaway. Yesterday morning I ain't even got jingling in my jeans and I got to make a brace, and the Bowery ain't so popular as it used to be with tourists, so touches ain't easy there. So I'm a little off my beat. I'm on Bleecker, which is usually all right for bracing stale rolls off bakeries, but ain't much good for a flop-stake or a booze-stake. Anyway, I'm figuring I'll work my way up to Washington Square, because at this time of day there is usually a lot of ladies with babies there, and sometimes if you goo-goo at the babies, you get a dime from them. The ladies, I mean, not the babies. Also there is usually some young punks hanging around which is working steady and killing their lunch hours, and some of them are marks which will maybe spring two-bits.

"But I am still on Bleecker when I see this mark, which is dressed too good for the place where he is walking. This well-dressed guy stops and pets a little cur dog which is lying outside a grocery store; then he reaches in his pocket and takes out a piece of dog biscuit and gives it to the pup, and so I figure he must be a soft touch which is anyway good for coffee money and maybe even a flop-stake, and I brace him.

"I give him the old routine about excuse me, Mister, but couldja maybe spare a few pennies for a cuppa coffee. And he straightens up from feeding the dog the biscuit and says: 'Why, you look to me like you could use a little brandy in your coffee. A café royale,' he says, 'is very stimulating, don't you think?'

"I tell him that the joints I patronize do not put brandy in your coffee, in fact you are lucky if they put canned cow and sugar with flyspecks in it. He laughs, and says to come along with him, and he will see I have some coffee which is laced with brandy.

"Well, I figure I have picked myself a screwball, like one of them guys which are always walking around the Bowery with petitions in their pockets for you to sign, so I say: 'Where do we get this coffee with the slug in it, Mister?'

"And he tells me: 'Well, I had thought it might be pleasant for us to go to my house over in Mulberry Mews, which is not far from here, and have our coffee and brandy in the garden, as it is a pleasant day, but I would like to walk around a bit first, and I would like to talk to you. However,' he says, 'I can see your need for refreshment is urgent, so let us drop into this place on the corner.'

"This place on the corner is called the San Remo, and it is a bar which has a big machine for making Italian coffee at one end which is as big as a diesel engine. This machine explodes and sputters a few times and the bartender gets some coffee out of it; then he gets some brandy out of a bottle and pours it into the coffee, and it is very refreshing, although I would personally have just as lief settle for a boilermaker at Grogan's Elite Palace Café and Bar on the Bowery. Well, we have two of these fancy drinks, and he introduces himself to me very politely as Professor Dean, and I tell him I am Cecil Vanderlip because that is the first name which pops into me head, and besides it seems appropriate under the circumstances. The Professor asks me if he might have the pleasure of my company for a stroll around the streets, and says that afterwards we can go to his house for more of the same we have been having, only better, because he owns some rare old Napoleon brandy. I do not figure how I have anything to lose, as he has not asked me to sign any petitions or even gone into the old routine about how did I become what I am, so I do not tell him anything at all about myself, not even that I am once a heavyweight who was good enough to get his fights promoted by the famous Tommy Twotoes.

"We walk up MacDougal Street but do not get very far very fast, because Professor Dean is a great animal-lover, and MacDougal Street is almost as full of animals as it is of people, and it is very full of people. The Professor stops to stroke the cats and regrets that he has no milk for them to drink. He feeds dog biscuits to half a dozen mutts in every block. He even stops and pats the nose of a bony old horse which he addresses as 'Percy' and which is hitched to a vegetable wagon. He puts his hand in his pocket, but I guess he is out of fodder and horses do not eat dog biscuits, because he says: 'Poor Percy, I have nothing for you today but we will meet again tomorrow and I will bring you something nice.' Only I guess he can't keep his date with the horse account of he is in the can today.

"Finally we get to Washington Square park, and he takes a bag of corn out of his pocket and feeds it to the pigeons. The pigeons seem to know the Professor personal, because they roost all over him until he looks like a fan dancer, and they eat corn right out of his hand. After a while we sit down on a park bench, and a minute later I nearly fall off the park bench because he says to me: 'Vanderlip,' he says, 'what would you do if your wife was trying to poison you?'

"Well, I tell him that my wife has been dead a long time but that she was a good cook and never tried to slip no rat poison into the corned beef and cabbage, and if she had of, I would of clouted her a left hook to the button which would of been a lesson to her.

"He then tells me that his wife is so young and pretty that he could not think of clouting her and risking marking her up with a busted nose or maybe a cauliflower ear. He says that his wife is in love with a young character who paints pictures and that they are planning to slip him a fast mickey and live happily ever after on the fifty gees insurance which he carries. I tell him maybe he is just imagining things, like guys on the Bowery which get the stuff in the wrong bottle and go into the rams and see lavender leopards. But he tells me this is not the case. He says he has overheard his wife and this picture-painter planning to slip a jolt of bug-killer into his coffee and brandy, and he says he is in the habit of drinking coffee and brandy at all hours of the day and night, so there is plenty of opportunity for his wife to sweeten it up for him.

"Then he says that he would like very much to have coffee and brandy in the garden of his house, which is just across the park, but he would not dare to drink his wife's coffee unless a third person is present, and he asks if I will go with him. I tell him I guess there is no harm in me going if he's sure his wife won't dunk the DDT in the wrong cup. He laughs and says there's no danger of that, because he has bought a antique coffee cup for himself up on Cape Cod some years ago which is four times as big as most cups and has old sailing ships painted on it. He says he is the only one at his house which ever drinks out of this big cup. Then he slips me a stake for listening to his troubles, and it is a double saw, twenty bucks! It is the biggest brace I ever made in my entire career on skid row, and the shape I'm in, I would of gladly drunk rat poison to get it.

"Well, this Mulberry Mews where he lives is a kind of little blind alley which runs off MacDougal Street, only it ain't a alley, because it has boxes filled with trees in it instead of cans filled with garbage. There are about half a dozen little houses, all old-looking and pretty much alike, on each side and the Professor lives in the next to the last house on the right-hand side. The house has a white door with a brass knocker and a brass bell on it and the Professor rings the bell to let his wife know he is coming, I guess, before he unlocks the door. His wife is a pretty piece who is young enough to be his daughter and it is not hard to see why she might wish to dose the Professor's coffee and brandy if she has a young picture-painter just around the corner. She does not appear to welcome me too heartily, maybe because I am not dressed up like most of her guests, although I am wearing a coat and pants I got practically new from the Salvation Army, I just washed all over three days ago in a public bath and I have recently had a close shave and haircut at the barber's college.

"The Professor's house is not like any which I am used to going into. It has wallpaper and pictures in gold frames and shiny furniture and long red curtains at the windows. And it is full of animals. There is two dogs and more cats than I can count and there are bright-colored fish in little glass tanks and there is a cage with two of those little green birds in it that sit smooching each other all day. The Professor introduces me to his pets, but I'm afraid I do not remember the names of all the little bright-colored fishes which he has in his glass tanks.

"We go out into the garden, although it is not much of a garden. It is a place which is paved with what they call flagstones and there is a umbrella and a table and some chairs and there are plants and little trees growing out of pots. The Professor tells his wife to make some coffee and we will all have coffee and brandy in the garden. The Professor and I and one of them big woolly dogs which are supposed to carry a shot of brandy hitched to their collars and one of them little dogs which look like a sienie sit out in the garden talking of this and that while Mrs. Dean is making coffee. Pretty soon she comes out with a tray. On the tray is three cups of coffee, two regular-sized cups and the big cup for the Professor, and a bottle of brandy which looks like it has been laying around somebody's cellar a long time, and a little silver thing with sugar lumps in it."

Romano asked: "Did she bring out the coffeepot or a cream pitcher?"

The Killer shook his head. "No sir," he said. "She must of poured the coffee into the cups inside the house. And we put brandy instead of cream into the coffee."

"Did all of you take sugar?" Romano asked.

"Yes sir," replied Killer Carney. "Everybody took sugar. The Missus and I took two lumps apiece, but the Professor took three or four because he had such a big cup."

"Who poured the brandy into your coffee?"

"The Professor. He poured a big slug in all our cups. His wife said he was pouring too much."

"And he poured from the same bottle into all your cups?" asked the Lieutenant.

"Sure. There wasn't but one bottle. A real old-looking kind of bottle it was."

"And did each of you drink the coffee with the brandy?"

"Well, Mrs. Dean and I start to drink ours, but the Professor says to his wife: 'My dear,' he says, 'do you really think it's safe for me to drink this?'

" 'What in the world do you mean, Stephen?' she asks him.

" 'Are you quite sure you haven't put something special in this big cup of mine?' he asks her. 'Something that might disagree with me?'

" 'Stephen!' she says. 'How absurd can you get?' she asks him.

" 'It's quite all right, my dear,' he tells her. 'I've told Mr. Vanderlip here that you are planning to poison me.'

"This makes me feel very embarrassed, so I drink my own coffee and brandy down at a gulp. Mrs. Dean is blazing mad. She says to the Professor, 'You fool!' she says, 'I wondered why you brought this man here! You must be completely insane,' she tells him.

"The Professor reaches over and slides the cup which she has been drinking from across the table and pushes the big cup with the ships painted on it, which he hasn't touched, towards his wife. He sips coffee and brandy out of his wife's cup and he says to her, 'If you're sure there's nothing indigestible in the coffee you prepared for me, why don't you drink it yourself, my dear?'

" 'You poor, crazy fool,' his wife says. 'You need a psychiatrist,' she tells him. Then she stares him straight in the face like she is kind of defying him and before anybody can stop her, she picks up the Professor's big cup with both hands, and drinks it down, even though the Professor jumps up out of his chair and starts yelling that she shouldn't.

"She puts down the cup and she stares the Professor in the face again, and then all of a sudden she has a funny look and she starts to choke and then she doubles up and falls out of her chair.

"Right there is where I lam. I run out of the house and I don't stop until I am in Grogan's Elite Palace Café and Bar on the Bowery. I tell Suds, the bartender, the funny thing which has happened to me, and he reminds me that Tommy Twotoes is a kind of a detective even if he ain't got a badge, so after I get the twenty that the Professor has give me changed, I have a few boilermakers and I take a train to Tarrytown and see Tommy Twotoes and today he brings me here and that's all that I know about anything."

"You know too damned much," said Romano. "You know enough to give Professor Dean a perfect alibi and to knock my case into the left-field bleachers."

The Lieutenant turned to Tommy and sighed. "The case was almost too perfect," he said. "Dean was a professor of chemistry at Empire State University. He had access to all the poison he could use. You see how smart he was? He decided to kill his wife by poison. So he alibis himself in advance by picking up a panhandler to witness the whole thing. This man can swear that Mrs. Dean prepared the coffee and that she poured it into three separate cups, one of them a very distinctive cup, while nobody was looking. He can swear that the brandy they all drank came out of the same bottle and the sugar they all used came out of the same bowl. He'll testify that although Dean goaded his wife into drinking the cup with the poison in it, she actually drank it of her own volition. He can even say Dean made some kind of effort to stop her—too late. I don't know how Dean got cyanide into the cup. He was smart enough to pour a lot of brandy in, too, so the fumes would disguise the bitter almond odor. Dean's guilty as hell. Otherwise he wouldn't have prepared such an elaborate alibi. But proving it is something else. I doubt the D.A. will even bring the case to trial after hearing Carney's evidence."

"Killer," asked Tommy Twotoes, "what kind of coat was Professor Dean wearing yesterday?"

"A sports coat with a kind of zigzag check," the Killer replied.

"Is that the coat he is now wearing?" Tommy asked Romano.

"Yeah," replied the Lieutenant. "A hound's-tooth tweed."

"Where is Dean now?" asked Tommy.

"Matter of fact, he's right in the building," Romano answered. "We brought him here this morning for what we politely term 'further questioning.'"

"Can you arrange to bring him here and allow me to question him in an ex officio capacity?" Tommy asked. "By staging a bit of mummery, I may be able to break him. You see, this whole matter hinges on a horse."

"A horse!" exclaimed Romano. "Why not the dogs or cats or

pigeons or tropical fish or lovebirds? It's irregular, of course, but I'll have him down. I'm like the Killer—I've got nothing to lose."

Romano spoke into a phone.

In a few minutes a detective arrived with Dean. You could tell the Professor was an immaculate, self-contained little man under ordinary circumstances, although his clothes were rumpled now from a night in jail and long hours of questioning by the police.

When the Professor saw Killer Carney, his face lit up. "Thank God you've come forward at last, Vanderlip!" he cried.

"This gentleman wants to ask you a few questions," Romano said to Dean, indicating Tommy with a nod of his head. "He's kind of a special investigator in this case."

The Professor regarded the grossly corpulent old man curiously.

Tommy Twotoes said: "Professor Dean, please remove your coat."

"My coat?" asked the bewildered Dean.

"Your coat, sir," replied Tommy. "You will hand it to Dr. Rooke, our police laboratory technician. Take his coat, please, Doctor."

I didn't quite know when I'd been awarded a doctor's degree, but I took the coat.

"Now, Professor Dean," continued Tommy, "you were accustomed to taking midday strolls in the vicinity of Washington Square, I believe?"

"Weather permitting, yes," replied the Professor.

"And you were accustomed to carrying with you tidbits for animals and birds you might encounter during your walks?"

"I was," replied Dean. "I have always been fond of animals."

"You often encountered a horse hitched to a vegetable wagon, a horse you addressed as 'Percy,' during these midday strolls?"

"I did," answered Dean, smiling. "I called him Percy because he had such a long, gaunt face, like the caricatures of typical Englishmen. I always found Percy standing hitched to his wagon at the corner of MacDougal and Minetta Lane, while his owner was crying his wares. Percy is a particular friend of mine."

"And you were accustomed to feeding sugar lumps to this horse, Percy?" Tommy asked.

Dean's eyes narrowed. "Yes," he said at length. "Yes, I was. But why on earth do you ask that, sir?"

"You encountered the horse, Percy, yesterday while you were in the company of Mr. Vanderlip here?"

"Yes," said Dean.

"But you did not feed him his usual tidbit of a sugar lump?"

"No. I had forgotten to bring any sugar with me, I'm afraid."

"Isn't that rather odd, Professor?" Tommy asked. "You carried biscuits for dogs and corn for pigeons. There was a bowl of lump sugar available in your house. Yet you forgot to bring a sugar lump for Percy, whom you describe as your particular friend."

"I simply forgot it, is all," said the Professor.

"No, Professor Dean," said Tommy, his tone very stern. "It won't wash. It won't wash at all. You had a sugar lump in your pocket. But it was not for Percy. Mr. Vanderlip here has testified that when you saw the horse, you reached in your pocket, took out a lump of sugar, but that on second thought you returned it to your pocket."

Of course, the Killer hadn't said anything like that. The old fighter's jaw gaped open, but a frown from Romano silenced him.

"You did not give Percy the sugar because it would have killed him," Tommy Twotoes continued. "And you did not intend to kill a horse. You intended to kill your wife. Cyanide of potassium comes in small white sticks which a chemist such as yourself could easily introduce into a sugar lump. A tenth of a gram is sufficient to bring death almost immediately. You could not risk carrying sugar for Percy yesterday because it might get mixed with the lump of sugar you were carrying about awaiting the opportunity to slip it into the coffee you would trick your wife into drinking. It was simple enough for you to drop the poisoned sugar into the big cup, along with the other lumps you took from the bowl."

"This is fantastic," said Professor Dean.

"I am surprised at you, sir," said Tommy Twotoes. "You are a chemist, and you should know that the modern detective depends more upon the laboratory technician than upon the rubber hose."

Tommy turned to me. "Dr. Rooke," he said. "You will take the coat to the laboratory and make the necessary tests. Pay special attention to any microscopic particles found among the lint in the pocket.

There is certain to be crystals of sugar—and of cyanide of potassium. We will expect your report as soon as possible. It will wind up our case against Professor Dean."

The Professor smiled. "I had to kill her," he said. "I could not have let her go to the arms of another man. But it doesn't matter much about your tests. I carried the poisoned sugar lump loose in my pocket, so I could reach it quickly when I needed it. Now she's dead, I have no desire to live."

When Killer Carney and I had settled Tommy in the Rolls Royce, the old man said to Ebony Black:

"Ebony, you will stop at a grocery store and procure a package of lump sugar. Then drive to MacDougal Street and Minetta Lane in the Village. We are going to make a present to a horse named Percy, with the compliments of Lieutenant Romano."

INSIDE STUFF   Jerome Barry

Some stories grow directly out of incidents in the life of the writer—amusing or terrifying, puzzling or sentimental. Years ago in the Philippines I narrowly escaped being minced by bolomen on suspicion of bringing on a cholera epidemic by poisoning wells. Result: a prize-winning story. More recently, on the telephone, a man threatened to kill me if I didn't stop meeting his wife. (I didn't know either him or his wife and had only a speaking acquaintance with the telephone.) Result: a suspense story for Redbook *magazine.*

Such fiction often has a strong impact because remembrance enables the writer to achieve a convincing mimicry of real life. Inside Stuff *is not of their number. It is, on the contrary, an exercise in pure gimmickry. It grows out of no personal experience. I've never been either a big-league catcher or a jeweler, although usually accurate sources report I was once a small boy.* Inside Stuff *is the product of the attitude that makes a mystery writer's mind sniff inquiringly at each thing he sees or reads or hears, asking, "Gimmick? Switch? Clue?"*

The launching platform for the present flight of fancy was a magazine or newspaper interview (I've forgotten where I saw it) with a famous catcher (don't ask me who) on baseball signs. The rest was a mortise-and-tenon job.

JEROME BARRY

The bell trilled on the front door of the little jewelry shop and young Tod zoomed in. "Uncle Rich, Chet says they got a lot o' good bunters. What do I do if they try a squeeze play on me this afternoon?"

Richard Fulhan, the old jeweler, who had spent twenty years behind the bat in the big leagues, rubbed a knotty hand over the boy's head. He didn't muss the hair. It was permanently untamed. "Sign for one low and away, bub. The man coming down from third'll be a gone goose. But don't get too technical in sandlot ball. That's big-league stuff, Toddy."

"What sign would you use?" the boy insisted.

The jeweler shoved back his green eyeshade. "Well, when I was behind the bat they'd look to me for the signs, and I'd fiddle around to cover up so the other team wouldn't spot 'em, but whenever I'd touch the bill of my cap, the next one was the real signal. Then I'd let 'em have it—maybe thump a fist in my mit for a quick throw to first to pick the runner off. Or wipe my hand on my shirt for a pitch-out. Or straighten my mask to tell the second baseman to cut in behind a runner on second for a snap throw from the pitcher. Then the man the signal was meant for would scoop up some dirt to show he got the sign, all right."

"Gee, thanks, Uncle Rich!" The boy's eyes were bright with anticipation as he padded out of the shop. Halfway through the door he called back, "Customer comin' in!"

The bell rang and the door closed.

A young man, hatless, in a light raincoat, stood at the counter. He had cold eyes and thin lips that hardly moved as he said, "This is it, Pop! I got a gun in my pocket. Now get the stuff out. A tray at a time."

Mr. Fulham took a tray of rings from the case. His hands were steady, but the palms were slippery with sweat. All at once his stomach felt sickish and quivery—through the shop window he saw Tod, the boy, coming back!

Thin Lips said, "Get rid of this kid quick. I don't want to blast him. And you."

The jeweler's heart went cold. He had been held up before. The last time—two gunmen—one of them cracked a customer across the face with a pistol out of meanness—broke his nose. If only he could keep Tod away—

But the bell tinkled and Tod's eager voice called, "Uncle Rich, I just wanted to ask you—"

"Not now, Toddy. Run along." The jeweler thumbed the eyeshade up so that he could see Tod clearly. "Go play, Tod. Right now." Trying to keep his voice unconcerned had him sweating. He wiped his palms on his coat.

The boy's rush carried him right to the counter. Thin Lips eyed him narrowly. "But, Uncle Rich, I only—"

"Go on Tod! Scram." He sounded crosser than he intended.

Tod ran his fingers fliply along the glass case. "Y'ought to keep your place cleaner," he said with sharp impudence. "It's all dusty." Then he ran helter-skelter out, whistling.

The jeweler breathed again. But it was not like Tod to be so insolent.

"O.K., Pop. Keep the trays coming." Slowly, Thin Lips scooped rings into his raincoat pocket. One gray eye was kept on the front window. "Now open the safe—" His voice broke as the front door whipped open.

Tod stuck his head in and yelled "Uncle Richy! Uncle Richy! Ha-ha-ha. Couldn't catch a caterpillar, yah-yah-yah!" He rattled a stick against the glass and made an obnoxious whistling sound.

The jeweler said, "Whatever has got into the—?"

"Get him away from here." Ominous strain showed in the tight mumble—strain to make a trigger finger itchy.

Then from the back of the shop a gun crashed. . . . A body was on the floor—in a raincoat. A heavy policeman covered Thin Lips, who whined and clutched at his injured arm . . .

Tod whispered, "I got your sign, Uncle Rich!"

"Sign, Toddy?" The jeweler was catching his breath.

"Yeah—when you touched your cap—I mean, your eyeshade—I knew the next one would be the real sign. So you wiped your hands on your shirt—I mean your coat—and that meant pitch-out. I couldn't figure it out until I was almost out of the store. Then I knew! The time you call for a pitch-out is *when a man is going to steal!* So I knew it was a stick-up, and I made like I was scooping up dust so you'd know I got the sign. Then I ran for the cop. He sneaked in the back way while I made a fuss out front." He was out of wind and gulped air excitedly. "That was real inside stuff—you being able to think so fast and give those big-league signs!"

The jeweler met the bright eyes looking up at him so proudly. It wouldn't be right to take anything away from a moment like that.

He rubbed the boy's head. "That's the way we use inside stuff, Toddy. Big-leaguers. Like me—and you."

DEAD MAN'S CODE   Brett Halliday

*Helen McCloy and I had been married almost eight years be-
fore we attempted to collaborate on a short story. It all started
at a party in Greenwich (at the home of Frank and Nan Taylor).*

*Among the odd and interesting guests the Taylors always man-
age to dredge up there was a very attractive girl sitting alone
on the floor drinking martinis-on-the-rocks (without too many
rocks), so naturally I gravitated to a spot on the floor beside her.
Turned out she was secretary to an editor of* This Week, *and she
started things out pleasantly by berating me for never having
submitted a story to* This Week.

*With a certain amount of Frank's excellent brandy under my
belt, I loftily told her I was too busy writing books to fool with
short stories for the sort of price I assumed* This Week *would pay.*

*So she knocked my ears back by glibly quoting a price that
adds up to about ten times the amount I used to receive for a
full-length serial from King Features. I managed to shrug off
the shock with a great show of nonchalance, and we drank more
martinis and brandy and had more conversation while the party
roiled around us . . . and she was pretty, and the floor was comfortable, and she had mentioned that nice round sum of money
. . . so I didn't see any reason to move for the rest of the evening.*

*Came midnight or perhaps a few hours past, and we were
rolling back to Westport on the Post Road, and Helen casually
inquired in dulcet tones, "Who was that charming girl, darling?
And what on earth did you find to talk about off by yourselves
the entire evening?"*

*Among my readers there will be some married men who will
understand why I hastily explained, "She's a sort of assistant
editor at* This Week. *Most unattractive, I thought, but she was
after me all evening to write a story for them." And I casually
mentioned the price she had quoted.*

*Helen said, "Why that's wonderful. Why don't you write one
tomorrow . . . before she fully recovers from all those martinis?"*

"But I don't want *to write a short story. I haven't any plot.*

You know I'm trying to get going on a new book."
Helen said, "All right. I'll write one and put Shayne in it."
So she did.

Dead Man's Code *was thirty-three pages of first draft when she handed it to me a week later. I cut it to eighteen pages and made Mike a little more rugged and forceful than Helen had managed . . . and mailed it in to the girl whose name I have now forgotten.*

A few days later Stewart Beach called from New York to say he'd buy the story if I would lop off a couple of pages. I muttered in my beard that I'd try, then hung up and told Helen bitterly that the sale was off . . . because I couldn't take another single word out of the story without ruining it. It was already stripped to the bare bones, etc., etc.

My efficient wife smiled happily and said, "I'd love to cut out a few hundred of your precious words."

So she did.

And this is it. The first collaboration from Brett Halliday and Helen McCloy.

BRETT HALLIDAY

The telephone in Michael Shayne's Miami apartment began ringing as the redhead entered shortly after eleven o'clock.

A man's voice answered Shayne. A precise, cultivated voice, with an unmistakable New England accent; it sounded thin and agitated over the wire:

"Is that Michael Shayne, the detective? Thank heavens I've reached you. This is Mr. Schoolman speaking. Harold Schoolman." The voice was reproving, as though Shayne were expected to apologize for having been out.

Shayne grinned slightly and said, "I don't know you, do I?"

"No, I'm staying at the Splendide Hotel on Miami Beach. Something terrible has happened, Mr. Shayne. I must consult you."

Shayne glanced at his watch and tugged at the lobe of his left ear. "If you want to come here?" he said tentatively. "If it can't wait until morning?"

"It definitely cannot." The precise voice became agitated again. "You see I . . . I hardly know how to say this, Mr. Shayne. I . . ."

There was a sound of a desperate gulp at the other end of the wire. "I've done a horrible thing. I'm . . . a thief."

"Wait!" Shayne came alert fast. "Splendide Hotel? Are you telling me you snatched the Montalba diamond this afternoon?"

"Good heavens, no! Nothing like that, Mr. Shayne. I wasn't even present at the concert when it happened, though my wife was. This is another matter entirely, but extremely embarrassing to me. I'm only a few blocks from your place at the moment, Mr. Shayne. If I could come up and explain. . . ?"

Shayne said, "Come along," and hung up, shrugging wide shoulders.

For a moment, he'd thought luck might be pushing something important his way. The fabulous Montalba medallion, boldly stolen from the Duchess at the Hotel Splendide that afternoon, was insured for two hundred grand. There would be a nice reward.

He was sure it must be Boston when Mr. Harold Schoolman arrived a short time later. He was a slight, middle-aged man with a bulging forehead and rimless glasses. From the dull gleam of his discreetly polished shoes to the neat bow tie, he was the embodiment of bleak, down-East decorum and probity.

He gave Shayne a limp hand. "This is the most upsetting experience of my life. I find myself a criminal, Mr. Shayne. Inadvertently, but a criminal nonetheless. I implore you to find the owner of the stolen property and return it at once."

"Sit down and tell me all about it." Shayne moved back to his chair. "A spot of brandy to settle your nerves?"

"No, thank you. I seldom indulge after dinner." Mr. Schoolman sat on the edge of a chair, reached in a side pocket and brought into view a small, exquisitely beautiful petit-point evening bag with enameled gold clasp and a loop of thin gold chain.

"I bought this for my present wife last Christmas. Note the distinctive, pastoral design, after Watteau. It cost three hundred dollars, Mr. Shayne, and you see there's a chain to go over the wrist for safety while it is being carried."

Shayne nodded and watched the Bostonian's strained face with some amusement.

"But my wife is exceedingly careless. She refused to use the chain, though I repeatedly warned her how easily a sneak thief might snatch it from under her arm. She was . . . ah . . . a member of the WAC before we were married, and the experience gave her quite an unfeminine feeling of self-sufficiency, I fear.

"I decided she should be taught a lesson. We were leaving the hotel at nine o'clock for a party here in Miami. It was raining hard and there was a crowd under the marquee waiting for cabs, pressed close together to avoid the rain.

"I left Alice to slip the doorman a dollar bill and when I pushed back to her side I saw the expensive bag just begging to be stolen. So I took it, Mr. Shayne. It was just as I had warned her. She had tucked the bag carelessly in the crook of her white fur sleeve, and she was not aware it had been taken.

"At that moment, some hearty football types shouldered their way between us and I momentarily lost sight of Alice. The doorman waved that he had a cab and we both pushed forward through the jam and drove away with the bag securely in my pocket.

"I then put my little plan into effect. Peering in my wallet, I said, 'Nothing smaller than a ten for the driver. Do you have a dollar bill in your bag, my dear?'"

Harold Schoolman paused in his recital and swallowed hard. "Mr. Shayne, you will never guess what happened."

Shayne grinned at him. "Your wife answered, 'Yes, dear,' and took a bill from her Watteau bag. You thrust your hand into your pocket and realized you were no longer a respectable member of society, but had become a sneak thief. In the crowd, you mistook another woman for your wife, one wearing a similar white fur jacket and with an identical evening bag. So you snatched the wrong one. Isn't there some identification inside?"

"There was nothing inside the bag."

"Nothing?" Shayne took the bag in his big hands. It was empty except for a small torn piece of coarse, grayish paper, with a wide margin on the right and portions of printed lines on the left.

"Only that," said Schoolman despondently. "A piece torn from a galley proof, with proofreader's corrections on the margin. Why any woman would carry it in her evening bag is beyond my comprehension."

"Galley proof?" said Shayne sharply. "How do you know?"

"It's obvious," said Schoolman impatiently. "I'm a publisher in Boston, you see. It can hardly be anything else with those proof corrections in the margin."

He pointed to the two penciled marks. "Quotation marks, you see. The next is the printer's symbol for more space. Then a single quote that has evidently been omitted, and the final mark indicates that a dollar sign should be inserted."

Shayne nodded. "Three of the printed words are underlined. *Not*. *Tonight*. And *danger*. Looks like a message. You have any galley proofs in the hotel, Mr. Schoolman?"

"Certainly not. We're here on vacation. And when I'm home, I seldom bring work from the office. A message? Yes. My wife deduced that, also. But what can it mean?"

Shayne shrugged. "That is what we'll have to find out. Were there many women wearing white fur coats like your wife?"

"Possibly. I didn't see my wife's face when I took the bag, of course. I was standing behind her. I saw the white fur and the familiar bag and naturally assumed . . ."

"I'd like to talk to your wife," said Shayne briskly, "and see if she noticed anything you didn't."

"Yes. Of course." Mr. Schoolman looked at his watch and stiffened. "I must be getting back to the hotel I expect a long-distance call at twelve-fifteen from my daughter in Boston—from my first marriage. I left Alice at the party while I came here, and she promised to meet me in our suite at twelve-thirty. Would you like to see her there?"

"Very much," said Shayne. His gray eyes were bleak as he studied the scrap of paper with three words underlined. He replaced it in the bag, tossed off the rest of his drink and rose. "I'll drive you to the Beach," he said.

It had stopped raining. A golden moon was riding high overhead as they reached the oceanside hotel. Shayne parked his car in the driveway and looked at his watch—a little after midnight. As they entered the luxurious lobby, he said, "Suppose you go up to wait for your call. I'll nose around downstairs awhile and join you in half an hour."

"Very well. Our suite is six-ten. Do you think . . . *can* you determine ownership of the bag and return it without publicity?"

"I'll try. There can't be too many identical Watteau bags in one hotel." Shayne left him as he hurried toward the elevator and strolled across a lobby that suggested the Arabian Nights in a gaudier moment, to a nail-studded, leather door. He knocked and entered.

A pudgy man, seated at a desk, looked up at the redhead with a soft, wise smile. "Hi, Mike. What brings you here?"

"Hello, Branson." Shayne slid one hip onto a corner of the security officer's desk. "Had any robberies lately?"

The man flushed. "Maybe you'd like to take over the job of riding herd on a crazy Spanish Duchess and her quarter-million-dollar diamond she insists on displaying like a glass bauble."

"How did it happen? All I got was a flash over the radio."

Branson shrugged. "A benefit concert in the main ballroom. A hundred or more guests milling around and I've got the Duchess myself, but you can't breathe down her neck every moment. So it happened at the punch bowl. A dame stumbled into her just as she was drinking a cup of punch. It spilled on her and there was a lot of confusion. A minute later she screams her damned medallion is missing. She's been begging for this for years, Mike. Wears it dangling from her neck on a thin chain.

"There were four persons close enough to clip the chain. A Mrs. Davis from Atlanta, who stumbled against her . . . insisted she was pushed. A Myrtle Hodson, unemployed secretary, who crashed the party. Lucille Lasalle, the movie actress, and . . . John Tarleton, who registered here yesterday."

"Gentleman John? Good Lord, Branson!"

"Gentleman John Tarleton," Branson agreed wearily. "With a record of arrests in every major world capital for suspected jewel thefts, and nary a conviction. Sure he got it. Right under my nose. I recognized him at once and grabbed him. We also grabbed the three women fast and they agreed to be searched, after we explained that John is suspected of always working with a woman confederate to whom he passes the loot. No soap. Tarleton pulled off another perfect one."

"So he passed the diamond and the chain-clipper to some other woman before you got him?"

"To any one of the two or three dozen who pushed forward when the punch spilled. He had sixty seconds. That's all Tarleton needs."

"Arrest him?"

"How the devil could we? We had to let him go with an apology. All we can do is tail him and wait for him to contact his confederate. Monitor his telephone line. He can't as much as speak to a dame without us grabbing her."

"You didn't search all the other guests?"

"Lord, no. We'd be up to our necks in lawsuits if we did."

"And you didn't search the Duchess either?"

Branson's mouth dropped open. "It was *her* diamond."

Shayne shrugged. "You're positive it was the genuine thing? I suppose she keeps it in your safe and you had a chance to inspect it carefully?"

"As a matter of fact, no. Each of our master suites is equipped with a small wall safe with a combination known only to the guest. She kept it there. What are you getting at, Mike? You suspect any funny business?"

"No. I dropped in on something else entirely. Any idea how many of your guests wear white fur coats?"

Branson scowled. "There were exactly three at this afternoon's shindig. I know because the Duchess wore one, and I checked the others to make it easier to keep an eye on the diamond."

"Who wore the other two coats?"

"Miss Lasalle, and a woman from Boston. Mrs. Schoolman. Why?"

"I don't know." Shayne drew the Watteau bag from his pocket. "Did your eagle eye notice any of these floating around this afternoon . . . preferably in conjunction with a white fur coat?"

Branson picked it up with a frown. "You can't expect a man . . ."

"Frankly, no. What I really hoped was that this one had been reported stolen this evening. About nine o'clock. While a lot of your guests were jammed up outside waiting for cabs."

"Sorry." Branson looked completely bewildered. "Nothing like that was reported stolen."

Shayne said, "See what you make of the paper inside." He lit a cigarette and studied Branson's face while he took out the scrap.

"Three words underlined," Branson mused. "Could be some sort of message. A warning?"

"Could be," agreed Shayne, cheerfully. "You say you've got men on Tarleton. What were his movements this evening?"

Branson shuffled papers on his desk, picked one up and read: "Directly to his room when we released him at five-thirty. Stayed until eight. Ordered two drinks and a sandwich from Room Service. Down to lobby at eight-twelve. Bought newspaper and cigar. Sat alone in chair and read till nine-oh-six. Spoke to no one. Went out at nine-oh-six where there was a crowd waiting for taxis as you seem to know. Stayed on fringe of crowd, closely observed, for ten minutes, evidently changed mind about going out in rain. Returned to room. I've got men on both front and rear exits and he hasn't showed again." Branson sighed. "He's undoubtedly laughing at us."

"Probably. One thing more. Do you have any way of knowing whether either the Duchess of Montalba or your movie queen wore their fur coats out of the hotel about nine o'clock?"

"No. They're not being tailed. We could ask them, I guess . . ."

The telephone interrupted him. He barked, "Security Office," listened a moment while his pudgy face went doughy. "I'll be up at once. Stay right there." He put down the phone and told Shayne heavily: "Harold Schoolman has just been murdered upstairs."

The woman who confronted them in the ivory-and-gold sitting room of suite 610 was obviously fighting hard to hold back tears that seeped from under her eyelids. Like her husband, Alice Schoolman seemed to carry a wintry climate with her. The crisp, freshly waved hair was the sad brown of autumn leaves. The blue eyes were pale as ice, with a network of fine wrinkles at the corners.

She looked an oldish thirty-five, with tensely anguished features and blue-veined slender hands that twisted together as she stepped mutely aside to show them the figure of her husband, slumped on the floor beside a small table where a portable typewriter stood.

The upper rear of Schoolman's head was crushed, and blood still flowed from the gaping wound onto the carpet. A heavy, blood-stained whiskey decanter lay beside the body. From his position, it appeared that Schoolman had been seated in a chair before the type-writer with his back to the door when the fatal blow was struck. A single sheet of white notepaper with the figures 2 and 3 typed on it.

The Bostonian had died instantly, and certainly not more than ten minutes before the detectives arrived. Mrs. Schoolman's white fur coat lay on the floor just inside the door, with a pair of long white gloves and a Watteau bag beside it.

"I returned from a party just a few minutes ago," she explained swiftly. "I expected Harold to be in because he was expecting a tele-phone call. I rang the bell but he didn't answer. I thought he was on the phone, and used my key. He . . . was like that. I knew he was . . . gone, so I called the operator." She slumped into a chair, cov-ering her face with both hands, and shuddered violently.

Shayne said, "I'll cover the door, Branson. Go through the suite and see if he's hiding. It's been only minutes . . ."

Branson nodded and strode away. Shayne stood quietly by the open door, looking at neither the corpse nor the weeping widow, his ragged red brows low over hooded eyes and a look of intense concentration on his rugged features.

Branson returned, shaking his head. "All clean. And now you come clean, Mike. You've been asking a lot of questions about white fur coats and fancy bags. What's it all about?"

Shayne shook his red head impatiently. "I still don't know. Check Tarleton's room. Is it on this floor?"

"One above." Branson turned to the phone. Shayne looked down bleakly at the dead man and the typewriter. "Did you or your hus-band use this machine, Mrs. Schoolman?"

"I . . . mostly. H-Harold could only hunt and peck."

"What do the figures two and three mean to you? Can you think why your husband might have typed those out before he was killed?"

"I don't know," she said brokenly. "A message? But *what?*"

Branson came from the phone. "Gentleman John is in the clear again. He's been on the phone in his room chatting with a friend in

New York for the past twenty minutes."

Shayne nodded. A trace of tightness left his face. He took out the petit point Schoolman had given him and asked Alice Schoolman, "Ever see this before?"

She looked at it with dilated eyes. "It's exactly like mine on the floor. Isn't it the one Harold grabbed by mistake, thinking it was mine? Didn't he explain how it happened?"

"He told me." Grimly, Shayne opened the bag and withdrew the scrap of paper and read, "Not tonight. Danger. He also showed you this. Do you agree these are proofreader's marks in the margin?"

"I suppose so. He said they were. He . . . was a publisher, you know."

Shayne told Branson: "Ask the Duchess and Miss Lasalle to come here at once bringing their petit-point bags with them. Have one of your men bring Tarleton also."

"Wait, Mike. I've got to know . . ."

"You want to get back that diamond medallion," Shayne reminded him harshly. "And clean up the murder. Get them here." He turned and stalked into the bedroom where he pulled a brocaded cover from one of the beds and brought it back to cover the body.

Branson turned from the phone. "Miss Lasalle is out. Her maid insists she has only jeweled evening bags. The Duchess refuses to come, and denies owning a bag like these two."

Shayne was looking down at the torn scrap of paper and the two digits on the sheet in the typewriter. "I think I know why School-man typed those two figures before he died. Where is the private safe in this room?"

Alice Schoolman gestured to an inconspicuous silver dial in the wall above the divan. Shayne went to it slowly, asking her, "What is the combination?"

"The combination?" she faltered. "I don't . . . know. Harold set it this morning and didn't tell me."

Shayne stopped in mid-stride and swung about with ragged red brows lifted unbelievably. "He didn't tell you? Why?"

"I don't know, really. I didn't think to ask him."

Shayne swung to Branson. "Can you get the combination?"

"Not a chance. Each guest sets his own when he checks into a suite. It's a simple one. Just two figures on the dial. You make two full turns to the right and stop. Then back to the second figure you've chosen. If Mrs. Schoolman doesn't know where her husband set it, we'll have to get an expert to open it."

Shayne turned the dial two full circles to the right, stopped on 2. Branson intervened when he started to turn back to 3.

"Not that way. The first digit has to be larger. You can't turn back past zero."

Shayne frowned, made two more complete turns, stopped at 3. He turned back to 2. Nothing happened. He turned from the safe to see Alice Schoolman watching, pallid and frightened.

Shayne strode to the typewriter and studied the scrap of paper again. He looked down musingly at the typewriter and pushed one of the keys with his forefinger. An 8 appeared behind the 2 and 3 already on the sheet. He pressed another key and had four figures in a row: 2384.

He told Branson grimly: "That's the real message that was hidden in the bag Schoolman stole. Not the three underlined words. They were camouflage to draw attention away from the four penciled symbols in the margin. Quotation marks, a space symbol, single quote, a dollar sign . . . as Schoolman explained to me."

He pointed to the symbols on the top row of the top line of keys. "Right in front of us. A beautifully simple code. The same key that has quotes is also the figure two. The space symbol is a three. Eight and four, corresponding to a single quote and a dollar sign."

"Two-three-eight-four," repeated Branson. "What do they mean?"

"Try eight-four on the wall safe," said Shayne grimly. "When it opens, reach inside and take out the diamond medallion Gentleman John snatched this afternoon and passed on to his confederate for safekeeping while he was being searched."

Branson was on his way to the safe when Alice Schoolman was out of her chair and on him like an avenging fury, clawing his face and screaming hysterically, every iota of her Boston calm forsaking her under stress . . .

"She had to kill her husband," Shayne told Branson later. "As soon as she walked into the suite and saw him at the typewriter picking out the two and three. He'd evidently remembered the proof marks and just noticed the juxtaposition of those symbols and numbers on the top row of keys. She knew the jig was up right then. Twenty-three and the combination to the safe in the suite."

"What was the twenty-three for?" asked Branson, wonderingly.

"Twenty-three hours. Eleven o'clock. Don't forget she was in the WAC and learned the military way of reckoning time. Those were the two items of information she had to pass on to Tarleton after bringing the diamond up and putting it in her own safe this afternoon. The two things they couldn't set beforehand when they planned this coup so carefully in Boston where Tarleton picked her up as his accomplice and made love to her. They couldn't afford to see each other or speak together after reaching the hotel, yet Tarleton had to know when the suite would be vacant and the combination Schoolman picked out this morning.

"He knew he'd be watched every moment after the robbery, and brought her another Watteau bag, identical with her own, as a device for passing the information. She had them both with her when she went down tonight, the decoy bag carelessly under her arm.

"Imagine how Tarleton must have felt when he followed her from the lobby to pick up his information . . . and had to stand helplessly by while her uncomprehending husband snatched it from her in front of his eyes. To teach his wife a needed lesson on the perils of carelessness," Shayne ended sardonically.

DIAMONDS IN PARADISE   Ellery Queen

In the language of philately, Diamonds in Paradise *is a "commemorative." It was one of two tales written for* Ellery Queen's Mystery Magazine *to celebrate the 25th anniversary of Ellery Queen's debut in print* (The Roman Hat Mystery, *first published August 16, 1929*).

Diamonds in Paradise *appeared in* EQMM's Sept. *1954 issue. Its companion piece,* GI Story *(set in Wrightsville), was published in the Aug. 1954 issue; and we thank David C. Cooke for adding kudos to our silver anniversary by selecting the latter tale for his annual,* Best Detective Stories of the Year—*1955.*

Our 25th anniversary was also marked by the publication of our 80th book and 28th novel, The Glass Village, *which was honored as one of the three novels to be nominated for the MWA "Edgar" award for "Best Novel of 1954."*

ELLERY QUEEN

Maybe Lili Minx was THE GIRL of your dreams, too. It's nothing to be ashamed of. Lili caused more insomnia in her day than all the midnight maatjes herring consumed on Broadway and 51st Street on all the opening nights put together since Jenny Lind scared the gulls off the roof of Castle Garden.

It wasn't just Lili's face and figure, either, although she could have drifted out on a bare stage before a two-bit vaudeville flat and stood there for two hours and twenty minutes just looking at you, and you'd have headed for your herring mumbling "smash hit." It wasn't even her voice, which made every other set of female pipes on Broadway sound like something ground out of a box with a monkey on it. It was the trick she had of making every male within eyeshot and mike range feel that he was alone with her in a dreamboat.

Of course there was a catch, as the seven yachtsmen she married found out. With all her wonderful equipment, Lili was a mixed-up kid. She was a hopelessly incurable gambler, and she was hipped on diamonds. And the two things didn't seem to go together. Let the psychologists explain it, but the fact is money didn't mean a thing to her. She could drop ten grand at the roulette wheel and yawn like a lady. Diamonds were another story. Let her temporarily mislay a single chip from her jewel box and she went into hysterics. Her press agent swore that she checked her inventory every night before going to bed like a kid casing his marbles.

Naturally, Lili's collection was the target of every itch-fingers out of the jug. But Lili was no pushover. When it came to her diamonds, she was like Javert in the sewers of Paris; she never gave up. The police were kept busy. They didn't mind. With La Minx on the broadcasting end of a complaint, every cop with a front porch and asthma felt like No-Hips Lancelot, the Terror of the Underworld.

Lili's favorite gambling hell, while it lasted, was Paradise Gardens. Those were the days when New York was wide open and everything went, usually before you could come back for more. Paradise Gardens had a longer run than most. It operated behind a frowsy old brownstone front off Fifth Avenue, in the Frolicking Fifties.

The ceiling was a menace to healthy eyesight, with its glittering stars and sequinned angels; you swallowed your buffalo steaks and cougar juice among tropical flowers under papier-mâché trees with wax apples tied onto them; and you were served by tired ex-showgirl-type waitresses wearing imitation fig leaves. So it was a relief to go upstairs where there was no mullarkey about gardens or Edens—just nice business décor and green baize-covered tables at which the management allowed you to lose your shirt or bra, as the case might be.

On this particular evening Lili Minx, being between husbands, was alone. She drifted in, pale and perfect in white velvet and ermine, unapproachable as the nearest star and tasty-looking as a charlotte russe. On each little pink ear glowed a cold green fire, like a radioactive pea, La Minx's only jewelry tonight. They were the famous mumtaz green-diamond earrings, once the property of Shah Jahan's favorite wife, which had been clipped to Lili's lobes by the trembling hands of an Iraqi millionaire, who was running hard at the time in the sixth race of La Minx Handicap. Lili prized her green diamonds at least as highly as the ears to which they were attached.

Everything stopped as Lili posed in the archway for her usual moment of tribute: then life went on, and Lili bought a stack of hundred-dollar chips at the cashier's cage and made for the roulette table.

An hour later, her second stack was in the croupier's bank. Lili laughed and drifted toward the ladies' lounge. No one spoke to her.

The trim French maid in the lounge came forward swiftly. "Madame has the headache?"

"Yes."

"Perhaps a cold compress?"

"Please."

Lili lay down on a chaise longue and closed her eyes. At the cool touch of the wrapped ice bag on her forehead she bestowed a smile. The maid adjusted the pillow about her head deftly, in sympathetic silence. It was quiet in the deserted lounge, and Lili floated off into her own world of dreams.

She awoke a few minutes later, put the ice bag aside, and rose from the chaise. The maid had discreetly vanished. Lili went to a vanity and sat down to fix her hair. . . .

And at that exact moment the gambling rooms of Paradise Gardens went berserk. Women shrieked, their escorts scuttled about like trapped crabs, the housemen struggled with their nefarious tools, and the massive door gave way under the axheads of the police.

"Hold it!" An elderly man with a gray mustache hopped nimbly onto a crap table and held up his arms for silence. "I'm Inspector Queen of police headquarters on special gambling detail. This is a raid, ladies and gentlemen. No sense trying to make a break; every exit is covered. Now if you'll all please line up along the walls while these officers get going—"

And that was when Lili Minx burst from the ladies' lounge like one of the Furies, screaming, "My diamond earrings! I been robbed!"

So immediately what had begun as a gambling raid turned into a robbery investigation. La Minx was in top form, and Inspector Queen did her bidding as meekly as a rookie cop. She had often enough disturbed his dreams, too.

As the axes rose and fell and the equipment flew apart, the Inspector was crooning, "Now don't you worry your pretty head, Miss Minx. We'll find your earrings—"

"And that creep of a maid!" stormed La Minx. "She's the only one who touched me, Inspector Queen. I want that maid clobbered, too!"

"She can't get away, Lili," soothed the Inspector, patting the lovely hand. "We've had the Paradise surrounded for an hour, getting set for the jump, and not a soul got out. So she has to be here . . . Well, Velie?" he barked, as the big Sergeant came loping from the ladies' lounge, furtively feeling his tie. "Where is the woman?"

"Right here," said Sergeant Velie, looking at Lili like a homesick Newfoundland. And he thrust into Inspector Queen's hands, blindly, a maid's uniform, a starched cap and apron, a pair of high-heeled shoes, two sheer stockings, and a wig. "Dumped in the broom closet."

"What does this mean?" cried Lili, staring at the wig.

"Why, it's Harry the Actor," said the Inspector, pleased. "A clever character at female impersonation, Lili—he's made his finest hauls as a French maid. So Harry's tried it on you, has he? You just wait here, my dear," and the Inspector began to march along the lineup like a small gray Fate, followed by La Minx, who waited for no one.

"And here he is," said the Inspector cheerily, stopping before a short slender man with boyish cheeks which were very pale at the moment. "Tough luck, Harry—about the raid, I mean. Suppose we try this on for size, shall we?" and he clapped the wig on the little man's head.

"That's the one," said Lili Minx in a throbbing voice, and the little man turned a shade paler. She stepped up to him, and looked deep into his eyes. "You give me back my diamond earrings, or—" She mentioned several alternatives.

"Get her away from me, get her out of here," quavered Harry the Actor in his girlish treble, trying to burrow into the wall.

"Search him, Velie," said Inspector Queen sternly.

A half hour later, in the manager's office, with the drapes drawn before the window, Harry the Actor stood shivering. On the desk lay his clothes and everything taken from his person—a wallet containing several hundred dollars, a pocketful of loose change, a ball of hard candy, a yellow pencil, a racing form, a pair of battered old dice, a crumpled cigarette pack and a booklet of matches, a tiny vial of French perfume, a lipstick, a compact, a handkerchief smeared with make-up and a box of Kiss-Mee, the Magic Breath-Sweetener. Everything in parts had been disassembled. The cigarettes had been shredded. The hard candy had been smashed. Harry's clothing had been gone over stitch by stitch. His shoes had been tapped for hidden compartments. His mouth and hair had been probed. Various other indignities had been visited upon his person. Even the maid's outfit had been examined.

And no green-diamond earrings.

"All right," muttered the Inspector, "get dressed."

And all the while, from the other side of the manager's door, Lili's creamy voice kept promising Harry what was in store for him as soon as she could get her little hands on him.

And it drove the thief at last to a desperate folly. In the midst of stuffing his belonging back in his pockets, he leaped over the desk, stiff-armed the officer before the window, and plunged headfirst through the drapes like a goat. It was a hard-luck night for Harry the Actor all around. The railing of the fire escape was rotted through with rust. His momentum took him into space, carrying the railing with him.

They heard the railing land on the concrete of the back yard three stories below, then Harry.

The officers posted in the yard were shaking their heads over the little man when Inspector Queen and Sergeant Velie dropped off the fire-escape ladder, followed—inevitably—by Lili.

If the thief had had any hope of cheating his fate, one glazed look at the furious beauty glaring down at him destroyed it. Either way he was a goner, and he knew it.

"Harry," said Inspector Queen, tapping the swollen cheek gently. "You're checking out. If you want a fair shake Upstairs, you'd better talk fast. Where did you stash 'em?"

Harry's eye rolled. Then his tongue came out and he said thickly, "Diamonds . . . in . . . the Paradise . . ."

"In the Paradise *what*, Harry?" asked the Inspector frantically, as Harry stopped. "In the Paradise *where?*"

But Harry had had it.

Ellery always said that, if it wasn't his greatest case, it was certainly his shortest.

He first learned about it when his father staggered home at breakfast time. Ellery got some coffee into the old man and extracted the maddening details.

"And I tell you, son," raved the Inspector, "we went back into that joint and tore it apart. It was rotten luck that Harry died before he could tell us just where in the Paradise Gardens he'd hidden Lili's diamonds. They had to be in the building somewhere, either in something or on someone. We still hadn't let anyone go from the raid. We not only took the Paradise apart piece by piece, we body-searched every mother's son and daughter on the premises, thinking Harry might have passed the earrings to an accomplice. Well, we didn't find them!" The Inspector sounded as if he were going to cry. "I don't know what I'll say to that lovely child."

"Diamonds speak louder than words," said Ellery briskly. "At least —from all I hear—in the case of Lili Minx."

"You mean . . . ?" said his father. "But how *can* you know where the Actor hid them?" he cried. "You weren't even there!"

"You told me. Harry was putting his belongings away in his pockets when he made his sudden break. Where is Harry now, Dad?"

"Harry? In the Morgue!"

"Then the Morgue is where Lili's earrings are."

"They were *on* him? But Ellery, we searched Harry outside and—and in!"

"Tell me again," said Ellery, "what he had in his pockets."

"Money, a dirty handkerchief, women's cosmetics, a hard candy, a racing form, cigarettes, a pair of dice, a pencil—"

"I quote you quoting the late Actor's dying statement," said Ellery. " 'Diamonds—in Paradise.' "

"Paradise . . ." The Inspector's jaw wiggled. *"Pair o' dice!* His dice were just shells—*they're in the dice!"*

"So if you'll phone the Morgue property clerk, Dad—"

Inspector Queen turned feebly from the phone. "But Ellery, it did sound just like the Paradise. . . ."

"What do you expect from a dying man," asked Ellery reasonably, "elocution lesson?"

A NAME FOR BABY   Thomas Walsh

A Name For Baby *was written, by not quite an odd coincidence, when a little stranger arrived at our house. There was the usual discussion about names, and a friend decided to help by sending along a booklet listing all feminine and masculine names from Aaron to Zebediah.*

Well, the booklet didn't help out much, since the name turned out to be Thomas, Junior, but one day not long afterward I happened to find the booklet in one of the desk drawers. I was occupied, at the moment, in thinking up a cop story—quite as usual—and "A Name For Baby" seemed to stick in my head for some reason. So, having the title to start with, the rest followed pretty much as a matter of course, after the usual struggle with fitting cop, baby and girl respectably together in a short-story plot. It was published originally in Collier's, *republished once afterwards and used as the basis of a TV half-hour show.*

THOMAS WALSH

It was no more than a few minutes past ten, on a slow and rainy November night, when Kilbane happened to meet up with her in the street corridor at headquarters. Just as she came out of the press-room on the mezzanine landing and tip-tapped down marble steps toward the lower hall Kilbane himself, pushing through the frosted glass doors of the detective bureau, paused by a convenient window to light a cigarette and glance out at the melancholy drizzle slanting down past the street lamps in City Hall Square. That was what allowed Miss Pulitzer to catch up with him. She came on fast, in her accustomed great hurry; at the front entrance, which they reached almost together, Kilbane looked sideways at her and then flicked a forefinger at his hatbrim in a negligent gesture of salutation.

She glanced up, too. "Kilbane," she said, with an offhandedly casual, man-to-man greeting that matched his own perhaps overdone disinterest. At the moment, a slim girl with black hair and dark eyes, dressed in a gray tailored suit and a plain little round hat like a boy's, she was nothing important to Kilbane regardless of how he chose to look at it.

He knew that she had covered the police news for the *Morning Tribune* ever since Jack Garrity left for the army, and he had heard somewhere or other that up in the pressroom, with exceptionally little friendliness, the boys had begun to refer to her as Miss Pulitzer, Scoop or By-line. That part, of course, was no concern of Kilbane's.

He opened the right-hand door for her by levering his arm against it, let her through, and went out after her. "It's raining," he said, unnecessarily, on the top step.

Miss Pulitzer nodded. Countless tiny drops sprayed up at them on a moody billow of wind; when she narrowed her eyes against them, peering down at a deserted taxi stand near the corner, he turned up his coat collar and mentioned his car and the possibility of a lift simply because there seemed to be nothing else for him to do.

Miss Pultizer did not jump at it; but after a moment, with an air of not asking for any favors, she admitted that she wanted to stop in at the *Tribune* office. If that was on his way—

Kilbane brought her down to the car and helped her in. He said, "I'll make a stop first, on Eagle Street. A couple of minutes. Okay?"

"Okay with me," Miss Pulitzer told him, dropping the hat into her lap and fluffing out the black hair carelessly. "Business, Kilbane?"

"I guess," Kilbane said. On that November night S. Pasquariella, who was being guarded against certain unpleasant possibilities by Kilbane on the night shift and Charley Harris on the day, was no topic for conversation with anyone from the pressroom. Kilbane sheered away from him at once. How was the reporting? he wanted to know. Quiet, eh?

"Deadly," Miss Pulitzer said. She gave him a level glance, as if she didn't want him to think anything he shouldn't think. "I'm not thrilled to death, you know. I've done it before."

Kilbane started the car. On the far side of the plaza, where they turned into Eagle Street, he offered the opinion that there was a swell bunch of fellows in the pressroom. Personally he liked them.

"Oh, fine," Miss Pulitzer said. But she had her head back against the seat and was smiling up scornfully at nothing. "Perhaps I'm not quite—meek enough, Kilbane. I don't ask advice and when it's given I don't follow it. That's bad. And then, of course, I don't intend to be a police reporter all my life. There you have the really unforgivable thing."

Kilbane, puzzled by what seemed to be a slight lack of continuity, stopped for a traffic light. "Like the town, maybe?"

"It's all right. It's any American town," Miss Pulitzer said. She blew an impatient stream of smoke against the windshield and then pursed her lips carefully. "I'll stick here six months," she said. "I might possibly need that. It—well, gives you prestige or something to say you've worked on the *Tribune*. I don't know why it should, but it does. Then—"

Kilbane cocked his nearer eyebrow at her. "Big stuff," he said. "New York."

"Why not?" Miss Pultizer said. She was very cool about it. "That's why I'm not liked, you know. I'm conceited, you understand. I know what I want and I mean to get it. And that's one of the things you mustn't let people see, of course. Never. You've found that out," she said. "You know that's true, don't you, Kilbane?"

"Once in a while I've got a hint of it," Kilbane said, deciding thoughtfully that here was a funny kind of girl. At the next corner he slowed long enough to see that the barbershop of S. Pasquariella had been closed for the night; then, a block down, he pulled into the curb before a two-story row house with a scrubbed white flagstone in front of it.

Miss Pulitzer sat in the car while he got out and rang the doorbell. He was admitted presently by a little girl with long black hair and enormous black eyes, who told him that Poppa had gone out but that Momma was upstairs. Momma was sick.

"That's too bad," Kilbane said, patting her head. "You're Angelica Therese. Your poppa told me all about you. Know who I am?"

"No," Angelica Therese said, incuriously. She was about eight years old. Behind her in the kitchen doorway a smaller-scale model began to emit wailing sobs without taking her eyes from Kilbane. Angelica Therese looked around at her unemotionally.

"She always cries," Angelica Therese said. "She's Christina Marie.

She's only six, mister. I think she's crazy. I can tell you what my momma's got—'pendectis. Poppa said so before he went for the doctor. It hurts her bad—awful bad. She—" Noise came from the second floor, and Angelica Theresa looked up there with some interest. "You hear her now?"

"Yes," Kilbane said. It seemed to him that he'd have heard her over at headquarters. "Your poppa put an ice bag on her before he left?"

"A what?" Angelica Theresa said.

Kilbane dropped his hat on the hall table. She should get some ice cubes out of the refrigerator and bring them upstairs as fast as she could. And she mustn't cry. That would only make Momma feel a lot worse.

"All right," Angelica Theresa said. "I won't cry."

She didn't. She was perfectly willing to be helpful. But when she went upstairs with the bowl of ice, Kilbane erupted violently before her in the bedroom doorway. Did she know what was happening up here? Kilbane demanded in a shrill voice. Did she have any idea— he stopped, added something in a low whisper, glared helplessly at her and slammed the door.

Three or four minutes later S. Pasquariella and the doctor broke in from the street and ran upstairs. It was all over then. The baby, S. Pasquariella's first boy, weighed eight pounds and seven ounces, and Kilbane hadn't done a bad job for a first-class detective lacking any kind of previous experience.

The doctor complimented him highly; S. Pasquariella, liquid-eyed, crushed his hand in a grip of steel. But Kilbane got out of there as fast as he could, his coat slung over his arm, his face glistening with sweat. Miss Pulitzer, who had a nose for news, was in the hall by that time talking to Angelica Therese. Kilbane looked at her; after a moment he remembered who she was.

"Come on," he said, going by her blindly into the rain. He did not pick up his hat; he did not put on his coat. And on the way to the *Tribune* office, unobservant of everything, he did not notice that Miss Pulitzer kept on staring at him with bright and interested eyes.

Next morning he read all about it on the back page of the *Tribune,* where the city news usually appeared. It was a two-column spread, signed by one Janet S. Harrington, and the heading was cute and explicit: "Doctor late, Baby Early; Detective Waylays Stork." Kilbane chanced upon those words after a late breakfast of ham and eggs, while he was sitting with his feet propped up on the table and a morning cigarette in the corner of his mouth. For a moment he did not move. Then he sat up slowly, spilling half a cup of coffee into his lap, and reading over the story itself as if it were—as if it had to be—some kind of horrible mistake.

It wasn't, of course. In the first paragraph Miss Pulitzer had done him off brown. There it was narrated that Detective Joseph J. Kilbane, at present attached to the headquarters squad, owned modestly to the principle that the finest was always prepared. Payroll bandits or traffic tickets, mad dogs, homicide or arson—Detective Kilbane took all those things in stride. Babies, too. What—and here Detective Kilbane was quoted directly—what was so exceptional about babies? A good police officer could turn his hand to a lot of things. Twins or triplets might have been considered extraordinary; but a single baby, even one of eight pounds and seven ounces—

"Nothing to it," Detective Kilbane was reported to have been said. "Wouldn't any of the boys have done the same?"

There was more, much more. Further down he was described as the "rugged-looking, Fred MacMurray type," and after that it was asserted that he had borne himself throughout the ordeal with the most incomparable *sang-froid*. Some people might have thought it a fairly amusing story on a night when nothing very much had happened; but Kilbane, who did not agree with their opinion for several grimly personal reasons, walked into headquarters at four that afternoon prepared for anything.

In that he was wise. When he passed the desk, Sergeant Mulligan referred to him in a deferential way as young Dr. Kilbane; when he entered the locker room he found a statement pasted up on the bulletin board outlining the duties of the newly formed maternity squad, Joseph J. Kilbane, acting chief; when he went upstairs to the chief inspector's office two or three persons waw-wawed blithely after him from the crowd gathered outside police court.

He endured all that; he had to. But at half-past five, as he came on Janet S. Harrington—Miss Pulitzer, Scoop, By-line—occupied with a cup of coffee and a sandwich in the basement cafeteria, he licked his lips gently and then touched her one on the tip of the left shoulder.

"Swell story," Detective Joseph J. Kilbane said; his dark blue eyes glittered down at her. "Nice going, I'd call it. There's the kind of stuff that's going to get you places fast, sister."

Janet S. Harrington thought it was pretty good herself. The *Tribune's* city editor had liked it. He—

"Sure. He knows first-rate stuff," Kilbane told her, with a painful grin she seemed to accept as quite in order. "Suppose I buy you a drink on it tonight? Ten-thirty, say. At the ramp entrance, By-line."

"By-line?" she said. "Oh! You're not angry about it, for heaven's sake?"

"Me?" Kilbane said. He went off, the grin clamped in place. It was later that night, when he had Miss Pulitzer secure from interruptions behind a table in the nearest cocktail lounge, that he drew up the points of arraignment over the one drink he ever intended to buy anyone like her.

"I wasn't anything much," he said, after a first few matters—common decency among them—had been made clear to her. "Just old Joe Stooge—Officer Pup waiting for the brick to hit him. You had a column to be funny in—that's what mattered. And if you had to crucify somebody in print, why that part was all right. It was nothing you—"

"Crucify?" Miss Pulitzer said. Now she seemed exasperated. "Of course that's ridiculous. I should think you'd be—"

"What?" Kilbane asked, his voice throbbing. "Pleased, maybe. Tickled to death. Because I got my name in a cheap rag, in a smart-aleck, smirking story—"

"Cheap what?" Miss Pulitzer demanded, with some excitement. "Let me tell you something. The *Tribune*—"

Kilbane thumped his chest. Afterward that seemed a lot too dramatic, but at the moment distinctions were beyond him. "I'm kind of proud of being a cop. I like it. It ain't funny to me and I'm the kind of guy that doesn't want it to be funny to other people. That's another laugh, I guess. That's not big stuff, like New York. You know it's a laugh because you're a couple of months off the *Yaphank Gazette* and you got everything and everybody figured out. But what you—"

There Miss Pulitzer, losing whatever remained of her self-control, pointed a trembling cigarette at him.

"You shut up," she said. "Shut up right now, do you hear? You don't even know what you're talking about. The—the *Yaphank Gazette!* I never saw—"

Kilbane reached for his hat. "There's a lot you never saw," he told her. His voice shook slightly, to his fury. "I guess there's a lot a girl like you is never going to see."

He stalked off without looking back, without stopping at the cashier's desk either; when he realized afterward that he must have saddled her with the check it provided him a moment of sullen satisfaction. From the cocktail lounge, still simmering inside, he visited S. Pasquariella for the regular nightly check up, and there he asked the usual questions without wasting very much time over them: Had anyone, Kilbane wanted to know, been around today to talk to him? Had anyone tried to bother him?

S. Pasquariella, a wiry little man with bushy black hair and glowing black eyes, dismissed that matter with a Latin gesture richly expressive of contempt. Those fellas kept away from him; you betcha, kid. Something else was on his mind. Last night he had not thanked Kilbane. Last night—he gripped Kilbane's forearm, smiling sheepishly and jerking his head toward the bedroom upstairs. The boy— he was a fine boy, eh?

Kilbane put his hand on the knob. Unmatchable anywhere, Kilbane assured him.

"Bambino," S. Pasquariella murmured in a tender voice to himself. "We call him—" He paused, took a deep breath before the plunge, and then without looking at Kilbane punched him slightly and very self-consciously in the stomach. "We call him Salvatore Kilbane Pasquariella. For me—for you. This thing what I say I no say so good. But what I mean, Joe—"

He nodded, very earnestly and at the same time rather shyly; his eyes searched Kilbane's astounded face. Nice guy, this Joe—S. Pasquariella got that out with some effort. All right, you betcha. S. Pasquariella liked and admired him. That's why he had thought—he stopped, smiling painfully at Kilbane's chin. He waited.

"Admired who?" Kilbane asked him after a moment, his ears and the back of his neck slightly flushed. "You ain't got much sense, Salvatore."

"No," S. Pasquariella said humbly. "But—you like it, Joe?"

"I don't know," Kilbane said. He was more in command of himself then. "Nobody ever wanted to name a kid after me before. It's okay, I guess. If you can stand it, I suppose I ought to be tickled to death."

He was, in a way, though he would never have admitted it to anyone. Still, when he thought of Miss Pulitzer eventually, and of the time Miss Pulitzer could have with something like this, he was not very much disturbed; but by that time, of course, after the third glass of wine in S. Pasquariella's kitchen, Miss Pulitzer was no one to worry about, no one to fret over, from there on in.

During the next ten days he ran into her occasionally at headquarters. Then the procedure never varied: Miss Pulitzer's cool stare would pierce all the way through Detective Kilbane; he would gaze absently at a point in space some two or three inches above her head. Miss Pulitzer understood that and so did he. Two Saturdays later, the afternoon before the christening, he bought a silver cup and spoon for Salvatore Kilbane Pasquariella at a downtown baby shop; and that night at ten o'clock, coming back to headquarters after a bit of excitement over by the waterfront, he picked up an early edition of the Sunday morning *Tribune*.

It appeared in there that Miss Pulitzer was doing all right for herself. Jack Garrity's weekly feature—"Over a Headquarters Desk" —had her name underneath it now, and Kilbane spared a moment to glance contemptuously through that pile of guff. . . . The last paragraph, in italicized letters was adorned by the picture of a crystal ball on the side. Inside stuff, Kilbane thought sourly. Right off the— His throat got very dry then, because in Pulitzer's chattiest style he began to read that odds on the conviction of Samuel J. (Little Sammy) Gordon at his trial for murder next month were now five to one in favor of the prosecution.

There was an eyewitness to the shooting, kept undercover and very hush-hush by the higher-ups, who would be the State's big surprise at the proper time. Miss Pulitzer advised her readers to watch for him. "Once over, but not too lightly," would be the D.A.'s watchword.

Kilbane read that part twice. No, he thought then, not even Miss Pulitzer would be dumb enough—he raced off to the chief inspector's office, clutching the paper, and about a minute and a half later, bursting out through the ramp entrance with Beatty and Tom Wilshaw, he rammed head-on into Miss Pulitzer.

"So you did it," he said thickly. "You went and—who told you about Salvatore?"

She blazed up at once. "Who told me?" She mimicked him. "Salvatore told me when I met him coming in here yesterday afternoon. Did you observe that I failed to mention his name? I'm not a fool, you know. And if you've got the faintest idea that you can bully me into ignoring legitimate news—"

"Legitimate news," Kilbane said. He could not seem to get enough breath into him. "He told you because he'd seen you with me. Because he never thought you'd go ahead and plaster it all over the city."

His right fist pounded the air. Did she know where Charlton Street was? Right by Salvatore's barbershop. That's where Little Sammy knocked off his friend; that's where Salvatore practically watched him do it. He was closing up that night—had the lights off—when it happened. The department hadn't let that get out because there were some others mixed up in it who'd do their best to take care of an eyewitness. They were still running loose. Now they saw what they had to do to protect themselves.

"But that's absurd," Miss Pulitzer faltered. She was just a little breathless. "From what I wrote they could never—"

Kilbane put his face close to hers. Maybe she forgot the phrase she used—once over, but not too lightly. They'd get it. Anyone with brains of a fly would get it. A barber, sure. They'd look for a barber and they wouldn't have to look past the corner of Charlton Street, where the shooting came off. Salvatore was the only barber in the neighborhood. Did Miss Janet S. Harrington understand everything now?

Tom Wilshaw honked at him from the car. "Wait," Miss Pulitzer said. "Kilbane—" He did not wait. He swung onto the car as it circled around the guard rail, and three minutes later he swung off it before S. Pasquariella's barbershop. That was locked and dark now, and after a hurried consultation they split up in front of it. Tom Wilshaw and Beatty sought information in a couple of near-by stores; Kilbane went on down to the house in the next square.

He had pushed the door open, not waiting tonight to ring the bell, when Miss Pulitzer got out of a cab behind him. She followed him into the hall without a word; she did not look or act like Miss Pulitzer at all. In the parlor Angelica Therese put down an accordion and Christina Marie slid off the piano stool. A stout woman, coming out of the kitchen, blushed rosily and hid her mouth with her hand when she saw Kilbane.

She told him that Salvatore was not in yet; on Saturday after work he did the marketing. But soon, any minute now—

"We'll wait a while," Kilbane said. His heart was pounding. They sat down in the parlor and the two girl children, preparing a repertoire for the celebration tomorrow, played something or other when Mrs. S. Pasquariella nodded vigorously at them. Kilbane was given some wine and managed to touch his lips to it; later, with Miss Pulitzer, he went upstairs and admired Salvatore Kilbane Pasquariella, an infinitesimal peanut snoring placidly in an old-fashioned rocker crib.

Downstairs again they listened to *"Santa Lucia"* as interpreted on the accordion by Angelica Therese and on the piano by Christina Marie. In the middle of it Kilbane answered the doorbell and held a low-voiced conversation with Beatty and Tom Wilshaw on the white flagstone. He learned that at a quarter past nine, not long after the *Tribune* appeared on the streets, Salvatore had walked out of the barbershop with two strangers. No one had seen him since.

For a moment after closing the door Kilbane leaned his shoulders against it. Then, his face much the same as ever, he went back to the parlor. "We'll get in touch with Salvatore," he announced loudly, surprised that the words came out as well as they did. "Now I guess we'd better be pushing along."

He drove Miss Pulitzer home. "They got men out," he told her quietly, after she whispered her address to him. "Better men than me. You don't have to worry about Salvatore. You aren't, are you?"

She did not answer him; she did not bawl either; whatever was inside her—and Kilbane realized soberly that there must be pretty much—she was managing to keep inside her. But over on Appleton Street, when he pulled up behind a maroon roadster parked in front of her apartment house, she failed to get out after he walked around the car and opened the door for her.

He glanced down at her, at the side of her face and at the hands all knotted up in her lap; then, because it seemed best to leave her alone there for a minute or two, he went on up to the stoop and into the vestibule that was already occupied. A redheaded man, very broad through the shoulders, looked up at him without friendliness and then shifted position on a stone bench near the stairs.

Kilbane did not pay any attention to him. He walked past him to the row of bells and fussed around there momentarily; then, as if he had pressed one without receiving an answer, he went out mumbling to himself. He had seen the redheaded man before, standing sullenly beside Sammy Gordon in a morning lineup. But at that time the redheaded man had been on an illuminated stage, while Detective Kilbane sat half a dozen rows back in a darkened auditorium. That was why he knew the redheaded man did not know him.

Before he reached the steps a good many details had dropped miraculously into place. They had Salvatore—they'd had him since nine-fifteen—but what Kilbane had forgotten was that Salvatore was nobody's fool. If he denied everything they'd be careful with him because Miss Pulitzer, as she said, had mentioned no names. They had a lead, but if they had not broken Salvatore they could not be positive that it was the right lead. So they got a phone book and looked up the Janet S. Harrington who had signed the column and after that they sent the redheaded man over here to talk to her.

It was not very complicated. By the time he reached the car Kilbane understood the main points well enough to shape them into eight or nine sentences directed at the top of Miss Pulitzer's round hat.

She looked up at him blindly. What was he trying to tell her? That—

"Keep it low," Kilbane warned her. He wanted to be very calm himself, but a couple of hundred pinpoints that were each as small and hard as the tip of an ice pick had drawn themselves up into a complete circle around his chest. "He won't want to bring you over where Salvatore is; you've got to make him. You've got to tell him that you don't know Salvatore's name, that you only saw him once when someone pointed him out to you at headquarters. You can't describe him very well, either, but you'd know him if you saw him again. Got that straight?"

He had pulled down ahead of the maroon roadster to the next corner. He parked there.

"Yes," Miss Pulitzer answered him very quietly and without a tremor. "I understand perfectly. I'll go with him and you'll follow us—"

Kilbane nodded. That was the ticket. She'd sit here for five minutes so that he'd have a chance to line things up. After that— He looked narrowly at her. She understood that this wasn't a picnic, didn't she? She understood that she didn't have to do it? It was a good way, but it wasn't the only way. They could—

Miss Pulitzer turned to him, her eyes blazing with cold excitement. If he tried to stop her now— "All right," Kilbane said. He patted her hand reassuringly, understanding that a girl like this was all right in fundamentals; she was a lot cooler now, for instance, than Joseph J. Kilbane. Before she left the car—a department car—he contacted headquarters by means of the two-way radio, and not very long after that several black sedans with no police insignia on them were cutting over to Appleton Street from City Hall Square.

They were all in place when Miss Pulitzer came down the stoop with the redheaded man and got into the maroon roadster with him. O'Hare and Conlon were two blocks ahead, near the park, and O'Hare and Conlon picked them up on the fly. That was the best arrangement since there'd be no car swinging out right after him to make the redheaded man suspicious, but it was one that was very hard on Kilbane. On another avenue a block west, hunched forward over the wheel, he followed the directions relayed to him—east on Appleton, north on Chestnut. It was a long ride, and all the way he kept telling himself senselessly that he should never have let her go off alone. But in the end nothing went wrong; when the maroon roadster stopped outside an apartment house at Thirty-second and Greenwood he was only two blocks away on a parallel road.

O'Hare and Conlon were right behind him; Ed Patterson, who had taken over for the last part of the trip, met them at the corner; Beatty and Tom Wilshaw also appeared from somewhere, but despite the crowd Kilbane got first into the lobby. Arrangements were made there after they found out that the apartment was 4E, and that in addition to someone who almost certainly was S. Pasquariella it held a girl and three men. They started upstairs in a creaking elevator, Kilbane breathing slowly and deeply. They got off at four and O'Hare stopped them all before a brass 4E glittering sleekly against dark wood.

"All right," O'Hare said. "Wait till we hear Beatty and Ed Patterson out back. Then!"

Kilbane looked at him. "To hell with that," Kilbane said, through his teeth. It was not time for waiting—not for Kilbane. He set his revolver almost flush with the lock, fired twice into it, rammed one heel viciously into what the bullets left and plunged far off balance into a long and empty living room.

The redheaded man appeared in a doorway across from him. He was shouting back at someone and trying frantically to get a gun out from under the left flap of his vest. After Kilbane shot him precisely through the chest without breaking stride, event seemed to move on into event without any intervening time lapse at all.

Later, much later—that was the way it came back to Kilbane, at any rate—he appeared to reach the inner doorway immediately after he burst through the outer one, and the very moment that he did reach it he sprawled forward over a little sallow-faced man crouched down just in front of him. He landed on a dining-room table that was eight feet long and as smooth as ice; he sped down it on his left arm and the side of his left leg.

It must have been an impressive entrance. The tablecloth wrapped itself around him and a bowl of flowers in the center got all tangled up in his left armpit. On the far end he sailed off into a chair and carried that majestically with him against the wall. He had one swirling glimpse of the sallow-faced man running out of the dining room and into O'Hare. Then he landed.

A dapper young man with crisp blond hair raced out of the kitchen and fired down quickly at him with his left hand. Kilbane shot back from an impossible angle, wondering for a moment—he must have been badly dazed by the fall—why left-handed people always had such a smooth, deft way of handling themselves. O'Hare, Conlon, Beatty, Tom Wilshaw and the sallow-faced man poured into the room; S. Pasquariella stood over the blond young fellow and waved the remains of a kitchen chair venomously in the air. Everyone was there—everyone but Miss Pulitzer. Kilbane himself moving only a pair of wild blue eyes, lay with his right shoulder piled into the wall, his knees drawn up under him and his nose dug deep into the carpet.

He breathed something when he could—he'd known it, he'd known it. Wobbling, the gun still in his hand, he got up and staggered out to the kitchen. Dark. Empty. And the incredible part lay in the fact that he was the only one worried about her. Back in the dining room O'Hare was lighting a cigar and stirring the left-handed man with a contemplative toe.

"Eh?" O'Hare said, when Kilbane croaked something, "What's the matter with you?"

Kilbane staggered by him into the bedroom. She was there, trying to light a cigarette and handle the phone at the one time—the same old Miss Pulitzer. He looked at her for a moment and then he attempted to help her. One sleeve was ripped away from his coat and his buttonless vest bore a fragment of tablecloth and a few crushed flower petals. His nose was bleeding. The moment she saw him Miss

Pulitzer said, "St-st-st-st," with progressive disapproval.

"I fell," Kilbane said. "Over the table," he added, with a vague gesture toward the dining room. "I bet you were beginning to think you lost me?"

"Oh, no," Miss Pulitzer said, sharp as ever. "I heard you come in." But after that, when her city editor's voice barked out of the earpiece, she took a moment to reach up one hand and brush a couple of the flower petals away from him. And she said, very softly for Miss Pulitzer, "I'm all right, you know. Were you afraid I wasn't?"

Was he? Kilbane couldn't figure anything out. He nodded, though. She spoke something into the mouthpiece and then she opened her handbag and took her handkerchief out of it.

"As if you had to do it all," she said. "Now sit down some place where I can't see you and wipe your nose."

She went with him to the christening Sunday afternoon, and when they got out of his car before S. Pasquariella's house Kilbane showed her the silver cup and spoon and asked her what she thought of them.

"They're very nice," Miss Pulitzer said. "Monogrammed, too."

"Well," Kilbane said, taking credit only where credit was due, "that was free. I think it looks pretty nice. S.K.P. You know what the K's for? Kilbane."

"Oh," she said, without adding anything smart about him and the presidents. There was no need for her to take his arm, either, but she did that, too, and Kilbane was not very much upset about it. Maybe it meant something; maybe it didn't. Kilbane intended to find out.

Inside, in a very busy parlor, the girl children of S. Pasquariella swung into something or other on a one-two-three piano and accordion duet. It sounded fine to Kilbane.

DEATH BEFORE BREAKFAST Q. Patrick

*Why does a novelist decide to write a short story? There are
many reasons. Some of these reasons, perhaps the most cogent
of them, have little interest except for the novelist himself. He
needs money; he has just finished a book and has some free working time; an editor has requested something of so many words
for such-and-such an issue of his magazine. But, even though
the pressures that give birth to a story are frequently as drab as
this, there is also the more personal and complex element which
results in the story becoming, not just any short story in a void,
but the particular story that happens to be written.*

*All novelists are, in part, wire recorders. They move through
life, going about their business and, at the same time, constantly
receiving impressions and ideas which are automatically pre-
served on wire and filed away for future consumption. A writer,
faced with the necessity of writing a story, reaches into his built-in
file more or less at random and plays back whatever spools come
first to hand. Eventually, out of the cacophony of warring sounds,
a theme emerges which whets his professional appetite. This will
do, he says. Or, if he is a little more conscious of his dignity:
This is a wonderful idea which demands to be written.*

As I recall, in the case of Death Before Breakfast, *I had played
back several spools of wire which ranged in subject matter from
the Swiss Guards at Vatican City to a waitress in a diner at
Amenia, New York. Then, barking its way out of the file, came
the playback of an extremely bossy dachshund which had run a
household where I had been staying in Southern California. As
a guest, I had been on friendly enough terms with this dachshund
but I had secretly felt that, if it considered itself to be* that *important, it might at least justify itself by doing something of benefit
to society.*

*And so—frivolously enough—*Death Before Breakfast.

Q. PATRICK

Lieutenant Timothy Trant of the New York Homicide Bureau followed the sedate waddle of Minnie, his sister's dachshund, through

the midwinter bleakness of Central Park. It was 7:30 on a Sunday morning, an unhallowed hour. But Minnie, who was temporarily boarding with Trant, believed in Rising and Shining.

As an Artic wind slashed around Trant, Minnie paused imperturbably to inspect a sheet of newspaper which had floated to rest at their side. She put her front paws on it and examined an advertisement for the Ice Follies at the Center Theater. Hopefully, Trant kept the leash slack. Minnie, however, merely sniffed at the Obituaries and padded ahead.

The park was almost deserted, but, coming up the path toward them, Trant noticed the now-familiar figure of the blind man with the Seeing-Eye dog. Every morning since Minnie had inflicted these sadistic pre-breakfast hikes on him, he had met this pathetic pair. Minnie had on previous mornings carried on a hopeless flirtation with the German Shepherd. However, between Trant's firm grip on her leash and the Seeing-Eye dog's apparent indifference, Minnie's progress had been halted.

Sometimes the blind man and his dog were accompanied by a pretty, Gallic-looking girl and sometimes they were alone. Today they were alone, and as the dog steered his master between a bench and a large clumsily boarded excavation in the path, Trant glanced sympathetically at the blind man. His youngish face with its dark glasses looked harsh and hostile. But suddenly he bent to pat his dog's head and his tenderness touched Trant's heart.

"I wonder," he reflected dubiously, "whether I could ever get that fond of Minnie."

It seemed unlikely, unless Minnie made a drastic change in her pattern of life. She dawdled to peer down into the perilous depths of the excavation hole; she inspected a bench nearby and yawned. Then, as if she hadn't a care in the world, she tugged Trant into a skittish gallop.

When Minnie's business was finally completed more people were about and, as Trant hurried homeward toward the life-preserving prospect of hot coffee, he noticed that an excited group was gathering around the excavation hole.

Congenitally curious, he picked up Minnie and walked to the brink of the excavation. In the bottom of the deep pit, sprawled across pipes and jagged fragments of rock, lay the body of the blind man, and the Seeing-Eye dog, moaning despairingly, crouched at his side.

One of the onlookers, a blond young army sergeant, was trying to lower himself into the pit, but each time he tried the dog leaped upward, snarling with bared fangs.

Trant called: "I'll go down, Sergeant."

The sergeant jostled toward him, his open overcoat revealing an Eisenhower jacket impressively hung with foreign and domestic decorations. "Are you a policeman? Listen, I saw it all. I was coming up the path. This guy was sitting on that seat." He pointed to the bench Minnie had inspected earlier. "The dog was off having its run. The guy got up to call his dog. I saw him headed for the pit. I yelled and ran toward him but he didn't hear and went over the edge. The dog rushed up, snarled at me, and jumped down."

"Get a cop," put in Trant.

As the sergeant hurried off, Trant squatted at the edge of the pit with Minnie in his arms. It was improbable that the German Shepherd would co-operate with Minnie but the improbable happened. Lowering demure lashes, she gazed down at the police dog and yelped coyly. The police dog cocked its head attentively. Trant called to it and it did not growl. With Minnie under one arm, he swung recklessly down into the pit. The police dog did growl then, but Minnie pranced toward it with great coquetry. While she charmed it, Trant examined the blind man. He was dead. The skull was crushed and a jagged lump of rock near by was thickly spattered with blood.

Feeling a kind of cosmic sadness, Trant slipped the wallet from the dead man's pocket and examined its contents—twelve dollars in cash, two ticket stubs for the Center Theater, an identification card giving the name of Andrew Stiles, and a battered photo. Trant peered at the photo. It showed Stiles in sergeant's uniform with the same pretty girl whom Trant had noticed in the park. They were standing in front of an ancient broken bridge, with a little chapel at its center.

Suddenly, as Trant fingered these objects, he experienced a thrill of astonished excitement. The idea was fantastic and proof was at the moment practically nonexistent, but instinct screamed that he was right. If he could bluff it out . . .

Above, two policemen and the blond sergeant were standing at the pit's edge, lowering ropes. Trant supervised the lifting of the corpse. He coaxed the police dog into letting itself be pulled up, too. Finally, with a smug Minnie under one arm and the blood-stained rock under the other, he was hauled up himself. A policeman, recognizing Trant, hovered respectfully. "Okay, Lieutenant, we take over now. Guess there's nothing special you want us to do?"

"I'm afraid there is." Trant turned to the army sergeant, intimidated by his own daring. "Arrest this man for murder."

The sergeant's jaw sagged.

"Murder!" gasped a policeman. "But he saw the blind guy fall . . ."

"He didn't." Inexorably committing himself, Trant held up the rock and indicated the evergreen bushes behind the bench. "He was hiding behind those bushes. He waited until the dog was off on its run, sprang out, hit Andrew Stiles on the head with this rock, and dumped the body and the rock into the excavation."

The sergeant's face was grayish green. "Lieutenant, you're crazy."

"That's what all murderers tell me. But we'll dig up your motive." He pointed to one of the sergeant's decorations. "That's the *Croix de Guerre,* isn't it? So you fought in France. Stiles did too."

In spite of the cold, beads of sweat were forming on the sergeant's forehead. Trant produced the photograph from the dead man's wallet. "Look at this snapshot. There only one broken bridge like that with a chapel in the middle. That's at Avignon. The Pont D'Avignon. And the girl—she's a cute little mademoiselle, isn't she? I've seen her right here in the park with Stiles. He stole her from you, didn't he? The two of you never got on overseas. Then, on top of it all, he snitched your girl and married her. Was that the way it happened?"

The sergeant stood as though stunned. Then, with a look of sheer panic, he spun around and started to run like a madman. As the policemen dashed after him, Trant's exultation welled up. *He's cracked,* he thought. *I've done it.*

In a few moments the policemen had dragged the sergeant back. Trant surveyed the young man's guilt-scared face. "Yes, I can see the whole picture. One of these mornings here in the park, quite by chance, you ran into Stiles and his wife and the Seeing-Eye dog. Suddenly, there he was—the guy you'd sworn to get, the guy who'd stolen your girl. And he was blind. What a temptation! All you had to do was to wait in ambush some morning when he came alone with the dog. With the excavation hole, it was a cinch. Blind man, left a few minutes without Seeing-Eye dog, stumbles into pit. A cut-and-dried accident case. And, in due course, what was to stop you showing up out of the blue and courting his widow?"

He shook his head. "Fine, but you shouldn't have stuck around. I see the advantage, of course. With you as a phony eyewitness, there'd be no embarrassing investigations. But, unfortunately, you overlooked one rather important point. Blind men trip and fall into excavations in broad daylight—yes. But *only* blind men. Not men who can see."

He paused. "And Andrew Stiles could see. Oh, he'd been blind. Probably one of those shock blindnesses. But he'd regained his sight. We can easily check with his doctors and his wife. But there's no real need. We've got proof enough."

From the wallet Trant produced the theater stubs. "Two tickets to the Center Theater, Radio City. Thanks to my dog's interest in reading the newspapers, I happen to know that the Center's current show is an Ice Follies. A man who can't see might go to the movies, to a concert, to a theater. But never in a million years would a blind man, however much he loved his wife, take her to the Ice Follies. It isn't worth anything to someone who can't *see* it."

The sergeant, completely broken, gasped: "But the dog . . . !"

"Oh, the dog." Trant shrugged. "Stiles undoubtedly thought that Seeing-Eye dogs pine away when they feel they're no longer useful to their masters. Stiles loved his dog. For the dog's sake, it wasn't much of a hardship, when he took it walking, to pretend for a while at least that he was still blind."

Minnie was gazing at the Seeing-Eye dog now with entranced adoration.

Her tail was thumping while she squeaked her delight. Slowly the

German Shepherd lowered its head and made a dab at her nose with its tongue.

Trant patted his head. "Okay, boy," he said resignedly, "if Mrs. Stiles doesn't want you now, I guess Minnie and I have house room for another boarder."

THE *AMATEUR* Michael Gilbert

"Such an unpleasant idea as—" Mr. Gilbert began his own introduction to this grim story, and the editors elected to stop him there. Mr. Gilbert went on, far too generously, to tell what the unpleasant idea is, and that sort of thing will never do. In due time, but only in due time, the reader will discover what is intended, and there is no doubt that his hair will rise. (It would be foolish, under the special circumstances, to contend that his blood will be chilled.)

"There are," Mr. Gilbert continued—and here we will not intervene—"two real heroes in the story. One is an ordinary man and the other a rather more than ordinary boy. The professional detective hardly features and indeed must always be at a comparative disadvantage in dealing with circumstances of the sort suggested here."

T<small>HE</small> E<small>DITORS</small>

We were talking about violence. "Some people," I said, "are afraid of people and some people are afraid of things."

Chief Inspector Hazlerigg gave this remark more consideration than it seemed to merit and then said: "Illustration, please."

"Well, some people are afraid of employers and some of razors."

"I don't think that sort of fear is a constant," said Hazlerigg. "It changes as you grow older, you know—or get more experienced. I haven't much occasion for bodily violence in my present job." (He was one of the chief inspectors on the cab rank at Scotland Yard.) "When I was a young constable the customers I chiefly disliked were drunken women. Nowadays—well, perhaps I should look at it the other way round. Perhaps I could describe the sort of man whom *I* should hate to have after *me*."

In the pause that followed I tried hard to visualize what precise mixture of thug and entrepreneur would terrify the red-faced, gray-eyed, bulky, equitable man sitting beside me.

"He'd be English," said Hazlerigg at last, "Anglo-Saxon anyway, getting on for middle age and a first-class businessman. He would have had some former experience of lethal weapons—as an infantry soldier, perhaps, in one of the World Wars. But definitely an amateur —an amateur in violence. He would believe passionately in the justice of what he was doing—but without ever allowing the fanatic to rule the businessman.

"Now that's a type I should hate to have after me! He's unstoppable."

"Is that a portrait from life?" I said.

"Yes," said Hazlerigg slowly. "Yes, it's a portrait from life. It all happened a good time ago—in the early thirties, when I was a junior inspector. Even now, you'll have to be very careful about names, you know, because if the real truth came out—however, judge for yourself."

Inspector Hazlerigg first met Mr. Collet (*the* Collets, the shipping people—this one was the third of the dynasty) in his managing director's mahogany-lined office. Hazlerigg was there by appointment. He had arrived at the building in a plain van and had been introduced via the goods entrance, but once inside he had been treated with every consideration.

Even during the few minutes which had elapsed before he could be brought face to face with Mr. Collet, Hazlerigg had managed to collect a few impressions. Small things, from the way the commissionaire and the messenger spoke about him, and more still from the way his secretary spoke *to* him: that they liked him and liked working for him; that they knew something was wrong and were sorry.

They didn't, of course, know exactly what the trouble was. Hazlerigg did.

Kidnaping—the extorting of money by kidnaping—is a filthy thing. Fortunately, it does not seem to come very easily to the English criminal. But there was a little wave of it that year.

Mr. Collet had an only child, a boy of nine. On the afternoon of the previous day he had been out with his aunt, Mr. Collet's sister, in the park. A car had overtaken them on an empty stretch. A man had got out, pitched the boy into the back of the car, and driven off. As simple as that.

"So far as we know," said Hazlerigg, "there's just the one crowd. I'll be quite frank. We know very little about them. But there have been four cases already, and the features have been too much alike for coincidence."

"Such as—?" said Mr. Collet. His voice and his hands, Hazlerigg noticed, were under control. He couldn't see the eyes. Mr. Collet was wearing heavy sunglasses.

"Well—they don't ask for too much to start with, that's one thing. The first demand has always been quite modest. The idea being that a man will be more likely to go on paying once he has started."

"Right so far," said Mr. Collet. "They asked for only five thousand pounds— They could have had it this morning—if I'd thought it would do any good."

"Then there's also their method of collecting. It's disarming. They employ known crooks. I don't know what they pay them—just enough to make it worth their while to take the risk. These crooks are strictly carriers only. We could arrest them at the moment they contact you without getting any nearer to the real organizers."

"The Piccadilly side of Green Park, at two o'clock tomorrow," said Mr. Collet. "I got the rendezvous quite openly over the telephone. Could they be followed?"

"That's where the organization really starts," said Hazlerigg. "Every move after that is worked out—and when you come to think about it the cards are very heavily stacked in their favor. All they've got to do is to hand the money on. There are a hundred ways of doing it. They might pass it over in a crowd in an underground train or a bus in the rush hour, or they might be picked up by car and driven somewhere fast, or they might hand it over in a cinema. They might get rid of the money the same day, or they might wait a week."

"Yes," said Mr. Collet, "a little organization and that part shouldn't be too difficult. Any other peculiarities about this crowd?"

He said this as a businessman might inquire about a firm with whom he was going to trade.

Hazlerigg hesitated. What he was going to say had to be said some time. It might as well be said now.

"Yes, sir," he said. "There's this to consider. However much the victim pays—however often he pays—however promptly he pays—he doesn't get the child back. You've given us the best chance so far by coming to us immediately." Mr. Collet said nothing. "You know Roger Barstow—he lost his little girl—Zilla was her name. He paid nine times. More than £100,000—until he had no more left and said so. Next morning they found Zilla; in the swill bin at the back of his house."

There was another silence. Hazlerigg saw the whites of the knuckle-bones start up for a moment on one of Mr. Collet's thin brown hands. At last he got to his feet and said: "Thank you, Inspector. I have your contact number. I'll get hold of you as soon as I—as soon as anything happens."

As he walked to the door he took off his glasses for the first time and Hazlerigg saw in his eyes that he had got his ally. It had been a risk, but it had come off.

Mr. Collet was going to fight.

When the door had closed behind the chief inspector Mr. Collet thought for a few moments and then rang the bell and asked for Mr. Stevens.

Mr. Stevens, who was a month or two short of fifteen, was the head of the Collet messenger service, and a perfectly natural organizer. He spent a good deal of his time organizing the messenger boys of the firm into a sort of trade union, and he had already engineered two beautifully timed strikes, the second of which had called for Mr. Collet's personal intervention.

It says a good deal for both parties that when Mr. Collet sent for him and asked for his help, young Stevens listened carefully to what he had to say and promised him the fullest assistance of himself and his organization.

"No film stuff," said Mr. Collet. "These men are real crooks. They're dangerous. And they're wide awake. They expect to be followed. We're going to do this on business lines."

That was Wednesday. At four o'clock on Thursday afternoon Inspector Hazlerigg again visited Archangel Street, taking the same precautions. Mr. Collet was at his desk. "You've got something for me. . . ." It was more a statement than a question.

"Before I answer that," said Mr. Collet, "I want something from you. I want your promise that you won't act on my information without my permission."

Hazlerigg said: "All right. I can't promise not to go on with such steps as I'm already taking. But I promise not to use your information until you say so. What do you know?"

"I know the names of most of the men concerned," said Mr. Collet. "I know where my son is—I know where these people are hiding."

When Hazlerigg had recovered his breath he said: "Perhaps you'll explain."

"I thought a good deal," said Mr. Collet, "about what you told me—about the sort of people we were dealing with. Particularly about the men who would make contact with me and carry back the money. It was obvious that they weren't afraid of violence. They weren't even, basically, afraid of being arrested. That was part of the risk. They certainly weren't open to any sort of persuasion. If they observed the routine, which had no doubt been carefully laid down for them, they would take the money from me and get it back to their employers, without giving us any chance of following them. Their position seemed to be pretty well impregnable. In the circumstances it seemed—do you play bridge, Inspector?"

"Badly," said Hazlerigg. "But I'm very fond of it."

"Then you understand the Vienna Coup."

"In theory—though I could never work it. It's a sort of squeeze. You start by playing away one of your winning aces, isn't that it?"

"Exactly," said Mr. Collet. "You give—or appear to give—your opponents an unexpected gift. And like all unexpected gifts it throws them off balance and upsets their defense. I decided to do the same. To be precise, I gave them five thousand pounds *more* than they asked for. I met these men—there were two of them as I told you— by appointment in Green Park. I simply opened my brief-case and put a brown paper packet into their hands. They opened it quickly, and as they were doing so I said: 'Ten thousands pounds in one pound notes—that's right, isn't it?' I could almost see it hit them.

To give them time to cover up I said: 'When do I see my boy?' The
elder of the two men said: 'You'll be seeing him soon. We'll ring you
tomorrow.' Then they pushed off. I could see them starting to argue."

Mr. Collet paused. Inspector Hazlerigg, who was still trying to
work out the angles, said nothing.

"The way I figured it out," said Mr. Collet, "they'd have all their
plans made for handing on five thousand pounds to their employers.
So I gave them ten thousand. That meant five thousand for themselves
if they kept quiet about it, and played it right. But I'd put all the notes
in one packet, you see. They had to be divided out. Then they had
to split the extra five thousand among themselves—they were both
in on it. Above all, they had to get somewhere safe and somewhere
quiet and talk it out. You see what that meant. Their original plan
—the careful one laid down for them by the bosses—had to be
scrapped.

"They had to make another plan, and make it rather quickly. It
would be something simple. They'd either go to one of their own
houses, or a safe friend's house—and it would probably be somewhere
with a telephone—because they'd have to invent some sort of story
for the bosses to explain why they'd abandoned the original plan.
That last bit was only surmise, but it was a fair business risk."

"Yes," said Hazlerigg. "I see. You still had to follow them, though."

"Not me," said Mr. Collet. "It was the boys who did that. The
streets round the park were full of them. They're a sort of car-
watching club—you see them anywhere in the streets of London if
you look. They collect car numbers. Boy of mine called Stevens ran
it. He's a born organizer. I went straight back to the office. Fifteen
minutes later I got a call. Just an address, near King's Cross.

"I passed it on to a friend of mine—he's quite a senior official, so
I won't give you his name. Inside five minutes he had the line from
that house tapped. He was just in time to collect the outgoing call.
That was that. It was to a house in Essex. Here's the address." He
pushed a slip of paper across. "That's the name."

"Just like that," said Hazlerigg. "Simple. Scotland Yard have been
trying to do it for six months."

"I had more at stake than you."

"Yes," said Hazlerigg. "What happens now?"

"Now," said Mr. Collet, "We sit back and wait."

Continuing the story, Hazlerigg said to me: "I think that was one of the bravest and coolest things I ever saw a man do. He was quite right, of course. The people we were dealing with moved by instinct —that sort of deadly instinct which those people get who sleep with one finger on the trigger.

"When their messengers reported the change of plan—I don't know what sort of story they put up—their bristles must have been on end. These people can smell when something's wrong. They're so used to double-crossing other people that they get a sort of second sight about it themselves. If we'd rushed them then, we should never have got the boy alive. So we waited. We had a man watch the house— it was a big, rather lonely house, between Pitsea and Rayleigh on the north of the Thames."

And, meanwhile, Mr. Collet sat in his mahogany-lined office and transacted the business of his firm. On the fourth morning he got a letter, in a painstaking, schoolboy script.

> *Dear Father,*
> *I am to write this to you. You are to pay five thousand pounds more. They will telephone you how to pay. I am quite well. It is quite a nice house. It is quite a nice room. The sun wakes me in the early morning.*
>
> > *Love from David.*
>
> *P.S. Please be quick.*

Mr. Andrews, senior partner in the firm of Andrews and Mackay, house agents of Pitsea, summed up his visitor at one glance which took in the silk tie, the pigskin brief-case and the hood of the chauffeur-driven Daimler standing outside the office, and said in his most deferential voice: "Certainly, Mr.—er—Robinson. Anything we can do to help you. It's not everybody's idea of a house, but if you're looking for something quiet and secluded—"

"I understand that it's occupied at the moment," said Mr. Robinson.

"Temporarily," agreed Mr. Andrews. "But you could have possession. The owner let it on short notice to a syndicate of men who are interested in a new color process. They needed the big grounds—the quiet, you understand, the freedom from interruption. The only difficulty which occurs to me is that you will not be able to inspect the house today. By the terms of our arrangement we have to give at least forty-eight hours' notice."

Mr. Robinson thought for a moment and then said: "Have you such a thing as a plan of the house?"

"Why certainly," said Mr. Andrews. "We had a very careful survey made when the house was put up for sale. Here you are—on two floors only, you see."

"Only one bedroom," said Mr. Robinson, "looks due east?"

"Why, yes." Mr. Andrews was hardened to the vagaries of clients.

"*'The sun wakes me in the early morning,'*" said Mr. Robinson softly.

"I beg your pardon?"

"Nothing," said Mr. Robinson. "Nothing. Thinking aloud. A bad habit. Would it be asking too much if I borrowed these plans for a day?"

"Why, of course," said Mr. Andrews. "Keep them for as long as you like."

Four o'clock of a perfect summer afternoon. It was so silent that the clack of a scythe blade on a stone sounded clear across the valley where the big gray house dozed in the sun.

As the double chime of the half-hour sounded from Rayleigh Church a figure appeared on the dusty road. It was a man, in postman's uniform, wheeling a bicycle.

The woman in the lodge answered the bell and unlocked one of the big gates, without comment. Then she returned to her back room, picked up the house telephone, and said: "All right. It's only the postman."

It was a mistake which might have cost her very dearly.

As Mr. Collet wheeled his borrowed machine slowly up the long drive he was thinking about the bulky sack which rested on the saddle and balanced there with difficulty. He knew that some very sharp eyes would be watching his approach. It couldn't be helped though. He had been able to see no better method of getting this particular apparatus up to the house.

He propped his bicycle against the pillar of the front door, lifted the sack down, keeping the mouth of it gathered in his left hand, and rang the bell. So far, so good.

The door was opened by a man in corduroys and a tweed jacket. He might have been a gardener or a gamekeeper. Mr. Collet, looking at his eyes, knew better.

"Don't shout," he said. The gun in his hand was an argument.

For a moment the man stared. Then he jumped to one side and started to open his mouth.

Even for an indifferent shot three yards is not a long range. The big bullet lifted the man back onto his heels like a punch under the heart and crumpled him onto the floor.

In the deep silence which followed the roar of the gun, Mr. Collet raced for the stairs. The heavy sack was against him but he made good time.

At the top he turned left with the sureness of a man who knows his mind and made for the room at the end of the corridor.

He saw that it was padlocked.

He put the muzzle of his gun as near to the padlock as he dared and pulled the trigger.

The jump of the gun threw the bullet up into the door jamb, missing the padlock altogether. He took a lower aim and tried again. Once, twice, again. The padlock buckled.

Mr. Collet kicked the door open and went in.

The boy was half sitting, half kneeling in one corner. Mr. Collet grinned at him with a good deal more confidence than he felt and said: "Stand out of the way, son. The curtain's going up for the last act."

As he spoke he was piling together mattresses, bedclothes, a rug, and a couple of small chairs into a barricade. When he had done this he opened the sack, pulled out the curious-looking instrument from inside it, laid it beside his homemade parapet, and started working on it.

"Get into that far corner, son," said Mr. Collet. "And you might keep an eye on the window, just in case it occurs to the gentry to run a ladder up. Keep your head down, though. Here they come."

Joe Keller had tortured children and had killed for pleasure as well as for profit, but he was not physically a coward.

As he watched his henchman twitching on the hall floor, with the indifference of a man who has seen many men die, he was already working out his plan of attack.

"Take a long ladder," he said to one man, "and run it up to the window. Not the bedroom window—be your age. Put it against the landing window, this end. You can see the bedroom door from there, can't you? If it's shut, wait. If it's open, start shooting into the room —aim high. We'll go in together along the floor."

"He'll pick us off as we come."

"Not if Hoppy keeps him pinned down," said Keller. "Besides I reckon he doesn't know much about guns. It took him four shots to knock off that lock, didn't it? Any more arguments?"

Half a mile away, at points round the lip of the valley, four police cars had started up their engines at the sound of the first shot.

Hazlerigg was lying full length on the roof of one of them, a pair of long binoculars in his hands.

The Essex Superintendent looked up at him.

"I made that five shots," he said. "Do we start?"

"No, sir," said Hazlerigg. "You remember the signal we arranged."

"Do you think he can do his stuff?" The Superintendent sounded worried.

"He hasn't done badly so far," said Hazlerigg shortly, and silence settled down once more.

It was the driver of their car who saw it first, and gave a shout. From one of the first-floor windows of the house, unmistakable and ominous, a cloud of black and sooty smoke rolled upward.

The four cars started forward as one.

In that long upstairs passage things had gone according to plan— at first. Covered by a fusillade from the window, Joe Keller and his two assistants had inched their way forward on elbows and knees, their guns ahead of them.

At the end of the passage stood the door, open and inviting. The outer end of Mr. Collet's barricade came into sight as they advanced, but it was offset from the doorway, and Mr. Collet himself was still invisible.

Five yards to go.

Then, as the three men bunched for the final jump, it came out to meet them. A great red and yellow river of flame, overmantled with black smoke, burning and hissing and dripping with oil. As they turned to fly it caught them. . . .

"There was nothing very much for us to do when we did get there," said Inspector Hazlerigg. "We had to get Mr. Collet and the boy out of the window—the passage floor was red-hot. We caught one man in the garden. His nerve was gone—he seemed glad to give himself up.

"As for the other three—an infantry flame thrower is not a discriminating sort of weapon, particularly at close quarters. There was just about enought left of them—well—say just about enough of the three of them to fill the swill bin where they found little Zilla Barstow. No, never tangle with a wholehearted amateur."

DEAD TO THE WORLD   John D. MacDonald

They keep telling me that the heyday of the pulp magazines was way back when Chandler, Hammett and group were doing work for Black Mask *as edited by Cap Shaw. My own heyday came considerably later, in '46, '47, '48 and '49. Those were the first four years of writing for me. Most of the ones I sold, and there were several hundred, went to Popular Publications where Mike Tilden and Harry Widmer did a good deal to stomp them into shape.* Dead to the World *is one from that era. I am sorry the pulp magazines withered. I liked doing the stories. I learned a great deal. Were the pulp magazines still active, I would be selling to them those stories which I now file away, those stories which I enjoy doing but are termed too vigorous for the smooth-paper magazine pattern.*

JOHN D. MACDONALD

I can probably explain why I got so upset about Howler Browne's troubles if I tell you that in our case it was a little different than the usual relationship between the owner of a roadhouse and the gent who plays his piano. After I was out of the army a year and still not getting anywhere, he took me on out of hunger, and also because twice while we were both working for Uncle Sugar, I pulled details for him so he could sweeten up a dish he had located in Naples.

He hadn't talked much about this club he owns, the Quin Pines, and after he met me on the street in Rochester and I told him my troubles and he took me on and drove me out there, I was agreeably surprised to see a long low building about two hundred feet back from the highway, with five enormous pines along the front of it. It looks like class and a high cover charge. It is. It pulls the landed gentry out of their estates and loads them up with the best food and liquor in the East. And the Howler makes a fine thing out of it.

I guess he got the name of the Howler because of the way he flaps his arms and screams at the ceiling when things don't go just right. He's a big guy, with a fast-growing tummy, a red face and crisp curling black hair . . . the kind of a guy who can wear a Homburg and look like the Honorable Senator from West Overshoe, North Dakota. But he has a large heart of twenty carat which probably wouldn't wear well on a politician's sleeve.

I'm Wentley D. C. Morse, the first name and the initials having suffered a contraction to plain Bud. I seem to appeal to the babes with frustrated maternal instincts, probably because I have a nice fresh round face and a well-washed look. I'm not above taking advantage of such inclinations.

I know that when the Howler took me on, he expected me to be a floperoo, a citizen he could stick up at the piano at times when the band happened to be tired. He offered me a room, food and thirty bucks a week. I snapped at it so quick I nearly bit his hand. I've been slapping a piano around ever since I've been able to climb up onto the stool. I have my own style, whatever that is, and a long string of startling failures at auditions. I have about twenty-nine varieties of rolling bass in my left hand. I like to mess around with improvised discords with the right. I can play the normal corn, just like any other boy with two hands, but I like my own way and sticking to it had kept me in bread crusts until I ran into the Howler.

I did about an hour the first night. I got some surprised expressions from the dowager clique and saw one old party choke on his celery when I stuck some concert counterpoint into the middle of Gershwin. When some kids tried to dance to me, I switched the beat on them until they stumbled off the floor, throwing ocular stilettos over their shoulders. I don't like being danced to. Somehow, it seems silly.

It was nice clean work, but I didn't have much chance to talk to the Howler. After a week, I began to build up a discriminating clientele. The Howler stopped and listened to the banging of hands after a long number and ordered me a blue spot. In two weeks I was set and beginning to get some small mentions in the trade papers. Then I began to notice things. The first thing I noticed was that the Howler's cheeks, instead of being nice and round and pink, began to hang like a couple of laundry bags on Tuesday morning. Once I walked out into the kitchen and heard him screaming. He was also flapping his arms. The kitchen help stood around with wide eyes, waiting for him to burst. I stood by to enjoy it.

"Why, oh why," he hollered, "did I ever get into this business? Am I nuts? Am I soft in the head?"

While he was gathering breath for another burst, I interrupted. "S'matter, Howler? Somebody get a buckshot in the caviar?"

He spun around and said: "Oh! Hello, Bud." He walked out of the kitchen. I shrugged at the pastry chef. He shrugged at the dishwasher, who grinned and shrugged at me. I went back out through the place and up to my room.

The next night, we had the fight. It didn't last long, but it hurt business. The cocktail lounge is to the right as you come in the front entrance. The dining room and dance floor is to the left. The joint was packed, as it usually is around eleven. The Howler wasn't around. I was due to play during intermission, so I was in the cocktail lounge waiting for the end of the set.

Two citizens in dark suits started arguing with each other at one end of the bar. One was tall and one was short, but they both had the same greased black hair and the same disgusting neckties. Before anybody could move, the big one backed the little one over to the door and across the hall. At the entrance to the dining room he wound up and pasted the little guy. It was a punch and a half. The little one went slamming back into a group of tables occupied by the cash customers. He knocked over two. One of them had four full dinners on it—half eaten. The big one left in a hurry before we could stop him. The little one got up and felt of his chin. He clawed the cabbage salad out of his ruffled locks and departed. He refused to leave his name. Then about forty very stuffy citizens departed with cold looks. I was watching the new hatcheck girl give them their stuff when the Howler came up to me and asked me the trouble.

"Couple of citizens had fisticuffs. A big one fisticuffed a little one right into two lobster dinners, a steak and an order of roast beef. These people figure you're running an abandoned institution, so they're shoving off."

He spun me around and his face was red. "You dope! Why didn't you hold them?"

"Me? I play the piano. Besides, the big one left in a hurry. And what could you hold the little one for? For standing in front of a big fist?"

He walked off, but I could tell from his back that he was as mad as he could get. I hurried in and started slapping the piano around. I probably didn't play too well, as I was wondering why I had been jumped. After my half-hour was over, I dug up the Howler. He was upstairs. He was still mad.

I walked up to him and said: "Am I a friend, or just another employee of the Great Browne?"

That jolted him. He grabbed my arm and said: "O.K., so you're a friend. Why?"

"Come on." I didn't say another word until I had led him downstairs and out into the parking lot. I picked a crate that looked comfortable. We climbed into the front seat and I waited until we both had cigarettes going before I continued.

"Look, my boy. I know something is eating on you. You don't act right and you don't look right. Now what is it?"

He waited a while and I could tell that he was wondering whether to tell me. Finally he sighed and sank down into the seat. "Shakedown, Bud. The curse of this business. You get going good and then some smart monkeys figure you got dough to give away just to stay out of trouble."

"How much?"

"A thousand a month."

"Are you paying?"

"Not yet. That's why the little scrap tonight. Just a warning. If I keep holding out, we get a free-for-all and then there's no more customers. Maybe the cops close me up. The county boys are tough."

"Can you afford it?"

"Maybe. It'll be O.K. for now while the boom's on, but come a slump and I dig into the bank to make payments. You see, I can't deduct the payoff as a business expense. I don't get any receipt. It has to come out of my end after taxes."

"Have you talked to the cops?"

"What's the use? The new group has hit all the joints for miles around. Some of them went to the cops—no help. We got no data on them. They're slick. That's why I wanted one or both of those guys who brawled. Thought I might squeeze something out of them."

"How did they contact you?"

"Phone. Very slick voice. Polite. Told me I needed assurance that my club would run smoothly. Told me he wanted a thousand in tens, twenties and fifties put in a brown envelope on the first of each month. Then I give it to my daughter Sue and send her walking up the road with it to the state highway in the middle of the afternoon. She's just turned eight. He says that if there's any trouble, they give Sue a face she won't want to grow up with."

I cursed steadily for many long minutes.

"That's just what I said," he remarked, "only I said it louder and faster."

"You couldn't take a chance on telling that to the cops and letting them try to get on the trail after the kid's O.K.?"

"Hell, no. If I pay off to these characters, I do it straight. I can't take a chance on the kid. There's not enough dough in the world to mean that much to me."

"Anything I can do?"

"I guess not, Bud. Just beat on that piano the way you've been doing, and we'll jam enough customers in here to make the thousand look like a fly bite. You're doing great, kid. But even if . . ." His voice trailed off and he snapped the butt out onto the gravel.

"But even if what?"

"I'm afraid that if we make more dough, they'll ask for more dough. I can't help but feel that they've got somebody planted on me. The guy on the phone knew a lot about the business. Too much."

"How many new guys do you have?"

"Maybe fourteen in the last two months."

"You've been watching them?"

"They all look O.K. to me. I can't figure out which one it could be. Maybe I'm wrong. Maybe the guy on the phone was guessing."

"I could help look."

"You could stay out of it. I hired you to give me piano music, not protection from a protection mob." He climbed out of the car and slammed the door. I heard his footsteps crunching on the gravel as he headed back for the joint. I sat and had another cigarette and did some thinking. A few couples came out and climbed into their cars —but they didn't drive away. The music rolled out across the green lawn and the stars seemed low and bright. It was a good night, but the taste for it had sort of left me. I wanted to help the Howler.

He paid off on the first. I stood with him and watched Sue trudge up the road in her blue dress, the big envelope in her hand. The sun was hot. She went over the hill and out of sight on the other side. We both wanted to run after her but we didn't dare. In the next twenty minutes I saw the Howler age five years. His face was white and his eyes were strained. He kept snapping cigarettes into his mouth and dragging twice on them before flipping them away.

I grabbed his arm when I saw something coming over the hill. Sue came into sight and the color came back into his face. We shook hands solemnly. When she was twenty feet away, he dropped on one knee in the dust and she ran into his arms, giggling. He held her roughly and slapped her where you slap children with either affection or correction.

He held her at arm's length and said: "Now tell Dad what happened."

"A black car stopped and a man stuck out his hand and said, 'Got that envelope for me, Sue?' and I gave it to him and they drove away."

"How about his voice?"

"He kind of whispered."

"What kind of a car was it?"

"I don't know but I think it was an old one. Black, too."

"Did you look at the license like Dad told you?"

"Sure, but it had dirt all over it. I couldn't read any numbers."

"Could you recognize him if you saw him again?"

"Golly, no! He held a handkerchief up to his nose like he was going to blow it, but he didn't."

We stood and looked helplessly down into her bland little face. She looked hurt, as though she had failed the Howler somehow. He patted her on the head and told her she had done O.K., so she went skipping off to her mother in the bungalow the Howler had built down over the crest of the hill from the Quin Pines. I had met Mrs. Browne, a tall blonde with steady eyes, but I didn't see her often, as the Howler has the excellent rule of keeping his wife away from the joint. More joint owners should try it. I wondered how she was reacting to the ugly choice of having to use Sue as a courier for a shakedown mob.

Even though I wanted to do something—anything—to help the Howler, I couldn't think of a starting place. For the next few weeks he walked around looking as gay as a wreath on the door. And still the customers flocked in. Nothing will ever beat the old formula of good food, good liquor, good music and no clip games. Whenever I asked him how things were going he would shrug and look grim.

It must have been the day before the second payoff day that I burst into the Howler's office without doing any knocking. I had dreamed up the hot idea of getting hold of a midget and dressing it in clothes like Sue wears and sending it down to the highway with a cannon and a chip on its shoulder. I was chewing over the idea and I didn't knock.

The Howler looked up from behind his big desk and he wasn't happy to see me. A man I had seen around the place sat in the visitor's chair. He was a tall slim blond gent with a steel-gray gabardine suit, white buck shoes, a hand-painted tie and a languid manner. He was real pretty with his suntan.

I said, "Excuse me, Howler. I should have knocked," and I turned to go back out.

"Wait a minute, Bud. You probably are going to have to look for a job soon, so you might as well know the score. Meet my lawyer, John Winch. John, this is Bud Morse, my piano player and good friend."

Winch jumped up and grabbed my hand. I liked his warm smile and tight handshake. "I'm glad to meet you, Bud. I've enjoyed your work a lot. I like your 'Lady Be Good' best, I think."

I like the way I play that one too.

I perched on the window sill and the Howler said: "It looks like we're at the end of the line. John can't think of a thing we can do, Bud. The mob, whoever they are, want two grand a month. I can't swing it. I told them I would have to go out of business and the guy on the phone said that was O.K. with him. I've gone over the books with John and we can't see any way out of it. I'm going to sell out and get out of here."

Winch looked steadily at me and said: "And the trouble with that is that he'll only get the value of the land, building and fixtures. You can't sell these places on the basis of a capitalization of the earning rate. It just isn't done."

I felt sorry for the Howler. His big red face sagged down over his collar. His eyes were as empty as yesterday's lunch box.

"Damn it, why don't you fight a while?"

He spread his hands. "Nothing to fight with, Bud. Nothing to go on."

"This doesn't sound like you, boy. Besides, give me another couple of days to poke around. I got a lead."

They both leaned forward. New life came back into the Howler's face. "What is it? Come on, give!"

I opened my mouth to tell him and then decided against it. It was too vague—it would sound silly. Once when I was in college I worked in a shoe store and I learned about shoes. I know good ones when I see them. Even though the Howler had told me just to play the piano, I had done some poking around among the new employees. I noticed that a fellow named Jake Thomason, the new dishwasher, was wearing a pair of beautiful shoes. Looked like a handmade last. Narrow and well stitched. For a guy making eighteen bucks a week plus two meals a day, they didn't look right. It made me wonder and I had been keeping an eye on him. But you can't tell a guy not to sell out because his dishwasher wears good shoes.

"I'm sorry, gentlemen, but I got to keep it to myself until I develop it a little more." They nagged at me for a while but I kept my mouth shut.

Finally the Howler said: "O.K., John. Forget the sale for a while.

I'll pay off the two grand tomorrow and take a chance on Bud."
Winch shrugged and I left before the Howler could change his mind.

The bee was on me. I had to develop the shoes into a big lead in
nothing flat. Because I had opened my big mouth, I was costing my
boss another two thousand dollars. I went up and sat in my room
and did a little thinking. I had thought about Thomason enough so
that it was easy to visualize him—a slight quiet little man of about
forty, with thin lips and oversize hands, receding hairline and a nose
that had been busted a few times. I had already found out that he
lived in the Princess Hotel, a flea-bag outfit in nearby Casling. There
was something about him that I couldn't put my finger on. Suddenly
I remembered what it was. I snapped my fingers and hit myself on
the head with the palm of my hand. I realized that without actually
noticing it, I had seen him coming out of the kitchen and hanging
around the new hatcheck girl.

Then I did some more thinking. I like the looks of the little gal,
a round-faced blonde with kind of a Dutch air about her. She looked
as though she scrubbed her red cheeks with a big brush. I remembered the lights in her blue eyes and the trim, pert little figure that
went with that pretty blond head. Jerry Bee her name was.

I glanced at my watch. Four-thirty. She would be coming back on
duty about now. I couldn't take the time to case her carefully. You
have to take some people on trust. I decided to enlist her in the save
Howler campaign.

I went downstairs and found her sorting out the tags for the evening
business. She smiled up at me with professional cheer and said: "I
didn't know you wore a hat, Mr. Morse."

"The name is Bud, Jerry, and I got to talk to you. Alone. Quick."

"Why . . . ah . . . sure, Bud. Is this a fancy line? You want to
try to make a date or something?"

"I would, sometime, but not now. I got other things to talk about.
You know where that grapevine thing is? That white wooden thing
over across the lawn? See you there in two minutes."

I walked off and went through the kitchen. Thomason was fiddling
with the controls on the dishwasher. He didn't look up. I went out

the back door and walked over the yard to the grapevines. I lit a cigarette and in about a minute she came hurrying across the grass, looking as cute as a bug and very earnest.

I gave it to her quick. "A mob is shaking the boss down. The mob has somebody planted in the joint. I figure it's Jake Thomason, the dishwasher. They're forcing the boss out of business. I've seen Thomason hanging around you. What's he said? What does he act like?"

Her mouth was a round O of amazement. Then when she realized what I wanted, she began to look disappointed. "Gee. He's just acted like any other guy. He all the time wants me to go out with him. I don't want to go out with no dishwasher."

"He hasn't hinted anything about having more dough than a dishwasher should have? He hasn't tried to sound important?"

"No. Nothing like that."

It was discouraging. I sighed and said: "O.K., Jerry. Thanks anyway. Guess I'll have to take it alone from here."

"What you going to do?" she asked, her eyes wide.

"I don't know. Follow him, maybe. Try to get into his room, I guess."

She stepped foward and grabbed a button on the front of my jacket. She twisted it in her finger and looked at it as she said: "Gee, Bud, that sounds so exciting. Do you think maybe that I could . . . help?" As she said the last word, she slowly raised her eyes up toward me. I was surprised to notice how long her lashes were. That slow look flattened me.

"Sure. Meet me as soon as the joint closes. Sure." I stood and watched her walk back across the yard toward the joint. She was put together in the proper manner. I tried to put my cigarette in my mouth and found that my mouth was open and I was still saying: "Sure." I stopped talking and chewed the end of the cigarette.

During the long evening I fretted about the job of following Thomason. I knew that having the gal along would make it easier if he noticed us. We could just be having a routine date. It wouldn't look as fishy as if he found just me on his trail.

The Howler is one of those people who like to have things all cleaned up before the joint is closed. That fit in nicely with my plans. It meant that Thomason would be running stuff through the dish-washing machine long after the last customer had left. I strolled out into the kitchen a few times between my shows and tried to get a good clean look at him without him noticing me. There was nothing to see. He stood beside the splashing, humming machine and fed in the dishes with quick easy movements. I felt an all-gone feeling in my middle, and hoped that I wasn't wrong—and yet there was the matter of the shoes. . . .

I told Hoffer, the statuesque citizen with the South Jersey accent who keeps a fatherly eye on most of the employees, that I was check-ing to see how many of our people brought their own cars. I didn't want to ask about Thomason by name, so I had to stand and look interested while he rambled through a long list. Finally he said: "And the dishwasher, Thomason, he drives an old heap that I make him park down in the pasture beyond the parking lot." I asked some more questions about matters I didn't give a damn about, and then drifted off.

The half-moon outlined the square frame of Thomason's car. Hoffer had been right when he called it a heap. It squatted in the tall grass looking like the nucleus for a junk yard. The fenders were frayed and it looked old enough to have a bulb horn. I stood in the night breeze and listened. The music blatted away in the club a hundred yards behind me. I suddenly realized that if I was right, I could be given a large hole in the head. I shivered slightly and stepped forward to where I could read the license number with a match. Then I hurried back.

Jerry finally scurried out of the barn that the Howler had converted into living quarters for the women. It was twenty to three. The last bunch of noisy customers had driven away. From where I stood I could see the kitchen lights still blazing.

I didn't waste time talking. I grabbed her arm and hustled her over to my coupe. I opened the door and handed her in. Then I ran around the car and jumped behind the wheel. As I backed out and turned around, I noticed that her perfume smelled good in the closed car.

"What are we going to do now, Bud? Where're we going?"

"Thomason's crate is parked back in the pasture. He'll be through pretty soon. We got to be where we can tail him no matter which way he goes."

She quivered and slid over close to me. "Gee, this is exciting," she said. I drove about two hundred yards down the road and backed into the driveway of our nearest neighbor. His house was dark. I cut my lights and we sat where some high bushes made the gloom thickest.

"We can have a cigarette, but we got to throw out the butts soon as he drives out. If he goes home, he'll go right by us here, out to the main drag."

She agreed and we sat quietly waiting. I found her hand and held it tight. Somehow it was less lonely, having her along—and yet I didn't let myself think of what I might be exposing her to.

Our cigarettes were well down when some dim lights flashed on in the pasture. I heard a roar as an aged motor clattered into life. We ditched the cigarettes, and in a few minutes the old car banged by the driveway.

Jerry gave a little squeak of excitement and I turned out after him. I didn't turn my lights on. I stayed well back. I figured that the noise of his motor would cover any sound we might make. I hoped that no eager cop would notice our lights and decide to get official.

The old car looked anything but ominous swaying along ahead of us. He kept up an average speed of twenty-five. He stopped at the corner and turned toward Casling. Somehow, that was a disappointment. I had wanted him to go off somewhere and report to somebody. I switched on my lights when we hit the town. He turned into a dark parking lot opposite the Princess Hotel. I drove on by and went around the next corner. I parked and ran back to the corner. I stuck my head around the bricks just in time to see him walk up the steps to the entrance. I gave him plenty of time to get out of the lobby, and then Jerry and I went on in.

Once upon a time, the Princess was a reputable second-class hotel. I could see from the lobby that it was now running about seventh. It smelled of stale cigars and cheap disinfectant. The sodden furniture and the greasy tile floor held the memories of ten thousand traveling salesmen.

There was one light in the deserted lobby. It was over the desk. A young citizen with a bald head, oversized teeth and a vile necktie gave us a quick glance as we walked up.

"Double room, sir?" he said with a faint leer, spinning the register around.

Jerry frowned at him and I said: "Wrong guess, friend. I got a present for you." I took out a five and creased it lengthwise and set it on the marble counter. It stood up like a little tent.

He reached for it and I tapped him on the back of the hand with my middle finger. They say that concert pianists can bust plate glass with their little finger. I can rap pretty good with my middle one.

He snatched his hand back and rubbed it. "Funny guy, hey?"

"Not at all. I just want to be understood before you fasten onto my dough. I got some curiosity about a guy who lives here. I want to know who comes to see him."

"Maybe I can tell you and maybe I can't. Some of the . . . uh, guests, pay a little extra so they won't be bothered with guys who are curious. Maybe the guy you want to know about has paid us some insurance."

I tried to think quickly. I decided that time was so short, it wouldn't hurt to let him know. "Jake Thomason."

"Let me see. Thomason. Thomason." He riffled through a visible file that hung on the side of the cashier's cage. "Room two-eleven. No insurance. Now what is it you want to know?"

Just then I heard steps clacking across the tile toward the desk. I winked at the desk clerk and slipped my arms around Jerry's waist. I edged her down the desk into the shadows and murmured in her ear: "Make out like you go for this." She put her hands on my shoulders and I went just a little bit dizzy.

I heard the man behind me say: "Give two-eleven a buzz. Tell him Joe is here."

The clerk stepped over to the switchboard. "Mr. Thomason? Desk. Man named Joe wants to come up. O.K.?" He yanked out the plug and said: "O.K., go on up. You'll have to use the stairs. Elevator man's across the street getting some coffee."

I felt Jerry stiffen a little in my arms. When the man had clumped up the stairs, she drew me away from the desk and pulled my head down so she could get her lips close to my ear.

"Hey, I know who that was. Mr. Sellers. He runs the Western Inn. I tried to get a job there just before Mr. Browne hired me."

I turned back to the desk. "You can keep the five. I changed my mind. I'm not curious any more." I tossed it onto the marble counter.

He snatched it up. "Sure, mister, sure. And don't bother telling me to keep my mouth shut. You're a five-dollar friend. I don't get so many of those. Maybe I can sell you something sometime."

I walked slowly out with Jerry on my arm. I walked back to the car and we sat and had a cigarette. She tried to ask me questions but I shushed her while I did some thinking. It had to be more than a coincidence. Night club managers don't go calling on other night clubs' dishwashers. It fitted in with the shoes.

I could tell by the set of Jerry's shoulders that she was getting annoyed with me. "Hey, Jerry. Wait up. I had to do some thinking. The way I figure it, this guy Sellers is running the shakedown. Jake has to be his plant out at the Howler's place. Now all I got to do is tell the Howler and we'll have the cops give Sellers a going over. But something may go on here. Do you think you can do something for me? Alone?"

I grabbed her hand again and she softened. "I guess so, Bud."

"You saw that all-night cafeteria across the street and down a ways from the hotel? It's got a big window in the front end. You go on in there and sit where you can see the front of the hotel. Nurse some coffee along and get nasty if they try to charge you rent for the table. I'll be back after you."

She didn't want to be left alone. She said no twice, and finally yes. I let her out and headed on back for the Quin Pines. I was restless and excited. I tried to shove my foot down into the motor.

I skidded into the parking lot in a shower of gravel. The club was dark. I slammed the door and sprinted over the knoll toward the Howler's house. I knew he would be glad to hear the new angle.

After about three minutes of leaning on the bell and banging the door, Mrs. Browne came and opened it a crack. Her hair was in curling gadgets and her eyes looked sleepy.

"Why, hello, Bud. What's the matter? Where's Stephen?"

I had to adjust to that. Finally I remembered that it was the right name for the Howler. I gasped. "Isn't he in there? Isn't he asleep."

"He hasn't come back from the club yet."

I stood on one foot and then on the other. I had seen that the club was dark. I didn't know what to say. She looked anxious and less sleepy. Then we both heard it—the thin sharp crack of a shot. Small caliber. From the direction of the club. I turned without a word or a look and raced back faster than I had come. I had to go over the knoll, across a corner of the parking lot and across the back yard of the club.

I was making such good time that I skidded and almost fell when I hit the gravel. As I raced onto the dark lawn, a dim shape loomed up in front of me. I swerved and stopped. I must have looked as dark and mysterious to him as he did to me. The fact that he didn't look big enough to be the Howler decided me. I hesitated a fraction of a second and then dove at his knees. It is the last time in my life that I shall ever dive at anyone's knees—even a four year old child's.

You leave the ground with your hands spread out. You can't turn in the air. All the opposite party has to do is sling a large fist in between your paws. Automatically it will catch you in the lower half of the face.

The world exploded in a ball of red fire and I lay on my back. The dank grass tickled the back of my neck. I heard footsteps hurrying across the gravel. I didn't want to sit up. I didn't want to move. I wanted to rest in peace.

I found something in my mouth. It turned out to be a small chunk of tooth. I sat up and grabbed the grass to keep from falling off the lawn. In the distance, a car roared away. Some late crickets cheeped at me. I got to my feet just as Mrs. Browne came up. Her terry-cloth robe was white against the shadows.

"Mrs. Browne," I said softly and she hurried over to me. "I just got slugged by somebody who was leaving in a hurry." I didn't talk so well with a piece of my front tooth missing. The cold air hurt it. It made me whistle on the letter *s*. My chin was damp and sticky with blood. "Maybe the Howler's around here someplace."

She held onto my arm and we circled the joint. We found him half in and half out of the side door. He moaned and I stumbled over him. I lit a match. He was face down, his hand opening and shutting against the concrete. Mrs. Browne moaned and slipped down beside him. I caught her before she hit her head. I slapped her conscious and made her wait while I brought my car over. We wrestled him into the front seat. She sat and held him up while I drove back across the field to their house. It strained me to get him in onto the day bed in the study. While she was phoning the doctor, I pulled his blood-stained shirt out of his pants and took a look. He had a small hole right in the center of the plump mound of his tummy. It looked bad.

He stopped moaning and opened his eyes. "Bud!" he exclaimed faintly. "These guys . . . awful rough . . . turned out the last light and started to go home . . . fella backed me back into the joint with a gun . . . told me to sell out . . . said the syndicate wanted to take over . . . made me mad . . . wouldn't let me turn on light . . . I tried to grab him and he shot me . . . burning hot . . . legs all numb . . . don't leave me."

I knelt down beside him and said: "Maybe it's all clear now, Howler. I found Sellers, the guy that runs the Western Inn, visiting our dishwasher. Hey! Did you hear me?" He didn't answer. His eyes were shut. He was breathing heavily.

Mrs. Browne came back in, her fingers woven together. "I don't know what to do. I telephoned the doctor. Should I phone the police right away?"

Just then we heard the door buzzer. She hurried to the front door. I heard her say, "Oh!" in a disappointed tone. John C. Winch, bland and tanned, walked into the room.

"Hello, Bud, I just stopped to see—" He saw the Howler on the day bed and saw the blood. His jaw dropped. "What? When did it happen? Was he shot?"

"Yeah. Shot about twenty minutes ago. The doc should be here. What'd you come over for?"

"I guess I was too late. I was sleeping and I got a phone call. The man didn't tell me his name. Just said that I better convince Browne he ought to sell out or he maybe would be shot. Told me that I better convince him quick. I dressed and hurried right over."

"Sell out be damned, Winch. That isn't the way to handle this thing. You got to fight."

"Sure, and get what Browne got. You look like you got some of it too."

I took a look in the mirror. I was a mess. My lips were three times too big and my chin and collar were blood-caked. Mrs. Browne had been standing by listening.

"I want my husband to get out of this, if he doesn't die." She sat in a chair and covered her face with her hands. Her shoulders didn't shake. She just sat there as still as the picture on the front of a movie house.

"What's the legal opinion about calling in the gestapo?" I asked.

He rubbed his chin and glanced at the Howler. "I guess we can take a chance on waiting to see what the doc says. Maybe we won't have to. It might be best all around if we didn't."

"Leave the cops out of it if you want to, Winch, but I got a lead and I'm going to chase it up. I'm beginning to get annoyed at this whole thing."

Before he had a chance to answer, the buzzer whined again and Mrs. Browne let the doctor in. He hurried over and started to push gently at the sides of the wound. I walked out without a word. I was scared, shaken and mad. I climbed into my car and drove back to the parking lot. I didn't have any idea where to go or what to do.

Just as I reached the lot, a taxi turned in. Jerry got out. I could see her by my headlights. I stopped, walked over and paid the man off. She stood there until he had spun around and headed out.

She grabbed me by the sleeve. "I watched and finally that man came out with Mr. Sellers. They went off in Mr. Sellers' car. I couldn't find a taxi to follow them. I don't know where they went."

"That's great. That's dandy."

"What's the matter, Bud?" she said, pouting. "Didn't I do it right?"

"Sure, you did fine. Only somebody shot the boss and he's in bad shape. It's probably too late."

"Oh!" She hung her head.

"If he's out, I'm going back and see what I can find in his room.

That jerk behind the desk will let me in for a few bucks."

"Can I come?"

"Not this time, honey. You'll just be in the way. You go on to bed and I'll see you in the morning. It's four o'clock already." She pouted again and walked off toward the barn. I wondered idly why none of the kids had been awakened by the shot. Then I realized that they probably had. In the club business, it turns out most times to be a good idea to stay away from places where you hear shots.

Thinking of shots reminded me that maybe I had better start running around with a gun like everybody else. I hurried up to my room and dug my .32 automatic out of my bureau drawer. I keep it under a green shirt. I seldom use the shirt and I have never used the gun. I won it in a crap game in San Diego, full clip and all.

I ran back out to the car and headed for Casling for the second time. I made good time getting in.

The clerk gave me a gentle sneer and said: "Back again, I see."

"No time for talk, sonny. Do I get a key to two-eleven for ten bucks, or do we argue some more?"

He shrugged and turned his back on me. Then he turned around again and slid a key across the counter. I hauled out a ten and gave it to him. He stuck it in his pocket as though it were an old gum-wrapper. "Any trouble about this, mister, and I say you snitched it while I was asleep."

I went on upstairs. Two-eleven was three doors on the right from the head of the stairs. I listened for a minute outside the door. The room seemed to be dark. No light showed under the door. I slipped the key in and it worked quietly. I shut the door gently behind me and found the wall switch.

It was the world's average cheap hotel room. A scratched walnut bed, one bleary window, pink and white cotton blankets, sagging springs, holes worn in the rug, only one bulb working in the over-head light, dripping faucets in the tiny bathroom, one cane chair, a bureau with a cracked glass top, an ash tray advertising beer, a glass half full of water and a liverish color scheme of soiled green and dusty maroon.

I tried the bureau first. Cheap clean clothes. Nothing else. I tried the closet. Cheap dirty clothes. Nothing under the mattress. I stood in the middle of the room and scratched my head. Where do the detectives look? I was wondering what was under the rug when I heard a stealthy clicking noise at the door. I snatched the gun out of my jacket pocket and stepped into the bathroom. I didn't have time to click the light switch. I felt cold sweat jump out on my forehead. I felt slightly dizzy. I pulled the door shut a little so I could see through the crack.

The door swung open so violently that it banged back against the wall. No one stepped in. I caught a flash of movement and tried to level the gun at it. A hand and arm reached quickly around the door and flicked toward the light switch. The room became abruptly black. A dim light from the hall silhouetted the door.

Then something moved quickly through the shadows and was in the room with me. I wanted to yell but my mouth was too dry.

Then a husky voice said: "O.K., Morse. Toss your gun on the floor."

The sound of my own name shocked me. I stuffed the gun down into the side of my right shoe and said: "I haven't got a gun. I haven't got anything, Thomason."

There was silence for a few seconds. Then, dryly: "I believe you. That's just the kind of a sucker play you'd make. Where are you standing?"

"In the bathroom."

"Stand outside the door of the bathroom."

I did as I was told. I heard the door shut again and then the lights clicked on. I had been straining my eyes in the dark and the sudden brightness made me blink. John C. Winch stood in front of me, an efficient-looking gun leveled at my middle. He had a smile on his tan face. He stepped forward and slapped my pockets and then stepped back.

"Surprised? Now go on over and sit on the bed."

I walked over. I had to move carefully to keep from dropping the gun out of my shoe. I hoped the pants cuff covered it enough. I tucked my feet back under the hanging spread when I sat down.

"You don't have to tell me, Winch. I can tell you. I've been a dope. You and Sellers and Thomason are behind this thing. You were in a perfect position to know how much the Howler could stand to pay. Now you're greedy and you want his place. You'll buy it through some dummy and start to rake off real profits."

He smiled down at me, but the muzzle of the gun didn't waver. "You're a smart boy, Morse, but not smart enough. You should have figured all this before. Then you could have handed me some real trouble."

"One thing I can't figure. Why let me know you're in on it? You won't be safe now, because you can't scare me."

"Scare you, Bud? Who wants to scare you? I wouldn't think of scaring you."

He stood and grinned down at me. I've never seen a colder pair of eyes. I realized then that he was probably a little insane. I knew that he wouldn't have to scare me. I wouldn't be able to talk with one of those little lead slugs nestling in my brain. The room seemed to sway around me. I sat on the edge of the bed and let my hands hang down. I couldn't reach the gun in my shoe without stooping over. The mouth of his gun was saying: "Don't move, brother!"

He stopped smiling and nibbled at the edge of his finger. "I wish you'd brought a gun, Morse. You make it tough."

I looked behind him and saw the doorknob move. I've never learned how to keep expressions off my pug face. He probably knew I couldn't swing a gag, and when he saw my eyes widen and where they were looking, he backed off so that he could cover me and the door at the same time.

I watched his eyes and saw them flick over toward the door. I swooped after the gun and brought it up, pressing hard on the trigger at the same time. "Drop your gun, chump!" I hollered. I rolled off the bed as I brought the gun up. Nothing happened. I realized with sudden horror that an automatic won't work unless you jack a cartridge up into the chamber first by yanking on the slide. I hadn't. His gun snapped and something picked at my sleeve.

I looked up from the floor and kept pulling on the useless trigger.

His cold right eye sighted down the barrel. I could look right into it. I shut my eyes, and another shot blasted in the room. I wondered if I was dead.

I opened my right eye. Winch was still looking at me, but the gun barrel had sagged a little. He was smiling. His eyes didn't look quite so cold. He leaned toward me, further and further and then I scrambled aside as he fell over toward me. His head crashed into my left shoulder and he bounded off. He lay on the floor with a neat hole through the top of his left ear. The hole didn't stop there. It went right on in.

I looked up. The door was open. Jake Thomason stood in the doorway, a gun in his hand. He looked down at me with an expression of infinite disgust. He shoved the gun into his pocket and stepped into the room. He kicked the door shut. He sat down on the wicker chair as I climbed up onto the bed again.

"You better have a cigarette, Morse. Your hand's shaking." He held out a pack and I took one.

"Hand, hell. I'm shaking all over. I'll be shaking just like this on my next birthday. I'm going to keep right on shaking for a couple of years."

"You ought to. So had every other amateur that fools around with stuff like this."

"I'm beginning to think maybe I had you wrong in this, Thomason."

"You sure did, and I knew you were digging around. I thought I'd let you. Thought it might stir up the big shot here." He reached his foot out and nudged Winch in the ribs. Winch seemed to be flattening out against the floor. "And the name's Burke. Jake Burke. I work for the Associated Restaurant Managers and Owners Group. I'm a trouble shooter. Sellers sent for me and I planted myself in Browne's place. You can figure the rest out. Winch, here, got greedy. He set up a shakedown racket. Then he decided he wanted Browne's place. Made the payments high. Tried to talk Browne into selling. Got Browne in the dark to scare him. Shot him. That was a mistake."

I raised my eyebrows and he said: "Don't look puzzled. I just came from there. Browne'll be O.K. Slug went right around him, under the hide, and wedged against his backbone. The doc has it out already. Give him a month and he'll be louder than ever."

"How did you know about me?"

"You! You looked at me like I had shot Lincoln. You followed me about thirty feet behind me. I could see the streetlights reflected on your headlights. I stayed at the top of the stairs and watched you and the gal talk to Jonesy down at the desk. Sellers thought you looked a little queer too. I told you this is no business for amateurs."

"If you're so smart, why didn't you pick him up quicker?"

"He was too smart, Morse. Used the telephone. Also, I couldn't step in on any of the payoffs. He had kids delivering the bucks in every case. Couldn't take a chance. Had to wait until he got worried about you catching onto him and about me. I don't think he had me figured, but I guess he was going to try to knock you off with my gun and me off with yours—if you had one."

There was a knock at the door. A gentle knock. Burke shouted: "Come in!"

The door opened and Jerry stepped timidly into the room. She looked down at the body of Winch, and her eyes widened. She circled widely around him and ran into my arms. She was shaking. I put my arms around her. Her hair smelled good. Burke started to laugh.

"This your girl?" he asked. I nodded. He stepped over and grabbed her wrist. He snapped something onto it and yanked her away from me. I started up with the vague idea of swinging on him. He was still laughing. She fumbled in her bag. He slapped the bag down onto the floor and a small automatic bounded out of it and balanced grotesquely between Winch's shoulderblades. She stopped struggling and hung her head.

"I told you you were an amateur. Why don't you think things out, Morse? Winch was in this with this gal. She was the plant in Browne's place. That's why I tried to date her. That's how he got on to me. She told him. And she told him about you wanting her to help follow me. That made him wonder who I could be. How did he know you were here? She waited until he came out of Browne's place and then told him. She saw his car out there. She probably waited in it. How did she get here? She probably came down with him. I figure she probably wore a man's hat and covered her face and helped him collect each month."

He tilted her chin up roughly and looked into her eyes. "I'll even bet she figured out that gag of using kids for the payoff."

She jerked her chin away from his fingers and said: "Suppose I did?"

There was a heavy fist banging at the door and Burke said: "That'll be the cops that I told Jonesy to send for. We'll all have to go down and make out statements and stuff."

He tugged at the steel bracelet on her wrist and whispered: "Come on, honey. Let's go answer the door." Dawn made her face look yellowish.

And suddenly I realized that when I got back to the piano I was going to do a cornball job on "Melancholy Baby." I was really going to do it up. I'd play it for the Howler.

THE SECRET OF FORT BAYARD   Georges Simenon

Translated from the original French by Anthony Boucher

To ask Georges Simenon why or how he wrote a particular story is to invite, not disaster, but a charming letter explaining that M. Simenon has written so many stories he has no idea how any one of them came into being. This is the case with The Secret of Fort Bayard, *which was born, obviously, within sight of a ruined French fortress and which doubtless took its present form in the mind of its prolific author almost without his being aware of the process.*

Simenon himself has no notion how many short stories, or for that matter, how many novels, he has written since, at the ripe age of 16, he first began writing for a newspaper in Liége, Belgium, his birthplace. Four years later he went to Paris where for many years he earned a living writing all kinds of stories for all kinds of people under all kinds of pseudonyms; later he turned to novels as well, and created the world-renowned Inspector Maigret, who does not, however, figure in The Secret of Fort Bayard.

Simenon, who has lived in many parts of the world, is now a more or less permanent resident of Connecticut.

THE EDITORS

We missed the most terrible part of this adventure, G. 7 and I. But the case remains my most vivid nightmare. The most sinister prison seems to me a delightful spot compared with Fort Bayard.

This fort is on an islet off La Rochelle. Two large islands, Ré and Oléron, here lie parallel to the coast, thus enclosing a magnificent roadstead which was formerly of strategic importance. Napoleon, among others, bestrewed it with forts which still stand amid the waves. The best known of these is Fort Bayard.

In the center of the roadstead, hardly a mile from Bayard, lies the island of Aix, on which a hundred or so inhabitants live—mostly on fish and particularly on oysters.

The setting is a harsh one, even in the summer season. In November it is sinister. The ocean roars and surges, and the people of Aix are sometimes cut off from the mainland for weeks.

When we arrived, the excitement aroused by the affair had not yet died down, but the worst was over. We landed on the island of Aix one foggy noonday. The gasoline lamps were already lit in the houses. You could believe that it was twilight.

G. 7 had George's house pointed out to him. This George was the only fisherman on the island who had his own small cutter to haul his net. We found him at home, before the fireplace, surrounded by his wife and three children. He was a man of about forty, large, strong, rough-looking, but with a disconcerting calm about him.

Despite which, public opinion had accused him of the most hideous crime. The woman's eyes seemed to me dead and lightless. Even the children seemed crushed by the atmosphere of suspicion that pressed down on the house.

The dialogue was brief:

"Will you take us to the fort?"

George didn't stir. "Now?"

"Yes, now." G. 7 showed his badge.

The man rose, took down his oilskin from a hook, threw it around his shoulders, and changed his wooden shoes for hip boots. For a moment he looked at us in our city clothes, then shrugged as though to say, "So much the worse for you. . . ."

A quarter of an hour later, we were on the bridge of the cutter, clinging to the rigging as we pitched unceasingly, our eyes fixed on the black walls of Fort Bayard as its outline slowly became clear through the fog.

At the helm, George never opened his mouth. There was such a calm in the man's blue eyes that it hurt me to look at him.

A week earlier, a yacht cruising through these parts had anchored by the iron ladder that still stands on one of the walls of Fort Bayard.

It's a dangerous spot, full of rocks. The fishermen never go there unless for some very good reason. The crumbling walls are a danger, too. Though there is a narrow opening through which you can get into what's left of the fort, no one ever had the curiosity to do so, for fear of a blow on the head from one of the rocks that fall from time to time.

The yachting party were strangers to the district and lacked the natives' prudence. That is how they came to make their monstrous discovery.

There was a being living in the fort. A human being. *A woman.*

You'd have to see the place to realize how much those words mean. The papers are fond of sob-stuff about the hard lot of the lighthouse-keepers, isolated out in the ocean. But lighthouses are livable. At least other men come there occasionally. At Fort Bayard, the wind whirls in through a hundred holes. The rain pours down through a roof that is now nothing but a few beams.

The woman was naked. When she saw strangers, her first movement was to flee.

And now, while we were sailing to what had been her prison, she was in a mental sanitarium in La Rochelle, surrounded by doctors.

She was eighteen. A girl.

But what a girl . . . ! Knowing nothing of human speech, casting frightened glances about her like a hunted animal, hurling herself avidly upon her food. . . .

As I said at first, we arrived only when the case was almost over. The photograph of the girl had appeared in all the papers. And already a man had come from Amsterdam who had recognized her, who had given a name to that enigmatic face: Clara Van Gindertael.

"Here! Grab the ladder!"

George held tight to the helm. We had reached the fort. The surf could shatter our boat against it. G. 7 grasped an iron rung and passed a mooring rope over it.

So this was the examination of the scene of the crime. What should one call it? A prison? But even prisons have roofs. . . .

Four ancient walls. Loose rocks. Seaweed. Rubble and rubbish of all kinds. I could imagine the girl crouching in some corner. . . .

I tried to imagine the man who must have brought her food regularly. Mechanically I turned to George, who seemed calmly detached from all that lay around us.

When the yachting party had found Clara Van Gindertael, there had been a stock of provisions for her not more than a month old. Public rumor accused the fisherman. People remembered that he was the only man who ever dared the dangers of this region and dragged his net near the fort.

I examined his features. I asked myself if it were possible that this man, whom I'd just seen at home with his children, could have been coming here for thirteen years, bringing monthly provisions for a human being.

Thirteen years! Clara was five then. Much the same age as George's children. . . . It was horrible. I felt unhappy. I was impatient to get away from this accursed fort.

The magistrates had already questioned the fisherman.

His answers had cast no light on the problem: "I don't know anything. I never saw the woman you're talking about. I used to fish around the fort, but I never set foot inside. . . ."

He ended his deposition with a question which embarrassed his examiners: "Where am I supposed to have picked up this little girl?"

The fact is that she was kidnaped in Paris, where George had never been. G. 7 had showed me an old newspaper clipping:

> A mysterious abduction took place yesterday in a hotel in the Avenue Friedland.
>
> For some days a Dutchman, M. Pieter Claessens, had been occupying a suite on the first floor of this hotel, which he shared with his five-year-old niece, Clara Van Gindertael, the child heiress, whose guardian he is, since she is an orphan.
>
> His personal valet looked after the child.
>
> Yesterday then, while M. Claessens was out, this servant went down to the kitchens where he remained about an hour, leaving the child alone in the suite. When he returned, she had disappeared.
>
> The description of the little girl is as follows: rather large for her age, slender, fair hair, blue eyes, wearing a white silk dress, white socks, and black patent-leather shoes.
>
> The police have begun an investigation.

Pieter Claessens had arrived at La Rochelle three days after the discovery of the girl who was still known only, in the phrase of the press, as "the Fort Bayard Unknown." He read in the papers the account of the yachtsmen's find. There was a photograph of the girl. And there was the statement that she had on her left wrist the scar of an old burn.

This was what clinched the identification for her guardian. He said that she had received the burn when she was only four, from the explosion of an alcohol heater.

That was as far as the affair had gone. You can imagine the many questions that arose:

Who had kidnaped Clara Van Gindertael thirteen years ago?

Why had she been taken to Fort Bayard?

Who had regularly brought her provisions?

What interests were at work behind this maddening drama?

The one most concerned, the victim herself, could not speak a word. According to the doctors, it would take many years to make a normal human being of her. Some specialists doubted that it could ever be done.

Reporters argued furiously over Fort Bayard. Photographs of the spot had appeared in all the dailies. The most unlikely hypotheses had been seriously considered.

It was a wonder that George was still at liberty. I knew myself that this was at the express order of G. 7, who had telegraphed from Paris to La Rochelle as soon as he got wind of the affair.

What was his own opinion? And why had our first step been to visit the fort, though it had seemed more logical to me to start off by seeing the victim herself, especially since we had to come through La Rochelle?

I had no idea.

G. 7 was as calm as the fisherman.

The two men were not without certain points of resemblance. One was as niggardly with words as the other. They both had the same clear eyes, the same imposing figure.

Was their silence with each other a sort of challenge?

I was ill at ease. I wandered clumsily around the square enclosure, my feet slipping on the seaweed. The empty food containers had a more sinister significance here than elsewhere.

There was a mountain of them.

It was beginning to get dark all around us, though it was only three o'clock. We heard the prow of the boat striking against the wall with every wave.

As for G. 7, he paced up and down with long slow strides, his head lowered.

"You've been married how long?" he asked suddenly, turning toward George.

The fisherman started, then answered promptly: "Eighteen years."

"You . . . you love your wife?"

I saw his Adam's apple quiver. It was some moments before he spoke. At last I heard a dull murmur: ". . . and the kids . . ."

"Let's go!" G. 7 concluded unexpectedly. He turned toward the only break in the walls through which we could get back to the cutter. He took my arm. And he whispered, while George hoisted the sails, "The affair has only begun!"

I heard the rest of his speech in snatches. There was a storm coming up. I kept my eyes riveted on George, who sat motionless in the stern, wrapped up in his oilskin, the helm between his legs, his attention fixed on the swelling of the sail.

"The guilty man," G. 7 said, "betrayed himself, you see. Reread that clipping I gave you. Reread the description of the child. The point at that time was to give the most complete description possible, wasn't it? A description that would help find her? It lists the details of shoes, even socks. And it doesn't say a word about the burn on the wrist. Why? *Because that burn didn't as yet exist!* Thanks to that, I knew the truth even before we came here. . . .

"Or listen: Pieter Claessens has no fortune of his own. But he's the uncle and guardian of Clara, who is very rich in her own right. At the same time he is the child's heir. . . .

"Is he afraid to commit, strictly speaking, a crime? . . . Does he fear that he'll be accused. . . . I don't know. . . . At any rate he shuts up Clara, or has her shut up, in Fort Bayard and there abandons her to her fate. . . . She is sure to die there. . . .

"After the delays of legal formalities, he inherits. He returns to his own country. He doesn't think of the child again. . . .

"Then why, suddenly, after thirteen years, does he feel this intense need of knowing what's become of her, of making sure that she's really dead? I'll bet anything you please that he had his eye on an inheritance which only the girl herself could receive. . . .

"Claessens tells himself that she may be alive, that people may have picked her up. . . . He comes back secretly to see. . . . At Fort Bayard, he finds her. . . .

"But still he has to find her *officially*. There still has to be his official *identification*. Merely a resemblance, after so many years, wouldn't do for the courts. . . . Some identifying mark is better. . . . a scar, for example. . . . He has only to burn the girl's wrist. . . .

"Claessens returns to Holland and waits long enough for the scar to seem reasonably old. The girl's exposed life would help there. His accomplices play out the comedy of the yacht and the discovery. The papers announce the find. He rushes to the spot—too fast, in fact. Beforehand he spreads the story of the scar. . . .

"There was the slip! I repeat, if that scar had existed at the time of the kidnaping, it *must* have appeared in the description. . . .

"Do you understand now that the affair has only begun? That man thinks himself safe, free from all suspicion. . . . Another man has been accused."

"George?" I asked.

G. 7 glanced at the fisherman and lowered his voice. "And George won't talk. . . . Why? . . . He found the child, long ago, by pure chance. . . . He hid his discovery for motives that I can't explain to myself too clearly. . . . These simple people can sometimes have horribly complicated souls. Was he afraid that they'd think his story was a myth? That his wife might suspect him of palming off as a foundling a child of his own? Again, I don't know. . . . He fed the child. Little by little she became a woman. . . . Now do you begin to see? It is monstrous, I know. They say that Clara, despite her strange life, is beautiful. . . ."

Up till then I had never stopped looking at George. Now I turned abruptly to the sea. It was a relief to lose myself in the tumult of the raging elements.

THE DOG DIED FIRST   Bruno Fischer

*As I remember, the opening of this story came to me one night
as I was waiting for my wife to come home from somewhere.
Unlike our heroine, I am happy to report, she doesn't play bridge;
her nocturnal activities are considerably more worth while, such
as P.T.A., Mental Hygiene and Socialism. Anyway, she was out
and I was in; and probably between the time I roused at the
sound of the car coming up the driveway and her entrance into
the house, it occurred to me that it would be an interesting gimmick if she had brought a murdered body home with her. Or
at least blood on the car floor.*

*Thus a writer feeds on his own, heaven help him. Including,
in this case, also the family pet when the developing plot required
a dog.*

*Naturally I used as a model the one at hand—our little black
mongrel with a white spot over her nose and white paws. Her
name was Maxine and she'd been with us since she'd been four
weeks old. Possibly this story of the untimely death of her fictional counterpart put the whammy on her. Shortly after it appeared in print, she too suffered a violent death, having lived
eight years and inflicted numberless progeny on the neighborhood. The theory is that her love of sweets was her undoing,
poisoned by strychnine on ant buttons carelessly left within her
reach.*

*Actually we don't know. Her death remains a mystery, and
there should be another story in that, but so far I haven't come
up with any.*

BRUNO FISCHER

Blood was on my mind that night, but it was blood of the French
Revolution. I was correcting Modern European History papers while
Dot was at a hen party at Marie Cannon's. At midnight I went to
bed, knowing that between bridge and chitchat there was no telling
when Dot would be home.

The sound of the car pulling into the driveway woke me. As we
have no garage in our bungalow-type stucco house, we leave the car

out in the open on the cinder driveway. I heard Dot enter the house through the back door, and then I was listening to water running in the kitchen.

It ran for a long time—too long for her to be getting a drink and she certainly wouldn't be washing herself at the kitchen sink. Drowsily I was wondering what she was up to now, and I wondered a lot more when she turned off the water and left the house again. The radium clock on the dresser said five minutes after one.

I turned on my side and looked through the window. Dot had left the car's headlights on and she was walking into their glare. The pail she carried in her right hand was evidently full of water. The weight of it made her neat hips sway. She opened the back sedan door, switched on the overhead light, dug a dripping scrubbing brush out of the pail and leaned inside the car.

So that explained her antics. No doubt somebody had spilled liquid on the upholstery and she was trying to scrub it off before it dried. I dug my head into the pillow to shut out the glow of the headlights coming in through the window.

I was almost asleep when the night lamp went on in the bedroom.

"Are you awake, darling?" Dot asked.

"Um, umph, um," I mumbled, turning my head to let her know I was too sleepy for conversation.

But as nothing ever stopped Dot from talking, my desire for slumber didn't. I'd trained myself to absorb her chatter without listening to it, and that was what I did then until a startling sentence jerked me fully awake.

"I couldn't get all the blood off," she had said.

"Blood?" I breathed, opening my eyes wide. "Did you say blood?"

Dot was taking a nightgown out of a drawer. "He died on the way to the doctor," she said complacently. "I feel like a murderer."

She straightened up with the nightgown in her hand. The soft, dim night light played over her tightly and precisely formed body, and her face was as guileless as a doll's.

"Who died?" I demanded hoarsely.

"The dog, of course," she said, dropping the nightgown over her head.

I sank back on the bed. A dog, of course. Well, what had I really expected?

"I wasn't going to tell you because you're always criticizing my driving," she explained. "Like when I smashed a fender last week. But I really couldn't help what happened tonight. The dog ran right under the wheel. Then when I got home I noticed the blood in the car and I tried to wash it off, but I couldn't quite because it had dried. I decided to tell you because you'll see it tomorrow."

I was drowsy again, but puzzled. "How does blood get inside a car when you run over a dog?"

"He was still breathing, so I took him to the vet, but he was dead when I got there. The dog, I mean. The poor little thing."

She put out the light and got into bed, but that didn't stop her voice. She told me about the dollar and seventeen cents she had lost at bridge and that Ida Walker looked dowdy and Marie Cannon stunning and Edith Bauer—

"How about some sleep?" I complained.

She was quiet—for about a minute, it seemed to me. Then she was shaking me.

"Bernie," she whispered, "there's somebody sneaking about outside with a flashlight."

The radium clock said ten minutes after three, which meant that I'd actually been asleep about two hours. Dot was sitting up, and past the vague outline of her shoulder and through the window I saw a splotch of light move along the side of the car.

"Maybe he's trying to steal the car," she whispered.

"Did you leave the key in the ignition?"

It didn't surprise me when she admitted that she thought she had. Snorting, I got out of bed and went to the window. Whoever held the flashlight seemed to have lost interest in the car and was walking toward the street.

"He's going away," I said hopefully. I was a man who liked to avoid trouble.

"I wonder what he wanted."

"I know what I want," I said. "Sleep."

I had one leg on the bed when the doorbell rang. I froze half on the bed, listening. There are few things more disturbing than a doorbell ringing at three in the morning.

"That must be the thief," Dot whispered.

I roused myself. "Thieves don't ring doorbells."

"Well, it's somebody," Dot pointed out.

It certainly was somebody. The doorbell kept on ringing. I fumbled into slippers and robe, went into the living room, turned on the light, opened the front door.

The man who entered held a flashlight in his hand, so he was the same one I had seen prowling outside. He had more paunch than chest and a lumpy face.

"Mr. Bernard Hall?" he said.

I nodded. "What is it?"

He didn't answer. He stepped past me into the living room, looked it over as if he were thinking of renting it, then fixed me with rather sad eyes.

"My boy Steve is in your History class. Stephan Ricardo."

"Ah, yes," I said, using my teacher-parent manner. But that was absurd. This man hadn't got me out of bed at three in the morning to discuss his son's scholastic problems. Then I remembered what Stephan Ricardo had told me his father did for a living, and I tensed.

"You're a detective," I said.

"That's right." Ricardo massaged his jowls. "Seems there's blood in your car."

"Is that what you were looking at with your flashlight?"

He nodded. "Uh-huh. There was an attempt made to wash it off, but it was soaked into the floor rug."

At that moment Dot came into the living room. She wore her flowered housecoat over the nightgown.

"I'm the one you want," she said. "I suppose I shouldn't have left the body in the bushes."

Ricardo pushed his hat back from his brow and blinked a couple of times. "You admit you did it, Mrs. Hall?"

"Should I have reported it to the police?" She handed him that disarming smile of hers. "The thing is, I didn't want any trouble."

"No," Ricardo said softly, "I guess you didn't want trouble." He kept looking at Dot as if he didn't quite believe she existed.

"Why did you do it, Mrs. Hall?"

"It was an accident. He ran in front of the car."

Ricardo shook his head sorrowfully. "That won't get you anywhere, Mrs. Hall. His head was smashed in, but there were no other marks on his body."

"But that's impossible. I held him in my arms and his head looked all right. He seemed to be injured internally. He died before I could get him to the vet."

"The vet?" Ricardo said, blinking.

"Dr. Harrison, the veterinary on Mill Street," she explained patiently. "Where else would you take a dog?"

Ricardo opened his mouth, but he didn't say what he started to. Instead he drew in air. "Suppose, Mrs. Hall, you tell me all about it."

Dot settled herself in the armchair and placidly crossed her fine legs. I stuck a cigarette between my lips and noticed that the match shook in my hand. I didn't for a moment believe that a detective would awaken and question her at three in the morning because a dog had been run over.

"I was driving to a bridge game at Marie Cannon's tonight," she said. "About two blocks from here a little black dog ran in front of the car and I couldn't stop in time. I got out and there was the poor creature in terrible agony. He was a little thing, all black with white paws and a white splotch on his face. I don't know what breed, though he had some Spitz in him, because when I was a little girl I had a Spitz that was the darlingest—"

"What time was this?" Ricardo broke in.

"Close to eight-thirty. Marie Cannon was anxious that we get to her house at eight-thirty, and it was just about that when I left here. I would be late, but I couldn't leave an injured dog lying in the road, so I put him in the car and drove to the vet."

"To Dr. Harrison on Mill Street," Ricardo said rather grimly. "A good seven miles away, though you were late."

"Do you know of a nearer veterinary?"

Ricardo admitted that he didn't.

"So I had no choice," Dot said. "But when I got there, I saw that the poor dog was dead, so there was no point to taking him in to Dr.

Harrison. I drove back to East Billford and left the dog in some bushes beside the road."

"Just like that," Ricardo sighed.

Dot flushed guiltily. "I suppose it was a cruel thing to do, but by then it was about ten minutes after nine and the bridge game couldn't start until I got there because I made the fourth and Marie Cannon would be furious with me. And, after all, the dog was dead, wasn't he? And I did look to see if he had a license, but he didn't have even a collar. He was obviously a stray dog, and I didn't know what else to do with him."

After that gush of words there was a silence. I filled it by saying, "I suppose killing a dog should be reported to the police. That's the law, isn't it?"

"Uh-huh." He glanced at me and then returned his sad gaze to Dot. "Did you get blood on your dress when you picked him up?"

"I'm sure I didn't. One of the women at the bridge game would have noticed if I had." She frowned. "He didn't seem to bleed at all, but he must have, because I saw blood in the car when I got home hours later."

"Where did you leave the—ah—body?"

"On Pine Road, in a section where there are no houses. Just this side of that dirt road."

"Wilson Lane," he said.

"Yes, that's it. A short distance past Wilson Lane, coming toward town, there are thick bushes on the right side. That's where I left him."

Ricardo nodded and scratched his cheeks with the backs of his fingers. He was a plump man with too much waist and jowls, but the set of his lumpy face frightened me.

"You better get dressed, Mrs. Hall," he said, "and go there with me."

Her blue eyes widened. "You mean right now?"

"Right now."

"I'm going too," I said.

"Sure," Ricardo said.

We went into the bedroom to put on clothes.

"I don't understand why they make so much trouble about a dog being run over," Dot complained as she slipped her shoes on. "Of course I feel bad about it, but getting people out of bed in the middle of the night! Why doesn't he just give me a ticket and I'll pay the fine?"

I didn't say anything. My stomach was sickishly empty.

We drove in Ricardo's sedan, the three of us in the front seat.

On the way, Dot said, "I suppose Al Wilcox saw me carry the dog into the bushes. He lives down the street and knows me. I saw his white police car pass when I returned to my car."

"That's right, Mrs. Hall," Ricardo said grimly.

It was less than a mile to the spot. Three cars were parked along the side of the road, and by the light of a couple of powerful electric lanterns I saw five or six men gathered on the narrow grassy stretch between the shoulder of the road and the line of thick bushes. One of them was Al Wilcox in his policeman's uniform.

"All these men because a dog was killed!" Dot said. Even she was catching on that something bigger than that must be up.

Ricardo had no comment. He led us across the road and then I saw the long shape under the canvas. The men had become silent and were looking at Dot.

"Mrs. Hall, is this the spot?" Ricardo asked.

She nodded and slipped her hand through my arm. She frowned at the size of the thing under the canvas.

"Give her a look, Cal," Ricardo said.

Wilcox bent over and gripped one end of the canvas and pulled it down. Dot uttered a shrill scream. I felt her sag against my side, clinging to my arm.

"Why that's—that's Emmett Walker!" she gasped. "I played bridge with his wife tonight."

It was Emmett Walker, all right, but no longer the handsome insurance agent Dot and I had known for years. His blond hair was matted with dried blood and some of it had run in ragged streaks over his face.

"Cover him up, Al," Ricardo said wearily. He turned to Dot, and there was controlled fury in his voice. "He was murdered, Mrs. Hall."

"But—but where's the dog?" Dot stammered.

"There is no dog, Mrs. Hall."

"But I left him right there in those bushes."

"No, Mrs. Hall," Ricardo said. "You struck Emmett Walker over the head with something and killed him. You dragged him into your car and drove here and dragged him into the bushes. That's how the blood got in your car."

"It's not true!" Dot had recovered from the shock and was now merely indignant.

At that point I should have said something. I should have come to my wife's defense. But even if I hadn't been too choked for words, I couldn't think of any that would do any good.

Al Wilcox spoke up. "I was passing here at a few minutes after nine, Mrs. Hall, when I saw you come out of these bushes and get into your car. At two o'clock I passed this way again, and by my head-lights I saw what looked like a man's leg sticking out of the bushes. I investigated and found him."

"Well, I didn't do it," Dot said angrily. "Why would I want to kill Emmett Walker?"

"Suppose you tell us, Mrs. Hall."

Dot turned to me in exasperation. "You try to make him understand, darling."

I gulped air into my lungs. I said, "Of course you didn't do it," but my voice quavered.

Ricardo moved away from us to consult with the other policemen in undertones. When he returned to us, he asked Dot if the dress she had on was the one she had worn at the bridge game. She said that it was. Then he asked me for the keys to my car and handed them to Wilcox.

"Okay, let's go," Ricardo snapped.

I didn't ask him where. I knew where.

This time there were four of us in the sedan. I sat beside Ricardo who drove, and Dot sat in the back seat with another detective. Ricardo didn't waste time. He had questions for Dot as we drove.

"Where did you say that bridge game was?"

"At Marie Cannon's house."

"Is she the wife of George Cannon, the lawyer?"

"Yes."

"Who else was there?"

"There were only four of us. Besides Marie and myself, there were Edith Bauer and Ida Walker." Her voice broke a little. "Poor Ida! Who is going to break the news to her?"

"She knows already," Ricardo said. "She didn't take the news too hard."

"They haven't got along too well lately. There were rumors that Emmett wasn't—well, exactly faithful to her." Dot leaned forward toward the back of Ricardo's neck, and her voice was breathless. "Do you think that Ida killed him?"

"I know who killed him," Ricardo said crisply.

That ended all talk until we reached the County Building, which also contained police headquarters and the county jail. Dot was taken into an office on the second floor, but I got no farther than the door.

"You might as well go home," Ricardo told me. "Your wife is being held."

"What are you going to do to her—give her the third degree?"

His lumpy face smiled a little. "We're going to question her."

"She's entitled to have a lawyer present."

"Sure." He waved a pudgy hand. "You'll find a phone booth down the hall."

I went into the booth and dialed George Cannon's number. His voice was drowsy, but it got wide awake when I told him what was up.

"I'll be right there," he said.

I waited out in the hall. In ten minutes George Cannon arrived. His hair was mussed and his suit looked like a sack on his frail body, but that wasn't because he'd dressed in a hurry. He always managed to look seedy and disheveled, though he was the most prominent lawyer in East Billford.

Briefly I gave him the details. His thin mouth tightened as he listened.

"Emmett was supposed to call for Ida tonight," he told me. "She waited in my house until one o'clock and then I drove her home. I think she suspected that he was out with another woman. And all that time he was dead."

"Don't stand here talking," I said. "God knows what they're doing to Dot."

"Oh, they won't be rough with a woman. You wait here, Bernie." He knocked at the door through which Dot had been taken and was admitted.

For a full hour I paced that lonely hall before George came out. Glumly he shook his head. "They've taken her up to a cell through another door. She hasn't been charged yet. There are still loose ends."

"How does it look?"

"It's too soon to tell," he said, not meeting my eyes. "If the blood in the car is a dog's, their circumstantial case will be shot." He patted my shoulder. "No use hanging around here. Go home and get some sleep."

He dropped me off at my house. Dawn was coming up, and in the grayness of it I saw that my car was gone. The police had taken it because it was evidence—evidence that might mean life or death.

The house was terribly empty. I went into the bedroom and there was her nightgown flung across the foot of the bed. I remembered how only a few hours ago I had watched her getting into that nightgown, and nobody could have looked less like a woman who had just murdered somebody.

She hadn't. She said so. She was flighty and talkative, but she had never before lied to me.

But she had never before had occasion to lie about murder. . . .

I tossed in bed for an hour and slept fitfully for another hour. Then the doorbell woke me. It was Herman Bauer, a fellow teacher at the high school. His wife Edith was an old friend of Dot's.

Herman, chubby and usually jolly, was glum and embarrassed. He said that he had stopped off on his way to school to tell me that the police had questioned him and Edith.

"They got us out of bed at six-thirty this morning," Herman said. "They asked Edith about the bridge game last night. When Dot arrived, when she left, if she'd been in the house all that time, and so on. They also asked how well Dot and Emmett had known each other." Uneasily he fumbled with the brim of his hat. "Neither Edith nor I mentioned that Dot used to go out with Emmett."

"That was years ago," I said. "Before Dot and I were engaged."

"Of course." Herman watched his fingers on his hat. "But the police mightn't understand." He turned to the door. "If there's anything I can do for you, let me know."

After Herman Bauer was gone, I stood in the same spot for a long time. He had it all figured out, the way everybody else figured it and the police certainly did. I couldn't know that they weren't right.

Rousing myself, I went to the phone to call the school that I wouldn't be in that day and maybe for the rest of the week. Before I could start to dial the number, the phone rang.

It was George Cannon, and he said, "Bernie, can you come over to the district attorney's office right away?"

"Did anything new break?"

"Yes, but I'm afraid it's not good. The blood in your car has been analyzed." He paused and then added tonelessly, "It's human blood, and it matches Emmett Walker's blood type."

There went the last hope, I thought as I hung up. Police science had proved Dot's story about the dog a lie, and if that was false, everything else she had said was.

I dressed and left the house. The police had my car, so I had to walk to the County Building.

Detective Ricardo and George Cannon were in the district attorney's office. John Fair, the D. A., was one of those backslapping politicians who never met a voter without heartily pumping his hand, but when I entered his office he merely nodded gravely and remained in his seat.

"The analysis of the blood in your car leaves no doubt of your wife's guilt," Fair began brutally. "It took her some forty minutes to arrive at the bridge game after she left home—a distance of little over a mile. We know now that her delay was not caused by killing a dog and driving out to Dr. Harrison's and back. She told the farfetched story about the dog to explain her delay and also the blood in her car. Obviously she met Emmett Walker and killed him with a blunt instrument, probably as he was sitting in the car with her."

"What time was Walker killed?" I asked, grasping at a straw. "I mean, if he died after she arrived at the bridge game—"

Ricardo shook his heavy head. "The medical examiner can't cut it that fine. Says he thinks Walker died between nine and ten-thirty last night, and he'll give or take half an hour at either end."

"What does my wife say?" I asked weakly.

Fair shrugged irritably. "In spite of virtually conclusive evidence, she sticks to her preposterous story about the dog. A very stubborn young woman and extremely foolish." He rose and came around his desk. "Hall, I'm not out for her neck. We have learned that she and Walker were sweethearts at one time. I'm sorry to have to say this to you, but it appears that she continued to be one of his women up until last night."

"No!" I heard myself shout.

"We haven't proved it yet," Fair admitted, "but that explains her motive for killing him. Let us say she struck him in jealous rage. In that case, I would not insist on a first-degree murder indictment. I want you to talk to her, Hall. I want you to make her see that it will be to her advantage to make a full confession."

"Prison," I said bitterly. "Is that what you offer her, years and years in prison?"

"It's better than the electric chair," Fair said softly and returned to his desk.

George Cannon hadn't said a word since I entered the office. He was our legal mind. I asked him for his opinion.

"Bernie, I'm against any deal," he declared. "I believe I can get her off free."

He believed! I looked at him standing there, seedy and slight and his pinched face with that perpetually hungry expression. He was the top lawyer in East Billford, but it was a small city and his reputation didn't extend beyond it. He didn't think her innocent—nobody did—but he was willing to risk her life to build up his reputation in a sensational murder trail.

"I'll talk to her," I told the district attorney.

Ricardo led me upstairs to a small bare room containing only a few chairs, and left me there. A few minutes later a matron brought Dot in.

There were tired lines about her eyes and mouth, but she looked beautiful. She felt wonderful in my arms and her tremulous mouth was unendurably sweet. The electric chair, I thought dully, or years in prison that would be a living death for her.

After a minute she slipped out of my embrace. "I'd like a cigarette, darling," she said.

I lit it for her, and she sat down and crossed her legs and drew smoke into her lungs. "Darling," she said then, "they're saying terrible things about me."

She sounded indignant. Not frightened, not broken up, but merely outraged that she should be accused of having done anything wrong.

"They're even saying that Emmett was my lover," she went on angrily.

"Was he?"

When the words were out of my mouth, I hated myself for saying them. But I had to know.

Her eyebrows arched. "Darling, you don't think that too?"

"Was he, Dot?"

"Certainly not." Again that vast indignation. "Emmett meant little to me, even when I went out a few times with him before I married you."

I bent over her and took her face between my hands and looked deeply in her blue eyes. They were grave and without deceit.

"Dot," I said, "did you kill him?"

"No."

"How did the blood get in the car?"

"From the dog I ran over."

But police science had proved that a man and not a dog had bled in the car. It didn't make sense that she would tell the truth about everything but that. It was all of one piece. Frantically I wanted to believe her, but deep inside of me I didn't know.

I straightened up. She was my wife and I loved her.

"We'll fight them," I said.

When I returned to the district attorney's office, the same three men were there waiting for me.

"Well, is it a deal?" Fair asked.

"No," I said.

Ricardo sighed. Fair pounded his desk. "Very well, it will be first-degree murder then."

I turned away. George followed me out of the office and put his hand on my shoulder.

"We've got a good chance to lick them," he said. "I don't think, at any rate, that Fair can get a jury to give her the chair. We may get away with temporary insanity if she'll co-operate. I'll tell her exactly what to say on the stand, and if she sticks to it—"

"She's innocent," I said and walked away.

I was running away from his legal logic, but I couldn't run away from my hellish doubts.

Emmett Walker had had an eye for pretty women, but he had married an unattractive one. He hadn't done well as an insurance agent. Financially, being the husband of a woman with a fat bank account had paid off better.

Ida Walker was dumpy, and she had a face to match. When she admitted me into the house, she didn't give the impression of a grieving widow. She was frank about it.

"I'm not a fool," she told me. "I was aware that Emmett was constantly betraying me."

"With Dot?" I asked, looking down at the carpet.

Ida's voice was gentle. "No, Bernie. I never suspected Dot." Then she added, "But a wife is the last to know."

Or a husband, I thought, and the silence that followed was more embarrassing for me than for her. After a minute I asked her what time Emmett had been supposed to call for her last night.

"He wasn't definite," Ida said. "He told me he had work to do at his office and at eight-thirty dropped me off at Marie's in the car. He said he would try to be back before ten to watch a prize fight on the Cannons' television set. At one o'clock I gave up waiting for him and George drove me home."

"Weren't you worried when Emmett didn't show up?"

"Worried?" Ida Walker's lips curled. "Not worried in the way you mean. I assumed that he was with another woman. Then the police got me out of bed and told me he was dead."

I stood up and Ida accompanied me to the door.

"I'm a lot sorrier for Dot than for Emmett," she said. "He deserved what he got. That devil had a way with women. Even I could forgive him a lot. I was willing to accept crumbs from him, but I don't regret that he's gone."

I wondered how much she had forgiven him in the end.

Edith Bauer was Dot's best friend. She was a high-strung, delicately formed woman whose figure would be a delight in porcelain. When I told her that Dot was being charged with first-degree murder, she burst into tears.

Her husband was there. Herman lived close enough to the high school, where he taught science, to walk home for lunch, and I found them seated at the dinette table.

After Edith dried her eyes, she asked me if I would care to have a bite with them. I shook my head. I'd had no desire that morning for anything but coffee. I sat at the table with them and asked Edith if any of the four women at the bridge game last night had left for any length of time.

"You mean left the house?" she said, frowning at the question.

"At least left the room."

"Not for more than a minute or two," Edith replied. "We four were playing bridge all the time, from about a quarter to nine until almost one o'clock when we broke off. Of course we took time off for a snack, but we were all in the same room."

"Who served refreshments?"

"Marie, naturally, but she didn't have to leave the house to do that."

"How could you start playing at a quarter to nine when Dot didn't arrive until after nine?"

"George Cannon made the fourth," she said. "He wasn't anxious to play, and when Dot arrived he gave up his seat to her and went down to the basement to work with his tools. Cabinetmaking is his hobby, and he showed us the record cabinet he's building out of bleached oak. It was one of the most attractive—"

She broke off. "How can I talk about furniture at a time like this?" she wailed and started to sniffle.

I turned my attention to Herman, whose chubby face was thoughtful as he chewed his food.

"Where were you last night, Herman?" I asked.

"Home alone, catching up on my reading." He scooped up a slice of tomato from his plate. "Why is that important?"

"Because," I said carefully, "Dot wasn't the only woman at the bridge game who used to go out with Emmett Walker."

"Meaning me," Edith said. "I had quite a crush on Emmett when I was a kid." She rose quickly—too quickly, it seemed to me—to go into the kitchen for the coffeepot.

Herman had his fork poised in mid-air, and he studied me over it. "What are you getting at, Bernie?"

"I'm not sure," I muttered.

And that was the truth. I was groping in the dark, trying to veer guilt away from Dot to somebody else. Anybody else.

I went to see Marie Cannon. Marie was a full-bodied, slow-moving woman who caught and held men's eyes when prettier women were ignored. The housecoat she wore had a tight, high waist and a wide, low neckline that accentuated her lushness. A handkerchief was balled in her fist, and like Edith Bauer she wept at the sight of me, for she too was a close friend of Dot's.

"I can't imagine Dot killing anybody in cold blood," she said. "It must have been an accident, or temporary insanity."

I didn't argue. I had come to ask questions, and my first one was whether Dot had been greatly upset when she had arrived last night.

Marie thought that over. "She seemed somewhat out of breath, but that was all. George played out the hand before he gave up his seat to her, and as she waited she rather calmly told us that she had run over a dog." Marie unclasped her hand to stare at her moist handkerchief. "George is afraid that the fact that she had a story about killing a dog all prepared before she got here will sound bad before a jury."

Somebody came down the stairs. Marie and I turned our heads as George entered the room. He wore a faded bathrobe and flapping slippers.

"I came home for a nap," he explained. "I had only a couple of hours sleep last night when your phone call woke me." He looked at me. "You can use some sleep too, Bernie."

Sleep? Could there be any sleep for me while Dot was shut in by four walls?

"Why would Dot have said she left a dead dog in the spot where she left the body?" I said. "If she'd killed Emmett, she would have known that his body would be found there instead."

George shrugged. "She was aware that Wilcox had seen her come out of the bushes and that when the body was found Wilcox would put two and two together. She was frantic."

"Marie says she didn't seem very frantic when she arrived here a few minutes later."

"No, she didn't," George agreed, "but it's hard to tell with a woman like Dot. She's always breathless and bubbling and excited anyway. And she's—well, Bernie, she's lovely and charming, but her mind jumps about. I mean, that farfetched story about a dog might have seemed like a valid explanation to her at the time, but she isn't exactly a logical person."

Not at all logical, I thought, and her flightiness used to annoy me. Now it might mean her death or imprisonment. Suddenly I was so tired that I could hardly stand. I leaned against the television cabinet, and I remembered that it was on that screen Emmett Walker had intended to see a prize fight last night. Or so Ida had told me.

I said, "The one who had most reason to kill Emmett Walker was his wife."

Marie sat down abruptly. "Yes," she whispered. "You mean before she got here last night?"

"It's possible," I said. "By the way, where was Emmett's car found?"

"At his house," George replied. "The police believe that he returned home after driving Ida here and then Dot picked him up in her car." He shook his head. "I've considered every angle too, Bernie, but they all lead to Walker's blood in your car and Dot's preposterous story about a dog."

I wasn't being logical either. I looked at Marie, who was opening her handkerchief to blow her nose, and at George, who tightened his lips glumly.

"I'll do my best to save her," George said. "The odds are that she can be got off within the law."

Odds, like gambling odds. Gambling against whether she would die or spend long years in jail or be released with the stigma of blood on her hands.

There was pity in their eyes. Pity for me, as well as for Dot. I could not stand it and I said good-bye and got out of there.

Sometimes, when I was worn out from a day of teaching and wanted quiet to read my paper, Dot's incessant and meaningless chatter would irritate me. Now the absence of her voice made the house terribly empty. I had come back home, but I couldn't endure being there without Dot. I was about to leave when the doorbell rang.

A ten-year-old boy stood there—Larry Robbins, son of the druggist who lived in the next block.

"Mr. Hall," he said, "did you see a little black dog?"

I stared at him.

"He got lost," the boy said. "I let him out for a few minutes last night and he never came back. So I'm asking all the neighbors if they saw him. Did you, Mr. Hall?"

With an effort I kept my voice calm. "What did he look like?"

"A little thing about so big. All black except for a white spot over his nose, and white paws. I got him only last week—my uncle gave him to me—and we didn't get a collar for him yet or a license. Maybe somebody thought he was a stray dog, fed him and took him in."

"What time did you let him out last night?"

"It was after eight o'clock. You didn't see him, did you?"

"Thanks, Larry," I said and patted his head.

He blinked at me. "Thanks for what, Mr. Hall?"

"Never mind," I said, and then added, "No, I didn't see your dog, Larry."

A couple of hours later, the small bulldozer I had hired arrived near the intersection of Pine Road and Wilson Lane. I'd been waiting there for some time. When the bulldozer had trundled off the truck, I told the driver where to start digging. Then I drove to the nearest phone and called Detective Ricardo at police headquarters.

"Can you come right away to where Emmett Walker's body was found last night?" I said.

"You got something, Mr. Hall?"

"I don't know," I said. "But if I have, I want you there as a witness."

I hurried back to where the bulldozer was ploughing up a fifty-feet-wide area that started at the bushes along the road. Though he'd dug some three feet deep and twenty feet into the field beyond, he had so far turned up nothing but boulders. I walked beside the bulldozer blade, my feet sinking into the loose, upturned dirt.

The scooped-out area doubled in size before Ricardo showed up. His fat hips waddled as he stumbled over the chewed-up ground. He brooded at the crawling, bucking bulldozer and sighed.

"Faith moves mountains, eh, Mr. Hall?" he commented dryly.

I told him about Larry Robbins' lost dog.

"So why didn't you come to the police and let them do the digging?" he demanded.

"Because there'd be too much red tape before I got them to move, if they moved at all."

Ricardo scratched his jowls reflectively. "This field belongs to Gridley. He wouldn't like what you're doing to it."

"I obtained his permission. I'm paying him and promised to have it leveled off after—"

The driver yelled. He was climbing off the seat. Ricardo and I ran toward him. There, on the ground, half covered by dirt, was a patch of the black fur. It was some fifty feet back in an almost straight line from where Walker's body had been found.

Ricardo stooped, brushed dirt away from the fur, pulled the dead animal out into the clear by one of its legs. I had never before seen that little black dog, but I had heard it described by both Dot and Larry Robbins.

Dot hadn't had a logical mind. She had only told the truth. Suddenly I was feeling fine. I had never felt better in my life.

"Do you believe now that my wife ran over a dog?"

Ricardo straightened up and dusted his hands. "Why should I?"

"W-w-why?" I stammered from sheer incredulousness. "Don't you believe what you see?"

"I see a dead dog, all right, but there are at least two things this dog didn't do. He didn't bleed in your car and he didn't leave Walker's body in the bushes. I think I know how the dog got here."

"He was buried by the murderer."

Ricardo smiled thinly. "That's what you'd like us to think. Early this morning, after you left police headquarters, you decided to try to save your wife by making her cockeyed yarn seem true. You found a little black dog and killed it and buried it here. Then you pretended to find it."

The bulldozer driver was listening open-mouthed. As for me, bitter anger had replaced my elation.

"Are you going to have the dog examined?"

"Sure, Mr. Hall, though it probably won't be possible to tell if a car or a club killed it."

There was nothing to be said. The finding of the dead dog proved everything to me and nothing to the detective. I told the bulldozer driver to shove back the dirt he had scooped out and walked to my car. The car had been returned to me a few hours ago by the police—with the bloody floor rug missing.

Ricardo moved at my side. "I guess I'd do about the same thing for my wife," he said sympathetically, "but I'd be smarter."

I whirled at the edge of the road to face him. "So you're smart! But not smart enough to see that a story can sound so farfetched that it has to be true. My wife isn't quite the fool all of you try to make her out."

Ricardo had no comment for long moments, and his sad black eyes were reflective. He wasn't a bad guy, I thought. Not one of those bullying, blustering cops. He was trying to do what seemed to him the right thing.

"You know," he mused, looking back at the splotch of black fur on the field, "there's another answer if your wife's story about the dog is true."

"It's about time you saw it."

Suddenly he grinned at me. "You wait here. I have to take the dog's body in. Might be evidence."

He waddled over the chewed-up field. It struck me that I could accomplish more than a policeman could, and by the time he caught up with me I could hand him something. I got into my car and drove off.

Marie Cannon came to the door. Those harsh, stricken lines at the corners of her eyes and mouth had deepened within a few hours.

"George isn't home," she said.

"I'm here to see you," I said.

She led me into the living room. She sat down, keeping her full-fleshed body stiff. I stood over her.

"Marie, you've been weeping all day for Emmett Walker."

She brought the handkerchief to her nose. "Of course I'm sorry he's dead. He was a friend."

"A friend and a lover," I said. "And maybe you're weeping a little for Dot too—or for your own conscience—because you know Dot is innocent. You know that Emmett was alive at around ten o'clock, which means that Dot couldn't have killed him."

I heard a car pull into the driveway at the side of the house. Ricardo, I thought, right at my heels. I hoped that he would have sense enough to let me handle Marie.

"No, no!" Marie was saying.

"We found the dog buried near where Emmett Walker's body was found," I told her. "That proves Dot's story, and it proves that one of the people who was in this house last night killed him. They were the only ones who knew where Dot had left the dead dog."

There was a whisper of feet on the porch. Then silence. That meant that Ricardo was playing along with me. He was letting me break down Marie while he listened through the open window.

Marie was sniffling into her handkerchief.

"This is what must have happened," I went on. "Last night, you went into the kitchen to prepare refreshments. Through the window you saw Emmett Walker arrive to watch the fight on your television. You slipped out through the kitchen door to talk to him."

"I didn't kill him!" she burst out. "Let me alone!"

"You didn't kill him!" I agreed. "None of you four women in the house could have, because none of you was out of the house long enough to drive the body away. But there was a fifth person in the house—your husband."

Now, beside the edge of the curtain on one of the two windows looking out on the porch, I could see a man's hip. Ricardo was taking it all in.

"No!" Marie was wailing. "No, no!"

"Yes," I said. "It's the only possible way it could have happened.

George was in the basement making a record cabinet. I've been down there a number of times. There's a ground-level window looking out to the side of the house. George saw you run out to meet Emmett. Maybe you kissed Emmett. Maybe you arranged a meeting with him. Then you returned to the kitchen and took the refreshments out to your guests. Emmett lingered outside so as not to enter the house at the same time you did and give his wife ideas. And George came out of the basement through the garage door, and in his hand he held a hammer, or whatever heavy tool he'd snatched up from his workbench."

Marie wept. In a minute she would be talking for Ricardo to hear.

I glanced toward the window and saw that Ricardo had shifted his position and that considerably more than his hip was now visible.

Only it wasn't Ricardo. The detective had a fat paunch, a padded hip. The man out there was thin, frail. George Cannon, who had seen my car parked in front of his house and had come up on the porch quietly.

All right, let him hear. Maybe he would break down when Marie did. Or he would flee and that would be as good as a confession.

I turned back to Marie. "So George killed Emmett Walker in blind, jealous fury. Then there he was with a murdered man on his hands. He had heard Dot tell that she had run over a dog and where she had left it. He saw how he could divert suspicion wholly from himself by shoving it all on Dot. He dragged the body into Dot's car, and the battered head bleeding on the floor rug fitted in with his scheme. He drove to where Dot had said she'd left the dog and found it and buried it in the fields behind the bushes and left Emmett's body there. He returned and drove Emmett's car to Emmett's house and walked back. The whole business had taken some time, but you women playing cards didn't know he was gone. Maybe he left one of his machine tools running so that you heard it upstairs and assumed he was in the basement."

"The disgrace!" Marie blubbered. "The scandal!"

And then I saw the gun. Outside the window George Cannon held it in his skinny hand against his hip. Rays from the sinking sun glinted on the barrel.

Breath clogged my throat. There was no chance in flight. Only in more words, and in not letting him realize that I knew he was there.

"So that's why you protected him," I said, "though he murdered the man you loved. You knew that George had killed him. Having seen Emmett alive and outside the house at ten, there was no other possibility. Yet you were ready to see Dot die for George's crime."

Her shoulders heaved. "George said he could get her off. And there would have been a frightful scandal if George had gone on trial. Everybody would have known that Emmett had been my— my—" Her voice went completely to pieces.

I looked at Marie as I spoke, but actually my words were directed to the man outside with the gun. "The police know the truth," I said. "When they found the dog's body, the pieces fell into place. With your evidence, there will be no doubt of his guilt. The police are on their way now to—"

Outside, somebody yelled. The man at the window jerked around, and all of George Cannon's slight body became visible. He held the muzzle of his gun against his temple.

The sound of the shot wasn't very loud. Then he crumpled out of sight below the window sill, and I saw Ricardo running up the porch steps.

I dashed out to the porch. Ricardo was looking down at the dead man.

"Shot himself when he saw me," Ricardo said. "Guess he thought I was coming to arrest him."

"Yes," I muttered. "I made him think so."

He raised angry black eyes to me. "Why didn't you wait for me?"

"Does it matter now?" I said, turning away from George Cannon's body.

Inside the house, Marie was sobbing brokenly.

"I guess not," Ricardo said softly. He went into the house.

I walked as far as the porch steps so that I would not be too near the dead man. In a little while, I thought, I would be bringing Dot home.

And I would buy Larry Robbins another dog.

ONE MORNING THEY'LL HANG HIM Margery Allingham

In this story I made an attempt to combine a human story with careful detection and for this reason it seemed necessary to have a less sympathetic police officer than I like to write about in the ordinary way. It was either a case of making Mr. Campion un-friendly or inventing a companion for him who would provide the necessary element and that is why this story has two detec-tives.

MARGERY ALLINGHAM

It was typical of Detective Inspector Kenny, at that time D.D.I. of the L. Division, that, having forced himself to ask a favor, he should set about it with the worst grace possible. When at last he took the plunge, he heaved his two hundred pounds off Mr. Campion's fire-side couch and set down his empty glass with a clatter.

"I don't know if I needed that at three in the afternoon," he said ungratefully, his small blue eyes baleful, "but I've been up since two this morning dealing with women, tears, minor miracles and this perishing rain." He rubbed his broad face, and presented it scarlet and exasperated at Mr. Campion's back. "If there's one thing that makes me savage it's futility!" he added.

Mr. Albert Campion, who had been staring idly out of the window watching the rain on the roofs, did not glance around. He was still the lean, somewhat ineffectual-looking man to whom the Special Branch had turned so often in the last twenty years. His very fair hair had bleached into whiteness and a few lines had appeared round the pale eyes which were still, as always, covered by large horn-rimmed spectacles, but otherwise he looked much as Kenny first re-membered him— "Friendly and a little simple—the old snake!"

"So there's futility in Barraclough Road too, is there?" Campion's light voice sounded polite rather than curious.

Kenny drew a sharp breath of annoyance.

"The Commissioner has 'phoned you? He suggested I should look you up. It's not a great matter—just one of those stupid little snags which has some perfectly obvious explanation. Once it's settled, the whole case is open-and-shut. As it is, we can't keep the man at the station indefinitely."

Mr. Campion picked up the early edition of the evening paper from his desk.

"This is all I know," he said holding it out, "Mr. Oates didn't 'phone. There you are, in the Stop Press, *Rich Widow shot in Barra-clough Road West. Nephew at police station helping investigation.* What's the difficulty? His help is not altogether wholehearted, perhaps?"

To his surprise an expression remarkably like regret flickered round Kenny's narrow lips.

"Ruddy young fool," he said, and sat down abruptly. "I tell you, Mr. Campion, this thing is in the bag. It's just one of those ordinary, rather depressing little stories which most murder cases are. There's practically no mystery, no chase—nothing but a wretched little trag-edy. As soon as you've spotted what I've missed, I shall charge this chap and he'll go before the magistrates and be committed for trial. His counsel will plead insanity and the jury won't have it. The Judge will sentence him, he'll appeal, their Lordships will dismiss it. The Home Secretary will sign the warrant and one morning they'll take him out and they'll hang him." He sighed. "All for nothing," he said. "All for nothing at all. It'll probably be raining just like it is now," he added inconsequentially.

Mr. Campion's eyes grew puzzled. He knew Kenny for a con-scientious officer, and, some said, a hard man. This philosophic strain was unlike him.

"Taken a fancy to him?" he inquired.

"Who? I certainly haven't." The Inspector was grim. "I've got no sympathy for youngsters who shoot up their relatives however selfish the old bottoms may be. No, he's killed her and he must take what's coming to him, but it's hard on—well, on some people. Me, for one." He took out a large old-fashioned notebook and folded it carefully in half. "I stick to one of these," he remarked virtuously, "None of your backs of envelopes for me. My record is kept as neatly as when I was first on the beat, and it can be handed across the court whenever a know-all counsel asks to see it." He paused. "I sound like an advertisement, don't I? Well, Mr. Campion, since I'm here, just give your mind to this, if you will. I don't suppose it'll present any difficulty to you."

"One never knows," murmured Mr. Campion idiotically. "Start with the victim."

Kenny returned to his notebook.

"Mrs. Mary Alice Cibber, aged about seventy or maybe a bit less. She had heart trouble which made her look frail, and, of course, I didn't see her until she was dead. She had a nice house in Barraclough Road, a good deal too big for her, left her by her husband who died ten years ago. Since then she's been alone except for a maid who cleared off in the war and now for another old party who calls herself a companion. *She* looks older still, poor old girl, but you can see she's been kept well under—" he put his thumb down expressively —"by Mrs. C. who appears to have been a dictator in her small way. She was the sort of woman who lived for two chairs and a salad bowl."

"I beg your pardon?"

"Antiques." He was mildly contemptuous. "The house is crammed with them, all three floors and the attic, everything kept as if it was brand-new. The old companion says she loved it more than anything on earth. Of course she hadn't much else *to* love, not a relation in the world except the nephew—"

"Whose future you see so clearly?"

"The man who shot her," the Inspector agreed. "He's a big nervy lad, name of Woodruff, the son of the old lady's brother. His mother, father, and two young sisters all got theirs in the blitz on Portsmouth. Whole family wiped out."

"I see." Campion began to catch some of Kenny's depression. "Where was he when that happened?"

"In the Western Desert." The D.D.I.'s protuberant eyes were dark with irritation. "I told you this was just an ordinary miserable slice of life. It goes on the same way. This boy, Richard Woodruff—he's only twenty-eight now—did very well in the war. He was in the landings in Sicily and went through the fighting in Italy where he got the M.C. and was promoted major. Then he copped in for the breakthrough in France and just before the finish he became a casualty. A bridge blew up with him on it—or something of the sort, my informant didn't know exactly—and he seems to have become what the boys call 'bomb happy.' It used to be 'shell shock' in my day. As far as I can gather, he always had been quick-tempered, but this sent him over the edge. He sounds to me as if he wasn't sane for a while. That may help him in his defense, of course."

"Yes." Campion sounded depressed. "Where's he been since then?"

"On a farm mostly. He was training to be an architect before the war but the motherly old army knew what was best for him and when he came out of the hospital they bunged him down to Dorset. He's just got away. Some wartime buddy got him a job in architect's office under the old pals' act and he was all set to take it up." He paused and his narrow mouth, which was not entirely insensitive, twisted bitterly. "Ought to have started Monday," he said.

"Oh dear," murmured Mr. Campion inadequately. "Why did he shoot his aunt? Pure bad temper?"

Kenny shook his head.

"He had a reason. I mean one can see why he was angry. He hadn't anywhere to live, you see. As you know London is crowded, and rents are fantastic. He and his wife paying through the nose for a cupboard of a bed-sitting room off the Edgeware Road."

"His wife?" The lean man in the horn rims was interested. "Where did she come from? You're keeping her very quiet."

To Campion's surprise the Inspector did not speak at once. Instead he grunted, and there was regret, and surprise at it, in his little smile. "I believe I would if I could," he said sincerely. "He found her on the farm. They've been married six weeks. I don't know if you've ever seen love, Mr. Campion? It's very rare—the kind I mean." He put out his hands deprecatingly. "It seems to crop up—when it does —among the most unexpected people, and when you do see it, well, it's very impressive." He succeeded in looking thoroughly ashamed of himself. "I shouldn't call myself a sentimental man," he said.

"No." Campion was reassuring. "You got his war history from her, I suppose?"

"I had to but we're confirming it. He's as shut as a watch—or a hand grenade. 'Yes' and 'No' and 'I did not shoot her'—that's about all his contribution amounted to, and he's had a few hours of expert treatment. The girl is quite different. She's down there too. Won't leave. We put her in the waiting room finally. She's not difficult—just sits there."

"Does she know anything about it?"

"No." Kenny was quite definite. "She's nothing to look at," he went on presently, as if he felt the point should be made. "She's just an ordinary nice little country girl, a bit too thin and a bit too brown, natural hair and inexpert make-up, and yet with this—this blazing radiant steadfastness about her!" He checked himself. "Well, she's fond of him," he amended.

"Believes he's God," Campion suggested.

Kenny shook his head. "She doesn't care if he isn't," he said sadly. "Well, Mr. Campion, some weeks ago these two approached Mrs. Cibber about letting them have a room or two at the top of the house. That must have been the girl's idea; she's just the type to have old-fashioned notions about blood being thicker than water. She made the boy write. The old lady ignored the question but asked them both to an evening meal last night. The invitation was sent a fortnight ago, so you can see there was no eager bless-you-my-children about it."

"Any reason for the delay?"

"Only that she had to have notice if she were giving a party. The old companion explained that to me. There was the silver to get out and clean, and the best china to be washed, and so on. Oh, there was nothing simple and homely about that household!" He sounded personally affronted. "When they got there, of course there was a blazing row."

"Hard words or flying crockery?"

Kenny hesitated. "In a way, both," he said slowly. "It seems to have been a funny sort of flare-up. I had two accounts of it—one from the girl and one from the companion. I think they are both trying to be truthful but they both seem to have been completely foxed by it. They both agree that Mrs. Cibber began it. She waited until there were three oranges and a hundredweight of priceless early Worcester dessert service on the table, and then let fly. Her theme seems to have been the impudence of Youth in casting its eyes on its inheritance before Age was in its grave, and so on and so on. She then made it quite clear that they hadn't a solitary hope of getting what they wanted, and conveyed that she did not care if they slept in the street so long as her precious furniture was safely housed. There's no doubt about it that she was very aggravating and unfair."

"Unfair?"

"Ungenerous. After all she knew the man quite well. He used to go and stay with her by himself when he was a little boy." Kenny returned to his notes. "Woodruff then lost his temper in his own way which, if the exhibition he gave in the early hours of this morning is typical, is impressive. He goes white instead of red, says practically nothing, but looks as if he's about to 'incandesce'—if I make myself plain."

"Entirely." Mr. Campion was deeply interested. This new and human Kenny was an experience. "I take it he then fished out a gun and shot her?"

"Lord, no! If he had, he'd have a chance at least of Broadmoor. No. He just got up and asked her if she had any of his things, because if so he'd take them and not inconvenience her with them any longer. It appears that when he was in the hospital some of his gear had been sent to her, as his next of kin. She said yes, she had, and it was waiting for him in the boot cupboard. The old companion, Miss Smith, was sent trotting out to fetch it and came staggering in with an old officer's hold-all, bursted at the sides and filthy. Mrs. Cibber told her nephew to open it and see if she'd robbed him, and he did as he was told. Of course, one of the first things he saw among the ragged bush shirts and old photographs was a revolver and a clip of ammunition." He paused and shook his head. "Don't ask me how it got there. You know what hospitals were like in the war. Mrs. Cibber went on taunting the man in her own peculiar way, and he stood there examining the gun and presently loading it, almost absently. You can see the scene?"

Campion could. The pleasant, perhaps slightly overcrowded room was vivid in his mind, and he saw the gentle light on the china and the proud, bitter face of the woman.

"After that," said Kenny, "the tale gets more peculiar, although both accounts agree. It was Mrs. C. who laughed and said, 'I suppose you think I ought to be shot?' Woodruff did not answer but he dropped the gun in his side pocket. Then he packed up the hold-all and said, 'Good-bye.'" He hesitated. "Both statements say that he then said something about *the sun having gone down*. I don't know what that meant, or if both women mistook him. Anyway, there's nothing to it. He had no explanation to offer. Says he doesn't remember saying it. However, after that he suddenly picked up one of his aunt's beloved china fruit bowls and simply dropped it on the floor. It fell on a rug, as it happened, and did not break, but old Mrs. Cibber nearly passed out, the companion screamed, and the girl hurried him off home."

"With the gun?"

"With the gun." Kenny shrugged his heavy shoulders. "As soon as the girl heard that Mrs. Cibber had been shot, she jumped up with a tale that he had *not* taken it. She said she'd sneaked it out of his pocket and put it on the window sill. The lamest story you ever heard! She's game and she's ready to say absolutely anything, but she won't save him, poor kid. He was seen in the district at midnight."

Mr. Campion put a hand through his sleek hair. "Ah. That rather tears it."

"Oh, it does. There's no question that he did it. It hardly arises. What happened was this. The young folk got back to their bed-sitting room about ten to nine. Neither of them will admit it, but it's obvious that Woodruff was in one of those boiling but sulky rages which made him unfit for human society. The girl left him alone—I should say she has a gift for handling him—and she says she went to bed while he sat up writing letters. Quite late, she can't or won't say when, he went out to the post. He won't say anything. We may or may not break him down, he's a queer chap. However, we have a witness who saw him somewhere about midnight at the Kilburn end of Barraclough Road. Woodruff stopped him and asked if the last eastbound 'bus had gone. Neither of them had a watch, but the witness is prepared to swear it was just after midnight—which is important because the shot was fired at two minutes before twelve. We've got that time fixed."

Mr. Campion, who had been taking notes, looked up in mild astonishment.

"You got that witness very promptly," he remarked. "Why did he come forward?"

"He was a plainclothesman off duty," said Kenny calmly. "One of the local men who had been out to a reunion dinner. He wasn't tight but he had decided to walk home before his wife saw him. I don't know why he hadn't a watch"—Kenny frowned at this defect—"anyway, he hadn't, or it wasn't going. But he was alert enough to notice Woodruff. He's a distinctive chap you know. Very tall and dark, and his manner was so nervy and excitable that the dick thought it worth reporting."

Campion's teeth appeared in a brief smile.

"In fact, he recognized him at once as a man who looked as though he'd done a murder?"

"No." The Inspector remained unruffled. "No, he said he looked like a chap who had just got something off his mind and was pleased with himself."

"I see. And meanwhile the shot was fired at two minutes to twelve."

"That's certain." Kenny brightened and became businesslike. "The man next door heard it and looked at his watch. We've got his statement and the old lady's companion. Everyone else in the street is being questioned. But nothing has come in yet. It was a cold wet night and most people had their windows shut; besides, the room where the murder took place was heavily curtained. So far, these two are the only people who seem to have heard anything at all. The man next door woke up and nudged his wife who had slept through it. But then he may have dozed again, for the next thing he remembers is hearing screams for help. By the time he got to the window, the companion was out in the street in her dressing gown, wedged in between the lamp post and the mail box, screeching her little gray head off. The rain was coming down in sheets."

"When exactly was this?"

"Almost immediately after the shot, according to the companion. She had been in bed for some hours and had slept. Her room is on the second floor, at the back. Mrs. Cibber had not come up with her but had settled down at her bureau in the drawing-room, as she often did in the evening. Mrs. C. was still very upset by the scene at the meal, and did not want to talk. Miss Smith says she woke up and thought she heard the front door open. She won't swear to this, and at any rate she thought nothing of it, for Mrs. Cibber often slipped out to the mail box with letters before coming to bed. Exactly how long it was after she woke that she heard the shot she does not know, but it brought her scrambling out of bed. She agrees she might have been a minute or two finding her slippers and a wrapper, but she certainly came down right away. She says she found the street door open, letting in the rain, and the drawing-room door, which is next to it, wide open as well, and the lights in there full on." He referred to his notes and began to read out loud. " 'I smelled burning' "—she means cordite—" 'and I glanced across the room to see poor Mrs. Cibber on the floor with a dreadful hole in her forehead. I was too frightened to go near her, so I ran out of the house shouting "Murder! Thieves!" ' "

"That's nice and old-fashioned. Did she see anybody?"

"She says not, and I believe her. She was directly under the only lamp post for fifty yards and it certainly was raining hard."

Mr. Campion appeared satisfied but unhappy. When he spoke his voice was very gentle.

"Do I understand that your case is that Woodruff came back, tapped on the front door, and was admitted by his aunt? After some conversation, which must have taken place in lowered tones since the companion upstairs did not hear it, he shot her and ran away, leaving all the doors open?"

"Substantially, yes. Although he may have shot her as soon as he saw her."

"In that case she'd have been found dead in the hall."

Kenny blinked. "Yes, I suppose she would. Still, they couldn't have talked much."

"Why?"

The Inspector made a gesture of distaste. "This is the bit which gets under my skin," he said. "They could hardly have spoken long —*because she'd forgiven him*. She had written to her solicitor—the finished letter was on her writing pad ready for the post. She'd written to say she was thinking of making the upper part of her house into a home for her nephew, and asked if there was a clause in her lease to prevent it. She also said she wanted the work done quickly, as she had taken a fancy to her new niece and hoped in time there might be children. It's pathetic, isn't it?" His eyes were wretched. "That's what I meant by futility. She'd forgiven him, see? She wasn't a mean old harridan, she was just quick-tempered. I told you this isn't a mystery tale, this is ordinary sordid life."

Mr. Campion looked away.

"Tragic," he said. "Yes. A horrid thing. What do you want me to do?"

Kenny sighed. "Find the gun," he murmured.

The lean man whistled.

"You'll certainly need that if you're to be sure of a conviction. How did you lose it?"

"He's ditched it somewhere. He didn't get rid of it in Barraclough Road because the houses come right down to the street, and our chaps were searching for it within half an hour. At the end of the road he caught the last 'bus, which ought to come along at midnight but was a bit late last night, I'm morally certain. These drivers make up time on the straight stretch by the park; it's more than their jobs are worth, so you never get them to admit it. Anyhow, he didn't leave the gun on the 'bus, and it's not in the house where his room is. It's not in the old lady's house at 81 Barraclough Road because I've been over the house myself." He peered at the taller man hopefully. "Where would you hide a gun in this city at night, if you were all that way from the river? It's not so easy, is it? If it had been anywhere obvious it would have turned up by now."

"He may have given it to someone."

"And risked blackmail?" Kenny laughed. "He's not as dumb as that. You'll have to see him. He says he never had it—but that's only natural. Yet where did he put it, Mr. Campion? It's only a little point but, as you say, it's got to be solved."

Campion grimaced.

"Anywhere, Kenny. Absolutely anywhere. In a drain—"

"They're narrow gratings in Barraclough Road."

"In a sandbin or a static water tank—"

"There aren't any in that district."

"He threw it down in the street and someone, who felt he'd rather like to have a gun, picked it up. Your area isn't peopled solely with the law-abiding, you know."

Kenny became more serious. "That's the real likelihood," he admitted gloomily. "But all the same, I don't believe he's the type to throw away a gun casually. He's too intelligent, too cautious. Do you know how this war has made some men cautious even when they're being the most reckless? He's one of those. He's hidden it. Where? Mr. Oates said you'd know if anyone did."

Campion ignored this blatant flattery. He stood staring absently out of the window for so long that the Inspector was tempted to nudge him, and when at last he spoke, his question did not sound promising.

"How often did he stay with his aunt when he was a child?"

"Quite a bit, I think, but there's no kid's hiding-place there that only he could have known, if that's what you're after." Kenny could hardly conceal his disappointment. "It's not that kind of house. Besides, he hadn't the time. He got back about twenty past twelve: a woman in the house confirms it—she met him on the stairs. He was certainly spark out when we got there at a quarter after four this morning. They were both sleeping like kids when I first saw them. She had one skinny brown arm around his neck. He just woke up in a rage, and she was more astounded than frightened. I swear—"

Mr. Campion had ceased to listen.

"Without the gun the only real evidence you've got is the plain-clothesman's story of meeting him," he said. "And even you admit that gallant officer was walking for his health after a party. Imagine a good defense lawyer enlarging on that point."

"I have," the Inspector agreed, dryly. "That's why I'm here. You must find the gun for us, sir. Can I fetch you a raincoat? Or," he added, a faintly smug expression flickering over his broad face, "will you just sit in your armchair and do it from there?"

To his annoyance his elegant host appeared to consider the question.

"No, perhaps I'd better come with you," he said at last. "We'll go to Barraclough Road first, if you don't mind. And if I might make a suggestion, I should send Woodruff and his wife back to their lodgings—suitably escorted, of course. If the young man was going to crack, I think he would have done so by now, and the gun, wherever it is, can hardly be at the police station."

Kenny considered. "He may give himself away and lead us to it." He agreed although without enthusiasm. "I'll telephone. Then we'll go anywhere you say, but as I told you I've been over the Barraclough Road house myself and if there's anything there it's high time I retired."

Mr. Campion merely looked foolish, and the Inspector sighed and let him have his way.

He came back from the telephone smiling wryly.

"That's settled," he announced. "He's been behaving like a good soldier interrogated by the enemy, silly young fool—after all, we're only trying to hang him! The girl has been asking for him to be fed, and reporters are crawling up the walls. Our boys won't be sorry to get rid of them for a bit. They'll be looked after. We shan't lose 'em. Now, if you've set your heart on the scene of the crime, Mr. Campion, we'll go."

In the taxi he advanced a little idea.

"I was thinking of that remark he is alleged to have made," he said, not without shame. "You don't think that it could have been 'Your sun has gone down,' and that we could construe it as a threat within meaning of the act?"

Campion regarded him owlishly.

"We could, but I don't think we will. That's the most enlightening part of the whole story, don't you think?"

If Inspector Kenny agreed, he did not say so, and they drove to the top of Barraclough Road in silence. There Campion insisted on stopping at the first house next to the main thoroughfare. The building had traded on its proximity to the shopping center and had been converted into a dispensing chemist's. Campion was inside for several minutes, leaving Kenny in the cab. When he came out he offered no explanation other than to observe fatuously that they had a "nice time" and settled back without troubling to look out at the early Victorian stucco three-story houses which lined the broad road.

A man on duty outside, and a handful of idlers gaping apathetically at the drawn blinds, distinguished 81 Barraclough Road. Kenny rang the bell and the door was opened after a pause by a flurried old lady with a duster in her hand.

"Oh, it's you, Inspector," she said hastily. "I'm afraid you've found me in a muddle. I've been trying to tidy up a little. *She* couldn't have born the place left dirty after everyone had been trampling over it. Yet I don't mean to say that you weren't all very careful."

She led them into a spotless dining-room which glowed with old mahogany and limpid silver, and the wan afternoon light showed them her reddened eyes and worn navy-blue housedress. She was a timid-looking person, not quite so old as Kenny had suggested, with very neat gray hair and a skin which had never known cosmetics. Her expression was closed and secret with long submission, and her shoulder blades stuck out a little under the cloth of her dress. Her hands still trembled slightly from the shock of the evening before.

Kenny introduced Campion. "We shan't be long, Miss Smith," he said cheerfully. "Just going to have another little look around. We shan't make a mess."

Campion smiled at her reassuringly. "It's difficult to get help these days?" he suggested pleasantly.

"Oh, it is," she said earnestly. "And Mrs. Cibber wouldn't trust just anyone with her treasures. They are so very good." Her eyes filled with tears. "She was so fond of them."

"I daresay she was. That's a beautiful piece, for instance." Campion glanced with expert interest at the serpentine sideboard with its genuine handles and toilet cupboard.

"Beautiful," echoed Miss Smith dutifully. "And the chairs, you see?"

"I do." He eyed the Trafalgar set with the cherry-leather seats. "Is this where the quarrel took place?"

She nodded and trembled afresh. "Yes. I—I shall never forget it, never."

"Was Mrs. Cibber often bad-tempered?"

The woman hesitated, and her firm small mouth moved without words.

"Was she?"

She shot a swift unhappy glance at him.

"She was quick," she said. "Yes I think I ought to say she was quick. Now, would you like to see the rest of the house or—?"

Campion glanced at his watch and compared it with the Tompion bracket clock on the mantelshelf.

"I think we've just time," he said, idiotically. "Upstairs first, Inspector."

The next thirty-five minutes reduced Kenny to a state of jitters rare to him. After watching Campion with breathless interest for the first five, it slowly dawned on him that the expert had forgotten the crime in his delight at discovering a treasure-trove. Even Miss Smith, who betrayed a certain proprietorial pride, flagged before Campion's insatiable interest. Once or twice she hinted that perhaps they ought to go down, but he would not hear of it. By the time they had exhausted the third floor and were on the steps to the attic, she became almost firm. There was really nothing there but some early Georgian children's toys, she said.

"But I must just see the toys. I've got a 'thing' on toys, Kenny." Campion sounded ecstatic. "Just a minute—"

A vigorous tattoo on the front door interrupted him and Miss Smith, whose nerves were suffering, emitted a little squeak.

"Oh, dear. Somebody at the door. I must go down."

"No, no." Campion was uncharacteristically effusive. "I'll see who it is and come back. I shan't be a moment."

He flung himself downstairs with boyish enthusiasm, Miss Smith behind him, and Kenny, seeing escape at last, following as quickly as the narrow stairs would permit.

They reached the hall just in time to see him closing the door. "Only the post," he said, holding out a package. "Your library book, Miss Smith."

"Oh, yes," she came forward, hand outstretched. "I was expecting that."

"I rather thought you were." His voice was very soft and suddenly menacing. He held the cardboard book box high over his head with one hand, and with the other released the flap which closed it. The soft gleam of metal appeared in the light from the transom, and a service revolver crashed heavily to the parquet floor.

For a long minute there was utter silence. Even Kenny was too thunderstruck to swear.

Miss Smith appeared frozen in mid-air, her hands clawing at the box.

Then, most dreadfully, she began to scream. . . .

A little over an hour later Kenny sat on a Trafalgar chair in a room which seemed to quiver and shudder with terrible sound. He was pale and tired-looking. His shirt was torn and there were three livid nail scratches down his face.

"God," he said, breathing hard. "God, can you beat that?"

Mr. Campion sat on the priceless table and scratched his ear.

"It was a bit more than I bargained for," he murmured. "It didn't occur to me that she'd become violent. I'm afraid they may be having trouble in the van. Sorry, I ought to have thought of it."

The C.I.D. man grunted. "Seems to me you thought of plenty," he muttered. "It came as a shock to me—I don't mind admitting it since I can't very well help it. When did it come to you? From the start?"

"Oh, Lord, no." Campion sounded apologetic. "It was that remark of Woodruff's you quoted about the sun going down. That's what set me on the train of thought. Weren't you ever warned as a kid, Kenny, and by an aunt perhaps, never to let the sun go down on your wrath?"

"I've heard it, of course. What do you mean? It was a sort of saying between them?"

"I wondered if it was. They knew each other well when he was a child, and they were both quick-tempered people. It seemed to me that he was reminding her that the sun *had* gone down, and he showed her he could have smashed her precious bowl if he had liked. It would have broken, you know, if he hadn't taken care it shouldn't. I wondered if, like many quick-tempered people, they got sorry just as quickly. Didn't you think it odd, Kenny, that directly after the row they should *both* have settled down to write letters?"

The detective stared at him.

"She wrote to her solicitor," he began slowly. "And he—? Good Lord! You think he wrote to her to say he was sorry?"

"Almost certainly, but we shall never find his letter. That's in the kitchen stove by now. He came back to deliver it, pushed it through the door, and hurried off looking just as your plainclothesman said, as if he'd got something off his chest. Then he could sleep. The sun had not gone down on his wrath." He slid off the table and stood up. "The vital point is, of course, that *Mrs. Cibber knew he would.* She sat up waiting for it."

Kenny sucked in his breath.

"And Miss Smith knew?"

"Of course, she knew. Mrs. Cibber hadn't the kind of temperament one can keep a secret. Miss Smith knew from the moment that Mrs. Cibber received the initial letter that the nephew would get his way in the end—*unless she could stop it somehow!* She was the one with the bee in her bonnet about the furniture. I realized that as soon as you said the whole house was kept like a bandbox. No woman with a weak heart can keep a three-story house like a palace, or compel another to do it—unless the other wants to. Miss Smith was the one with the mania. Who was to get the house if the nephew died in the war? Mrs. Cibber must have made some provision."

Kenny rubbed his head with both hands. "I knew!" he exploded. "The lawyer's clerk told me this morning when I rang up to find out if Woodruff was the heir. I was so keen to confirm that point that I discounted the rest. If he died the companion was to have it for her lifetime."

Campion looked relieved.

"I thought so. There you are, you see. She had to get rid of them both—Woodruff and his new wife. With a young and vigorous woman in the house there was a danger of the companion becoming

—well redundant. Don't you think?"

Kenny was fingering his notebook.

"You think she'd planned it for a fortnight?"

"She'd thought of it for a fortnight. She didn't see how to do it until the row occurred last night. When she found the gun on the window sill, where young Mrs. Woodruff left it, and Mrs. Cibber told her that the boy would come back, the plan was obvious." He shivered. "Do you realize that she must have been waiting, probably on the stairs, with the gun in her hand and the book box addressed to herself in the other, listening for Woodruff's letter to slide under the door? As soon as she heard it, she had to fly down and get it and open the door. Then she had to walk into the drawing room, shoot the old lady as she turned to see who it was, and put the gun in the book box. The instant she was certain Mrs. Cibber was dead, she then had to run out screaming to her place between the lamp post and the mail box and—*post the package!*"

Kenny put down his pencil and looked up.

"Now here," he said with honest admiration, "there I hand it to you. How in the world did you get on to that?"

"You suggested it."

"*I* did?" Kenny was pleased in spite of himself. "When?"

"When you kept asking me where one could hide a gun in a London street with no wide gratings and no sandbins. There was only the mail box. I guessed she'd posted it to herself—no one else would have been safe. Even the dead letter office eventually gives up its dead. That's why I was so keen to get her to the top of the house —as far away from the front door as possible." He sighed. "The book box was misguided genius. The gun was an old Luger, did you notice? Loot. That's why he never had to turn it in. It just fitted in the box. She must have had a thrill when she discovered that."

Kenny shook his head wonderingly. "Well, blow me down!" he said inelegantly, "Funny that *I* put you onto it!"

Mr. Campion was in bed that night when the telephone rang. It was Kenny again.

"I say, Mr. Campion?"

"Yes?"

"Sorry to bother you at this time of night but there's something worrying me. You don't mind, do you?"

"Think nothing of it."

"Well. Everything is all right. Smith had been certified by three medicos. The little girl is very happy comforting her boy, who seems to be upset about his aunt's death. The Commissioner is very pleased. But I can't get off to sleep. Mr. Campion, *how did you know what time the afternoon post is delivered in Barraclough Road?*"

The lean man stifled a yawn.

"Because I went into the chemist's shop on the corner and asked," he said. "Elementary, my dear Kenny."

HOMICIDE EXPERT Lawrence Treat

Homicide Expert *was written because I was literally on pins and needles. I told my wife that I wanted to do a short Mitch Taylor story, but that I had no ideas. She was on one of her sewing binges, and she didn't appear to give me her usual attention. She sews erratically, moving from chair to chair and leaving her pins and needles behind, along with buttons and other obstructions. I never sit down with any confidence until the cushions have been tested out.*

However, I must have been preoccupied that evening, for I sat down and received the prod which gave me the idea for Homicide Expert. *The rest of it came to me while eating soup, although the character of Mitch Taylor dominated the story and gave it its form.*

The point is that my best stories are written in collaboration with my wife, whose ways are often devious, and exceeding strange.

Lawrence Treat

If ever a homicide looked routine, this was it. Except for one thing, Detective Mitch Taylor could have wrapped it up in half an hour and gone back to his doodling in the squad room.

Except for the knife.

He was the first one to get there, he and his partner, Keenan. The pair of them went up in the newly painted self-service elevator, marched down the short corridor and knocked on the door with the Sperber nameplate. Keenan, a big man, long-nosed, with great, meaty paws. And Taylor, shorter, cocky, wearing a suit that cramped his shoulders. His brown eyes, lively and brimming with energy, gazed up from their long, dark lashes.

They both loosened their coats, touched their holstered guns, just in case. They both drew back as the door opened, both flashed a sharp glance at the man who stood there, and then they both relaxed a little.

Sperber was built broad, with power, and he was young, but his eyes were bleary and dazed. He gulped and rubbed at his face.

Beyond him, Mitch could see the empty bottle and the stale glasses, the dirty ash trays, the overturned chair. Hangover, Mitch decided. Sperber'd killed her while he was drunk, and now he could hardly remember why. The thing was to throw it right at him, before he started thinking his way out.

"Police," Mitch said. "Where is she?"

The guy blinked. His reactions were slow, from shock, and he stammered, "Th-there," without even pointing, Mitch shouldered past him and walked back to the bedroom.

Dorothy Sperber was lying on the floor. She was still blond and you could see she'd been pretty, and she was dressed in black lace underwear. The stab wounds had ripped it up plenty.

Mitch shuddered and closed his eyes. Sperber must have hated that underwear.

Keenan made coffee.

The lieutenant showed up next and began firing questions. All he could get, at first, was that Sperber was a bus driver and his wife's name was Dorothy.

After the coffee, Sperber got hold of himself. He admitted he'd been having trouble with his wife. Sperber said it was his fault, he hadn't treated her right, but he claimed they'd made up and everything would have been fine.

They'd had a party last night to celebrate the reconciliation. Sperber said he didn't remember a thing from the time the guests left until he woke up with a hangover and a dead wife. So he called the cops.

The lieutenant got a list of the guests. There were four of them, and a precinct team picked them up and had them at the apartment almost before the high brass and the experts arrived.

Meanwhile, the lieutenant tried to get a confession. When he saw he wasn't getting anywhere, he told Mitch to look for the knife. Mitch couldn't find it, but he did come up with a button. A fancy green one, that Sperber said had come off Marian Benton's dress last night. The button had bounced out of sight, and she'd been upset because nobody could locate it.

"Upset?" said the lieutenant sharply.

"Just for a little while," said Sperber. "Then she forgot about it. We were all pretty high. We got laughing. Dorothy, she was the life of the party."

"That why you got sore at her?"

"No," said Sperber uncomfortably. "You don't understand. She was cute. She had a way, kind of innocent." He shook all over and began falling apart again.

The first of last night's guests to be brought in were the Chuck Browns. They lived in the neighborhood. They'd left the party around one A.M. and gone straight home. It didn't look as if they could be involved.

Sperber's friend, Jack Pinney, arrived next. He was a tall, lanky guy with sharp, dark eyes and hollow cheeks. Mitch took him into an empty apartment and found out he was a bus driver, too. But that was as far as Mitch got.

The door opened and a big, healthy guy wearing a new suit strode in. He said, "Hello, Taylor. Get anything out of him?"

"Not yet," said Mitch. "I just—"

"That's okay," said Dickinson. "I'll handle him."

Mitch bristled. He'd tangled with Dickinson before, on other cases, and Mitch knew that the big guy would try to step all over him. And particularly with all this brass around.

"Look," said Mitch. "I only started—"

But he didn't finish the sentence. He was talking at Dickinson's back, and Dickinson's deep, confident voice drowned him out. Mitch edged over to the window, took out his pad and made notes.

Pinney stated that after the party he'd taken Marian Benton to the subway, then had a cup of coffee and gone on home. His parents had heard him come in a little before three in the morning. He'd called out to them and said he was tired and wanted to get to sleep.

The deputy inspector nodded at Mitch and told him to check with the restaurant and with Pinney's parents. Mitch maneuvered a couple of the boys into doing the leg work, so that he could hang around while the medical examiner looked over the body. He placed the time of death somewhere between two and three in the morning, which meant Dorothy Sperber had been killed pretty soon after the party broke up.

After that, the medical examiner went into a huddle with Dickinson and a couple of lieutenants, and came up with the news that there'd been a lot of blood, and that the killer must have got spattered with it. Dickinson made chalk marks on the floor, to show where the killer had stood.

Mitch wished he'd thought of making chalk marks, and then he spotted Keenan coming in with the clothes Pinney had been wearing last night. Mitch grabbed them and brought them over to the deputy inspector. He took them without glancing at Mitch and he examined them for stains. There weren't any.

A couple of minutes later, Mitch got his reports saying Pinney's story looked okay. So Pinney was released and told he could go to work.

When Mitch got back to the empty apartment, Dickinson was questioning Dorothy Sperber's girl friend, Marian Benton. For once, Mitch was glad he wasn't carrying the ball, because you'd never impress anybody working on a dame like this. She just didn't react.

Mitch heard her flat, squeezed voice before he got a look at her face. You wanted to slap some life into her, and you knew it was a waste of energy.

She answered all the questions and corroborated all the stories, but she seemed dazed as she gave the information. That the Chuck Browns had gone home first, that Pinney had left with her, and that the Sperbers could hardly stand up at the end of the evening. She identified her missing button, and she wanted to get it back so she could sew it on and wear her dress. She kept saying in her dull, hopeless voice that it was the only decent dress she had, and she needed it.

She claimed she'd got home around two-thirty A.M. and that her roommate had awakened and could vouch for the time. Dickinson kept Marian waiting while he checked her alibi and examined her dress. It had a button missing, and it didn't have any stains. That cleared her, so Dickinson sent her home and told her to take the dress with her. But he stuck the button in a small envelope and kept it.

With all the guests questioned and their actions accounted for, it looked as if everything was back where Mitch had lined it up four hours ago—either you had to get a confession, or else the knife. Mitch saw that the next step was looking through the garbage pails downstairs, and he felt he'd be elected. So he elbowed his way out to the hall, where Dickinson couldn't order him around.

In front of the elevator, Mitch went into two minutes of heavy thinking. The thing was, Dickinson was betting everything on Sperber's guilt, but Dickinson had to be wrong once in a while. So why not pick another angle and follow on it?

Mitch told himself that Dorothy had been playing around. Sperber had said so. And if she'd been playing around with Pinney, then Pinney was in this right up to his neck. That would give Pinney a motive for killing her. And as for the bloodstains—well, let Dickinson worry about that.

Mitch began to like his theory.

He realized he might run into a little trouble with the lieutenant, going off on his own like this. But if he stuck around, Dickinson would only make a sucker out of him. And tonight, when Mitch came home, he'd have to tell his wife he'd spent the day sorting garbage.

That settled it. Mitch ambled down the street, thinking of her and thinking maybe he'd hit on a bright idea. At the next drugstore he turned in, entered a phone booth and called her. Mostly to hear her voice.

"Hello, Amy?" he said.

"Hello, fella," she answered, speaking softly and yet with a lift that went right through him and perked him up. "How are you?"

"Fine. I got a homicide."

"Mitch!" she said, and the concern poured out of her. "Where are you?"

"I just left the place. It's routine."

"Well, I'm glad of that. Mitch, try to get home on time, will you? The Morrisons called and they have a new TV set. They thought you might like to look at the fights tonight."

"Oh," he said. "Sure, I'll wind this up before dinner. All I got to do is find a knife, and then write out the report. I'll be home in plenty of time. What are you doing with yourself?"

"Sewing those curtains."

"Oh," he said. That meant pins all over. In the chairs, stuffed under the cushions—there wouldn't be a safe place to sit.

"Well," he said, "don't leave too many pins around. And Amy, what do you know about black underwear?"

"With lace?" she said excitedly. "Oh, Mitch!"

"I was just thinking," he said.

He hung up. Funny how a homicide could give you an idea what to get your wife for her next birthday. The trouble was, he'd feel a little embarassed buying it, unless he knew exactly where to go. Now if he could find out where Dorothy Sperber's had come from, for instance—

He went down to the bus garage to pick up a little gossip. He knew from experience that sometimes the cops were the last people in the world to get information. So he'd go to the source and listen.

When he got there, he could tell by the way they clammed up that they'd been talking about the homicide. He hung around, though, not asking questions, and after a while they began talking again.

They were sorry for Sperber. He was a right guy, they said. He and Pinney worked different shifts, and everybody knew where Pinney went while Sperber was driving his route. But that was what you got for marrying a flashy dame. With the plain ones, you didn't have to worry. But with somebody like Dorothy, you were asking for it.

Mitch listened and decided he had something. He phoned the precinct and found out they were still looking for the knife, and that Sperber still couldn't remember.

Mitch said he was working on a lead, and he asked his partner, Joe Keenan, to meet him down at the garage with a squad car. Then Mitch went out for a late lunch.

When he got back Keenan was there.

"Well," said Keenan, "what happened to you? Dickinson wanted you to look for the knife."

"Garbage pails?" asked Mitch.

Keenan nodded, lifted his big, meaty paws and smelled them with disgust. "Yeah," he said. "Garbage. What gives here?"

"We're waiting for Pinney," said Mitch. "He's out now, but he's due back around four. I figure we'll see what we can get out of him."

"The lieutenant won't like this," said Keenan.

"That's tough," Mitch snapped. "But when a big sap like Dickinson—"

"Forget it," said Keenan. "He's out of your class. These homicide boys, they know their business."

"Look," said Mitch. "Whose side are you on, huh?"

"He worked it out with charts," said Keenan. "They none of them had time to go back and get other clothes, and they none of them had stains. Dickinson, he figures Sperber must have been wearing pajamas, and then put them down the incinerator."

"Maybe some sneak thief got in the apartment," said Mitch, "and had to kill her to get away."

"The way her underwear's sliced up," said Keenan, "that's personal."

"Yeah," said Mitch. "Now where would you buy stuff like that?"

"How would I know?" said Keenan.

"You'd feel like a fool going in there and asking for it," said Mitch. "Explaining what you wanted." He frowned and thought about Amy. Then he and Keenan sat down and waited.

Pinney came back a little after four, spotted the cops and glared at them and went into the washroom. Mitch got up and followed, but he didn't say anything. He just watched.

After a while it was too much for Pinney. He spun around and said, "Well? What do you want?"

"Where'd you put the knife?" asked Mitch.

"Knife? I didn't have a knife. I didn't have anything to do with it."

"We know you did," said Mitch. "We want that knife."

"You're nuts," said Pinney. But his voice was shaky.

After he'd changed his clothes, Mitch and Keenan walked up to him, one on each side.

"Come on," said Mitch.

Keenan drove the squad car and Mitch sat behind with Pinney.

"We know you were playing around with her," said Mitch. "We know all about it."

Pinney licked his lips. "I thought Sperber did it. You said so this morning."

"We got some more evidence," said Mitch. "We know better now."

"What evidence?"

"You'll see."

Keenan drove to the Sperber house, and in front of the door Mitch said to Pinney, "All right now. What I want is, you show us where you went when you left here last night. Which side of the street you walked on, what you saw, what you did. Everything, see?"

"We just walked," said Pinney. "Marian and me."

"You took her to the subway and then came back. You were seen."

"Nuts," said Pinney angrily. "Don't pull that. I didn't come back. I took Marian to the subway, like I said this morning. Then I had a cup of coffee. I told you where, and you checked, didn't you?"

"What did you talk to Marian about?"

"Not much. She wasn't feeling good, and I was afraid she'd get sick or something. I just wanted to get rid of her."

"Kiss her goodnight?" asked Mitch, to needle him.

"Me?" said Pinney. "That face?" He snorted sharply. "She didn't go for me, and I didn't go for her. Just because she was a friend of Dorothy's I had to be polite. So I took her to the subway and handed her a dime."

"Yeah," said Mitch. That was the sort of thing that could be checked on, it was a wedge. He called to Keenan, "Let's go," he said. "Marian's."

But Mitch wasn't happy. Usually you kind of sense things. Except for professionals, most guilty people want to be caught, they do something dumb, they shove the evidence right at you, they can't help it. But Pinney, he was just mad. The only reason Mitch didn't give up was he could tell that Pinney didn't want to see Marian.

"You give Dorothy that black underwear, with the lace?" Mitch asked suddenly.

Pinney jerked up. "Oh," he said. "That's why."

"Why what?"

"Why you think I had something to do with it."

"You bought it," said Mitch. He made the statement casually, as if he knew it for a fact.

Pinney closed his eyes for a couple of seconds. Then he shook his head as if to clear out the cobwebs.

"Where'd you buy the stuff?"

But Pinney wouldn't tell him. "Come on," Pinney said. "If I got to see Marian, let's go and get it over with."

She lived in one of those places where you rang a bell downstairs and then a buzzer sounded and you opened the door. There was no elevator, and Marian Benton's apartment was on the third floor. Mitch parked Pinney on the second, in Keenan's charge, and went up alone.

Marian looked bad. She was pale and splotchy to begin with, and she'd had a rough day, what with having her best friend killed and then being questioned most of the morning. Apparently she'd just finished cleaning up. The two-room apartment looked scrubbed, and you could smell the soap and the wetness.

Mitch started off politely. "I'm Taylor," he said, showing his badge. "We got Pinney downstairs, and there's a few questions I'd like to ask you."

"Jack?" she said. "You mean—" She didn't finish the sentence, and Mitch didn't finish it for her. He waited a few seconds before tackling her from another angle.

"We been checking on what happened after the party," he said. "Tell me how he took you to the subway, what he said and all that."

She stared at Mitch in amazement. "He didn't take me to the sub-way," she said. "I went alone."

"But you said this morning—"

"I didn't," she interrupted. "Nobody asked me that. I wondered why, because I think he went right back. We went downstairs to-gether, but he left me there, in front of the Sperber house."

Mitch walked to the door and opened it. "Hey, Joe," he called. "Bring him up."

From the moment Pinney entered, Mitch could feel the atmosphere building up. He knew he had something, but he wasn't sure whether it was hooked up with the homicide. He studied Pinney, and then turned to Marian and hoped something would happen.

Nothing did.

"Let's see the dress you wore last night," Mitch said to Marian.

"Of course," she said. "But I showed it before." She opened a closet and pulled out a green print. Mitch took it and held it up for Pinney to see.

"Is that where the button came off?" asked Mitch.

Pinney nodded. "Sure," he said.

Mitch was still fishing. He sat down in the easy chair. There was a pin stuck in the arm, and he wondered whether there was more pins in the seat. Women that sewed, they were all alike, they all had the same habits. He put his hand down beneath the cushion and felt something. He knew what it was even before he held it up.

"Button!" he said. "The extra button!"

Marian ran at him and made a grab for it, but he got hold of her arm and twisted. She began screaming.

"Shut up," said Mitch.

She tried to slap him, and he ducked back. "You did it," he said. "You were carrying the torch for Sperber. That's what I missed out on."

"He didn't do it," she said hysterically. "He didn't—he didn't."

"Sure, but you did. You knew you didn't have a chance to marry him while Dorothy was alive. And you figured if you could kill her and frame Pinney, Sperber would practically fall into your arms. But instead everybody thought Sperber had killed her, so you decided to do something. That's why you said Pinney left you in front of the house and went on back. You wanted to make a liar out of him and frame him."

"No!" she screamed. "No—no!" And then she broke.

Back at the precinct, after she'd confessed, Mitch went over it all with the lieutenant.

"She bought two dresses," said Mitch. "Duplicates. The one she wore and that had the stains and the button torn off, she hid it in the basement, where we found it along with the knife. The other dress, that was her alibi.

R0109090133

R0109 090133   S
                      808.83872
                      M998

MYSTERY WRITERS OF AMERICA
CRIME FOR TWO

R0109 090133

HOUSTON PUBLIC LIBRARY
CENTRAL LIBRARY
500 McKINNEY